LESBIAN PULP FICTION

The Sexually Intrepid World of Lesbian
Paperback Novels 1950-1965

LESBIAN PULP FICTION

The Sexually Intrepid World of Lesbian Paperback Novels 1950-1965

Edited by Katherine V. Forrest

Published in the United States by
Cleis Press Inc., P.O. Box 14697, San Francisco, California 94114.
Printed in the United States.
Cover design: Scott Idleman
Book design: Karen Quigg
Cleis Press logo art: Juana Alicia
First Edition.
10 9 8 7 6 5 4 3 2

The publisher wishes to thank Bruce Brenner at www.VintagePaperbacks.com for providing the artwork on the front cover and Kathy Belge at http://lesbianlife.about.com for the image of *Twilight Girl* on page 297. All other images are courtesy of the James C. Hormel Gay and Lesbian Center at the San Francisco Public Library. Thank you to Jim Van Buskirk, Mike Levy, and Adam Markosian at the library for their generous help.

Library of Congress Cataloging-in-Publication Data

Lesbian pulp fiction : the sexually intrepid world of lesbian paperback novels, 1950–1965 / edited by Katherine V. Forrest.—1st ed.
p. cm.
ISBN 1-57344-210-0 (pbk. : alk. paper)
1. Lesbians' writings, American—History and criticism. 2. Homosexuality and literature—United States—History—20th century. 3. Paperbacks—Publishing—United States—History—20th century. 4. Women and literature—United States—History—20th century. 5. American fiction—Women authors—History and criticism. 6. American fiction—20th century—History and criticism. 7. Lesbians—United States—Intellectual life. 8. Pulp literature—History and criticism. 9. Lesbians in literature. I. Forrest, Katherine V., 1939-
PS153.L46L453 2005
813'.54099206643—dc22

2005004799

For Ann Bannon
with gratitude that has no bounds
nor adequate words

ACKNOWLEDGMENTS

The James C. Hormel Gay and Lesbian Center in the beautiful main branch of the San Francisco Public Library is a national treasure, and a must destination for gay and lesbian visitors to San Francisco. My profound thanks to Jim Van Buskirk, Program Manager of the Hormel Center, for his invaluable assistance, advice, and encouragement, and to the staff of the San Francisco History and Special Collections Department for their kindness, patience, exemplary cooperation, and good humor during my many visits to their sixth floor domain.

To my partner Jo, who has shared so many adventures with me, especially this one.

To the pioneers I was privileged to consult with personally and to come to know during the process of putting this collection together: Julie Ellis (Joan Ellis) and Sally Singer (March Hastings).

To the pioneer I have had the great joy of knowing and calling my friend over the past two decades, Ann Bannon.

To the wonderful women of Cleis Press, Frédérique Delacoste and Felice Newman, pioneers in their own right. When they invited me on this journey I never dreamed it would be so emotion-laden a rediscovery and reinterpretation of my own past.

To the researchers whose diligent and loving work made my path so much smoother, many of whom are mentioned in the bibliography. I must single out these three: Jeannette Foster for her vital *Sex Variant Women in Literature* (Vantage Press, 1956), Jane Rule for *Lesbian Images* (Doubleday, 1975) and Barbara Grier for her truly indispensable *The Lesbian in Literature* (Naiad Press, 1981).

To the contributors to this collection: thank you on behalf of myself and the thousands of women whose lives you helped, for coming into our lives with your words when we most needed you.

Contents

Introduction

A lesbian pulp fiction paperback first appeared before my disbelieving eyes in Detroit, Michigan, in 1957. I did not need to look at the title for clues; the cover leaped out at me from the drugstore rack: a young woman with sensuous intent on her face seated on a bed, leaning over a prone woman, her hands on the other woman's shoulders.

Overwhelming need led me to walk a gauntlet of fear up to the cash register. Fear so intense that I remember nothing more, only that I stumbled out of the store in possession of what I knew I must have, a book as necessary to me as air.

The book was *Odd Girl Out* by Ann Bannon. I found it when I was eighteen years old. It opened the door to my soul and told me who I was. It led me to other books that told me who some of us were, and how some of us lived.

Finding this book back then, and what it meant to me, is my touchstone to our literature, to its value and meaning. Yet no matter how many times I try to write or talk about that day in Detroit, I cannot convey the power of what it was like. You had to be there. I write my books out of the profound wish that no one will ever have to be there again.

Having lived through this era, in all these years afterward I was certain that I knew in general outline an early literature so very close to me. What I understood of the paucity and the aridity of lesbian literature was the impetus for my own first novel, *Curious Wine*. Yet in compiling this collection, I discovered the range of our early books and some wonderful, revealing, ongoing scholarship about them. We had more books than I knew, better books than I had thought, and some of them were by writers of international reputation.

I grew up in the post-war 1950s, an idyllic world if you were a straight white male or if you were naïve enough to believe TV's idealistic "Leave It to Beaver" image of the average American family. It was 1960 when I discovered the seedy lesbian bars of Detroit, when I found my community and came of age. The birth control pill had just been introduced into the United States; it was a mere nine years after our first lesbian and gay organization, the Mattachine Society, had begun in Los Angeles; and five years after Daughters of Bilitis, our first national lesbian organization, had formed in San Francisco. According to the American Psychological Society, I was sick. According to the law, I was a criminal.

From the beginning of the '50s, popular fiction increasingly reflected the hypocrisy of the times. Tereska Torres's *Women's Barracks* was released in 1950 by Fawcett Gold Medal Books, one of the first books to be published in the brand new paperback format. A publishing sensation, it ushered in what is today termed the golden age of pulp fiction, an era of books so inexpensively produced and priced so low that, as Ann Bannon has said, "You could read them on the bus and leave them on the seat."

The enormous sales of Torres's novel ignited an unprecedented boom in lesbian-themed publishing never since duplicated, and the lurid suggestiveness of the three women on its cover became the template for lesbian pulp fiction. *Women's Barracks* was the book that led Gold Medal Books pulp fiction editor Dick Carroll to seek out Vin Packer to write *Spring Fire*, and to advise the young Ann Bannon to rewrite her first novel so that the lesbian subplot would become the central story.

With "morality" seemingly pervasive in the land, lurid covers of paperbacks screamed sex from every retail bookshelf and Americans gobbled up the books by the millions. A new breed of publisher emerged to reap huge profits. For lesbian books, cover copy proclaimed our evil in order to meet morality requirements while the come-hither illustrations beckoned the reader into their pages and promised lascivious details. Publishers were not the only ones who profited; popular paperback writers of the time made more money than their hardcover-published counterparts, Vin Packer's *Spring Fire*, for example, selling a million and a half copies its first year of publication.

Virtually all writers of homosexual material in those days used pseudonyms, and the men often used female ones—e.g., Lawrence Block, who penned several quite good lesbian novels under the name Jill

Emerson: *Enough of Sorrow* is excerpted here. A considerable number of male writers authored lesbian fiction in the '50s and '60s, either from prurient interest or, more likely, to cash in on a publishing boom; their books outnumbered the women's perhaps five to one. For pre-1970 male-authored works with lesbian content I refer interested readers to Barbara Grier's invaluable compilation, *The Lesbian in Literature* and will mention here only a few notable authors: Lawrence Durrell (*Clea* from *The Alexandria Quartet*, 1960), D. H. Lawrence (*The Fox*, 1923), John D. MacDonald (*All These Condemned*, 1954), John O'Hara (*Lovey Childs*, 1969; plus numerous short stories), Theodore Sturgeon (*Venus Plus Ten*, 1960), and John Wyndham (*Consider Her Ways*, 1957).

Such scant personal information exists about many of the authors that I cannot guarantee the gender of everyone I've included. Of necessity, given the times, with one or two exceptions such as March Hastings and Valerie Taylor, the pulp fiction lesbian writers were deeply closeted, and some have dissolved into the mists of history like Cheshire cats, leaving only their printed words behind. Others settled into another kind of invisibility. Marion Zimmer Bradley, who achieved international fame as a prolific fantasy writer (*The Mists of Avalon*; the Darkover novels), married and had three children, divorced, and began her writing career in the '60s, writing her lesbian novels under the names Miriam Gardner, Lee Chapman, and Morgan Ives. In later years she refused to acknowledge this work or to discuss any of this aspect of her life.

In the past three decades Valerie Taylor (Velma Young), Ann Bannon (Ann Weldy), and Vin Packer (Marijane Meaker) have emerged to discover our warm welcome, indeed our celebration of them. Valerie Taylor (now deceased) was perhaps the first of our pulp writers to be relatively open and visible, leaving her marriage and conventional life to live in the gay area of Chicago. Militantly active in the gay liberation movement, in 1974 she formed the Lesbian Writers Conference and delivered its keynote address.

Prolific Marijane Meaker (pseudonyms in addition to Vin Packer: Ann Aldrich, M. E. Kerr) reveals in her fascinating memoir, *Highsmith* (Cleis Press, 2003) that she was a presence amid the Greenwich Village bar scene where she met and became involved with the more famous Patricia Highsmith. *Spring Fire* (Vin Packer, 1952) owns the distinction of being our first original paperback novel with purely lesbian content. In subsequent years, writing as M. E. Kerr, Meaker has become, according to *The New York Times,* "One of the grand masters of young adult fiction."

Ann Bannon, who married early and had two children, held her conventional marriage together while spending weekends in Greenwich Village and portraying in her books the lesbian life she saw, imagined, and longed to live. Her eloquent introductions to the reissued *I Am a Woman* (Cleis Press, 2002) and *Journey to a Woman* (Cleis Press, 2002) provide rich reading about how her novels came into being, as does Marijane Meaker in her introduction to the reissue of *Spring Fire* (Cleis Press, 2004). We will soon learn much more about these writers and their times; both Meaker and Bannon have memoirs in the offing.

Joan Ellis (Julie Ellis), like Ann Bannon, married and had children, and like Meaker, continues a flourishing writing career to this day. A playwright and extraordinarily prolific novelist, she's written dozens of novels in the family saga, contemporary, and suspense fields for major publishers.

Paula Christian, one of the best known and most popular of all the pulp writers, died in 2002. She did see some of her work return to print; *Another Kind of Love, Twilight Girls* (a compilation of the novellas *Edge of Twilight* and *This Side of Love*), and *The Other Side of Desire* are today available from Kensington Books.

Sloane Britain (Elaine Williams), the author of *These Curious Pleasures* (1961) was an editor at Midwood Tower, one of the top pulp fiction publishers; she committed suicide many years ago.

March Hastings (Sally Singer) was sitting in a restaurant across the street from the Stonewall Inn the night the riots began in 1969. She has lived as a lesbian all her life, and for a time was partnered with Randy Salem (Pat Pardee), whose novel *Chris* (1959) is excerpted.

Tereska Torres is so interesting a figure in the history of the lesbian pulps, her contribution so singular, that she deserves additional mention. After her family fled Europe during World War II, Torres joined De Gaulle's Free French Forces headquartered in London and for five years came into contact with young women of widely varied backgrounds and sexual proclivities. This experience formed the basis for *Women's Barracks*, a fictionalized account of women in wartime, including a bold and candid portrait of a lesbian named Claude. Torres's later fiction was queer-tinged but never again so notably lesbian nor remotely successful as the book that launched the tidal wave of lesbian fiction.

Fawcett Gold Medal was the leading publisher in pulp fiction (Tereska Torres, Ann Bannon, Vin Packer), but other significant publishers were Avon (Randy Salem); Bantam (Shirley Verel, Della Martin); Beacon

(March Hastings, Randy Salem, Artemis Smith); Hillman (Kay Martin); Monarch (Marion Zimmer Bradley writing as Miriam Gardner); and Midwood Tower (Randy Salem, Joan Ellis).

The diversity and quality of what I found not only surprised me, it dictated a necessity for parameters. So, before proceeding further, I'll explain what those are and why you will not see excerpts from books you may fully expect to find here.

Since the intent (and title) of the collection is *Lesbian Pulp Fiction*, the decision to do it justice by confining the selections to books published as original paperbacks seemed obvious. Hardcover fiction could be its own separately rewarding venture, at another time. To my dismay, the decision immediately led to the first major omission, the beloved classic novel *The Price of Salt* by Patricia Highsmith, written under the pseudonym Claire Morgan. Some of us (including myself) first found and read it in paperback; but its initial 1952 publication was in hardcover from Coward-McCann.

The golden age of the lesbian pulps by definition limited the historical timeframe: the first paperback was issued by Pocket Books in 1950. This precluded prior decades and superb novels, including that cornerstone of all our lesbian literature, Radclyffe Hall's *The Well of Loneliness* (1928). Hall's decade, by the way, saw major lesbian-themed work by giants of world literature, Virginia Woolf and Gertrude Stein. Notable pre-1950 and hardcover novels are listed in the bibliography.

One book excerpted here, *The King of a Rainy Country* by Brigid Brophy (1957), requires mention for an odd reason: its publisher. Anyone with knowledge of the publishing industry would challenge the presence of Alfred A. Knopf on a list of paperback publishers. But the novel is indeed a paperback, its publisher explaining on the back cover its reasons for this "experiment." Obviously the format was subsequently deemed an unsuccessful experiment for Knopf.

In Lee Server's *Encyclopedia of Pulp Fiction Writers* (2002), Marijane Meaker recalled the instructions given to her by Gold Medal editor Dick Carroll: "The only restriction he gave me was that it couldn't have a happy ending... Otherwise the post office might seize the books as obscene." Her introduction to *Spring Fire*'s 2004 reissue addresses at greater length the conversation with Carroll, and how the mandatory ending of the book—madness and suicide—came to be.

When *Three Women* (1958) by March Hastings (Sally Singer) was reissued by Naiad Press in 1989 she insisted on revising it to the positive ending she would have given it had she been allowed to do so by editors at Beacon. "To compare the two endings of *Three Women* would require a book of its own," she says today. "We all know the publishing climate in those days: same sex affection is out of the mainstream loop in this country, therefore, give it to us overtly for fun and games (hetero titillation) but make sure you tack on an ending of misery, punishment, sadness—that was the commercial voice, loud and distinct." But she also remembers, "The voice of survival said to me, 'Give them what they ask for now. You will have your way, later.' Personally, I was both optimistic and nervous. I had a true and beautiful readership that I cherished. I gave them my integrity in the story-middle, and the feelings there implied our secret pact that one day it would all come right—which it did."

Ann Bannon remembers no specifically stated restrictions for her first Gold Medal novel published five years later, and avers that not one word was changed in the manuscript of *Odd Girl Out* she turned in to Dick Carroll. No matter. The tenor of the times, its rigid moral framework, were crystal clear to her, and she produced remarkable, vivid, crucially important fiction within the dictates of that framework. Ironically, a great value of her books today is their unvarnished reflection of their times. Irony indeed when books of this period were for a time regarded as an embarrassment and generally repudiated by feminists during the '70s and '80s for their depiction of a "self-hating" world. The historical perspective of our post-feminist world has restored the luster these books deserve for their sexual courage, exemplified by Cleis Press's reissues of *Spring Fire* and the Ann Bannon novels with covers reflective of their initial publication.

Back in those days, when the vast majority of lesbians were like isolated islands with no territory other than risky lesbian bars to call our own, and no way of finding more than a few of one another, we were in every way susceptible to accepting and even agreeing with the larger culture's condemnation of us. We despairingly hoped that stories in the original paperbacks would not end badly but realized that in the view of the larger society, "perversion" could have no reward in novels about us, even those we ourselves wrote. For unrepentant lesbian characters who did not convert to heterosexuality, madness, suicide, homicide awaited, or, at best, "noble" self-sacrifice, such as Stephen Gordon surrendering Mary Llewellyn to Martin Hallam in *The Well of Loneliness*.

The good news: it's not true that all but a precious few of these books ended badly.

Most of us believe that *The Price of Salt* is the first lesbian novel with a happy ending—Therese and Carol end up together—although it's tempered by the steep price Carol pays for her relationship with Therese, the loss of her son. Aside from the lyrical beauty of Highsmith's writing ("It would be Carol in a thousand cities, a thousand houses, in foreign lands where they would go together, in heaven and in hell..."), the affirmation of the ending is a prime reason why the novel is treasured by so many lesbians.

The first unadulterated happy ending actually belongs to a novel published more than a decade earlier, in 1938: *Torchlight to Valhalla* by Gale Wilhelm (reissued by Naiad Press, 1985). A slender, elegant, finely written novel despite its heavily Hemingwayesque prose, its main character is Morgen, a writer; and much of the novel is taken up with her resistance to her persevering male suitor, Royal. When she first sees Toni she understands instantly her every reluctance toward heterosexuality: "I didn't know what I was waiting for, I didn't even know I was waiting, but when I saw you I knew." The love scenes between the two are spare, delicate, and exquisite; and the two women end up together.

Some pulp novels of the '60s have alternative outcomes, if not precisely happy ones. In *Chris*, Randy Salem's classic 1959 novel, Chris rejects both Carol and Dizz to salvage her self. *In the Shadows* by Joan Ellis (1962) ends with Elaine, who is in love with her brother's wife, leaving her possessive husband to find her own future. In the final scene of Ann Bannon's *Odd Girl Out*, Laura is in a train station going off to "live my life as honestly as I can."

Some endings are even better. In *These Curious Pleasures* by Sloane Britain (1961), it's a triumph for the lesbian reader when Sloane, the novel's main lesbian character, asks Allison to see if a reservation is available on Allison's flight to the coast (the equivalent, in those dark times, of asking Allison to marry her)—only to discover that Allison, in hope, had made one for the two of them the day before. In *The Third Street* by Joan Ellis (1964), Karen leaves her husband for Pat; and in *Odd Girl* by Artemis Smith (1959), Anne ditches husband Mark, and chooses Pru over two-timing married Esther. All five of the Bannon novels end either with women together or going off to an open future. Paula Christian's *Edge of Twilight* (1959) and *Another Kind of Love* (1961) end positively, as do Valerie Taylor's *The Girls in 3-B* (1959) and *Return to Lesbos* (1963).

The Third Sex (1959) by Artemis Smith is notable on several counts. Its last line is a celebratory toast: "To Ruth and Joan, who are no longer alone." Like the Ann Bannon oeuvre, it takes place in an authentic gay milieu, contains portraits of gay men as well as lesbians, and features a marriage of convenience—lesbian Joan is married to gay Marc for mutual protection. It also portrays a stone butch (Kim) with a femme (Joan), and Joan's sexual exploration and fluidity of sexual roles are a precursor to lesbian behavior today.

Clearly, many of the writers of that era, like March Hastings, maintained an integrity of vision and did their best to write what they wanted to write. The jacket copy writers were the ones who did society's work of condemnation to pass any censorship/obscenity scrutiny. There's no better case in point than the novel titled *Twilight Girl* by Della Martin, published in 1961, apparently the only book by this writer—or perhaps the only one she wrote under this name. It's the story of an innocent teenage butch named Lorraine (Lon) Harris who discovers the shadowy world where she belongs, journeys to self-discovery within that world, but lacks the inner strength to withstand condemnation by the larger society that has all the power over her life and will not allow her to be any part of the person she is. *Twilight Girl* (to be reissued by Cleis Press) is a fine and remarkably well-written novel, psychologically true and deeply affecting and timeless, one of my major finds. The somewhat awkwardly phrased blurb on the front cover appears in surprising agreement with my assessment: "We sincerely believe this the finest novel ever to treat of the third sex." Then there is the back jacket copy: "...For unless the blight [lesbianism] is understood, it cannot be curbed...this book should be read by everyone bent on combating the lesbian contagion."

An inverse law seems to be at work on pulp fiction novels: the better and more honest the book, the more its jacket copy must moralize against it. For lesbian readers, mixed messages indeed. There is real, honest, and painful truth in *Twilight Girl*, and it raises important questions about the nature of what it is to be lesbian. Its author without doubt knew whereof she was writing. The viciousness of the jacket copy is designed not only to hold off censors but to short circuit any insights by lesbian readers who might add up the truths in this book and begin to question the inimical judgments made of them.

For this reason the original jacket copy on each of the novels precedes each of the excerpts. Judge for yourself the tenor of the times and the differences between packaging and content, how the copywriters wrote for the censors while the writers wrote about lesbian lives as honestly as they could.

Some of the settings reflect the real world of lesbian society. The pervasive presence of the lesbian bar in *Twilight Girl* and a number of other novels (Ann Bannon, Paula Christian, Valerie Taylor, Joan Ellis, et al) illustrates how crucial the bar society was for gays and lesbians as our only vestige of visible community and support. Alcohol infused this fiction as it did real life. However destructively addictive, it was the necessary ingredient for breaking down inhibitions and fueling courage, and as medication for the chronic pain of being an outcast.

If a lesbian bar setting is the leitmotif of much early lesbian fiction, other lesbian novels tend to be set everywhere else that young women congregate. *Spring Fire* takes place on a college campus in the Midwest, in a sorority. Bannon's *Odd Girl Out* has virtually the same setting. Some titles are self-explanatory: Torres's *Women's Barracks*, and *Summer Camp* by Anne Herbert. Novels set within the general confines of heterosexual society show a pattern of being those with the most tragic outcomes: *The Whispered Sex* (1960) by Kay Martin, has a night-club setting; *My Sister, My Love* (1963) by Miriam Gardner (Marion Zimmer Bradley), involves the world of music; *Three Women* (1958) by March Hastings, is set in the art world. Shirley Verel's exceptional novel *The Dark Side of Venus* (1962) features novelist Diana Quendon and Mrs. Judith Allard in the upper-class environs of London.

The success of Ann Bannon's novels is rooted in their urban setting. Rather than an invented setting, they take place in an actual society and community where isolated lesbians of the day longed to be.

So, what kind of excerpts are here, and why did I choose them? *Women's Barracks* and *Spring Fire* were obvious choices because of their pioneering status. Imagine, as you read these two pieces, their impact on readers as the button-down 1950s began. A number of others are included for their sexual content. Lesbian sex is vibrant during any era (somehow we manage), and you'll see how these writers portrayed our love with smoldering candor during an era of unrelenting repression. In other excerpts you'll find some of those happy endings I've mentioned. A few, like Fay Adams's *Appointment in Paris*, demonstrate the variety of background. I chose others for their palpable reflection of what the times were like, what being a lesbian was like. Quality of the writing is another reason why Brigid Brophy's *The King of a Rainy County* and Shirley Verel's *The Dark Side of Venus* are here. Writers Ann Bannon, Paula Christian and Valerie Taylor are showcased with more than one excerpt because they have earned an enduring popularity over the decades.

Ann Bannon's five books in particular are by far the most celebrated of our early literature, and she is called "The Queen of Pulp Fiction" for good reason. The author and her books are in a class by themselves. When her five novels were reprinted in Naiad Press editions in 1983, lesbian readers found that she had all this time been in academia (she retired as assistant dean at Sacramento State College), and she herself received the gratitude, acclaim, and embrace of her community. While the Naiad Press reprints in 1983 were instrumental in her rediscovery by readers who first encountered her in pulp format, the recent Cleis Press reissues have revealed her not only to an entirely new generation of readers learning of this history for the first time, but to the media. She has once again found a huge fan base of lesbian, gay, and queer readers, this time looking to her as living history. She has been featured in film documentaries, radio and television interviews, and in many appearances across the country where she speaks in detail about her novels and their times.

Although several of Paula Christian and Valerie Taylor's stories follow a lesbian character (Val McGregor and Erika Frohmann, respectively), the Bannon novels form a one-of-a-kind saga featuring three characters. They begin with Laura and Beth in *Odd Girl Out*, and continue in *I Am a Woman* with Laura and her volatile relationship with quintessential butch Beebo Brinker in Greenwich Village. The dark-edged (in more than title) *Women in the Shadows* resumes their story. In *Journey to a Woman*, Beth seeks out Laura in New York, resulting in an explosive mix of all three characters. *Beebo Brinker* is the final book, a prequel to the four books, delineating the origins of the title character, arguably still the most iconic figure in all of lesbian fiction.

The five books, vividly written and textured with characterization and setting, charged with passion and color, are especially treasured because they portray the only community most of us knew we had back then, the almost mythic Greenwich Village. The Beebo Brinker series without question will remain a part of our permanent literature.

The importance of all our pulp fiction novels cannot possibly be overstated. Whatever their negative images or messages, they told us we were not alone. Because they told us about each other, they led us to look for and find each other, they led us to the end of the isolation that had divided and conquered us. And once we found each other, once we began to question the judgments made of us, our civil rights movement was born.

The courage of the authors of these books also cannot be overstated, pseudonyms be damned. Anyone who has ever written a book can testify to the feeling of personal risk we experience, the sense of stark exposure. The writers of these books laid bare an intimate, hidden part of themselves and they did it under siege, in the dark depths of a more than metaphorical wartime, because there was desperate urgency inside them to reach out, to put words on the page for women like themselves to read. Their words reached us, they touched us in different and deeply personal ways, and they helped us all.

In my case, and with specific reference to Ann Bannon, they saved my life.

Katherine V. Forrest
San Francisco
March 2005

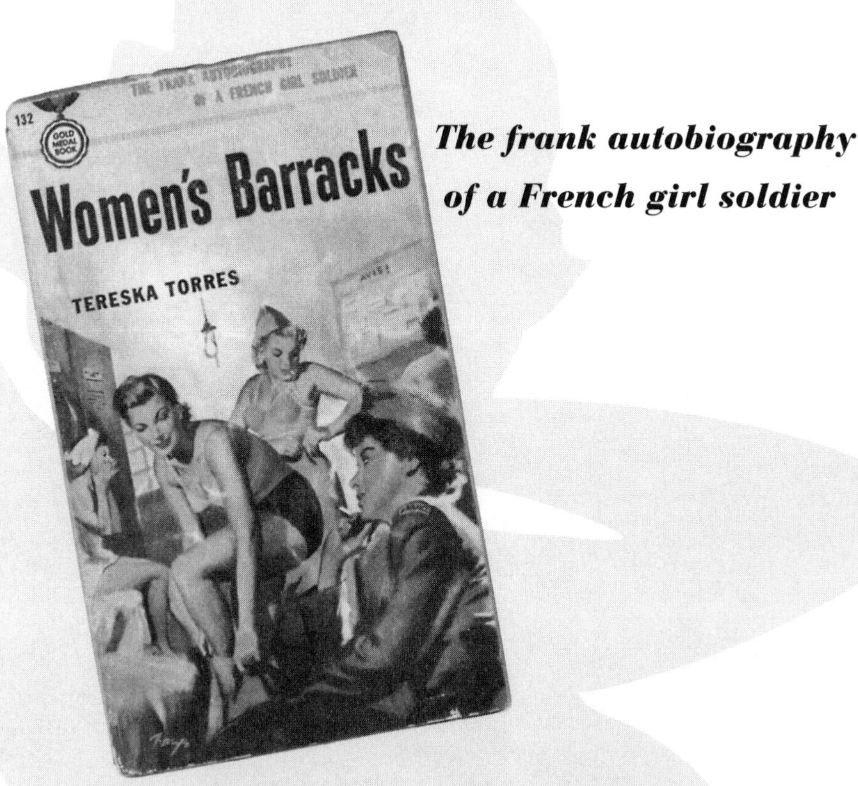

The frank autobiography of a French girl soldier

Women's Barracks

by Tereska Torres

This is the story of what happens when scores of young girls live intimately together in a French military barracks. Their problems, their temptations, their fights and failures are those faced by all women who are forced to live together without normal emotional outlets.

The girls who chose Tereska Torres, the author, as their confidante poured out to her their most intimate feelings, their secret thoughts. So this book, with all of its revealment and tenderness, is an important book because it tells a story that had never been truly told—the story of women in war.

Women's Barracks

That day, too, we were assigned to housecleaning.

Toward evening, a truck unloaded straw for mattresses—and also a batch of five new recruits, who were immediately sent off to peel vegetables in the kitchen. Ursula and I had just finished cleaning the three bathrooms. She had been chattering rather easily most of the day and I had begun to feel that I understood this frail girl who nevertheless was streaked through with decided, even passionate elements of character.

As we came out on the stairway we noticed one of the newcomers crossing the hall, laden with a huge pile of straw. It was a lady. A lady such as one saw in films. At first glance, the lady appeared fairly young—thirty or thirty-two. But on closer scrutiny one saw that she was somewhat older.

Ursula stood still and murmured, "Isn't she beautiful?"

The woman was tall and extremely blonde—a peroxide blonde. Her hair curled in ringlets over her forehead and fell in waves alongside her face. Her nose was fairly long, but quite narrow and very slightly arched, giving her an air of distinction. She was heavily made up. Ursula stood stock-still, a wisp of a girl wrapped in her long beige smock, watching the passage of this beautiful creature. The woman had such a marvelous scent! And in passing, she threw Ursula a smile that was as perfumed as the woman herself.

At that moment our sergeant-cook appeared, roaring, "Hey, you there, the new one—Claude! What are you doing with that straw? You're supposed to be in the kitchen!"

To our astonishment, we beheld the one called Claude raise a snarling face over her pile of straw, and from her artfully made-up mouth there came forth one of the most violent replies that I had ever heard. As for Ursula, she stood agape. "You can go to hell!" the lady spat at the sergeant. "Just because you're a sergeant, don't think you can get away with anything! First, I'm going to fix my bed and when I'm through, I'll come and peel your potatoes, and if you don't like it you can kiss my behind!"

The sergeant-cook must have realized that this was no little girl from Brittany, for she went away without saying a word.

Now Claude turned toward us. "Can you imagine, talking to me in such a tone of voice! What does she take me for—her servant? More likely, she'd be mine! I volunteered out of patriotism, and not to be treated like an inferior by a *conne* like that!"

It was strange, but the coarse words with which her speech was peppered seemed to lose their vulgarity when they were spoken by Claude. She had a very beautiful voice, cultured and modulated, the sort that could permit itself the use of slang.

"Can you tell me where to find the switchboard room?" Claude then asked. "That's where I'm to bunk. I've got to take charge of the telephone."

An assignment of this sort seemed prodigiously important to us. Full of respect for Claude, we showed her the little room near the entrance that had been set aside for the telephone operator.

Claude dropped the straw on the floor, went to the window, opened it, and leaned on her elbows, looking out into the street.

Facing our barracks was a large hotel, and in front of the hotel entrance stood the doorman, very tall, very thin, with graying hair and thin lips. His cheeks were highly rouged, his eyelids were painted a bright blue, and he bowed with feminine grace before every man who entered the hotel. Then he resumed his haughty nonchalant stance, staring directly before him at the windows of our barracks.

"You could take him for the ambassador of Peru," murmured Claude. We had no idea why "ambassador" and why "Peru," but the phrase enchanted Ursula and she started to laugh.

"How old are you, child?" Claude asked her.

This time Ursula replied, "Seventeen," without hesitation.

Claude placed her hand on Ursula's head and stroked her soft hair. I felt as though I were intruding. "You have the air of a tiny little girl, and you're ravishing—you're like a little bird," Claude said.

It was obvious that this was the first time anyone had told Ursula she was ravishing. And yet, because it was said in another person's presence—mine—it was quite normal, almost a conventional remark.

Ursula never forgot her feelings at this first meeting. When she spoke about it to me later she said that Claude's voice was so gentle, Claude's hand was so soft that she wanted to reply, "Oh, and you are so beautiful!" but she didn't dare, and she uttered the first banality that came to her. "I've been here since yesterday. I'm from Paris. Where are you from?"

Claude was about to answer when a corporal appeared—a third one. We seemed surrounded by corporals. This was a large girl, rather gentle and reserved, she had charge of the office. She had some forms in her hand and she gave them to Claude to fill out.

Ursula tugged at me, and we left.

Our aristocratic Jacqueline was the first to receive a secretarial post. She would always be first everywhere, with her enchanting face and her air of being owed the best, and yet this was so natural to her that we could not resent her manner. She returned at noon, absolutely delighted with her office. Her lieutenant was a man of excellent family, she announced to us, highly cultured. And he had already invited her to have lunch with him tomorrow. Of course, he had a wife and children in France.

Soon most of us were assigned to work in various offices at GHQ. I became, for the time being, a file clerk and the operator of a mimeograph machine in the Information Bureau. But the Captain had no idea what to do with Ursula. Most of us could type, at least; Ann could drive a car; but Ursula had no accomplishments. Finally the Captain put her down as sentry for the barracks.

Ursula remained seated all day long at a little table by the entrance, keeping a registry book in which she noted down all of our comings and goings. Opposite her was the switchboard room, where Claude was stationed. Through the half-open door she could glimpse Claude's glistening blonde hair. From time to time, Claude came out of the little room for a chat. She still wore that same wonderful perfume. But with tender dismay one night Ursula asked me if I had noticed that Claude had little creases at the sides of her mouth, and white hairs mingled with the blonde. Indeed, Claude could have been her mother. And in those first days I felt that this was what drew Ursula to Claude, the wish that she had had a mother as gay and amusing as this woman, with her inexhaustible store of gossip about all the celebrities in Paris.

But soon the stories Ursula brought back from Claude were less innocent. Ursula was fascinated and yet a little puzzled by the ease with which Claude related her bedroom experiences; she had slept with most of the currently fashionable actors and writers of the capital, and she kept up a continuous stream of intimate chatter about her lovers to the girl. Ursula would repeat Claude's gossip, somewhat in awe, and somewhat as though wanting reassurance that there was nothing wrong in her adoration of Claude. Claude would tell her, "I absolutely adored that boy, and then suddenly I had enough of him. My only love was always my husband, but he's a dog. He drinks too much, and he's a fairy, damn him! As soon as we're together, we fight. Luckily, I had Jacques. He was my great consolation. He was still a child, a high-school boy. He used to come to me after school. I trained him. I made him my best lover."

Ursula couldn't get over her astonishment at this woman who adored her homosexual husband but fought with him, and who had so many lovers, and who was so much at ease about it all. The world of grownups had always seemed distant and mysterious to Ursula. With Claude, that world became even more distant, and all the values that Ursula had so painfully established for herself were overturned.

But one thing was certain: Ursula felt that the one person who really cared about her was Claude. Big Ann was pleasant and sometimes brusque; the aristocratic Jacqueline irritated her, perpetually wanting to fuss over her and take charge of her; Mickey was a clown who made her laugh; and I suppose I was just someone who listened, someone she found it easy to talk to. Ursula complained that the corporals scolded her endlessly, and the Captain could scarcely remember her name. But Claude talked to her, confided in her as in a friend, called her her little bird, stroked her hair, smiled at her with her perfumed smile. Claude knew so many stories, she was afraid of no one, and she had a way of looking at Ursula with her black eyes, a way that made Ursula forget every desire except to remain close to Claude as much as possible.

One night there came an order for the sentry to sleep in the switchboard room with the telephone operator, so as to make sure that the service would continue in case of a serious air attack. I helped Ursula drag her iron cot into the little telephone room. Her heart must have been beating with joy. What heavenly evenings she would pass with Claude!

That same evening, Claude decided to throw a secret little party in the switchboard room. We organized it among a few of the girls, and sent Ursula out to the corner pub to fetch some bottles of beer.

Ursula put on her cap and hurried out. It was the first time she had been out since her arrival at the barracks. It was raining. Down Street was narrow and dark. Ursula found her way to the pub, which was brightly lighted and full of smoke, and crowded with soldiers in various degrees of drunkenness. They called out to her, "Oh, Frenchie! Look at the French girl!" Ursula told me later that she didn't know what to do with herself. The soldiers' eyes shone and their lips were wet with beer. They had thick red hands. Ursula's heart fluttered. She kept her eyes fixed at a point on the wall while she was being served. Finally it was finished. The soldiers tried to catch hold of her arms, but she freed herself and ran out. Ursula plunged toward the barracks as to a refuge.

I was standing in the doorway of the switchboard room when we heard Ursula's hurrying footsteps on the stairs outside. Claude brushed past me into the hall and opened the door for her. She stood there in the doorway, so shining, so blonde, with her khaki shirt partly open, revealing her white throat. Ursula pressed herself suddenly against the woman, and Claude held her in her arms. Her hands gently caressed Ursula's hair.

I can only suppose that Claude forgot my presence, or perhaps she thought I had gone on into the switchboard room. But I remained in the doorway, and I saw Claude gently press Ursula's head against her full breasts, separated from Ursula's cheek only by the khaki shirt.

It was not hard for me, then or later, to understand Ursula's feelings. After her first, unnerving visit to a pub full of roistering soldiers, she had hurried along a dark, alien street and found again at the end of it Claude—beautiful, shining Claude—who at that moment must have seemed to her the very embodiment of warmth and safety and gentleness.

Claude raised Ursula's chin with one hand, drawing her face closer, and suddenly, in the dimly lighted hall, she kissed Ursula on the mouth. It was a quick light kiss, like a brush of a bird's wing, a kiss so discreet as not even to startle the girl.

Just then Ann and Mickey came along, with their drinking glasses hidden under the jackets of their uniforms.

In the switchboard room, a little clock sounded nine. The corporal of the guard had closed her eyes to our soiree, since Ann had given her to understand that Warrant Officer Petit was invited, and, naturally, any corporal reporting our little party would only be making trouble for herself. (I had already noticed that Ann seemed to be born with a sense of how to manage things in the Army.)

Petit was the last to arrive. The little room was filled with cigarette smoke. Claude had taken off her uniform, and was now wearing a dressing gown—blue with little white dots. She was seated on the bed with one of her legs folded under her, and the other kicking a red slipper. A lock of platinum hair fell over her forehead. A cigarette trembled in her lips, while she was engaged in reading Mickey's palm.

Petit surveyed the room, with her scrunched-up eyes of a man of the world. Petit might readily agree that Claude was beautiful, but a woman like Claude had no interest for Petit. To our warrant officer, Claude was only a dilettante. One might pass a pleasant evening with a woman like that, but nothing else. At bottom, to the Petits of the world, Claude was a pervert, a perverted woman of the sophisticated milieu, but a woman in spite of everything. As for Ursula, Petit scarcely glanced at her, obviously summing her up as a nice little thing, but nothing special. She looked at Mickey. Her expression said, "A little fool."

Ann was standing against the table with her arms crossed. She had rather thick muscular arms and broad masculine hands. Petit poured herself a glass of beer, and drank it down without stopping; she was satisfied. It was said that her last two intimate friends had remained in France on the farm where the three of them had lived before the war. She was all alone here, and felt herself aging. Soon enough she'd be fifty years old. In Ann, she must have seen herself as she had been at twenty-six—solid and robust, with a deep voice and a man's hands. Ann looked directly into her eyes, and from her relaxed and satisfied expression Petit seemed to know that everything was going well. It was probably then that Petit decided to use her influence to have Ann made a corporal as soon as possible. That would make things a lot simpler.

Much was to happen between the women who were at Claude's little party, and when I traced back their stories, I found that the threads began to be woven together on this night.

Mickey was laughing as usual and playing the little comedian. Claude knew that she was making no mistake; she had wide experience with men, with women, and with life: Mickey would go far for adventure, even though she was still a typical *demi-vierge*. She was pretty, in her gawky way, she was ready for anything, she was gay, a good comrade, and well liked by everyone. Claude predicted a rich lover and a long voyage for her. Then Claude turned her gaze upon little Ursula, sitting silently at the foot of the bed, and Claude's face filled with tenderness for the child. A girl still so young, so new, altogether inexperienced and untaught. She must have thought of her own life as a little girl, for despite her bravura manner of an adventuress and a *femme fatale*, she was born of a provincial middle-class family. Ursula had already brought me Claude's story of how she had been lifted out of her small-town shell when quite young, through marriage to an elderly, dissipated Parisian who had initiated her into the city's circles of debauch. He had finally succeeded in completely disorienting a character that was at bottom healthy. Claude had left him at last, and married a younger man, an engineer by profession. But her second husband had his special passion, and had taken a job in London so as to be near one of his male friends. Claude had followed him in May, just before the fall of France, for she was in love with him despite his habit. She was a woman overfilled with love, and her love had to be dissipated. All the love that she might have had for a child had to be used somewhere. And here was this girl, this little Ursula. I think there was the same mothering desire in her love for Ursula that she had felt when that boy Jacques had come to her with his schoolbooks under his arm. And yet there was with it a devouring avidity for something as delicious as a slightly green fruit. It was strange, absurd, but when Claude talked of Jacques one could see that it had seemed to Claude as though she were carrying on in a motherly role, continuing a boy's upbringing, just as someone who had taught him to wash, to eat, to walk. She, Claude, was also a mother in her way. She had taught him to eat of another sort of food—and she was proud of his progress, with a maternal pride. And little Ursula—how wonderful it would be to watch her little mouth open for the first time, and to see her overcome with happiness, like a child to whom one has just given a beautiful toy!

Even while she kept chattering with the rest of us, Claude studied the girl through the corner of her eye. She smiled at Ursula, and drew her nearer, putting her arms around her, living again the intimate moment in the doorway.

Petit was watching, with a malicious and slightly obscene light in her eyes. She had the air of saying, "I leave her to you. That one doesn't interest me at all." But it was flattering to Claude that Petit understood at once. Claude always enjoyed the idea of being considered a dangerous woman.

The barracks had been in existence for more than a month. Every morning we went through our drill in Down Street before hurrying off to our various jobs. One day the Captain announced that a military ball was taking place, to which all of us had been invited.

That evening we were all loaded onto trucks and carried across blacked-out London. As we bumped along, Jacqueline regaled us with tales of the formal balls she had attended before the war, dressed in white tulle. She remembered the family limousine, with the chauffeur in uniform, bowing as he opened the door for the young lady. I suppose she could not help feeling her superiority to most of the girls in the truck, who behaved with a good deal of vulgarity. And I suppose that Jacqueline really had no desire to go to a dance at a training camp, where she might be pawed by any soldier from anywhere. But neither did she want to remain alone in Down Street. Besides, it might be amusing to see what a soldiers' dance was like, just once.

The truck made a few too many sudden stops. The driver must have found it amusing to jolt our bunch of girls so that we fell all over each other. Most of us laughed, but Jacqueline protested, for her back was again giving her trouble. One of the women called her a snob, and told her to cut out her mannerisms.

When I really came to know Jacqueline, I understood that she suffered from a perverse need to impress everybody. That night, she hoped that she would faint, so as to make that woman regret her words. But it didn't happen, and she didn't quite feel like feigning a loss of consciousness, as she sometimes did by letting herself slide into a kind of feebleness that readily took hold of her. But the bouncing truck brought tortures to her back. She had been suffering these odd spells ever since that night of her flight and her accident. I knew the pain was real enough, but I sometimes wondered why she had jumped from the roof of the house in the first place. Was it really because of that pair of perverted drunkards whose children she was taking care of? Was it really to escape from them? Or had she done it because of some need she carried within herself, a need for drama and for disaster?

I was astonished, and filled with admiration for her honesty, when Jacqueline told me once that she often asked herself the same questions.

"There seems to be a tradition of melodrama in my family," she said. "One of my first memories is of being surrounded by people, all of them talking about the airplane crash that killed my father."

Soon after that, Jacqueline told me, there had been a stepfather, elegant, attentive. She recalled the household scenes, later on, between her mother and her stepfather because he would kiss her when she came home from school. She spoke of the attempted suicide of her stepfather.

She had left home to escape this concentration of hatred and misfortune, veiled by riches and good manners. But her fate followed her wherever she went. Or was it perhaps that she carried it with her? Jacqueline wondered.

A week after her arrival in England, in the first family to which she had come on an exchange visit, the husband had died of a heart attack. After that she had lived with a couple, a man and his wife, who came in turns each night to knock on her door. She hated them. She wanted to punish them, to bring about some sort of explosion, to provoke a drama. Yes, she said, she knew now that it was drama that she wanted most of all. She could just as well have left quietly. No one would have kept her back by force. But she had preferred to stage an escape—to jump. She had had visions of herself as a beautiful corpse beside their house.

But instead, Jacqueline had howled in pain under their windows all night long and no one had come. In the morning she had dragged herself to her room. It was finished. The drama had failed.

Soon afterward, she had read a newspaper item about a feminine contingent being formed in the Free French Forces. That was her salvation. All the history of France passed before her eyes—pictures remembered from her childhood: the parades of July Fourteenth, Jeanne Hachette, Ste Geneviève, the queens of France, the *Marseillaise*, Verdun—she was going to become part of all that! To save France! To avenge the armistice, the great shame! Her father would have been proud of her—that legendary father who had fallen from the sky like Icarus.

As soon as she was well, she had volunteered. And now she was a soldier, mingled with the women of the people. There were indeed several girls of good family—Ursula, Mickey, a student of pharmacy, the daughter of a consul—but they were the exceptions. Most of Jacqueline's comrades now were women of an entirely different sort from any she had ever known before.

She spoke with contempt for all the members of her self-satisfied family—so sure of their prerogatives, so certain that it was a great distinction for anyone to be invited to their table—and yet, was she herself so different from them? Since she had come to live at the barracks, I knew that Jacqueline had her doubts. It was true that she accepted any sort of physical task without the slightest complaint, and that she did her best to accomplish it through pride—just to show us that she was perfectly capable of scrubbing the floor or peeling potatoes. But there were so many coarse women, with the tales of their cheap affairs with men already resounding through the barracks—she hated them all. They permitted themselves to be taken to filthy little hotels. They went to bed with sailors, copulating like animals. She, Jacqueline, would never permit a man to take her at his will. When the others talked of their cheap affairs,

Jacqueline said nothing. But I knew she was thinking of the lieutenant in her office, so eager to please her, bringing her books and flowers and gifts, inviting her to the Mayfair or to the Claridge. All the men were in love with her; Jacqueline had become used to that, and she would have been astonished if it were not so. She loved to watch the shine come into their eyes, and to provoke their compliments. The other evening in a taxi, after being taken to dinner, she had permitted a young officer to kiss her on the mouth and then had come running in like a child, her eyes sparkling, to tell me about it. It was fun, it was really like one read in stories, like playing with fire, to feel him burning close to her, and to be able to put him off whenever she wished. Before the war, in France, she had been engaged to a handsome lad, quite well-to-do, belonging to her own world. Jacqueline had permitted him to kiss her and to fondle her breasts, and she had found it amusing to hold him off after that, and to feel him trembling with desire, a slave of his desire for her. It was as though she had made a discovery, that in addition to being born to an aristocracy in which one always was in the position of deciding how other people should behave, she had been born into the aristocratic sex, for it was the woman who could always decide, always command, in relationships with men. It had been a pleasant discovery. Jacqueline had been seventeen at the time.

The dance was in full swing when we arrived. The men welcomed us with shouts and cries of joy; they were mostly French, though there was a scattering of uniforms from other nations—Polish, Norwegian, and Belgian. I liked dancing, and found myself in a little circle of swing enthusiasts. Everybody was learning the Lindy, and I danced with one after another in a strange exhilaration so that I scarcely knew or remembered with which boy the dancing went well. They were still all boys to me.

Mickey was seized by a master sergeant of the Air Corps, who squeezed her tightly as they danced. He was short and slightly bald, but Mickey said he was nice enough. Mickey was never especially particular. She liked to have fun and was willing to taste out of any dish, finding them all pleasant. As she danced, soldiers called to her. They assessed her with an expert air. Her mouth especially excited them—an arched red mouth with the upper lip slightly advanced, as though the girl were constantly ready to be kissed.

While they danced, the sergeant kissed her throat. For form's sake, Mickey pretended to be shocked. But even the sergeant could see well enough that she was not at all offended.

I looked around for Ursula, but she didn't seem to be anywhere in the room. I learned later that, after having danced with a fat soldier who was nearly drunk, she felt that she had had enough, and sought to escape. The cigarette smoke was so thick that it stung her eyes almost to the point of tears. She was afraid of these men, didn't know what to say to them, and was terrified merely at the idea of being touched by any one of them. She saw a door and fled outside. There was a little courtyard, and the fresh evening air made her shiver. Ursula sat down on the steps. The cool air caressed her cheeks, and she shook out her hair, relieved in her escape. Then she noticed that a soldier, quite young, was sitting on a crate in the courtyard, and watching her. There it is, she thought. I have to leave this place, too.

But in order not to appear ridiculous, she told me with her quaint nicety, she remained for another moment, planning to get up and leave as though she had just come for a breath of air.

She kept her eyes averted from the soldier so as not to give him an excuse to speak to her. The music came from the hall—muted, but reaching them nevertheless. In there, a voice was bellowing "Madelon."

Suddenly the soldier said to her, "It's better out here than inside, don't you think?" And as soon as she heard his calm voice, tinged with a slight foreign accent, Ursula felt reassured. Now she looked at the soldier. She could scarcely see him in the darkness, but he had a very young air and seemed rather small in stature. She replied, "Yes," and didn't know what else to say.

They remained silent for a long while. Ursula was suddenly quite astonished to hear her own voice break the silence.

She said, "Have you been in England long?"

The soldier answered, "I've been here three days. Last week I was in Spain, and it's only about fifteen days since I was in France."

Now Ursula looked at him with a kind of awe. He came from France! Only fifteen days ago, he had walked on the earth of France and spoken to the people of France and looked at the trees, the sky of France. It seemed to her that she had been in London for years rather than months.

She raised her head and watched the searchlights sweeping the sky. It was beautiful to see. The alert had sounded, just as it did every evening, but there had been no sound of aircraft. The German planes must have headed somewhere else instead of coming over London.

"Aren't you cold?" the soldier asked. He spoke so nicely, with so much gentleness in his voice, that Ursula said she was touched. She shook her head. He was probably not French. He had an accent, but Ursula couldn't tell from what country. And yet he spoke perfect French.

He was silent again for a little while, and then he said, "I admire you for joining the Army. It's not much fun for the men, but for women it must really be hard."

And now Ursula began to speak. Whenever she knew she was to be in the company of young men, she worried her head for days in advance to prepare some conversation, and she confessed that her voice always sounded affected to her own ears. Young men had always seemed members of another race to her, mysterious beings with whom she had no point of contact.

But this evening in the dim courtyard, Ursula found herself talking freely to the unknown soldier. She told him about her life in Down Street. She described Jacqueline, "absolutely ravishing, but a little bit artificial." Mickey, "a good comrade, and so funny"; Ann, "everybody thinks she'll be the first to get her corporal stripes"; Ginette, who "talks nothing but slang, used to be a salesgirl, and can sew her own uniforms to measure." She spoke of Claude, "very intelligent, very generous," who was her protectress. Then suddenly she saw it all, all of her comrades as we were in the mornings, tense, badly adapted to this life, ready to find distraction in anything, hungry for love, each hiding her homesickness at the bottom of her heart. Ursula saw the main hall of Down Street, and her little sentry table. And all day long the phonograph that we had just acquired kept playing the same records, "Violetta" and "*Mon coeur a besoin d'aimer.*" She spoke about our captain, hurried and distant, a smile always on her lips, calling us her "dear girls," always giving the impression that she was really going to do something, that she was going to help us somehow, that she was going to create an atmosphere of friendship in Down Street. She talked about this at every opportunity, but after each of her speeches one found oneself just as lonesome and empty as before.

The soldier listened without interrupting her, and when she had finished all he said was, "I understand," and Ursula felt herself to be truly understood, although she didn't really know what there was to understand. It seemed to her that this boy comprehended things even before she had grasped them herself. This comforted her, like finding a schoolroom problem solved without having to trouble over it.

We were all ready to go home, and had been hunting for Ursula. Jacqueline opened the door to the courtyard and called, "Ursula, are you there? Ursula, where are you?"

Several voices shouted, "Blackout!" But we just had time to make out two forms, like little children clutched together in the dark. They started up, coming toward us.

"Hurry!" Jacqueline called. "What a relief! At last we can leave," she said to me.

Ursula came slipping through the door.

The truck was waiting outside, and we piled in. This time I suppose the driver was too tired for his game of jolting us against one another. It was far past midnight, and some of the girls slept, leaning their heads on each other's shoulders. Suddenly I heard Ursula murmur, "Oh. I forgot to tell the soldier good-bye."

Just across from us sat Claude; she was holding Mickey's head on her shoulder. I could feel Ursula stir unhappily. It must have seemed to her that Mickey had stolen her place.

We jumped from the truck, one after the other, and were swallowed in the barracks hall. The house seemed to come awake, invaded like a beehive. Doors slammed, women ran up the stairway, women called to each other from room to room.

Mickey, in pajamas, began to dance in the middle our dormitory. Jacqueline was dressed in one of her elegant flowered linen nightgowns. She sat massaging her face with cold cream. Ann, who was already carrying out the duties of a corporal, even before being promoted, came to remind us that the reveille for tomorrow was for six o'clock, as usual, and to put out the lights. One door after another was heard closing, and the night quieted. There were still a few whispers from bed to bed.

"I was dancing with a sailor, and he's crazy about me."

"He's a perfect dancer. He wants to take me out someplace where we can have fun. You know."

"He's going to phone me tomorrow."

"But honey—it's amazing—he knows my brother! They went to the same school in Lyons."

As for myself, I hadn't met anyone special. I had given my name to a few of the men, perhaps for one of the evenings when a girl is so lonesome she'll go out with anyone. I'd seen some of the girls do things they probably wouldn't do otherwise, out of this loneliness, and I hoped it wouldn't happen to me.

The whispering gradually ceased. Ursula slipped through the room in the dark. She had been in the bathroom, as she was still modest about undressing; she had put on her regulation rose-colored pajamas. This was one of the nights when she slept in the switchboard room and she slipped out of the dormitory, going downstairs.

When Ursula reached the little switchboard room Claude was already stretched out on her narrow camp bed. A storm light stood on the floor. In the feeble light Claude's bright hair shone. Everything else was in shadow. Outside, the guns began to roar.

Ursula went to sit on the edge of Claude's bed. The alternate nights that Ursula was assigned to sleep in this room were impatiently awaited. For on these occasions Claude talked to her at length about her husband, about her lovers, about her life before the war. Claude told about places where opium was smoked, and about her travels, and about her pets. It was always passionately absorbing, and Ursula would listen without saying a word, extremely impressed by the number of important people Claude knew, by her countless adventures, and flattered to be spoken to with such intimacy. No one else had ever been like a real friend to her. Especially a really grown-up mature woman.

Ursula adored Claude, and was attracted to her in a special way she could not explain to herself. Sometimes it seemed to her that Claude took particular pains to charm her as though she, Ursula, were a man. But that would be absurd, and Ursula rejected so ridiculous an idea.

That night as she sat on the edge of the cot Claude said to her, "What a whorehouse that dance was! Where did you hide yourself? I drank I don't know how many glasses of port. Everyone offered me port to drink. I'm sleepy. Kiss me, Ursulita." She drew Ursula against her as she had that evening by the door, and suddenly she kissed her on the mouth. But this time the kiss was not so short. Ursula felt Claude's lips burning hers. She didn't know what was happening to her. She was lost, invaded, inflamed. She tried to get hold of herself as though she were drowning, dissolving in Claude's arms. Claude drew her into the bed.

Ursula felt herself very small, tiny against Claude, and at last she felt warm. She placed her cheek on Claude's breast. Her heart beat violently, but she didn't feel afraid. She didn't understand what was happening to her. Claude was not a man; then what was she doing to her? What strange movements! What could they mean? Claude unbuttoned the jacket of her pajamas, and enclosed one of Ursula's little breasts in her hand, and then gently, very gently, her hand began to caress all of Ursula's body, her throat, her shoulders, and her belly. Ursula remembered a novel that she had read that said of a woman, who was making love, "Her body vibrated like a violin." Ursula had been highly pleased by this phrase, and now her body recalled the expression and it too began to vibrate. She was stretched out with her eyes closed, motionless, not daring to make the slightest gesture, indeed not knowing what she should do. And Claude kissed her gently, and caressed her.

How amusing she was, this motionless girl with her eyelids trembling, with her inexperienced mouth, with her child's body! How touching and amusing and exciting! Claude ventured still further. Then, so as not to frighten her, her hand waited while she whispered to her. "Ursula my darling, my little girl, how pretty you are!" The hand moved again.

Ursula didn't feel any special pleasure, only an immense astonishment. She had loved Claude's mouth, but now she felt somewhat scandalized. But little by little, as Claude continued her slow caressing, Ursula lost her astonishment. She kept saying to herself, I adore her, I adore her. And nothing else counted. All at once, her insignificant and monotonous life had become full, rich and marvelous. Claude held her in her arms, Claude had invented these strange caresses, Claude could do no wrong. Ursula wanted only one thing, to keep this refuge forever, this warmth, this security.

Outdoors, the antiaircraft guns continued their booming, and the planes growled in the sky. Outside, it was a December night, cold and foggy, while here there were two arms that held her tight, there was a voice that cradled her, and soft hair touched her face.

A story once told in whispers now frankly, honestly written

Spring Fire

by Vin Packer

There was a girl named Leda who was Queen of the Campus. There was a girl called Mitch who desperately wanted to be loved. Suddenly they belonged to each other.

Not since *The Well of Loneliness* has there been such an honest, provocative novel on a theme too important to keep from the light.

Spring Fire

It was a gray afternoon, and the sun was hidden behind a sheet of dull sky, with the wind kicking the leaves along the curb in front of the Tri Epsilon house, where they stood talking.

"I'll pick you up after the meeting," he said. "We could squeeze in a few beers at Rick's."

"Not tonight, Jake-O. I'm tired. Think I'll catch up on sleep. Those Monday night chapter orgies wear me down."

She was thinking that Mitch would be waiting in the room. Before dinner she would tell Mitch that she was going out with Jake when the chapter meeting let out, and then she would surprise her. She'd say, "Do you think I could go out with him when I knew you were up here? I can't kid myself any longer, Mitch." Maybe that would erase the nervous undercurrent of tension between them since Jan had gone. It would be more dramatic that way, surprising her like that.

"OK, I'll give you a ring." He took the pipe out of his mouth and leaned over to kiss her quickly. Jake was funny the way he sang aloud in the streets. He walked away singing, "Oh, here by the fire we defy the frost and storm," and Leda heard him as she walked up the steps and came into the front room of the house. The thought came that if Jake were gone forever, it would be strange, but if the choice were to be made, it would be Jake who would go. Not Mitch. Was she upstairs? She teased her own curiosity, prolonging it, sweetening it by tarrying in the hall downstairs.

To the left of the dining room there was a small alcove, with square boxes and names printed evenly above each one. In her box there was an envelope with her name scrawled on the outside, and no postage or address. Girls were coming down the stairs, milling around in the hall waiting for the dinner gong. They were reading papers, playing cards, singing at the piano, and talking together in close, separate groups. Leda took the envelope to the scarlet chair in the corner near the entrance to Mother Nessy's suite. She ripped the seal open and held the thin notebook paper in her hand.

Dear Leda,

This letter is for you alone. Please tear it up when you are through.

More than anything else I want you to understand what I'm going to say here, and why I'm saying it. I want to leave the sorority and become an independent. Maybe it'll be the best thing for me, and maybe it'll be just another defeat, but I have to do it. Leda, darling, you know that I love you. You know it, even though I haven't shown it the past few days. I've been worried and afraid, and now I know for sure what's wrong with me. I suppose I should go to a doctor, but I don't have the nerve, and I'm going to try to help myself as best I can.

Lesbian *is an ugly word and I hate it. But that's what I am, Leda, and my feelings toward you are homosexual. I had no business to ask you to stop seeing Jake, to try to turn you into what I am, but please believe me, I didn't know myself what I was doing. I guess I'm young and stupid and naïve about life, and I know that you warned me about the direction my life was taking when you told me to get to know men. I tried, Leda. But it was awful. Even Charlie knows what I am now. I think that if I go to an independent house, away from you, the only person I love, I'll be able to forget some of the temptation. If I stay in the sorority, I'll only make you unhappy and hurt you. I love you too much to do that.*

Please announce that I am leaving during the chapter meeting tonight. Don't tell them why, please, because I want to straighten myself out and I don't want people to know. Tell them that I thank them for all they've done, but that I'd rather live somewhere else because I don't fit in here.

I know how you'll feel about me after reading this. I'll try to stay out of your way. Tonight I am going to eat dinner downtown, and then during chapter meeting I'll pack most of my things and move to the hotel until I get a room at the dorm. Robin Maurer is going to help me.

There's nothing else to say but good-bye, I'm sorry, and I do love you, Leda.

Mitch

The dinner gong sounded out the first seven notes of "Yankee Doodle." Mother Nesselbush stood in the doorway of her suite. She looked down at Leda, who was sitting there holding the paper the note was written on, not moving. It was customary for one of the girls to lead her in to dinner. Marsha usually handled the task because she was president, but Marsha was hurrying to finish the last-minute preparations in the Chapter Room for the meeting. Mother Nesselbush cleared her throat, but to no avail. Leda sat still and pale and Nessy bent down.

"Are you all right, dear?"

"Yes."

"That was the dinner bell, you know."

Leda said, "Yes."

"Would you like to escort me to my table?"

Leda looked up at her, a thin veil of tears in her eyes, so thin that Mother Nessy did not notice. She could sense the waiting around her, the girls waiting to go into the dining room, Nessy waiting, the houseboys who served the food waiting for her. Standing slowly, she crooked her arm and felt Nessy's hand close on it as they moved across the floor into the brightly lighted hall, past the six oak tables to the long front table and the center seats.

A plate of buns went from hand to hand, each girl taking one and passing the plate mechanically, reaching for it with the left, offering it with the right, as they had been taught when they were pledges. The bowl of thick, dried mashed potatoes came next, and the long dish of wizened pork chops, the bowl of dull green canned peas, and the individual dishes of cole slaw. When Leda tasted the food, she felt an emetic surging throughout her body and she laid her fork down. Around her there was a churning gobble of voices that seemed to slice through her brain like a meat cleaver. Mother Nessy stared after her when she went from the room.

"She said she was sick," she told Kitten, "and I knew it when I saw her before dinner. Poor thing. There's a flu epidemic going around, and I'm willing to bet my life she's got the flu."

The car was gone from the driveway. Leda put on the sweater she was carrying and ran down the graveled drive. In her hand she clutched her felt purse, and at the corner she caught a taxi.

At the Blue Ribbon there was a crowd of students waiting at the rail with trays, sitting in the booths with books piled high beside their plates, pushing and standing near the juke box with nickels and dimes, the pin-ball machines ringing up scores in her ears as she looked for Mitch.

The Den was quieter, and the waitresses were lingering lazily around the front of the room near the bar, where a few boys munched liverwurst sandwiches and drank draught beer. The bartender dropped a glass and cursed enthusiastically. Leda pushed the revolving door and felt the cold autumn wind.

Mac's, Donaldson's, the Alley, French's, Miss Swanson's, all of them alive with hungry students swarming in and out, the smell of hamburger predominant in each cafe, the sizzling crack of French fries cooking in grease on hot open grills.

"Ham on rye."

"One over easy."

"Hey, Mary, catch the dog."

"Well, hell, you're almost an hour late!"

Leda stood finally on the curb in front of Miss Swanson's. She fumbled in her pocket for a nickel and ran into the drugstore on the corner. She made a mistake dialing the number, and she held the hook down until the nickel came back and then tried again. When the voice answered, there was a long wait, the far-off sound of voices shouting down the halls, and then the answer, quick and flip. "Robin's out to dinner. Call back later."

Her heart was pounding, and she could feel the perspiration soaking her body. If Mitch was eating with Robin, she might have it arranged already. Where was she eating? With the car, she could be anywhere, but it was unlike her to drive far at night. The clock read seven-thirty. In half an hour the chapter would meet and Mitch would go back to the house for her bags. Leda shivered in the night air and wished she had found Mitch before she had a chance to see Robin and carry her plan through. Now Leda would have to tell Marsha she was sick, that she had gone for medicine because she was sick and she could not attend the meeting. She would be in the room waiting for Mitch when she came.

A car swerved away from her as she stepped off the sidewalk into the street. The cab driver grunted, and skirted the curb narrowly as he drove fast.

"Hurry!" he said. "You girls always gotta be someplace fast. That's all I hear is 'Hurry, driver!' Hurry, hurry, hurry."

"Marsha's in the Chapter Room," Kitten said. "Thought you were sick."

Leda said, "I am." She found the door to the room locked, and she knocked three times fast and once slow.

"Who goes?" she recognized Jane Bell's voice.

"Pledged in blood," Leda said. "Promised in the heart."

"Enter."

The bolt was slipped off and Jane Bell stepped back. She was wearing a silky white gown with a deep red scarf on her hair, drawing her hair back behind her ears. There was a sharp odor of burning incense in the dark room, lighted only by five single candles on a small table covered with the same silky white material. Marsha knelt at the table, arranging a red velvet-covered book with a black marker on the open page. When Leda walked in the room, panting, her face damp and hot, Jane stared at her.

"My gosh," she said, "you look feverish."

"That's what I came about. I can't attend the meeting tonight. I feel lousy."

Marsha looked up from the book at Leda. There was an angelic look to her face by candlelight, a look that she was fully aware of, cultivated and practiced. When she conducted the weekly chapter meetings, this look lent an air of piety to the conduct of the service. With the members of the chapter standing in a solemn semicircle before her, she felt that there was something spiritual about her leadership, celestial and sacrosanct.

"We're having a formal meeting tonight," she told Leda, as if to persuade her sickness to end.

"I see you are. I'm sorry. I just feel lousy."

"You look feverish," Jane Bell remarked again.

"I hope you feel better." Marsha smiled. "Did you know that Mrs. Gates, our Kansas City vice-counsel, gave us three new robes? Jane has one on."

Jane twirled and the robe floated on her gracefully. Inwardly Leda thought, Jesus! Oh, silly Jesus! but she pacified them by touching the material and exclaiming, then apologizing again. She backed out of the room just as the electric buzzer gave the signal for the members to line up in the hall and prepare to enter in single file.

The halls were still, the pledges confined to their rooms for study hour. Leda found the room dark. Mitch had not come yet. She struck a match and lit a cigarette, and in the blackness she went to the window and watched the street. Ten dragging minutes later the convertible pulled up in front of the house, and Mitch slammed the front door and hurried up the walk. Leda lay down on the bed, watching the cigarette smoke curl to the ceiling, and waited.

After the light went on in the room, Mitch felt a flood of surprise in her stomach as she saw Leda. She shut the door and set Robin's large empty suitcase on the floor. Leda sat up and looked at her.

"You're going to pack now?" she said.

"Yes. I thought you'd be in chapter meeting." She tried not to look at Leda, but she could feel the girl's eyes piercing her, stopping her attempts to avoid those eyes, and she went to the bureau and began removing socks and handkerchiefs and scarves.

Leda let her click the suitcase open, and watched her while she placed the things inside it. She could feel the sharp edges of the letter against her chest there near her bra where she had put it before dinner. With her left hand she reached down and fished the letter out and stuck it under her pillow.

"I decided," Leda said finally, "that the least I could do was to say good-bye to you."

Mitch felt choked up and agonized with desire. She scooped out an armful of slips and panties and pajamas, and thrust them in there with the other clothes. Her lips formed the word "Thanks," and she meant to say it, but there was no sound. On the floor of the closet there were fluffy swirls of dust near her tennis shoes, and she brushed them away with her hand. She tossed the shoes onto the bed, and took the chair from the desk over to the closet to reach the boxes at the top.

Leda said, "Want any help?"

"No. Thanks, though. I can do it myself."

"You've got an idea," Leda said, "that you can do everything yourself. I don't know where you got that idea."

"Sometimes it's up to yourself," Mitch said.

"You've got a lot of ideas, I bet. I bet you've got thousands of good ideas."

The box slipped from Mitch's hand and fell to the floor, spilling out two round hats, one black, one brown, both alike—round and plain.

"Someday you'll find out that most of the ideas don't work. None of them work."

Mitch stopped tying the strings on the top of the box and looked up at Leda. "What are you trying to say?" she asked. "What are you trying to tell me? You never say anything right out. You always talk around and make it hard."

"I'm trying to say, don't go. Going isn't the answer." The tears came in her eyes, and Mitch looked away at the shoe bag on the closet floor. She thought of Robin, her friend, of the swimming team, of other years and anything to keep them from being the same, but this made it worse and the sob started low in her throat. Then Leda bent and caught her shoulder and held her, kneeling on the rug, listening to the stifled crying.

"Mitch," she said, "don't go. Don't leave me, please."

"But you know what I am. I told you what I am in the letter."

"I don't care. Mitch, I don't care."

"I can't stay with you. I won't feel right, I—"

Leda put her hand on the girl's face and felt the tears. She turned her face and put her lips on the salty moistness. "Come on over to the bed," she said. "Get up, Mitch, and come on over to the bed."

Mitch lay down with her face buried in the pillow, and Leda sat on the edge, her hands stroking Mitch's hair.

"Can you hear me, Mitch? Listen, it doesn't help to run away. You don't think it helps, do you? It doesn't help."

"No," Mitch sobbed. "I can't stay here. I can't bear to see you every day and know what I'm doing to you."

"What are you doing to me? What in hell are you doing to me?"

"I'm a Lesbian," Mitch answered. "That's how I feel about you, too. I'm not like you—with Jake and everything."

"Oh, God, Mitch! All right, listen. I love you, you crazy kid. I don't have to label my love, do I? Do I have to say that it's Lesbian love? OK, then that's what it is. It's Lesbian love, pure and simple. Ye gods, I've known about myself for years. I didn't run away. I didn't walk out and run away. You gave me plenty of reason to. You were the first one to come along and blow up my little plan for hiding the way I am. You think you're doing something to me! Oh, Mitch! If anyone's doing it, I'm doing it. I'm doing it because I love you."

Mitch brought her head up from the pillow and turned over on her side. "But you said it," she said. "You said you couldn't love a Lesbian. You said—"

"I said so damn much, didn't I? You've got to understand, Mitch. I don't like what I am. If Jan ever knew, I'd take a razor and slash my wrists. I couldn't live with people knowing, and pointing and saying, 'Queer' at me. No one knows but you, and I guess I never would have told you if you hadn't started to leave. Do you think it's easy to admit it? It was different when I could say it wasn't this way, that I was bisexual and all that rot. Bisexual—that's sort of like succotash, isn't it? Only this succotash hasn't got any corn in it. It's straight beans!"

"What about Jake?" Mitch blew her nose and sat up. "What about all the time you spend with Jake?"

"Maybe I'm trying to prove something to myself. Part of me is trying to say that I'm not what I am. That's the part of me that everyone knows—the alluring Leda, the queen, Jan's daughter, an apple never falls far from the tree. Out with Jake every damn day to keep myself away from what I really am. Want to know what sex with him is like? It's like dry bread, that's what it's like. Like dry bread!"

Leda got up from the bed and reached for her cigarettes on the desk. She felt relieved, cleansed, as though her mind had been emptied and she was free. She walked over to the suitcase on Mitch's bed and picked up the clothing, taking it in her arms to the drawer. "You want this all put back, don't you?" she said to Mitch. "You won't leave me?"

"No," Mitch said. "I'm going. Robin arranged everything, and—oh, Leda!" They stood in the center of the room holding one another, their lips fastened hard, their arms strong around each other. Leda's hand reached for the buttons on Mitch's blouse.

"Just stand still," she said. "Just let me take everything off and look at you. I want to look at you."

The skirt fell to the floor, and the blouse. Mitch stepped out of her shoes and stood before Leda.

"I want to love you," Leda said.

Her hands stroked Mitch's body gently. She leaned over to kiss her lips and her forehead and the closed eyelids. She said her name and held her, feeling the fast beat in her pulse and knowing that she had almost lost her.

The blood beat furiously in Mitch's throat and she could feel a mounting strength in her legs and arms. With the arrogance of a master, Mitch's nails dug into Leda's flesh as she began to pull the sweater and the thin blouse from her shoulders. She let her teeth sink into Leda's neck.

"No, faster!" Leda cried. "Faster, Mitch!"

Leda's gasp was one of pleasure and desire and it moved Mitch to more violence, pinning Leda's wrists behind her back and jerking at her skirt.

Neither of them heard the door open.

They turned in time to see Kitten and Casey framed in the doorway, eyes big, mouths dropped, and they fell apart from one another when the door was slammed, and the sound of feet running down the hall was as loud and fast as the beating of their hearts in that room.

It was a long time before they talked. Mitch lay dumb with horror, never forgetting the look on their faces as they had found her that way with Leda, unclothed and wild like a fierce animal. Sitting with her head hung, her hands pressing at her eyes, Leda was the first one to speak after the minutes passed as they would in a slow nightmare when nothing is real.

She stood up and picked the blouse off the floor. "Look," she said. "I'll go and talk to Marsha. That's where they ran to. I'll go and straighten it out."

"How?"

Leda reached in the closet for a fresh blouse, and straightened her skirt so that the zipper was pulled and on the side. She ran a comb through her long hair, and her hands were trembling.

"I'll explain it somehow. Marsha's gullible, and I'll explain it. I have to go now, or they'll have a chance to talk and spread the story."

Mitch said, "'I'll go too, Leda, I'll go too. What'll we say?"

"No!" Leda put her hands over her face and shook her head. "I'm sorry I yelled. We've got to handle this just right. You stay here. It's better for me to go alone."

"Are you sure?"

"Yes. Look, get into bed. I'll turn the light out and you stay here. If anyone else comes by, pretend you're asleep.

She waited while Mitch pulled her pajamas from the suitcase on her bed and threw the suitcase down on the floor, before she stepped into the pants and the coat. After she got in bed, Leda snapped the light out and went back by her own bed before she opened the door to go.

"Don't worry," she said. "Don't worry at all. And stay here!"

In her hand, as she walked toward Marsha's suite, Leda clutched Mitch's letter, wrinkled and folded on the long sheet of notebook paper. Her eyes were set and determined, and there was a tight line about her lips.

Under the heavy violet and black quilted robe, Mother Nesselbush wore a voluminous peach-colored flannel nightgown. Her hair was rolled on large black pins so that it pulled at her scalp and gave her round face a bizarre expression like that of a mild Jersey cow. Her skin shone with "night cream," and until everything began, it was with conscious effort that she stifled the great yawns that exposed her pressing lethargy, as well as her gold-studded molars.

Everything began when Marsha shut the door to Nessy's suite and pressed the lock down to secure it. Beside those two, Casey, Kitten Clark, Jane Bell, and Leda shared the secrecy of the meeting that was about to commence. Marsha stood while the others sat in various positions around the small anteroom.

"I don't need to tell you that this gathering is an extreme emergency. We must all pledge never to reveal what we hear. Our whole reputation as a national sorority is at stake, to say nothing of the reputation of Tri Epsilon on the Cranston campus. I've asked Jane to come because she's a member of the Grand Council. Fortunately, our other two members were on the scene when this thing happened. And Leda will explain her part in it. Nessy, we've inconvenienced you tremendously, but this is too terribly serious."

Mother Nesselbush protested that she was not disturbed, and that she was only too thankful that she was called on. She straightened her drooping shoulders and sat forward intently.

"Maybe you better tell how it started, Casey," Marsha said, leaning against the small mahogany table with the vase of daisies set on it.

Casey was excited. Her face was animated and colored with the heat of her adventure. She uncrossed her legs and leaned forward from the couch.

"It was right after chapter meeting. Kitten and I were going up to talk with Leda about her being nominated for Christmas Queen, and about the campaign we were going to plan. Well, we were kind of pleased and everything and I guess we just never thought of knocking, and when we got in there—well, this is kind of hard to say—we found Mitch naked and she was attacking Leda. I mean, she was kissing her and pulling at her clothes."

"What!" Mother Nesselbush paled and caught her jowls with her pudgy hands. "Oh, no!"

Leda's knees felt watery and loose, and her knuckles were white in a tight fist.

"Well," Casey went on, "Kitten and I ran like the devil—"

"I'll say we did," Kitten broke in. "I was never so scared in my life. If you could have seen it! I didn't know what to think. I didn't even think when I was running."

"What did she do when you opened the door? Gosh, Leda, you must have been crazy with fear." Jane Bell looked over at Leda after she said it, and shook her head and wrinkled her forehead in disbelief. "Absolutely crazy with fear!" she repeated.

"You poor, poor darling," Nessy said. "To think of it!"

Marsha moved forward and held her hand up for silence. "After that," she said when everyone settled down, "Leda came to me in the suite. Luckily, Kitten and Casey had come right there, so the story hasn't spread."

"What about Susan Mitchell?" Mother Nesselbush snapped. "Where is she now?"

"You better carry on from here, Leda." Marsha sat down on the floor, close to Nessy's chair, and waited while Leda found words. Of course, they believed the story. It had been easy to tell it, Leda thought; not easy, but the only way. It had been the only way to tell it. Strange how she had thought that she would do it just this way if they were found, in that quick flash of intuition a second before they were found. She remembered another day when she was a child alone in her room, and in the midst of it she had heard Jan's footsteps down the hall. If they stopped, if Jan came in the room, then she would say that she had shooting pains from cramps, and that she had been tossing on the bed and was hot and out of breath, and she would even cry to show that the pains were bad ones. But she would not spoil that moment there with herself for anything. All of the thoughts came quickly to Leda, solved in seconds, so that there was never any defeat. Now again she was not defeated, because they believed her. There was Mitch upstairs, waiting, trusting, but the time was now, downstairs, and Leda began slowly, her words careful and well remembered.

"Mitch is upstairs in bed. She'll stay there, and she won't talk to anyone. I told her that I would explain it, and I'm going to try to. I can't explain it so that everything is over and forgotten as I know she hopes I will do, but I am going to try to be fair to her.

"First of all, with everyone's permission, I'd like to read a letter."

When she finished the letter, Mother Nesselbush rolled her eyes in utter horror. "I declare," she said. "I do declare!"

"You see," Leda said, "I suspected that Mitch had a crush on me. She was jealous of Jake and of the time I spent with him. I knew that, but I never dreamed the kid was in love with me like this. You know how I am. I call everyone honey and darling, and I guess the kid took me to heart. Then, after I told her to get some boy friends, she got mad and tried to ignore me. I didn't pay any attention until I found this note in my mailbox before dinner tonight. Well, you know how I acted at dinner."

"And I thought it was just the flu," Nessy said. "Land!"

"So I decided that the only thing I could do was to try to help the kid. At least persuade her to wait until morning. I didn't know what kind of condition she was in. She might do something dumb like confiding in that Robin Maurer. Then the whole campus would know. I didn't know what to do. I couldn't wait till chapter meeting and talk it over with you kids, because she'd be gone by then. I tried to handle it myself."

"Who's Charlie?" Kitten said. "Is he that independent? What does she mean, he knows?"

"She imagined that, I'm sure," Leda answered. "I guess they had a fight or something and she thought he knew. The kid is really naïve."

"She didn't look naïve when Casey and I saw her."

"Let me finish, Kitten."

"Well, Lord, we don't want it all over campus that one of the Tri Ep pledges is queer. That's all the independents need."

"I tell you, he doesn't know. No one does!"

"Let Leda finish," Marsha said.

"She brought a suitcase with her and was ready to go. I persuaded her to wait until morning. I thought that by that time I'd be able to do something—talk to Nessy or Marsha or someone. She got undressed to go to bed, and—then she—attacked me. Thank God you kids came along at the right time."

"What did she do after they left the room?" Jane Bell asked. "I can't even imagine this!"

"That brought her to. You see, she really went out of her mind for a minute. After the door slammed, she came to and became herself. I quieted her as best I could, and told her it would all be OK. She was scared to death, poor kid."

"Yeah, poor kid!" Casey sneered. "She belongs in a cage!"

"I don't know," Leda said. "I can't help feeling sorry for her."

Nessy said, "You showed great presence of mind, Leda. Why, if it had been me, I would have just shrieked my lungs out!"

"You weren't even yelling," Casey said.

"And it's a good thing she didn't. If it ever got around the house—Lord, I hate to think." Kitten reached for a cigarette and snapped the flame on her lighter. "That's one thing we've got to be damn careful about. We've got to keep it between us. We'll have to think of some other reason for getting rid of her."

"Maybe I can do it," Leda said. "Look, maybe I can convince her that the best thing for her to do is to go to the Psych Department. I'll tell her I think she was right to want to move to the dorm, and then we'll be rid of her and she'll never know the difference. We can keep it all hush-hush."

Jane Bell groaned and scratched her head. "No, that's no answer. She'd blab it to one of the doctors and then it'd get back to Panhellenic. Besides, no telling what she might do at the dorm."

Inwardly Leda shook at the danger of her own suggestion. But no matter where Mitch went, there was the danger of her telling her side of the story. Of someone believing it. Who'd believe it? The letter was written perfectly, leaving Leda free of any implication, and there was no other proof. Nothing. She felt stronger then, fear lending new armor.

"You know," she said, "the kid will probably try to blame me. She'll probably say I had something to do with it. You know how people get when they're up against a wall."

Mother Nesselbush giggled. "Leda, our queen," she said. "Now really, do you think anyone would believe the child? She's obviously demented!" Her face changed and became grave. "Girls, I don't think the decision is ours to make. We must think of the reputation of the house. Tri Epsilon stands for honesty and loyalty, to ourselves and to the school too. This is a matter for the dean's office, girls, and I assure you, Dean Paterson is a very discreet person. She'll handle this with utmost concern for our welfare."

"I agree with Nessy," Marsha said. "It isn't anything we can decide. We can only pledge ourselves to secrecy. No other member of the sorority is to know about this. Now, let's promise it."

"Promised!" Kitten said. "That's for sure."

"I'd be embarrassed to tell anyone else," Casey commented. "Even now it embarrasses me."

Jane Bell stubbed her cigarette out in the ash tray. "I don't have to remind anyone," she said, "that if the pledges ever learn about this, we'll be in danger of losing the entire pledge class."

Marsha stepped forward to the middle of the room. "We all know the consequences. It could be anything else but this. Homosexuality just leaves a horrid taste. We'd all have to pay, even though we had nothing to do with it, just because it happened under our roof. We'd be the brunt of thousands of miserable jokes. You remember the year the Sigma Delts had those two terribly effeminate boys in their pledge class? Remember what happened the day they woke up and found the signs all over their front yard? That's just half of what we'd get."

Leda remembered the signs. They were large cardboard ones with bright red paint. They said, "Fairy Landing," and "Sig Delt Airport—Fly with our boys!" For weeks, the jokes out at the Fat Lady and down at the Den and the Blue Ribbon centered around the Sig Delt house. No one ever knew how it all started, or whether there was any basis to it all, but everywhere you went you heard the sly remarks, and saw the wry grins that attended the cracks about "those fairy nice Sigma Delts." She had been a freshman then, but after two and a half years it was all very fresh in her memory. Everyone remembered, long after the boys left campus.

"I'll call the dean," Mother Nessy said, "the first thing in the morning. The only thing we can do tonight is go to bed and try to sleep. Leda, you'd better make up the couch in here."

"I'm afraid Mitch will be suspicious. I mean, I told her I'd explain everything. She'll probably wait for me to get back."

"Oh, joyous reunion," Casey said. "Holy God!"

"You mean you're going back to that girl, Leda? Why, I won't hear of it!"

"Look," Marsha said calmly, "maybe it's the only way. We can't have her getting out in the halls and trying to find Leda. I mean, she won't be violent like that again, will she, Leda?"

"No, I know she won't. You don't understand. The kid is scared out of her wits now. She wouldn't lift a finger." Leda felt queasy, listening to them picture Mitch as a wild beast roaming the halls for prey. She would have to make them believe that she was wise to go back up there to Mitch. But not too anxious. "Of course, I confess it isn't going to help me sleep any to know she's in the room, but—"

"No!" Nessy said. "I simply can't have it. I'm responsible."

Mitch would be waiting. Leda would have to go back, or Mitch might run to Marsha and confuse the story, ruin it—even if they didn't believe her.

"I know," Marsha said. "Kitten and Casey and I will wait in the bathroom. Leda, you go in and see if it looks OK to stay there. If it does, you can tell us by coming down to the john. If it's not OK, then you can tell and we'll think of something else. I mean, if you think Mitch is going to act up."

"That's fine," Leda said, "and I think it'll be OK. You don't know this kid like I do."

Kitten grinned. "Obviously," she said. "Who'd want to?"

"All right," Nessy consented reluctantly, "but I won't sleep a wink. Not a wink!"

Marsha moved the tab back on the door and opened it. "Now, for heaven's sake," she whispered, "look nonchalant. Pretend we were all in talking to Nessy, and that's all. Some of the kids might still be up. And Leda, when you come down to the john, make it subtle if anyone's there. Then we can go to the suite and talk."

Mother Nessy took Leda's arm before she left the room. "You promise me," she said, "you promise me that if that girl gives any indication of acting up again, you'll just jump right out of that room and come down to me. I don't care what the *hour* is."

Leda said, "Don't worry, Nessy, and I promise."

The five girls climbed the main stairs slowly, Marsha attempting vaguely to whistle a bit from "On, Wisconsin."

It was taking Leda a long time. What could she say to them? Mitch was numb with torment, and the sheets on her bed were wrinkled and halfway off the mattress from her perpetual turning and moving as she waited. The ticking of the tin clock on the dresser sounded frantic and Mitch made the ticks come in three beats in her mind—Les-bi-an, Les-bi-an, tick-tick-tick. Leda was one too. The thought foamed in Mitch's brain and hurt her. She did not know why she felt dirty when Leda told her that she was a Lesbian. She thought she should have felt happy and glad that they were two. But she did not want to be one. Abnormal.

From far off she could hear the sweet voices of a fraternity serenading a sorority house down the street.

She turned the light on and looked at the face of the clock. It was eleven-thirty. Leda had been gone too long. She saw Leda's half-full package of cigarettes on the desk, and she took one from the pack and lit it. It tasted strong and sour and she squashed it in the ash tray and turned the light off again.

Tomorrow, she decided, she would move out of Tri Epsilon and into the dorm with Robin. If she and Leda weren't put out of the sorority, she would leave anyway. But she could not leave Leda. "I love Leda," she said softly to the darkness, "even though we're both that way. I wish she wasn't that way."

The dream came in a half fit of consciousness. Her mother was very beautiful, with black hair that came to her shoulders, and clear green eyes. Mitch loved her. She wore pants and shirts and combed her hair back, wet from her swim, and went to her mother with jewels and furs that she had stolen for her to have. Her mother smiled and accepted them. Mitch heard her say, "You'd better not steal all the time. I couldn't love a thief." She ran down a long alley to escape the police who were looking for her. It was late when she got back to the Tri Epsilon house and her mother was there with the police holding her arm. Her mother was laughing. She said, "You didn't know I was a thief too," and the policemen led her away. Diamonds were spilling out of her mother's pocket as she went down the steps with them.

She thought she had been asleep for hours, but it was only twenty minutes to twelve. Leda must be in trouble. The dream put a ragged edge on her anxiety. The bed was a sight, rumpled and torn apart as though it had been ravaged. Mitch straightened the sheets and fluffed the pillow. In the corner of the room by the bureau her clothes lay where Leda had taken them off, kicked to the side. Mitch picked them up and brushed them off.

Les-bi-an, Les-bi-an, tick-bi-an...

Mitch thought, I can get a job. Leda and I can run away and I can work someplace. If they put us out of the sorority I won't go home. Leda won't either, because of Jan. Colorado is nice, or California. She had a vivid picture of the open convertible speeding through purple and rust landscapes and along white desert with the cactus along the roadside. She added glorious black nights and ten thousand brilliant stars, and a warm wind whipping at their faces. It was no good. She hated the picture. Why? A slow self-disgust chewed at her and called her coward, but she was still afraid. She promised herself to be strong when Leda came back, no matter. Whatever Leda said, Mitch would not reveal her fear. Leda loved her and this was the price. Be strong for two. The words on the storybook she'd had as a child came dancing on the scene of her mind: "Now We Are Two."

Part of it was the way Leda acted when she had said "No, faster! Faster, Mitch!" It seemed far away and morbid, as though there was an insane spark to their love that made them fierce and careless. Sitting on the side of her bed, under the harsh light of the electric bulb overhead, Mitch could not know herself in that scene. She reasoned that she was not violent. Never violent. Yet there was still the faint taste of blood on her tongue, and the way she knew she had been strong there with Leda.

Don't blame Leda. You're trying to blame Leda.

There was a sound of steps in the hall. Mitch caught her breath when they came to the door. It was Leda returning.

"What are you doing with the light on?"

"I had to find out the time."

"I told you not to leave it on. I told you to go to bed."

"I just turned it on. I was afraid."

"Well, it's over, so go to bed."

"Over?"

"Yes. It's all right."

"Wh-what did you say? How did you explain it?"

Leda's face was composed and placid. She took her soap from the tray on the rack behind the door. Her washcloth hung over the bar above the shoe bag and she put that with the soap. "I'm going to wash my face. I'll tell you when I get back. Look, it's over. There's nothing to worry about."

Mitch just sat there staring.

"Get in bed. I'll be back."

"I'll come too," Mitch said. "I didn't wash yet. Wait for me and I'll come too." She started toward the bureau.

"No!" Leda's tone came out sharper than she had meant it. She could not look at Mitch's face, which was alive with a new hope. Her words went to the rug. "No, it's better if you stay in bed. I told them you didn't feel well. You see, that's how I explained it. I said you were sick."

"Oh," Mitch said. "I—" She sat back on the bed and rubbed her forehead.

Leda walked toward the door. "Look, just get in bed. I'll be back in a minute. I'll tell you then."

"OK, Leda."

Before Leda turned the doorknob, Mitch's eyes met hers.

"Leda?"

"What?"

"Thanks."

When she was gone, Mitch felt sick and dull all over. She was ashamed of the way she had thought about Leda. The thoughts seemed to tease her still, pricking her knowledge that Leda had made everything all right, that now there would be no reason to run and hide. Steadily she rebuilt the structure of their love, amplifying it with Leda's courage and with her own indebtedness to Leda. She could feel the physical ache for her down to the tips of her fingers, replacing the enfeebled numbness, charging it with renewed vigor. Healing time had conquered the doubt and fear, and her servility was sworn in that moment. Mitch felt humble and brave in the darkness of the room.

A tongue of light cut through the black as Leda opened the door and slipped back in. Mitch could hear her putting things away and getting out of her clothes. The thud of her shoes on the floor sounded unusually heavy in the silence. Mitch threw the sheets and blankets back and went over to her.

"For God's sake, no! We just got out of one mess."

"I'm sorry, Leda. I just feel so—"

"Get back in bed. My God!"

The covers felt itchy on her chin and she pulled the sheet up higher. She could hear Leda getting in bed.

"I know you're upset," she said. "I should have known better than to come over to you, Leda. I'm sorry."

"Forget it."

Mitch waited. Leda would tell her now—everything that had happened. The minutes crept and the clock began the game, ticking out the word.

"Leda?"

"What?"

"You said you'd tell me." Mitch's voice was thin and meek. She didn't mean to keep at Leda like that, but she had to know.

"OK. I said you were sick. I said you went to bed sick and you were feverish when you came after me."

"D-did you say that I came after *you*?"

"Well, hell, I had to say something! When they came in the door, that's what they saw."

"Oh."

The wind blew papers off the desk and they ruffled along the floor, the noise quick and airy.

"Leave them," Leda said. She settled back and the noise stopped.

"Well, did they believe you? What about—My God, I was naked!"

"You were sick! I told them you were sick, Mitch!" Mitch wanted to stop the angry tone. She lay quiet and another paper chased across the room and landed on top of her on the bed.

"Mitch, I'm sorry I'm so snappish. I just feel like hell. It wasn't easy."

"I know what it must have been like, Leda."

"It was hell."

"Does—does anyone know? Anyone else, I mean?"

"Just Marsha and those two."

"It'll be hard tomorrow. What'll I tell them when they ask what was wrong?"

Leda turned her pillow over on the side. Then she got up and put a bottle of ink on top of the papers so they wouldn't blow any more. "It won't be hard," she said. "They won't even talk about it. Just go along as though nothing happened."

"Leda, I don't know how to thank you."

"Quit saying that! What in the name of God do you think I am, your holy savior?"

The night air was crisp and Mitch snuggled down in the covers. She closed her eyes and tried to sleep, but she kept listening for Leda to say more. When she didn't, Mitch said, "I just want to say one more thing, Leda. I'll always stick by you—always. You mean more to me than anyone I know."

Leda didn't answer.

The unashamed story of a girl's journey to the well of forbidden knowledge

Summer Camp

by Anne Herbert

It began at the summer camp, when Peggy Matthews and Lillian Parker met in the counselors' cabin. After that, curiosity and desire had their way, but Peggy had no idea of what she was getting into....

Dr. Herbert Greene says: "The *Summer Camp* is the unforgettable story of an eighteen-year-old girl losing control of her emotions. Her affairs with men as victim, then aggressor...her affairs with women, tentative, then greedy and unashamed...are delineated with valid insights. This is nothing less than a classic case history of modern lesbianism."

Summer Camp

"Peggy, I wish I could. But I—I just can't. If I speak that name, all of us will be destroyed."

"Is it Mike? It must be. It's Mike, isn't it? It can't be Pam or Lilian or anybody like that. Dorothy and Ruth have a crush on each other—surely neither would be interested in me. So it has to be Mike. Mike made a play for me. She—"

"Watch your mouth! Lots of girls get crushes on each other, but that doesn't make them gay."

"Gay? What's gay?"

"Oh, skip it. Peggy, I simply can't mention names. I refuse to discuss Mike or anybody else." Beth gazed down at Peggy, huddled at her feet. Suddenly the nurse kneeled, lifted the girl's chin with a finger, forcing Peggy to look at her. In a kindlier tone, she said, "You're afraid, aren't you? You've been afraid all this time."

Beth's voice was calm now, natural, not insinuating. "You're afraid of this girl who violated you—and you're afraid of yourself."

Peggy's eyes flashed to the nurse.

"You're afraid that you liked it too much," Beth said.

"Yes!" In that instant a tumult of confusion rushed over Peggy. She wanted to throw herself into those compassionate arms and cry on the golden shoulder as she had not done since she was a child; she wanted to unburden herself as never before. "Beth, whether I'm afraid or not, I've got to know. I've got to discover what I am."

"You're a nice, perfectly healthy girl. You have nothing to worry about." The nurse edged nearer. One hand fell to Peggy's arm. "All right, so you had an episode with a woman. But it meant nothing. Happens every day. Often young girls like you come into bodily contact with other girls, feel some sort of physical sensation, and immediately begin to have doubts about themselves. They are afraid of their reactions—and ashamed—but that doesn't make them one of my kind—"

"Your kind?"

"That's right. I'm a genuine lesbian, truly twisted, and I know it."

"But what if I am, too?" Peggy said, thinking of her aversion to the male sex. "How am I to find out?"

For an instant she was sure she saw a different expression in Beth's eyes. The kind of expression Ted used to get when Peggy would pull away from him in order to take off her clothes.

But Beth had control of herself again. She smiled, and tried to answer Peggy's question. "You'll find out in time. Try not to let it bother you now. You're much too young to become enmeshed in this sort of thing—no matter what you are."

"Beth, I've got to know." And with more resolution than she would have thought possible, Peggy said, "I want you to kiss me."

The nurse looked away. "No."

Peggy scrambled to her knees. "Please, Beth," she pleaded. "You mean so much to me. Help me."

"Peggy, I—"

Peggy lifted her face. "Please." She moved a little closer. Her mouth was almost touching Beth's.

With a cry that was like a sob, Beth clutched Peggy to her. Beth's lips, soft and warm, touched Peggy's.

At last they broke away. Peggy's heart was pounding. Fever seemed to have possessed her blood. Strange hot prickles assailed her nerves. She looked at Beth—soft and warm and alluring. The nurse was not in uniform now, but in blue stretch slacks donned against the rain and damp. Her womanly hips were faithfully outlined. Her breasts strained against the blue of the button-down man's oxford shirt she wore. Her hair fell in soft waves to her shoulders. How beautiful, thought Peggy. How utterly beautiful. She put an arm around the nurse's waist.

"Oh, Beth—"

"No, Peggy, no more." She started to rise, but the younger girl, stronger, held her down.

Peggy said once again, "I have to know."

"You don't make love to find something out, Peggy."

The girl tossed her head, yellow ponytail flicking like a banner. "I'm not attractive to you? You don't want me?"

"Want has little to do with it."

Peggy forced Beth's hand to touch her full young breast. "Tell me you want me."

"Don't do this to us," Beth begged. "Don't do it to yourself."

"I have to know," Peggy insisted.

"God help us," moaned Beth. Her arms went around Peggy.

The two fell back upon the soft, damp grass, their eager lips clinging. For the first time Peggy knew the sensation of another woman's tongue darting and circling against her own. So acute was the thrill that her bones seemed to turn to water.

Then Beth came up for air. Pulling away, she slowly opened Peggy's simple camp blouse. Loosening the bra, she exclaimed with delight as Peggy's breasts tumbled forth. At first Beth was gentle as she kissed and fondled the trembling, youthful bosom. Peggy's heart jumped as the woman's lips touched each rosy nipple, hands stroking all the while, searching sweetly, trailing fire from the fingertips.

For a while Peggy lay still, basking in every touch, every tender kiss, every deliberately inciting stroke. But as Beth's hands and lips roamed, Peggy began to writhe on the ground. She burrowed closer to the older woman, sent her hand up under the oxford shirt. When her hand touched the soft roundness of Beth's quivering breasts, a glorious burst of white-hot bliss lashed Peggy's body. With reckless lust she loosened Beth's slacks, touched the nylon beneath. At the same time she felt Beth's clever fingers at her shorts. The fingers cunningly slid and stroked. "Oh, sweet Beth," groaned Peggy.

No longer could she concentrate on every touch and kiss. Her whole being seemed engulfed by wave upon wave of fiery pleasure. Then, in a burst of purest ecstasy, she crested. The whole world seemed to explode inside of her. Slowly Peggy drifted down to earth. For long minutes she lay quietly, her head on Beth's lap, a hand still on Beth's bare breast.

A sense of utter peace, of profoundest fulfillment, possessed Peggy.

"We'd better pull ourselves together," Beth said softly. "We have to be on our way. They'll be wondering what happened to us."

Peggy sat up, buttoned her blouse, then followed Beth across the bridge. In the station wagon, they both repaired faces and hair.

As the car rolled onto the road, Peggy slouched against the door, wishing she could cuddle against Beth.

Neither spoke during the ride back to camp. Skillfully Beth swung into the parking lot, cut the motor. She turned toward Peggy and was about to say something when she saw Miss Duncan approaching.

The older woman told them that the most recent weather forecast had reported an end to local thundershowers. The staff had decided to chance a swimming session so the hikers could rinse off some sweat.

"You join them, Peggy. I think you deserve a refresher. We can take care of these things later."

Peggy thanked the director, then sat unmoving, hoping for a chance to be alone with Beth. But one glance at Miss Duncan told her that she was excused.

To Beth, she murmured, "See you later." Then Peggy left the two women.

Life took on a whole new color for Peggy. During the following twenty-four hours, her mind was filled with visions of Beth—sweet, kind Beth, lovely Beth with her fragrant brown hair and dark-blue eyes and gentle hands. No longer did she fear or reject lesbian love. How could anything so good, Peggy argued, not be right? At least for Beth and herself.

Now that she was not obsessed with doubts about herself and about the lesbian existence, she was free to enjoy all the more her wonderful relationship with Beth. The prospect intoxicated Peggy. She did not weigh consequences.

She looked forward with deep excitement to their next meeting but forced herself to avoid the nurse still one more day. She did not want to become a pest or presume on Beth. But by noon, Peggy knew she could no longer contain herself.

She was standing at her table while the campers filed in for lunch. A cool breeze blew into the screened lodge porch. Peggy took a deep breath of pine-scented air, flavored by aromas rising from tureens of hearty soup in place on each table.

Peggy went through her serving duties mechanically, filling plates, passing them down the line, saying, "You have to eat at least three spoonsful," when the girls objected to the vegetable. She answered questions automatically, and somehow got through the main course. Then dessert was brought out. The jello and cookies lasted longer than she thought they should but it was mail call afterward that seemed unbearable.

And then a song or two....

At last, if was over, the whole ordeal. Beth, thought Peggy. Beth...

The girls scrambled from their seats, running every which way. Most of the counselors drifted toward the lounge for a quick smoke before rest period. Peggy started quietly toward the door, but was stopped by a voice calling her name.

"Phone for you," a junior counselor yelled.

With a sigh of distaste, Peggy followed the girl, sure it would be Ted on the line.

Gingerly, she picked up the receiver.

"Hi, Peggy. This is Kirby. How are you doing?"

Peggy was stunned into silence. What colossal brass!

"I want to apologize for the other night," he said. "I mean—well, I guess I shouldn't have done what I did. I'm sorry."

Peggy's mind darted back to the quick kiss, the slap. "Oh," she said nonchalantly, "I had forgotten all about it." Which was no lie, she thought.

"Is that a compliment or a slam?"

"Just a remark."

"Meant to put me in my place, I presume." He seemed hesitant to continue. "Uh—there was one other thing," he said. "I was wondering if you would reconsider getting together some time."

"I told you the other night, Kirby—"

"I know what you told me the other night. I just hoped maybe you would have a change of heart."

"No. In fact, I'm more certain now than before," she said, thinking of Beth.

"Is it me personally you object to?" he asked.

Again Peggy was taken aback by his brass. "You've got a nerve! Of course it's you personally. That was a hell of a thing to do—grabbing me, kissing me—"

"Peggy, we hardly know each other, but please listen," he said. "I never saw a girl so attractive as you. You're the most beautiful thing alive. Sure I lost my head—what guy wouldn't? I'm not sorry, if you want to know the truth. I'll carry that kiss for the rest of my life. I would have risked a hell of a lot more than a slap for it—"

Peggy could not help being a bit moved. "Look, Kirby," she said in a less chilly tone, "I've got to run now. I don't want to go out with you, so let's just drop it, okay?"

"I'd better warn you—I don't give up easily."

"And I don't give in easily," she retorted.

Peggy hung up, amused and a little touched by his compliments and his ardent wooing. However, when she glanced at her watch she cursed him under her breath.

Kirby's phone call had deprived her of a chance to see Beth. This put a damper on Peggy's high spirits. She sulked through the rest period but afterward, on the basketball court, as the minutes slipped by, her anticipation began to mount once more. At last the whistle blew, signaling the end of the period.

Peggy bounded from the court. Quickly she changed into a fresh outfit.

She brushed her hair while her young cabin mates, most of them already in swim suits, dawdled away the last few minutes before swim period.

"Miss Peggy, aren't you coming with us?"

"I don't have waterfront duty today," Peggy answered brightly.

Another girl said, "You look so pretty!"

Peggy glowed inwardly. "Thanks, honey," she said, inspecting herself in the mirror. A mint-green blouse topped rich brown Bermudas that were cinched at the waist by a wide dark belt. A green band held her corn-blond hair away from her face.

Peggy fluffed the blondness and left the cabin, calling, "I'll see you at dinner."

She sauntered downhill, past the lodge and into the Pillbox. There she slouched in the clinic's one large chair while Beth finished with her patients.

The nurse was carefully inspecting a little girl's foot. At last she straightened and said, "I guess you can go swimming today. But keep putting the salve on before you go to bed." She walked to her desk, scribbled something on a piece of paper and said, "Give this to Miss Mike. Then go up and change into your suit."

The girl was radiant as she bounced off the stool. She took the note from Beth. "Thank you," she said. "Thanks, Miss Beth."

"And make sure to dry your feet," Beth called, as the child ran out the door.

Beth turned back to her desk, glanced at some papers, then up at Peggy. She smiled brightly. "Hi. What brings you—business or pleasure?"

"Strictly a social call," Peggy told her.

"Well, step into my social department, said the spider to the fly." She led the way into her room. "Have a seat. I want to get into my suit."

"Are you going swimming?"

"I thought I'd soak up some sun."

Peggy's face fell.

"Is anything wrong? Did you have something you wanted to talk about?"

"No. I—I just wanted to see you."

Beth stood planted in the middle of the room, watching Peggy. "Does this have anything to do with that business the other day?"

"That business!" flared Peggy. "Is that all it meant to you?"

"Listen, Peggy—" The nurse walked over to where the girl was sitting. "I'm sorry about that. I was hoping you had already forgotten it."

"Forgotten?" Peggy was incredulous. "How could I forget it, ever? Why, since it happened, all I've been thinking about is the next time. I could hardly sleep last night. I—"

"There's not going to be a next time, Peggy." Beth spoke slowly, deliberately. Her voice was calm, her tone low.

Peggy sat with her mouth open. "What did you say?" she asked finally.

"I said there is not going to be a next time."

"But why not?" Peggy cried despairingly.

Beth lowered herself to the arm of Peggy's chair. Her eyes rested on Peggy's tortured face. She took the girl's trembling hand in her own. "Peggy," she said carefully, trying hard to choose the right words, "Peggy, you mean too much to me—I can't let you lead a twisted, miserable life. And lesbians are miserable."

"Then why—"

Beth put her finger to the girl's lips. "No questions. If I knew all the answers, maybe I wouldn't have given in to you. Just because I did, and you found kicks in it, doesn't mean you're abnormal. It was a new experience for you, that's all. The fun would wear off with the novelty. And I'm certain that some day you'll find a man who can do as well for you, and probably a lot better."

Peggy glared at the nurse. "How can you say that? I dug it to the limit, Beth. Every minute of it. You know that. I remember everything you did. I—"

"Liking it doesn't make it right, Peggy."

Something burst inside of Peggy. "Right or not," she exploded, "you like it, too! Don't deny it, Beth. I may be a kid, but I know you want me as much as I want you, and maybe more. Do you think I'm blind to the way you're always watching me? Your eyes are on me all the time—in the lounge, at the lake, here. Every time I glanced up, you used to be looking at me. At first I didn't realize why, but now I know. And right this minute—even if you won't admit it—your eyes tell me that you're hungry for me, crazy to have me. Why fight it?"

Beth's stony gaze met her. "You'd better leave, Peggy."

Peggy's spirit wilted. Her idol was displeased with her. "I'm sorry,

Beth." Her voice was barely audible. "I didn't mean to offend you. It's just—" she hesitated—"I want you so much, Beth. I want to do all those things again...look at you, touch you, kiss you." She seized Beth's hand. "Please, Beth," she begged. "Let me."

Pulling away her hand, Beth snapped, "Just leave."

"Don't be angry," Peggy pleaded.

"You know, you can't make a habit of coming over here every free minute you have. People may begin to get ideas."

Everything strong and hard within Peggy seemed to melt. She felt her insides slouching. She started for the door, but paused and over her shoulder threw a pleading glance at Beth.

The nurse was watching her.

Peggy turned." I'm sorry, Beth. I didn't want to make you angry. I don't know what got into me. Our love was so wonderful—I've never felt like that before—I couldn't get it out of my mind. I've been thinking about you every minute. I couldn't wait to be with you."

Beth unbent a little. She took a couple of steps toward Peggy.

"I need you," Peggy whispered. "Really need you."

"Hush." Beth patted the girl's cheek. "I know how you feel, Peggy. I'll always be here. I'm your friend. Come back in a day or two, after you've cooled off. You will, you know. It's all in your mind. Ninety percent of all sexual desire is in the mind," she finished.

Beth kissed her on the forehead.

Peggy walked out, her shoulders slumping.

Peggy wrestled with her conscience for the next couple of days, longing all the while for Beth's company, yet conceding it would be best not to court temptation by returning to the nurse's quarters. She wavered between periods of extreme moodiness during which she was ashamed of the commotion she had caused, and long hours of utter bliss because, in the end, Beth had said that she would always be there, that she was Peggy's friend.

Peggy spoke casually on occasion to both Mike and Lilian, but only in connection with their work. Even in the counselors' lounge, Peggy indulged in only enough conversation to preserve the amenities.

Then Kirby Davis telephoned.

Peggy was sitting in the lounge after free swim. She went to the phone reluctantly, heard Kirby plead again for a date, and again refused him.

"Don't you think you'll ever give in?" he asked.

"Look, Kirby—"

"You don't have to hang up already, do you?"

"No," she said. "I'm not busy at the moment. I don't have to hang up."

"Good. You know, what I'd like to do is take you for a nice long walk among the open fields."

"I get my share of walking. Hikes every week."

"But they're not at all the same. To begin with, hikes are part of your job. In the second place, walking on dirt roads or through woods can't compare with tramping over open fields and nice soft grass."

"And where would you find open fields to roam around in? Most of them are planted with corn, or have cows all over them."

"When you get curious enough, let me know."

"I'll do that."

They talked a few minutes longer, Peggy keeping an eye on the clock.

Finally, when she told him her time was up, Kirby said: "Maybe I shouldn't mention it, but I made some progress—at least you talked to me a while."

Peggy could not help smiling.

She thought about Kirby's call again that evening after she had left the throng at the lodge. You couldn't fault a guy for trying, she thought, as she strolled the camp grounds, savoring the quiet.

At the bottom of the hill, Peggy turned, her eyes raised to the mammoth lodge, looming dark and somber except for the yellow light bursting through all the windows. Snatches of song and of laughter came rolling down the hillside. Peggy smiled inwardly, thinking of the youngsters in the big building, each one absorbed in the night's activities, her little mind filled with nothing else.

Suddenly a wave of loneliness surged through her poignantly. She turned toward the lake, a limitless pool of ink bathed in white moonlight.

Walking along the lake fence, kicking at an occasional stone, Peggy thought again of Kirby, of their telephone conversation that day. She wondered why she would not date him. Was she so far gone that a man could not appeal to her at all? Were her feelings, all of them, wholly directed elsewhere? Raising her eyes from the ground, she saw her answer. Standing at the gate was a womanly figure in white.

Peggy's heart hammered.

The nurse turned. "Hello, there," she called, glimpsing Peggy but uncertain of her identity.

Peggy moved closer, her loneliness replaced by wild excitement.

"Peggy!" the nurse exclaimed, recognizing the girl. "How are you? Want to walk along the shore?" she asked, unlatching the gate.

Peggy passed through, brushing against Beth's arm. The touch sent an electric current charging through the girl. Beth seemed not to notice.

"I've been expecting you at the Pillbox," she said.

Chills crawled up Peggy's spine. But inside her, heat was gathering.

They stood at the edge of the water, where wavelets washed upon the sand, darkening it, then rolling back again.

"I've missed our talks," Beth said, her eyes following the broad path of the moon upon the lake.

Peggy kicked at a pebble. It rolled into the water noiselessly.

The night air was warm and humid. There was no breeze. All was still save for the lapping of the water; leaves did not rustle, no laughter floated from the lodge anymore, even the crickets were not singing.

Peggy fought down the turmoil in her mind. She did not think; she waited.

Beth sauntered along the beach. She stopped when she reached the dock, turned, waited for Peggy.

Peggy joined her. "Let's talk, shall we?" Beth said, her voice cool in the hot night, cool as a breeze.

Peggy nodded dumbly. They sat down on the foot of the dock, a girl and a woman silhouetted against the moon-glow.

Peggy pulled off her shoes, dangled her feet in the wavelets.

"I regret that I had to be so short with you the other night," Beth said. "But the way you were carrying on was unbearable. It wasn't like you at all." Beth paused. "I realize," she said, "that you're under a tremendous strain, Peggy, and I know I've had a part in causing it."

Peggy dragged a toe through the water, concentrating on the ripples it left.

"Do we have to discuss it, Beth?"

"I think we should, don't you?"

Peggy shrugged.

"Peggy, your age is a trying one for most girls. But you've been exposed to more than the run-of-the-mill problems. You're riding the horns of a most serious dilemma." As Beth spoke, the moon hid behind a cloud.

In the thickened dark, Peggy began to swing her legs, feet splashing lightly.

"I can sympathize with you probably better than anyone else you know," Beth said sadly. "I want to help you, Peggy. I—"

Peggy jumped erect on the dock. "I don't want your sympathy. I don't want your help—or your pity or anything else…" She grabbed her shoes. "Just leave me alone," she sobbed hurrying away.

"Peggy!" The nurse scrambled to her feet. "Peggy, wait a minute."

As Beth tore after her, Peggy broke into a run. She was rounding the far end of the bathhouse, planning on a cut through the woods to the seclusion of her cabin.

The sand was cool and damp on her bare feet. She stopped crying, took a deep breath, clutched her shoes to her chest and sprinted across the beach. She could hear Beth running across the wooden planks of the bathhouse float, taking a shortcut in hopes of catching up.

Peggy stumbled, dropped a shoe. She backtracked, picked it up, started on her way. Beth, right behind her now, caught her by the arm, knocking her off balance. Peggy sprawled on the ground.

"I wasn't finished," Beth said breathlessly.

Peggy sat up. She glanced at the nurse, then away. She contemplated the beach in front of her. The moon emerged from the masking cloud, rendering the sand a silvery gray.

"Don't you see?" Beth asked, dropping down next to Peggy. "It won't do you any good to run away. Face things squarely. Get yourself under control."

Peggy said sullenly, "I don't want you to feel sorry for me, that's all." She pulled on her shoes. "You said it's partly your fault. Well, it's not Beth. You can't help the way I am, any more than you can help the way you are. It's not your fault at all. Besides, you've done me a lot of good. Really, you have." She was looking at the nurse now, talking to her rather than some spot on the ground. "You were doing lots of good even before—before anything happened between us, before I told you I heard you that night down here. Just being with you has always made me feel better."

Beth waited until she was certain Peggy had finished. "I understand," she said. "And I'm glad. But now that I know what's bugging you, I can do you even more good. I can open your eyes to what lesbianism is, Peggy. It's not a game, or a habit you fall into or out of at will. A lesbian is something you are—or aren't. If—"

"How do you know I'm not?" Peggy demanded.

Beth's gaze did not waver. "How do you know you are?"

"Because I've had a taste of being one. Because I want it more than I want love with boys."

"Peggy, try to understand. You were here, one day, at a strange place, with strange people—strange girls. You learned another girl wanted to seduce you. You were terrified by the prospect, but at the same time excited. After that, a row with your boy friend. Tensions mounted. And then—" Beth hesitated—"then you found out what it is like to make love with another woman. That served as both an emotional and a physical release, and a powerful one. So you decided you were a lesbian."

"Maybe I am. Maybe I'm not. I only know that a few minutes ago, when I saw you, I was bursting with want of you. I wanted you to kiss me, thrill me—and instead, you pitied me." Peggy paused. "Beth, you said yourself I'd find out eventually whether I were a true lesbian. So what difference does it make if I find out here, now, this summer with you—or if I wait till next year or some other time?"

Beth looked at the girl steadily. "Because if you wait only six months, that will be six months' less torment for you."

Peggy frowned. "Is it really that bad?"

Beth nodded emphatically in the moon's platinum glare.

"What I can't understand," Peggy said, "is your concern. Someone must have initiated you, and I'm sure you didn't hate her."

"It's not that I'm worried about your hating me some day, Peggy."

"Yet it means something to you that I don't succumb."

"Of course it means something."

"But why?" Peggy demanded. "Why should you care? You enjoyed our sex together as much as I did. You must still want me. And you certainly know that I want you. So why can't we please each other? Why can't we act the way we want to when we're alone? What difference does it make, as long as we both know what we're doing—as long as we both want to? Why should you care what I am, what I become, if we can be happy together even for a little time? Why should it bother you if I become a confirmed lesbian because of this summer?" Peggy gazed up into the nurse's eyes. "Why, Beth?"

"Because I love you."

Beth sucked in her breath, completely startled by her own words. Obviously, she had not meant to go so far.

Her eyes locked with Peggy's. Then the nurse recovered herself and broke the trance.

Forcing a smile, she said, "Yes. I mean in my own peculiar way, I feel affection for you. A kind of motherly love, you might call it. A protective instinct."

"You're not old enough to be my mother," Peggy said quietly.

"Well, I sort of feel that way toward all the girls at camp. I love them all—you know?"

Peggy shifted position so her body was closer to the nurse's. "Beth, you don't have to hide it. Don't you know that I love you, too?"

Peggy had not considered it before, but now she was certain of her feelings for this woman who had befriended her, stood up for her, guided her in a strange, new kind of consummation.

Before coming to this camp, never in her wildest imaginings would Peggy have conceived of two women making declarations of love to each other. Yet it did not now strike her in the least strange that Beth and she were speaking to each other as if one of them were of the opposite sex. The only thing strange, as far as Peggy was concerned, was that she had not realized before that she was truly, gloriously, irrevocably in love with Beth.

Yes—she was wholly certain of her feelings for this woman who had befriended her, defended her, and guided her to the most profound physical fulfillment.

"Oh, I do love you," Peggy swore. "I need you. Why can't we make each other happy? Why must we fight ourselves? Why can't I touch you—" Peggy's hand reached out, her fingers trailing over Beth's cheek—"feel how soft and delightful you are, whenever I want to? That's not wrong, is it, Beth—to want someone, want to touch her? It's not wrong when you love somebody, is it?"

Beth brushed a wisp of hair from Peggy's face. "No, Peggy, it's not wrong. But we must be sensible and draw the line. There's no reason we can't see each other often, have our usual talks, go—"

"Everything but make love, right? Well, I'm sorry, Beth. Sex is a part of love. Everyone knows that. I can't be with you and not want you—and I won't fight it anymore. So make up your mind. Either we must part entirely—or you must be mine entirely." Peggy rose.

Beth reached out, pulled the girl down. "Why do we always have to argue?"

"We don't have to." There were tears in Peggy's eyes.

"Peggy—" It was barely a whisper.

In the silence that followed, the two hearts were pounding as one. Bathed in moonlight, the women stared hotly. Then the air stirred. The gentle breeze seemed to be all that was needed to move them together. Their lips met.

With that kiss, the floodgates burst open. The pent-up passions of the young counselor and the mature nurse emerged in a hot, rushing tide that flooded them both. Tensions were washed away. Fears and hesitations were drowned by surging lust.

Yet both knew that this was not the time or the place. They might be seen. They might be overheard.

As if the thought had struck the two simultaneously, they drew apart sharply. Beth threw a cautious glance over her shoulder. Peggy's eyes warily searched the shadows on every side. Reassured, they turned back to each other, smiling fondly, tenderly.

"No more arguments?"

"No more arguments," Beth promised. "I may as well enjoy you while I can."

Peggy sat up straight. "I wish you wouldn't talk like that."

"Why not? I think of you as a butterfly—liable to take wing at any moment. Young people do tend to be flighty."

"But this is different. We love each other!"

Beth laughed. "Don't start that again, or I'll be ravishing you right here on the beach. You're a terribly tempting little hussy, you know."

"Your hussy."

Beth rose reluctantly. "I think we'd better get back," she said.

Peggy nodded, slipped on her shoes.

Together they left the lake, careful to latch the gate behind them.

Halfway up the flagstoned path that led to the lodge, Beth said, "I think I'll stop at the Pillbox a minute. I'll be in the lounge later. If we run into each other there, be careful. Let's not act particularly interested in each other."

The pair halted. In the ghostly lunar glow, their eyes met and held. Beth's look was a caress, Peggy's an embrace. It was their only farewell.

Peggy watched until the figure in white disappeared into the night, then continued on toward the lodge. Strange, she mused. Her body no longer ached with passion. The flood of desire had waned. Instead, she felt satisfaction, content, a welling of affection and tenderness.

A joyful shout ahead of her broke into Peggy's thoughts. Pushing the past minutes with Beth into a secret place in her heart, she hurried up the lodge steps. She collected her kids, herded them to the cabin and into bed. She decided to stretch out on her cot in the dark, and think over the events of the day.

She was asleep before her campers were.

The following day passed swiftly, but too slowly for Peggy. After dinner she was making her way up the lodge steps once more, when she was stopped by Ruth, the petite blonde.

Involuntarily, Peggy looked around for Dorothy. This time, the tall riding mistress was not in evidence.

"Say, Peggy," said Ruth, "my girls are planning a masquerade ball for their program night, and we wondered if your cabin would like to help out."

Peggy considered. "We haven't decided on anything for our night yet, and that sounds like fun. I'll ask them."

"Good. Let me know as soon as you can."

"Will do," Peggy promised, continuing on her way.

That evening's activity was being organized on the basketball court, leaving the lodge quiet and desolate. The silence permeating the big structure seemed to jar more profoundly than noise ever had. Peggy's footfalls echoed hollowly as she walked into the lounge, a book and writing tablet under her arm. She wondered if she were the only one in the building.

It was not yet dark, but a stillness had settled over the grounds, broken only by cricket calls.

Peggy sat down at the conference table and contemplated the paper in front of her. Then she jotted a quick note to her parents, telling them all was well.

Finished, she folded the letter, stuffed it into an envelope which she addressed and stamped, then gathered her belongings and left.

It should be time, she thought. It was too late for any more kids to visit the infirmary, unless some emergency developed. She fervently hoped there were no patients staying overnight.

At the door of the Pillbox, she rapped soundly and called, "Anybody home?"

Beth came to greet her, bright and even more cheerful than usual. "For you, always," she said pushing open the screen door. "But aren't you supposed to be other places?"

"It's my night off," Peggy answered, walking toward Beth's room. "Those of my colleagues who are unassigned, like me, are driving in to a movie that I've already seen. I told them I was going to stay behind to do some letter writing and catch up on my reading."

She lowered herself into one of the chairs, dropping her book and pad to the floor.

"So why aren't you?"

"Writing and reading? Because I'd rather be with you."

"I'm flattered." Beth curled up in the other large chair, asked, "What are you reading?"

"A book of short stories. I just finished that famous one by Somerset Maugham about a missionary and a prostitute. He—"

"I saw the movie they made from it," Beth said. "It just proves how weak the flesh is."

Peggy glanced away. "How weak men are, you mean." She was suddenly compelled to tell Beth about Kirby Davis, about the time the big goof had had the effrontery to kiss her. But no sooner had she mentioned Kirby's name than Beth interrupted.

"Oh, you mean Lelia's nephew. I know him. He comes around every summer. A nice boy."

"Nice?" Peggy laughingly told of the stolen kiss and mentioned his attempts to wheedle her into going out with him.

Beth said, "I think you should."

Peggy stopped laughing. "Should what? Go out with him?"

"You should make it a point to meet people."

There was a pause.

"Especially fellows, you mean," Peggy said.

"Not necessarily. Just people who can broaden your outlook, widen your horizons. People can be an education, you know."

"Hm. You're right," Peggy said, rising. "Take, for example, what I've learned from you." She perched on the arm of Beth's chair.

"Be serious," Beth said, her breath coming a little faster.

"But I am." Peggy bent to kiss the nurse on the mouth. When she pulled away, she looked at Beth with wide eyes. "Serious enough?"

"Too serious," Beth answered tensely.

"That's just a taste. Go over there," she said, waving toward the bed, "and I'll show you how really serious I can be." Beth hesitated, not smiling now. "Come on," Peggy said, taking the nurse by the hand. "No more arguments, remember?"

She pulled the nurse to her feet, drew her to the covered bed.

They fell to the bed together. "Undress me," Peggy begged. "Take my clothes off and kiss me."

Beth yielded, eagerly peeled off the sweatshirt Peggy wore. There was no bra under the baggy garment. Peggy's girlish yet copiously developed breasts, vibrant with life, crowned by pink, virginal nipples, drew an agonized cry from the nurse. She buried her face in the soft, lovely mounds. "Oh, Peggy, my darling," Beth whispered against the delicate flesh.

At the touch of Beth's cheek upon her bosom, Peggy felt heat leap in her veins. Then Beth's hands were drawing off Peggy's slacks, at the same time fondling the girl's lithe thighs, the long legs so adorably molded and curved.

Peggy's impatience gathered. She sat up, seized Beth by the hips, kissed her on the lips with ferocious hunger. Why, the woman drove her wild! Now it was she, in her turn, who tore at clothing. She pulled off Beth's shoes, drew down her white stockings. She loosened the white uniform at the sides, jerked it from Beth's body. The nurse stretched out on the bed, a fine figure of a woman, clad only in pale bra from which spilled rich creamy mounds, and in silky white briefs that clung to her milky thighs, her rounded and velvety hips. Even these garments annoyed Peggy. She fussed with them until they were off. Beth lay unclad at last—breathtakingly seductive, her voluptuous charms wholly revealed, wholly accessible.

"Beth?"

"Yes, honey."

"Which am I, the aggressive partner, or the passive?"

Beth laughed. "Where did you hear of such things?"

"Read about 'em in a book, once," Peggy said.

"Well, don't you know which you are?"

"Guess I'm both," Peggy confided mischievously, blushing.

"Little minx. In that case—let's take turns. You make love to me—then, well, I'll do the honors."

Peggy joyously threw herself into the nurse's arms. But passion was so strong upon her that she quickly withdrew her mouth from Beth's, filled her hands with Beth's heavy, delicately textured bosom. In her palms Peggy felt the nipples, in rosy glory, swell and stir. Beth squirmed with delight. Peggy boldly probed lower. Her fingers, with a timeless knowledge of their own, seemed to home unerringly on the unutterably secret nerve clusters that bestowed on Beth the sharpest bliss.

The effect was to evoke in Peggy a feeling of power, of mastery. She controlled Beth. Beth was her slave. She pushed buttons, and Beth danced. Lust came down on Peggy like a red cloud, and in her new wild power, she viciously pinched Beth's soft thigh. "Oh!" groaned Beth. Peggy gritted her teeth and with one heave turned Beth over on the bed. She sent a stinging slap to Beth's quaking buttocks. "Oh!" gasped Beth. "Please. Please, Peggy?"

"You pretty bitch. Tell me you love me. Tell me, or—"

"No! Don't hit me again. I love you, Peggy. I love you."

Peggy thrust her forearms under Beth's armpits, cupped the big breasts. She wrestled the nurse into a supine position, then threw herself upon her.

Wildly, the girls locked to each other. Their bodies were gleaming now with sweat. Lip to lip, breast to breast, thigh to slippery thigh, they heaved and gyrated, ecstasy rising like a lava wave. Eyes rolled, fingers clutched, light hair mingled with darker. Skin slithered slickly and long legs kicked. Murmuring endearments, panting like beasts, the counselor and the nurse felt the white-hot wave engulf them, drown them in fiery exaltation while their very guts shook and convulsed.

"God!" intoned Peggy, limply falling back on the bed.

"Leave God out of it," whispered Beth. "This is devil's work, pure and simple."

"Pure and simple?"

They both laughed. But Beth, perhaps because of exhaustion, nevertheless seemed somber, even sad.

For many minutes they lay side by side, Peggy curled up, her hand resting affectionately on Beth's breast. After a time, she felt Beth's nipple alive again in her palm.

"Oh, Beth, you do want me don't you? You didn't mind my being a little rough—"

"No, dear. I understand about that." She drew Peggy's hand away from her breast, raised it to her lips and kissed the fingers.

"Beth," whispered Peggy, eyes shining, "it's your turn now. Do everything. Teach me all about what lesbians do."

The nurse could not help smiling at Peggy's ingenuous eagerness. She sat up. "I've said it before and I'll say it again. You're a hussy. A shameless hussy."

"A delicious hussy! Try me."

Beth bent breathlessly to minister to Peggy, who now was the one lying supinely on the bed.

But unlike the prior wooing of the younger girl, the attentions of Beth seemed deliberately void of fondling, of stroking, of any bodily contact at all, save that established by the nurse's fragrant, tender kisses. First they were devoted to Peggy's mouth, sucked and savored like a crushed red berry under Beth's lips, probed and wickedly eased by Beth's flicking tongue.

Then the lips nibbled delicately at Peggy's earlobe, sending the softest of sensations coursing through the girl, sensations building and broadening as the nurse kissed her neck, her shoulders—and then, as Peggy stiffened in taut response, her passion-swollen breasts. Each nipple was moistly enfolded, wetly warmed. Beth's lips artfully tormented. The tip of her tongue rasped and tweaked. Then when Peggy thought she could stand this cruel titillation no longer, when she thought her bosom was about to burst with bliss and she pleaded for mercy, for respite, Beth's mouth moved on.

Peggy felt the brush of Beth's cheek on her navel. She flamed as Beth's hair trailed a prickling caress along the sensitive skin of the torso. "Damn it, Beth. Please," she pleaded, as Beth had pleaded before. "Oh, please, Beth!" Beth kissed on. Her lips were wet and lined with silk. Her tongue fluttered like a butterfly...

Later—much later—when the heavy breathing of the two unclad forms on the bed had quieted to normal, when only the sounds of the night were to be heard in the room—the crickets' chirping, the rustling of the warm night breeze, the trees, the soft lapping from the lakeshore—Peggy spoke up. "People are an education, all right." Beth shifted, propped herself on an elbow.

"I hope by the end of the summer you'll have learned more than that from me," she said.

Peggy lay against the coolness of the fluffy pillow, her blond hair rumpled, her eyes closed. A look of complete satisfaction etched her face.

"I've learned enough for two summers," she murmured, but on opening her eyes to look at Beth, she noted the gravity of the woman's expression. She said, "I hope you know what I mean, Beth. I've learned what happiness is."

Beth said nothing, nor did her face become less grave. Her eyes bored into Peggy, studying her, weighing her, and—so Peggy felt—accusing her.

"Look," Peggy burst out, "none of this is anyone's fault. And we—we enjoyed it, didn't we"?

"Too much, maybe. Peggy, don't you realize you may be marking yourself for life? Don't you think you should make some effort to fight it?"

"Oh, if it will make you feel any better," Peggy retorted, "I'll go with Kirby the next time he asks."

"Promise?"

Exasperated, Peggy said, "I promise." And then, with a grin: "Always worrying about me, aren't you?"

"Always," Beth answered.

"Well, don't. This is my off time. I don't have to show up at my bunk until morning."

Beth moved closer. Kirby and everything else were forgotten for the remainder of the night.

Ravaged by three men...
she sought the tenderness
of love in another woman

These Curious Pleasures

by Sloane Britain

They were celebrating the filming of a new TV show...and Allison's debut as a star. The party was wild and drunken...then it got out of hand and Allison found herself in the bedroom with three men...one held her, one stripped her... and they all raped her.

It was then that Allison turned to Sloane for affection...and gratefully entered the forbidden world of lesbian love.

This novel examines that love with provocative understanding and insight.

These Curious Pleasures

Allison was a big help. She thought my idea about getting zonked a splendid one. We bought enough booze to float the Saratoga, set it up with ice, glasses, etc. on the sideboard and proceeded to goof it up. I was half-drunk already from not sleeping and the firewater finished the job. Allison got loaded for the first time since I had met her. She was even more adorable that way. Maybe I thought so because in the condition I was in the view from left field made almost everything look good. Like I was digging her the most. It matters why?

While I could still articulate, I told her about what had happened. Not only that day, I filled her in on all the smut I had learned about during the preceding six months.

When I finished, Allison said, "Now I know who killed Cock Robin."

"Who?"

"Happy Broadman. He didn't do it himself, of course. He made Cinderella do it by hitting him with her glass slipper. Then, when she married the Prince, Happy was the caterer for the reception. The Prince and Cinderella had a baby boy named Twinkletoes. Happy had a contract with them so they had to let him perform the circumcision. He used a serpent's tooth instead of a knife so the child was traumatized and grew up to be Rumplestilskin."

"Brother, you're gone, my love. Like way out. Before you lose contact altogether, what about helping me decide what to do?"

"That's simple, come to California with me."

"Whether or not I go to California with you will be decided independent of my employment status. The question is, for the sake of argument presuming that I'm going to keep living and working in New York, should I quit my present job?"

"I refuse to accept the basic premise. Therefore, I can't help you decide. I will not even think of your staying in New York. You're coming to California."

"Dictating to me again?"

"No, using Pavlovian conditioning. I figure that if I repeat it often enough I'll brainwash you till you can't do anything else but come with me."

"There's another word for it," I said.

"Nagging?"

"Precisely. I had enough of it at home. My mother could have won prizes if they held contests in nagging."

"So now I'm like your mother?" Allison said teasingly.

"Yes, and I don't like it. Cut it out."

"What's the matter with you? You're supposed to go for it."

"I don't want you to be a mother to me," I protested.

"Nonsense. You're gay and therefore you're seeking mother substitutes with whom to re-enact the primal situation. I read that somewhere once."

"You read books?!!! Thank God that I found out before it was too late. I've heard about people like you. Your kind is trying to undermine the very foundations of this country. I heard that once at a Ku Klux Klan meeting. Fellow who had the local tar and feather concession was talking. Very interesting talk, very timely. I learned all about you all city folks that night. You people with book larnin' is a menace to decent folks."

Allison crossed over to in front of the television set. "May I take this occasion to announce that one member of the Literate Society to Stamp Out Mom and Apple Pie is in her cups? In fact, you might say I'm inebriated. No, I like four sheets to the wind better. All my sheets unfurled and spread out to catch the vagrant winds." She spread her arms out wide to illustrate. The gesture knocked her off balance and she swayed back against the TV set. It knocked the rabbit ears antenna down and it fell around her, one limb on each side of her shoulders. Allison pondered this for a moment and then looked up with a profound expression. "That's me...symmetry always."

I roared. When I recovered myself, I said, "I have just discovered that I'm in love with the kookiest woman in New York."

"You just find that out?"

"No, I've known it right along but that last bit finished me. Allison my love, you win the prize for irresistible insanity. You're marvelous, my love, simply marvelous."

"You really mean that?"

"As James Joyce would put it, 'Yes.'"

That cracked her up. She fell all over me with love. Ever been kissed by someone who can't stop laughing? Their lips keep sort of trembling. It tickles.

I mixed us another drink. Halfway through that one I began to get "Sloane's Reaction" (that's the name I gave it. If Bright could have a disease named for him, why couldn't I have a response to liquor in my name?). "Sloane's Reaction" consisted of most of the effect of the alcohol being concentrated in one particular area. Some people get weak in the knees from booze. Up about a foot and a half was bull's-eye for anything I drank.

If we were going to come to any solution that night I'd have to push the conversation right then, before my mind goofed off with my body.

"Allison."

"Yes, baby?"

"Ugh. Don't use that word now. Since you brought up that mother substitute routine I've gotten self-conscious about it."

"You never objected when I used it before."

"I know. But now it's too blatant. I crave subtlety in my regressive acting outs."

"Who's been reading books now?" She lifted one eyebrow mockingly. Allison did this as she winked, by closing both eyes and then opening one. Perfectly adorable. "Anyway, tell me how I can subtly shanghai you aboard the plane to California next week?"

"Allison! Please, baby...I mean, darling...try to be serious for a moment. We could reach a conclusion about this in a few minutes. Then, I promise you, I won't bother you with any more of my troubles for the rest of the night."

Allison composed her face into that absurd caricature of attentiveness that drunks wear. It was ludicrous. She looked as if she were trying to convince an arresting officer of her sobriety.

"Don't you have any thoughts on the subject?" I asked.

"Sure," she said, looking very grave. "To me it's all very simple. I don't know why you insist on making a prime spot production out of it."

She stopped speaking. I could see the alcoholic fuzziness creeping back into her eyes. I fought it fast.

"So it's simple. So tell me about it," I said.

"Very simple. Lovely girl, Sloane Britain, wonderful girl... but she's got some strange idea about herself."

"What do you mean?"

"Like she thinks she's some kind of real down cynic. A mentally retarded orangutan would see through that pose five minutes after meeting her. But she's lived with herself for over twenty years and she still believes most of the nonsense she tells herself. Very sad."

I was beginning to feel highly uncomfortable. The truth doesn't always hurt. More often it is just embarrassing as all hell.

"So, being the adorable idiot that she is, she thinks that she can work in an office where honesty and sincerity are dirty words," Allison continued. "She thinks that she ought to believe that all human beings are out to exploit each other. So what difference does it make if Happy Broadman happens to have carried exploitation to the point of being an art? Cynic Sloane wants to think that working for him might be a good idea. She might learn the fine points of being self-seeking from her boss."

Allison stopped and stared at me fixedly. Then she stretched out on the couch with her head in my lap.

She was still staring at me with eyes that held a potpourri expression of amusement, compassion, mischievousness, and advanced inebriation.

I was no temperance advertisement myself. Otherwise, I don't think I could have taken her observations. That she was saying those things at that time didn't bother me too much. What got me was realizing that she had most likely held the same opinions for a long time. All the while that I had been trying to come on as a juvenile delinquent version of a composite of Messrs. Shaw, Wilde and Voltaire, with a dash of Dorothy Parker thrown in, Allison had been seeing through it.

"My beloved Miss Britain," she went on, "I have news for you. You're no cynic. Sure, you see that life and people are ludicrous. It's the foundation of your humor. You laugh at the absurdity of everything and everybody, including yourself. Nothing wrong with that, human beings are ridiculous and some people, I among them, suspect that life is nothing but a cosmic joke."

She raised one finger, like a platform lecturer about to make a point. Instead, she continued the gesture upward and grasped a strand of my hair with it. She continued to play with the lock of my hair throughout the remainder of her discourse.

"In fact, at the risk of having you throw an apoplectic fit, I will go so far as to say that I think you're almost naïvely idealistic. Emotionally, I mean. Intellectually you know that the great majority of people will be doing more good when they're fertilizing the flowers than they ever did in their lifetimes.

"Now, to the point of all this: In the light of your aforementioned idealism, it is my opinion (don't blame me, you asked me for it) that for you to continue working for Happy Broadman would be self-destructive. In fact, I would predict that before too long one of two things would happen if you did. Either you'd get the screaming meemies or an ulcer or some other form of hysteria...or you'd blow the whole works one day by denouncing Happy to his face and putting yourself through a highly unpleasant scene. So, wouldn't you agree that it's a better idea for you to quit your job now before things get any easier than they are?"

"I...I guess so," I said weakly.

"Good. I'm glad that's taken care of. Now, Sloane," Allison's voice became pathetically beseeching, "could I get drunk again? I had such a lovely buzz on before."

Placing me on an equal footing again. Restoring the frayed edges of my ego by asking my permission. Having me mix the drinks for us both like I was the efficient hostess and she only an invited guest dependent on my largesse. What a woman!

More than ever before I was aware of my luck. Allison was the kind of woman most men looked for all their lives and never found. Warm, loving, intelligent, beautiful, charming and completely feminine. And she was in love with me!

My moment of humility didn't last but at the time I was filled with wonder...what did someone like Allison see in me? Could it have something to do with the rotten things that had happened to me before? Maybe there was something to that idea of suffering being rewarded?

I stayed deeply engrossed in remembering what Allison had said. Not that I was thinking about it or analyzing it. It was more like I kept repeating her words to myself. Like it was religious. Like I had had a mystical experience or something.

All right, so everything Allison had said was so true of me it hurt. So what? This proves I should pack up and follow her across the country? Maybe I was making too big a deal over it? After all, she hadn't told me anything new about myself. I knew those things about myself, I just acted as if I didn't because I fully expected by doing the right things I would someday become more like what I was on the outside.

That naïve idealist routine, for instance. I knew that underneath my assumed hard exterior (hard like glass...impervious to all but the sharpest assaulters but likely to shatter if hit by the wrong tone of voice) I was like somebody's overgrown dog, ready at any time to pledge undying devotion to any slob who threw me the right bone. Lucky for me no one did. The gimmick was that I thought that continually assaulting my naïve convictions with the seamy facts of reality would eventually penetrate and teach me to be less trusting. The way I saw it, you had to be tough. Real hard, like steel or the world would walk all over you. I was in great shape. I thought I was like the most mature, well-informed on all the latest trends in morbidity, a regular Hedda Hopper of neurotica. The truth was that I had gotten older but not much smarter. I was still mentally only on the second landing and the window wasn't open.

The big deal was that someone else had seen through the façade. It's possible Allison wasn't the first one to do so. I was having conniptions because she was the first one who had the conviction to let me know what she saw. Can't blame most people if they kept their thoughts to themselves. Usually, I had had an aversion to people giving me their analyses of my psyche. Among the literati of New York City that's the favorite indoor sport. Like charades, every goof who had read a magazine article about psychology felt qualified to play the game, what was the other guy acting out? That jazz gave me the chills. Those lovelies wouldn't dream of diagnosing a physical illness but they had no qualms about regarding themselves experts in the science of psychology. I didn't go for it and I wouldn't put up with hearing half-baked interpretations of my unresolved Oedipal conflict and all that sort of stuff. That stuff's for the professionals. I must have frustrated a lot of armchair Freuds in my time. Tough, baby dolls, real tough.

What really counted was that Allison loved me. She saw through me but that didn't mean she didn't like what she saw. That meant that she had a right to see the personality I presented to the world and the private one I had gone to such lengths to submerge. After all, she loved both sides of me and that's what really mattered.

"Hey, come back. You haven't said a word for ten minutes."

"I was thinking about one of the reasons why I love you," I said.

"What's that?"

"Let me try and illustrate it this way: if you hadn't been able to eat for three days, what would you say was wrong with you?"

Allison looked at me as if she were afraid that I had finally flipped out so far I'd never come back. "I'd say that I was hungry."

"That's what I thought. And that's one of the reasons I love you."

"Because I get hungry? Girl, I've heard of being weird, but this beats all."

"Really? You should read Stekel. However," I explained, "that is far from being my hangup. No, the point I'm trying to make is that you can get hungry without calling yourself oral-retentive. That's one of the reasons for my loving you. I've known too many of the other kind. People who can't enjoy eating an artichoke without thinking they're oral-regressive."

"I know the type. Sounds like some of the friends I made when I first came to the city. They bored me stiff."

"Yeah. You know, I've gotten revoltingly sober in the last hour. What about you?"

"Me too. I thought this drink would get me back where I was before but it hasn't. We're almost out of Scotch too."

"I could go down and buy some more," I suggested.

"Hey, I just got a better idea. Ever had a Sidecar?"

"No."

"You've been missing something. It's my favorite cocktail but I seldom drink it because after three of them I've been known to start thinking I was Madame Butterfly."

"That must be quite a scene," Allison said.

"You shouldn't know from it. Once, at a party, I lost count of how many I drank. All I know is that at one point I came out of the john with the end of a roll of toilet paper in my hands. I unwound it all the way into the living room where I proceeded to announce that I was that Butterfly cat. All the time I was tearing the tissue into little pieces and tossing them about like they were flower petals."

"You're making it up."

"So help me Giacomo Puccini, I'm telling the truth. At least that's what I'm told I did. I don't remember that night too clearly," I protested. "Anyway, I have a bottle of brandy in the kitchen and some Cointreau somewhere around the place. A smidgeon of lemon juice and we've got a Sidecar. How about it? Should I mix up a batch?"

"On top of Scotch? Oh, what the hell, let's try it anyway. But please," Allison requested, "no Madame Butterfly tonight."

"Don't worry, I passed the Puccini stage long ago. It'll be Der Rosenkavalier, at least."

"H-m-m-m. As I remember, the opening scene holds some interesting possibilities."

"Hold it. We better take this topic up again after I've made the drinks or we'll never get around to them."

I had never mixed a Sidecar before. I guess it takes practice. Anyway, mine were palatable...but just barely. We had three each. I was seeing the world through rose-colored glasses...someone else's prescription.

We were sitting on the floor, leaning back against the couch. I felt safer down there. Allison had her head on my shoulder and my arm was around her.

Suddenly I became aware that she had her tongue in my ear. No, that couldn't be right. She wouldn't just start out that way. She'd build up to something like that. Guess I had been drinking up such a storm I hadn't known that she had been kissing my neck.

When she withdrew her lips I turned and gathered her to me. "Well, hello there, pretty girl. Where did you come from?" I teased as I took liberties with her clothing.

"Glad you're back. For a while there I thought you were more interested in your drink than you were in me."

"Baby, you know I'm weak for you. Wait a minute and I'll prove it," I said, standing up and unfastening what appeared to be a million zippers.

"You should have music." Allison got up and put a stack of records on the phonograph. She turned the volume control way up. She had selected some jazz records of the Kansas City and Chicago barrelhouse and blues styles. Old stuff like they used to play in the speakeasies and brothels. It came swinging out of the speaker real raunchy and low-down. So right for the occasion. It was very definitely not the time for Italian opera.

"OK, you've got your accompaniment. Now do your bit," Allison said.

I didn't get what she meant at first but then I dug it and I goofed. I mean, like brother, I flipped. That wasn't my bit.

Allison was still standing by the phonograph. "Come on, I'm waiting. The curtain's up. The music's playing. What are you waiting for? A fan?"

"Allison, I couldn't. I'd be too embarrassed."

"Nothing to it. Just make like you're in bed. Let the music reach your hips. Like this." She came toward me slowly, giving it back to a frantic bass fiddle with bumps and grinds that would do credit to a shake dancer twenty years in the business.

By the time she reached me she had me in a sweat. I grabbed her and ripped off what few clothes she still had on. She let me but when I tried to kiss her she backed away and began moving around again.

They hadn't taught her that in her ballet classes. But the training had helped make her graceful. There wasn't much room for her to show her stuff but she didn't need much. She mostly stood in one spot and made her body go places while her feet stood still.

Man, I was kicked right out of my mind. But I really cracked up when she pulled a bit I had seen once at a strip joint on Third Street in the Village. When I watched that professional stripper do it I had been a little embarrassed but mostly as bored as the dancer had been. When the woman I loved did the same thing the effect, to understate to the point of absurdity, was different.

Allison extended her tongue out as far as it would go. She brought her hands up and licked the palms of each. Then, arching her body back from the waist so that her gorgeous breasts swelled out full and inviting toward me, she brought her hands down and cupped her breasts, like she was offering them to me. Then, she placed her palms flat against the pink tips and caressed them, her body swaying longingly, an expression of languid sensual delight on her face, her eyes open and staring at me with defiance and excitement.

With an involuntary moan, I fell to my knees before her, clasping her legs tightly and burying my lips in the silken pliancy of her thighs. Allison swayed sinuously in my arms.

Ardent pulsations coursed through the writhing body in my arms. My legs had lost their power. I couldn't rise. My body stretched upwards, stretching, straining for fulfillment. Up, up, my body pressed against the muscular hardness of her legs, my lips and tongue seeking, needing. Allison was shivering, small meaningless sounds coming from the depths of her throat.

Allison tossed limply, leaning against me for the support her trembling legs could no longer give her. A thin high-pitched scream and long shudders wracking through the length of her body and then my name repeated and repeated over and over again.

We were lying on the floor, the rayon rug prickling my bare skin. I was too relaxed to bother moving.

Allison was lying with her face cradled in my bosom. Her body was limp, her eyes closed. I could tell that she wasn't sleeping, though, by the rhythm of her breathing and by the small grasping motions she made at me every time I shifted my position slightly.

She stiffened one arm against the floor and propped herself up to a near sitting position. Her face was almost white, drained, exhausted. I noticed that the arm she was using to support herself was trembling as if too spent to expend any effort.

She stared at me long and hard without speaking. Then, in a voice that was heavy with desperation said, "I love you so much. Too much. I'll have to pay for this, Sloane. It must be sinful to get so much pleasure from one person. Somehow I feel that there must be something evil in my wanting to have you be the center and meaning of my life. Sloane, I want that so very much. God help me, I adore you!"

"Darling, you shouldn't look at it that way. That way of thinking's merely a carry-over from the medieval..." I never got to finish my statement. A look of longing had come over Allison's face. Feverish desire set her eyes aflame. She cut me off in mid-sentence with an insistent kiss.

Her lips, which I had always known to be soft and gentle, bore down on me inflexibly. I was taken aback and put off by the punishing fierceness of her kiss.

It was Allison who was kissing me, however. Allison who was roughly fondling me. The woman I loved whose body was crowding mine. As the initial surprise passed away, I began to respond. I could feel my taut muscles relaxing. My lips parted and I invited more sensual kisses.

Allison reacted by lessening the whiplash ferocity of her lovemaking. She became tender and adoring.

Briefly, she raised herself a few inches, to tell me, "Every time we touch, I feel as if a miracle were happening." Then she came back to my lips. But in the brief moment when she had her eyes open I had seen passionate desire that bordered on desperation.

I wriggled free and stood up. "I got up because I can't really believe that you want to make love again. Not so soon. I think you're doing it for some other reason. I don't know what it is but I'm highly suspicious of its being something other than sexual."

"Wrong, my love. I want you because I love you. If you think I should be some sort of limp lily now, I'm sorry to disappoint you. Sloane, I want you. I'm aroused again, honest. Maybe I'm turning nympho in my old age."

"Sure?"

"Dammit, what do you want? A signed affidavit? Let me put it this way, if you don't stop questioning me this instant and get back here in my arms where I can say whatever I have to say in sign language, I'll make you stop."

"Oh? You're also getting pretty cocky in your old age," I said. "What makes you so sure you can stop me?"

Allison smiled. Now I know what they mean by that Cheshire cat bit. She looked as if swallowing the canary were her hourly habit. "The records are still stacked. All I have to do is put them back on the changer and start the music playing. I don't think you'd keep giving me such a hard time if I were to start dancing again."

"Aah, I've seen that act already. Your performance would suffer from repetition. It just wouldn't have the same effect," I lied. "You know, like a mystery story. Once you know the ending, there's not much point in re-reading the story again."

Allison stretched luxuriously, emphasizing the slim voluptuousness of her figure. Then she put her hands on her sleekly rounded hips and gently kneaded the supple flesh. "You only saw the first act. There are two more and an encore. Shall I begin?" she cooed.

"D-don't bother. Any more of that and I'd be a candidate for a nut hatch." I meant it. I was so steamed up it was killing me to keep up the teasing and not just fall to it. Another performance of Allison's and I'd be locked up for loving her to death.

"There's only one way to keep me from dancing again. Come over here, darling," Allison cooed.

"Do we have to use the floor again? My back already feels like the bottom of a birdcage. If you want me, come after me." I turned and ran into the kitchen.

Allison ran after me, laughing. We were both giggling so much we could hardly keep running. Guess we were both racked up by the same thing, an image of how we would look to an observer, running around the apartment naked.

I barely escaped her grasp as I headed out of the kitchen, through the living room, to the foyer. It was a long narrow hall with the bedroom at one end and the door to the outside at the other.

I ran until I collided with unyielding wood. The outside door. In my excitement I had run in the wrong direction.

Allison had me trapped. There was only room for one person to walk down the hall at a time. She surged up against me, not able to break the momentum she had built up while running. The impact crushed me to the door. The wood protested loudly and the thud of my impact gathered volume in the empty halls and stairwell. Oh Christ, and with the landlord living right in the building! I was sure there would be an eviction notice for me the next day. You understand, I didn't know exactly what time it was but it had to be some time after midnight.

The unexpected noise flipped us both. We thought it was funny. We goofed it up laughing and making guesses about what the other tenants had done when they heard the sound. Like what they had been doing when it happened and how they might have interpreted it. We were breaking each other up.

Allison stopped laughing first. There was nothing humorous about the way her fingers were probing my body. What there is to do with hands in order to achieve certain effects, she was doing. Anything else, there isn't.

My laugh went to a grin to something quite other than hilarity. Allison had her hand behind my head, tugging a handful of my hair until my head was inclined backward. She bent over me and brought her mouth to mine. Instead of kissing me, she kept her lips a fraction of an inch away and traced the outlines of my mouth with the tip of her tongue. Playing with the contours of my parted lips.

She was using her hands and fingers to fondle me like a bibliophile examining the Guttenberg Bible. A delicious languor spread through me. My heart was beating frantically, blood spurting lustily through me, throbbing inside me that blocked out sight and sound, present and future. Only Allison and the exquisite sensations of her touch were real.

"No, no, Allison. Please, not here. Not so close to the door. The neighbors...they'll hear us." Some part of my mind that I wasn't in touch with was being rational. I heard myself speaking but wasn't aware that I was articulating, nor had any idea where the logical, coherent thoughts came from.

"They can't hear me making love to you, baby. That's just between us," Allison said. She followed her words with a probing kiss and then her mouth was roving my body, just the tip of her tongue extended.

Her mouth was on my breast, the wet pink wonder teasing the tips. I was sinking further and further into ardent urgency. My body had gone slack with need and it was only the pressure of Allison's body propping me against the door that kept me upright. I was falling limply. Allison started easing me down to the floor, not stopping her stroking.

"No. Please," I said weakly. "I don't want to here. Not on the floor. Not in front of the door."

Allison's voice was tight and husky. She had to take a deep breath before speaking. "I guess you're right. That might wake someone." She swayed against me and buried her head in my shoulder. "Oh, dearest, it's so wonderful when you finish. I love the way you go out of your mind and become so free and wild and unrestrained. My baby, it's so good to see you when you're like that. You're a different person, primitive, uninhibited and so completely mine. And the things you say at that time! Like they came from deep inside you where your sincerest feelings are. You say such lovely things to me then, Sloane precious. As if you had no control over what you were saying, sometimes you whisper so that I can hardly hear you, other times there are no words, just rapturous sounds, and sometimes you just let go and proclaim your ecstasy. Those times you usually call out my name. Like it was something of great beauty. Or loudly, as if you wanted to tell the world that I was the one you love." She picked her head up. "Yes, I guess you have a point. We had better get away from the door."

Allison helped me get up. Every bone and muscle in my body had turned to jelly. She propped me up in front of her as we went down the hall to the bedroom. Allison kicked the bedroom door shut behind us with the heel of her foot.

I was on the bed. Allison was standing next to the bed staring down at me. Then Allison was embracing me, the slippery velvet of her perspired body pulsating against me. Mouth on my mouth. Silken lips against mine. Hands and fingers stroking, clasping, fondling. Lips touching, brushing, sliding over my body. Agonizingly exquisite tongue seeking, caressing. I in the torturous ache of ecstasy, in the rapture of transport, then, quickly, knotted up with tension...release and flowing out and, "Allison, Allison, Allison, I love you. My precious darling. Allison, Allison, Allison, Allison..."

What was probably much later, I realized that sunlight was coming in the room from around the edges of the drapes. There was a clock on the bedside table. I twisted myself up and to the side in order to read its face which was turned away from me. I was very careful not to awaken Allison who was sleeping in the embrace of my left arm. I picked up the clock and brought it close to my eyes. Myopia and a hangover made me tempted to use Braille. Finally, I was able to make out the time.

"Is it very late?" a sleepy voice inquired from the other side of the bed.

"We must have fallen asleep. It's 9:15 already. I'm going to have to hustle to get to the office in time."

"Damn! I've got an appointment with a photographer for this morning. I'm due there already and I don't even know where the hell I left my clothes around this voyeur's dream. And I have to go back to my place to pick up my stage makeup. Oh, I hope he waits for me. I don't care if he kills me for being so late, just so long as he's there. He's one of the best cameramen in the business and I've waited months to get this appointment with him. I need a lot of new stills for distribution on the Coast. They're going to know Allison Millay is in town if I have to send them pictures and bios every day for a year."

"You better have some breakfast. Posing under those hot lights will knock you out if you don't. Remember, you've had hardly any sleep. Couple that with not eating and holding poses in the glare of those hot spotlights and they'll have to carry you out frothing at the mouth."

"You're right. I'll grab something to eat while I'm in the taxi. I won't have time to sit down to breakfast."

I let Allison have the bathroom first because she was so late. I'd never make it to the office on time but, if Judy or Happy had anything to say about it they'd be sorry. I was in no mood to put up with their nonsense that day. I would only be half to three-quarters of an hour late. They had no right to make a big deal out of that. Every human being is a little late for work once in a while. Once in a while? Face it, Sloane, I told myself, you've been late so often in the six months you've been there that the elevator operators probably think you're due at work sometime around eleven. So what? Just let one of them say anything today and I'll make them wish that they had stayed in bed. With my voice, I can make almost any line sound like an impeachment proclamation if I'm careful of my delivery.

Allison finished washing and was standing before the bathroom sink, putting layers of greasy makeup over the dark circles around her eyes and on the pink and blue blemishes around her mouth, the ones I had put there. She was looking at her reflection in the mirror as if she saw there some sort of hag. I should look half as ugly as she.

I got into the shower while she was making with the paint and took a quick one. Allison was combing her hair when I came out. She must have seen my reflection in the mirror because all of a sudden she whirled around toward me.

"Sloane, baby, did I do that? You look like you've been through the wars. You're covered with bruises. How did you get a black-and-blue mark there?"

"Don't tell me you've forgotten last night?" I was on the verge of tears. It would've been too much if Allison had been like those drunks Banner, Perry Matthews and Herb Talman...if her passion had come from a bottle and was a thing that meant no more to her than a hangover the next day.

"I remember what I felt last night. My emotions, most of the action and that it was divine. The exact continuity of events is a little mixed up in my mind. I do know that we were both pretty frenzied and that things were done by both of us last night that we'd never gone in for before. As I recall, it seems to me that we made love all over this apartment. However, I don't remember the exact sequence of events. No, I couldn't give a detailed plot outline of last night. Is that important?"

"No, of course not. I don't think I could either. There is one thing that will bother me if I don't ask about it now, though. Last night, when we started making love, you know, when you danced to the phonograph music...well, what happened after that worries me. You were sort of, well, hard like. I'm not referring just to your actions. There was a lack of your usual loving warmth and tenderness. I'm talking about an emotional quality that wasn't there. It was somewhat like the difference between love and lust."

Allison breathed a deep sigh and bit down on her lower lip. "I know. I'm always that way. When I'm hurt, I withdraw. Because of the way I feel about you I couldn't just keep away from you. Instead, something inside me shut off. I suppose you've got those bruises because, and I assure you I wasn't conscious of it, I wanted to hit back at you for hurting me so much."

I had been standing like some kind of idiot with the sopping wet towel held before me, dripping puddles onto the floor. I started to speak but a gurgling croak came out...I hadn't remembered to close my mouth before speaking, it had been agape all through Allison's reply.

"Baby," I finally managed, "I don't know what I did but if I hurt you, I'm sorry, genuinely so. But I can't imagine what I did wrong."

"You didn't give me your decision about coming to California with me. It was our last night together and I expected you to say something. Even if you had said no, it would have been kinder than not saying anything. You acted as if whether you came with me or not was an unimportant matter. I wasn't going to force you to put anything into words. I've got a little pride left. Not much, I admit, but enough to keep me from humiliating myself any more than I had already. I suppose your silence meant that you've decided not to go to the Coast. Is that right?"

"Just a little old minute. I mean no such thing. What's the rush? 'The Singer Show' isn't leaving for two more weeks. I could get plane reservations by calling in a week in advance. It's a big decision. I wanted as much time as possible to think it over. I didn't think you'd mind if I didn't let you know until next week. What's this bit about last night being our last night together. Why, for God's sake?"

"Because of yesterday's new development. I got in touch with you just as soon as I knew about it myself." Allison must have seen the complete bewilderment on my face because she looked at me incredulously and asked, "You got my message, didn't you?"

"What message?"

"The one I asked Judy to give you. I called while you were out to lunch. I was going to be busy the rest of the afternoon and couldn't call back so I dictated a message for you to Judy. She said she'd give it to you as soon as you came back to the office. I made everything clear in that message. That's why your acting as if everything was just the same hurt me so much."

"Allison, I swear to you, Judy didn't give me any message yesterday. She didn't even tell me you had called." Damn that freak Judy! That wasn't the first time she had "forgotten" to tell me about personal calls that had come in for me when I was away from my desk. Don't tell me her memory had been bad. If anyone called Happy, Judy would remember it all right. She could be dying and she'd gasp it out with her last breath. She didn't have the gumption to tell me she didn't like my getting personal calls at the office so she let me miss about half the calls she answered for me. I guess I was supposed to interpret this to mean that I shouldn't use the phone except for business. I knew what she was getting at but I hadn't let it stop me. The messages I hadn't gotten probably weren't all that important. If someone urgently needed to talk to me, they'd call back. But this time Judy had gone too far. This was being malicious, not just petty. "It's the truth, Allison. This is the first I've heard of your calling the office yesterday."

She collapsed against the sink, weak with laughter. "It's too incredible," she gasped. "I thought things like this only happened in Restoration comedies. The crucial message that goes astray and the ensuing farce scene where the boy and girl meet and insult each other because they don't know what's happened and each of them is talking about something different. Oh-oh, this is too rich. Somebody ought to have said that they'd never darken the other's door again. That's all we would have needed to make this period piece complete." She broke up in helpless laughter again.

I waited until she had subsided to giggles before asking, "Just what was it you asked Judy to tell me?"

"I called you right away because the Crystal soap people want me to start filming those spot commercials Monday of next week. That means that I've got to fly out to the Coast in four days. No, three days. It was four yesterday. Anyway, they're going to keep me busy for the two weeks until 'The Singer Show' arrives and I have to start rehearsing for that. I won't have a chance to come back to New York. When I leave a few days from now it'll be for good. At least, for the next three years. So, you understand now why last night was the last one I could spend with you? I have only three days and nights to do a mountain of packing, close out my bank account, say good-bye to all my friends, buy a load of new clothes, return the books and records I've borrowed from friends, take care of ten thousand business matters. I'm going to be too busy to blow my nose for the next three days. Coming here last night was allowing myself a luxury which I really couldn't afford. Now, do you understand why I was hurt? Remember, I had no idea that you didn't know it was our final chance to be alone."

"Allison, now that I know, I wouldn't have blamed you if you had told me to go to hell in a wheelbarrow."

"Thank the Lord I didn't do something like that. Then we would never have straightened this out."

"Yeah. Well, frankly I'm so taken off guard by this that I don't know what to say. Would you hate me very much if I didn't let you know until tonight? I could call or maybe come over and help you with your packing."

"It's all right, darling," Allison said. "I'll wait for your call tonight. In the meantime, I'll be praying to every god, saint, angel, prophet and holy man I can think of from every religion known to me that you will be on the plane to California with me. Look out the office windows during the day. If you see a girl doing what looks like a demoniac mazurka around one of the trees in Central Park, it'll be me. I think I'll try invoking the Druid deities too, I'm afraid to leave anything out."

I finally got to the office a few minutes before eleven. Happy was giving dictation to Judy in his office. They both looked up as I got off the elevator. I stared down anything they were about to say. There was blood in my eye that morning, I tell you. To rub things in a little more, I disappeared into the john for ten more minutes. By the time I finally sat down at my desk Judy was ready to have apoplexy.

She brought some work out for me to do and lingered in my office, waiting for me to give some excuse for my tardiness. I didn't say a word. Instead, I pointedly got out an ebony and silver cigarette holder that I had never before used. It was a real classy thing that a client had given me, six inches long and mucho impressive. I stuck a cigarette into it, lighted it and waved the thing around affectedly. Hip Judy was not but she got my message that time. She went back to her own office like a whipped puppy.

Happy was having a ball with one of his chicks on his private phone. I don't know what the girl was saying to him but I could get a good idea from the way he kept squirming around as he talked to her. Every once in a while he'd get a real sappy grin on his face as if she had just said something especially toothsome.

Meanwhile, the phones were ringing like crazy and I was trying desperately to get him to answer a few calls. Some of them were real important business calls but Happy didn't seem to care. He just went on talking and twitching.

I had my hands full with the phones until about one o'clock when things quieted down. That was the first chance I had had to look at the work Judy had given me to do. It was time for me to go out to lunch but I decided to have a sandwich sent up. I wanted to be fair, coming into work two hours late was enough, I'd make up the time by working through my lunch-hour.

There were tons of bills from the Ferguson pilot that had to be taken care of. That meant mailing out checks for about a third of them. The remainder received letters of acknowledgment. Harold Broadman informs you that he knows he owes you money and requests that you get the hell off his neck as he will pay up when he damn well gets around to it.

I came across one bill that was a whopper. A couple of thousand dollars for a blonde mink jacket. Originally contracted for rental, the jacket had been lost. Broadson, Inc. would have to pay the full price.

A blonde mink jacket. The one that Amy had worn for the pilot. The one that looked so much like the jacket Happy had bought for Pat Donnelly. Looked like? Oh, no!

That was going too far. It couldn't be true. I stared at the bill in my hand as if it were an hallucination. It wasn't. It was real and Happy Broadman was cheating the daylights out of Amy Ferguson so he could give his mistress a big deal birthday present. Amy Ferguson who was his most loyal, nicest, most financially valuable client. And he was robbing her at the one time in her career when she had suffered a setback, when she needed all the support she could get.

I had had it. It took a lot but I had finally reached the point of no return with Mr. Broadman. I was leaving. Immediately, that afternoon.

No two week's notice, decency wouldn't be appreciated in that office. I was going to play the game their way. When in Sodom, do as the Sodomites…no, that wasn't right. Anyway, as soon as Happy came back from lunch I told him I was quitting, and I told him why.

Happy tried to deny that he was a crook but I wasn't having any of it so he gave up that approach. He began giving me his usual garbage, tried to outshout me, bully me into staying. Guess he was afraid I'd leave that office and start telling tales out of school.

"Scream at me quietly, Happy," I told him. "I don't go for the megaphone bit."

He tried, he honestly did but it was like he was allergic to peace and quiet, he couldn't keep his voice down. Judy joined in. I just ignored them and cleaned out my desk as if they weren't there.

I was waiting for the elevator when Happy switched his pitch and began pleading with me to stay because I was such an irreplaceable employee. The office would just fall apart without me. He sounded like a beseeching lover.

The elevator came. "Why, Mr. Broadman, how you do go on," I said. "You're enough to turn a girl's head." With that I stepped into the elevator. The door closed behind me. End of an era.

I called Sylvan and told him what had happened. He was working on a rush project and could only spare an hour but he insisted that I come down and have a drink with him.

I wasn't very good company for him. I had been angry, I had expressed the anger and then I got depressed. I knew I had done the right thing. Big consolation, I still felt lousy.

"Trouble with you is you're free. Freedom is an awful burden," Sylvan said.

"Yeah, it's a drag. I always thought I'd love being this way. No ties, no attachments. I can decide on doing anything, going anywhere. Trouble is, I don't want to do anything. I just want to sit still for the next twenty or thirty years."

"Impossible. You can't. You're one of those people with built in ants in the pants."

"Thanks," I said ruefully. "That's the sweetest thing anybody ever said to me. Sylvan, what am I going to do? I want to get out of this town. I want to get away from all the dirt and mess of New York. But I don't know where to go."

"Sloane, Allison called me this morning," he said quietly. "She told me about leaving for the Coast Saturday. Why don't you go with her?"

"Because I waited too long to tell her I'd go. Because she might think that I was going with her because I want to sponge off her. I have no job, no money. I'd have to borrow from her until I got back on my feet. If only I had told her I'd go before all this happened. Then it would have looked as if I was going just because I wanted to be with her. This way, it looks fishy."

"Bull. Thank God you're telling me this instead of saying it to Allison. Maybe you don't realize it, but you're insulting her horribly. Sloane, Allison loves you. Remember that. She won't mind laying out a few bucks if it means having you near her. Go with her. Please, for her sake as well as your own."

"I don't know. I just don't know. Sylvan, something tells me you're right but I just can't make up my mind. Let me think about it a while longer."

"There isn't very much time left to think."

"I'm aware of that. Oh hell, let's drop it. I'll be able to think more clearly when I'm alone."

"You sound real low."

"I am."

"Maybe you shouldn't be alone. Look, I'll call the office and say that I took sick or something. Then I could stay with you for the rest of the day."

"Thanks but don't bother. I need to be alone."

I walked Sylvan back to the building where he worked. Just before we parted he said, "Be sure to write."

"Write? Oh, you mean from California. What makes you so sure I'm going?"

"You're going."

"Glad to hear it. Especially since I haven't made up my own mind yet. You seem to think you can make it up for me. Haven't you ever heard of free will?"

He smiled patronizingly. "Yes, I've heard of it. And that's why I know you'll be flying to the Coast on Saturday. Well, cheerio my deario and I'll be expecting a letter from you next week." And with that he disappeared into the building.

I went down to the Harbor. A few girls always came in around that time for cocktails on their way home from work. There were about ten women there when I arrived.

I recognized Dinah sitting in a booth with a vacuous looking redhead. Both women looked like they had been run over by tanks. They had bruises and bandages on their faces.

I approached them. Dinah remembered me and invited me to join them. She saw me staring at the wounds and explained them to me.

"We had a fight last night. Mary just had to find out who was boss. She found out all right. That's right, isn't it baby?"

Mary nodded dumbly.

"I ain't mad," Dinah went on. "These things happen. Mary won't pull anything like that again. She knows who's the daddy now."

Dinah went on telling me about their fight. She bragged about the way she had beaten Mary to insensibility. The point seemed to be that this proved she was worthy or something.

I'm telling you, Dinah's bilge got me down. It was like I was seeing what I would be letting myself in for if I went back to cruising the gay bars. Sure, I knew there were other types of girls. But when gay girls act out the forms of love without the content existing, things like what happened between Dinah and Mary are all too common.

Maybe somebody up there arranged the whole thing so that Dinah and Mary would have a fight one night and the next afternoon be in the Harbor when I got there and that Dinah would turn my stomach by telling me about it. I don't know. All I do know is that it turned the trick. I finished my drink out of politeness and lit out of there.

I didn't bother calling. I just grabbed a cab and hightailed it up to Allison's. I was there in fifteen minutes and up the stairs and knocking on her door.

Allison answered the door. She looked surprised and pleased. I didn't say anything. I just walked past her into the apartment, checked the place to make sure Ruth wasn't there, then came close to breaking Allison's ribs in an embrace of relief, and love and peace and decision.

We kissed for a long time. Not one of those kisses where we teased each other. Just a matter of contact that took the place of words that would say I need you, I love you, you give me strength, I want you near me always.

I took my lips from hers and looked down at her lovely face. She was leaning back in my arms, her eyes half closed, the corners of her mouth turned up in a slight smile. I love you, I thought, I love you because of what you are and not just because I need to love. I love you and nothing in this world is more important to me than being with you.

I thought those things but the only thing I said was, "Call the airline. See if you can get a reservation for me on the flight you're taking."

Allison nodded wordlessly and went to the telephone. While she was dialing the number I sat down on the couch and lit a cigarette. If she could get a reservation for me, I'd have to leave in a few minutes and go home to pack. That cigarette would be the last one I'd ever have in that apartment.

I listened while Allison talked to the airline ticket agent. She didn't make a reservation for me. She confirmed the one she had made the day before for both of us.

They walked together into a world of exotic evil

The Third Street

by Joan Ellis

This was where they came…the lonely and love-starved, the lovely and promiscuous, seeking new thrills, searching for a partner…a special kind of partner.

This was where they met…the tormented female artist and the amoral young model, baring their secret needs and feeding their secret hungers… needs and hungers condemned by society.

The Third Street

Pat opened the shop with a sense of renewed life. It was rash to feel this strange upsurge because of the encounter last evening, yet she couldn't restrain herself. Tonight she would go back to the studio again because there was no question of her moving back into the apartment now. Karen was coming at six. On impulse she had invited Karen to have dinner with her before the session. She would leave the shop early. Tony wouldn't mind.

Pat was glad that the morning was so rushed. She didn't want to think too much about Karen Coleman. There could never be anything for Karen and her, Pat's mind exhorted. Karen didn't belong to her shadowed world. Logic warned her she was stepping upon a treadmill to grief. And yet there was this buoyancy at knowing she would be in the same room with Karen tonight. That she could renew her memory of the appealing nakedness that quickened her pulse, and made her hands ache yearningly. She hadn't slept last night, but it had been a different kind of wakefulness from the other bleak, painful nights.

It was nearly noon when Tony rushed into the shop with a flurry of apologies for being so late.

"Sweetie, forgive me for leaving you alone all morning, but I was a total wreck. We just never got to bed last night." He was at the desk now, glancing over memos.

"Everything's under control." Pat smiled in affection. For all Tony's appearance of flightiness, he was sharp as an efficiency expert when it came down to cases. He knew how to manipulate his life, she thought with something like envy, again.

"Oh, I've been thinking about that mailing we discussed. Let's get it out, huh? Very chi-chi on the stationery. Maybe bring a girl in so you can keep an eye on how it looks."

"I'll call a temporary agency," Pat said, then stopped dead. Karen. She needed the work. From even that casual contact last night she knew that Karen would be competent. "I know someone we can buzz direct," she said offhandedly. "I'll have her come in tomorrow." She refused to meet the quizzical glance Tony shot at her.

The rest of the day held a special quality of excitement because she knew that tonight Karen would be at the studio and the sweet, attractive face would light up with pleasure because of the typing job, even though it would be only for two or three days. Her husband must have been an awful rat, Pat decided. Karen Coleman was the kind who would put up with a lot before running.

"Tony, you don't mind if I run off early, do you?" she asked, when the smart wall clock indicated that five was approaching. "I have some odds and ends to do about my apartment."

"Getting ready for a little New Year's Eve party?" he asked archly. New Year's was one time Paul and he always went out of town, to Philadelphia or Atlantic City.

"Nothing like that. I suddenly can't bear the way the place looks." Yet Tony had planted a seed in her mind. If Karen were new to the city, she would be alone on New Year's Eve—and that was ghastly when you were upset and lonely. Was there some casual way she could invite Karen to spend the evening with her without giving the invitation any special meaning? Did she dare? She could be simply cynical about men at this point, couldn't she? It would be easy to throw some remark about hating New Year's Eve brawls and the way men took it as an open season announcement. Karen could have no ideas she wasn't "straight."

"Do you have our little girl set to come in for the typing?" Tony asked casually as he settled down at the desk to make phone calls.

"I'll phone her tonight." Pat beat a retreat for the rear. She didn't want to talk about Karen to Tony. And doubt was creeping in. She made such a point of keeping the studio and the shop separate. She wouldn't want Karen to drop any hint to Tony. The typing job would be over in two or three days. Surely she could manage to keep the two of them apart with little difficulty, she coddled her unease. She knew she was all wrong to harbor any hopes about Karen, yet she was helpless to stem her plottings. It couldn't be wrong to spend time with Karen if nothing *happened*. There were friendships between two women without anything else.

On the way to the studio Pat shopped for dinner. The menu would be simple because she had little patience with kitchen preparations. She also remembered to pick up logs for the fireplace. In the studio she changed rapidly into slacks and a tailored blouse, nothing so stark as what she had worn last night, though Karen had not seemed to notice anything offbeat. She tossed the steak beneath the broiler, taking a chance on Karen's being on time. She was. To the minute. The doorbell rang and Pat forced herself to walk with normal speed to answer it.

"Hi." Karen was breathless from the climb. "I thought you might like these." She held forth a bunch of miniature chrysanthemums.

"They're lovely." Why had Karen spent money on her, when she was so short herself? She didn't have to repay her for dinner. "A cheery note for an uncheerful period," she said with deliberate flipness. "I mean, New Year's has a way of depressing me." Here was the chance to suggest the New Year's Eve bit, but Pat felt unsure.

"Can I help with anything? Set the table or put up coffee?"

"You can put these in water if you will." Pat felt herself heating up inwardly at the closeness of Karen. There was the dinner ahead, and then the hour of modeling. Oh, she was going to have to be so careful! So careful because her instinct was to pull this insecure, sweetly lovely girl into the comfort of her arms. And then to teach her about her kind of love. The kind no man could ever know.

"You wouldn't know of a rooming house anywhere around that isn't expensive, would you?" Karen asked in a rush of eagerness. "That hotel where I'm staying is crippling me. It's crazy, isn't it?" she laughed self-consciously. "I mean, normally I would never let myself get into such a rat-race."

"I'll ask around," Pat promised, and fought a suffocating urge to invite Karen to move into the studio. That would be impossible, of course.

Dinner progressed easily with Karen relaxing beneath Pat's adroit efforts to draw her out because she knew Karen had a need to talk. She could picture Karen as a child now, and the vision evoked a deep tenderness in her.

"I suppose you think I'm pretty silly," Karen said disparagingly as they sat over coffee. "Running off half-cocked the way I did, not really planning anything."

"Not at all," Pat insisted. Karen hadn't told her in so many words about her husband, but the portrait had been starkly drawn, nevertheless. There was this narrow, delicate possibility that kept pushing itself into Pat's mind, that Karen had been so hurt by this Stan that she might never want a man's love again. Yet Karen needed love and therefore might—just might—be receptive to the other kind, that was gentle and understanding, and still passionately satisfying.

"Tell me about the portrait you're doing," Karen said on impulse, and Pat was shaken off-balance by the demand.

"I told you—I'm not very good," Pat hedged.

"I don't believe that." The candid admiration in Karen's voice startled her. "You're the kind of person who wouldn't do anything unless she were good at it."

A need to vindicate herself enveloped Pat. "Painting is really an avocation with me. A compulsive drive—I told you that before." A wry smile touched her pale mouth. "Actually, I'm an interior decorator. I know you'd never guess it by looking around this place." And then she remembered about the typing. "Heavens, I meant to tell you as soon as you came in. If you'd like to do two or three days typing, I can arrange it in the shop where I work. We have a mailing to get out."

"Oh, wonderful!" Karen glowed. "You're good luck for me, you know, Pat? I was so low yesterday—I couldn't have sunk any further. Now..." She spread her hands eloquently. "I have a friend, some work, and hope."

"I was wondering...about New Year's Eve," Pat blurted our nervously.

"I hate to think about New Year's," Karen said with unexpected heat. Her hand toyed compulsively with the tablecloth. The amber eyes were almost black, and some of the youngness evaporated. "New Year's Day would have been my first wedding anniversary. It's pretty sad, isn't it, when you can't even keep up the pretense for one little year."

"Better to quit now than put yourself through further torture," Pat consoled. "When you know something is wrong, that's the time to pull out. You're young—you're entitled to one mistake."

Karen lifted her head, her jaw tightening. "Once is enough. I'll never get married again as long as I live. I've had it, believe me!"

"About New Year's Eve," Pat said, suddenly confident. "I make a point of steering clear of those awful brawls. If you have no other plans, why not come up here for dinner? We can listen to some records or watch television. We can be smug and satisfied because we're not involved in one of those madhouse parties."

For an instant something in Karen's eyes terrified her, but then that oddness disappeared and Karen was beaming.

"I'd love that, if you're sure you want me. I'd probably go stir crazy alone in my room."

"Good, then that's settled." Pat swung about towards the kitchen. "More coffee?"

"Let me get it." Karen sprang to her feet, raced with her quick graceful steps towards the kitchen.

Pat leaned back and slowly reached for a cigarette.

Karen sat behind the typewriter on the ultra-feminine desk at one side of the shop, and tried to concentrate on the mailing before her. She enjoyed the relaxed yet highly glamorous atmosphere of the shop and the air of luxury that permeated it. Pat had seemed oddly uncomfortable, though, when she had introduced her, this morning, to Tony. He insisted she call him Tony—and he'd gone out of his way to be solicitous about her comfort.

Was Pat upset because of Tony, because he was gay? Pat couldn't honestly think that this would bother Karen, could she? In a way, it was a relief. You didn't have to play games with the gay fellows. And she liked him, no matter what his personal inclinations. That was his business. It would be nice to work here permanently, she thought wistfully.

"Are you having any trouble with the writing on the card files?" Pat came over anxiously. "Both Tony and I write so atrociously."

"Oh, no, I can manage fine," Karen reassured her, thinking how different Pat appeared in these surroundings. The perfectly groomed, efficient career girl. She must be terrific at her job, too, Karen decided. You could tell that by the way clients listened to her when she talked. It was pleasant to know the other Pat, who relaxed in old clothes without makeup. It was like seeing deep inside, being welcomed into friendship. It was fantastic that meeting Pat could make such a difference in her attitude towards living. Never in her life had she encountered an honestly deep and lasting friendship. In the years with her mother it seemed as though they were always packing up and moving from one apartment to another. After a while she didn't trust herself to make friends because it would be such wrench when the next move came along.

"Karen, be a love and brew us some coffee," Tony sang out from the other side of the room where he was deep in conference with a client over swatches of material.

"Right away," Karen rose to her feet, exchanging a smile of amusement with Pat. "Tony's very nice," she whispered, and was glad she had said it because Pat was concerned about her reaction to him.

Even before Pat suggested it, Karen guessed she would invite her up to the studio for dinner again since she was scheduled to do an hour's modeling that evening.

"If you'll let me fix dinner," Karen stipulated. "I feel awful, sponging on you the way I am. May I cook tonight?"

Pat flashed her a brilliant smile. "I'd love it," she admitted frankly. "I hate anything to do with the kitchen. About the modeling tonight—if you think you'll be too tired—"

"Oh, no," Karen said quickly. "I rather like it. I mean," she flushed to a delicate pinkness, "it's so different from posing for Stan." There was a feeling of restfulness when she had sat for Pat last night. It hadn't even bothered her that she had been unclothed because there had been nothing ugly in Pat's eyes as she looked at her.

"I may be a bit late in getting out tonight," Pat warned thoughtfully. "We'll be in the shop tomorrow—you and I—Tony's taking off. We'll close early, though, because of the holiday. There won't be a soul coming in or phoning."

"Would you want me to go on ahead and get dinner ready?" Warmth encircled her. She felt needed, appreciated. "I could have everything ready by the time you got home."

Pat's eyes were strangely soft. "That would be nice," she said after a moment, and yet Karen was puzzled by the wall that Pat seemed to have dropped between them. What had she said that was wrong? Pat agreed to her going ahead.

"Would you rather I stayed here and worked on the mailing?" Karen said after a moment, her face troubled. "I didn't mean to sound as though I were running out on you."

"I know that, honey," Pat said sharply. "I think it's a great idea for you to go on ahead and spoil me that way. My mind had wandered on something I had forgot to do earlier," she alibied. "Call I should have made."

By five thirty Pat was insisting Karen call it a day. She fished in her wallet for a bill and pressed it on Karen.

"Let's go hogwild," she coaxed. "Buy everything wildly extravagant. After all, tomorrow's New Year's Eve. Let's jump the gun and celebrate tonight. And tomorrow," she added quickly, and again something in Pat's eyes reached out to Karen with a message she couldn't quite interpret. "Take a cab down town. We'll put it on the expense sheet." Her smile was warmly intimate, and Karen enjoyed the inclusion in Pat's confidence. It was amazing that a girl like Pat, so strangely attractive, so clever, so talented, wasn't knee deep in men. But it must be because she turned them away, Karen decided with satisfaction. Any man would be glad to nab somebody like Pat Conway. For a moment she thought of Stan. Wouldn't he love to throw Pat across a bed? And then she flushed because it was somehow dirty to think about Pat and Stan at the same time.

Karen moved about the studio in a comforting solitude, her eyes shooting regularly in the direction of the clock. Pat had said she couldn't possibly make it before seven. That assured her plenty of time for everything. The shrimps were cooling in the refrigerator. The tiny chicken had been stuffed and was a bronzed beauty in the oven now. The salad was crisp and cold on a bed of ice cubes. Funny, she had never enjoyed preparing a meal for Stan. In the beginning she had tried, but Stan would say he'd be home at seven and then show up at two the next morning, half-loaded and with rape on his mind. Because every time her husband touched her it was rape. She shivered in remembrance. But at the same time, an emptiness taunted her, because Karen Coleman needed to be loved.

What about Pat, Karen wondered? Was she so self-sufficient, so in control of herself, that it was enough to have her job and non-emotional diversions? Didn't Pat feel this yearning for something, somebody? She wasn't cold; Pat was warm and alive and deep of feeling, Karen was sure of that. Maybe it was your attitude, the way you approached life, she considered. Some time she would sit down and talk to Pat about this. They weren't alone; Karen was certain of this. And she refused to accept the alibi that she was a frigid woman. That was a lie. An outright lie!

Pat didn't use her key. She rang the bell.

"Hmm, everything smells wonderful," she greeted Karen with a smile of satisfaction. "I'm starving. And it's getting so cold out. Did you notice when you came home?"

"I thought you would like the fire." Karen turned to the logs crackling in the deep fireplace, the scent of the wood burning blending aromatically with the oven makings. "Doesn't it send a lovely glow about the room?"

"You're lovely," Pat said, then swerved away as though shocked at herself for verbalizing the compliment.

"I hope you like roast chicken." For no reason at all, Karen felt ill at ease, as though she might not measure up to Pat's appraisal of her. "I stuffed it, too."

"Mmm." Pat was off at the closet, reaching in for a hanger for a coat. "You're spoiling me like crazy."

"People are having their New Year's parties early this year, aren't they?" Karen felt compelled to talk, without knowing why. "I kept running into the tail end of parties—you know how little clusters carry office parties out into the street with them." Karen frowned, remembering. "I hate office parties, don't you?"

"Loathe them," Pat agreed. She was searching around for a cigarette with a vague restlessness in the deep blue eyes.

"Here," Karen offered a pack, then reached quickly for a match. "You're tired."

"Not really," Pat hedged. She seemed undecided for a moment, and Karen wondered what she was thinking about. "Sweetie, would there be time for me to take a shower before dinner?"

"Sure." Pat was tired, Karen thought with a rush of sympathy. "A hot shower does wonders for getting rid of kinks, doesn't it?"

"Sometimes." Pat's gaze rested on Karen with a veiled speculation that disturbed her. Was she talking too much, Karen asked herself in panic? Was Pat sorry for starting up this friendship? "I'll only be a few minutes, though." Pat went back to the closet, fished around for clothes, then disappeared into the oversized bathroom.

Karen hesitated for a moment, then went ahead with her plans for dinner music. The music would help Pat to relax. Something in the light classical field, of which Pat had much. She made her choice, dropped the needle into the groove, keeping the volume low. Just a thread of music to seep through the room.

When Pat emerged from the shower, in slacks and a blouse, her feet in sandals, Karen had dinner waiting on the table. She flushed with pleasure before Pat's compliments. She found herself talking as she had never talked with anyone before. Openly and without embellishments, about the uneasy childhood and adolescent years, the muddled year of her marriage. How easy it was to talk with Pat, she marveled! How good to spill out the dark, stored up memories that ever ate away at her sense of well-being.

"Stan was a mistake from the first minute," Karen said with a wry smile as she poured a second cup of coffee for Pat. "If I hadn't been so horribly lonely, I would have realized that right away."

"I'm glad you had the sense to break away," Pat approved. "You might have spent the rest of your life being miserable." Pat was staring into space, long slender fingers drumming on the table. "Of course, I have no right to be talking this way. Marriage is a deeply personal thing for the two people involved."

"That was no marriage," Karen denied passionately. "How could it be, with somebody like Stan? I'm glad I walked in on that party of his the way I did. I needed to be hit over the head to make the break."

"Everything'll be easier for you now," Pat said slowly. "You'll have no trouble getting a job. Tony and I both know lots of people, if nothing shows up right away. We'll ask around."

"I don't know why you're so good to me," Karen burst out.

"Don't be silly." Pat seemed to stiffen, and again Karen felt a wave of uncertainty, that she might spoil this friendship so newly found. "How are you managing with money?" Pat took on an air of crisp competence. "Will you be all right?"

"Oh, yes, thanks to you." Karen managed a smile, yet she couldn't fight off the suffocating fear that Pat was looking at her and finding her wanting. She needed Pat's friendship now as she had never needed anyone in her life.

"I have an idea." Pat took a moment to ditch her cigarette while Karen clung to her because there was something behind those few words that reached out with hidden depth. "I suppose I should have explained right away. I keep the studio here as a sort of hideaway. Nobody knows about it—not even Tony." Her eyes met Karen's in an exchange of candor. "I've been scared to death you might accidentally say something to him. What I'm getting at is this—I have an apartment up town. Why don't you move in here, right away? Then, as soon as you get a regular job and save some money, you'll find yourself an apartment. There won't be any rush about it—you can wait until something right pops up."

"But I couldn't throw you out of your studio!" Karen protested, bright spots of color in her cheeks. "That would be wrong."

"It's wrong for you to be plagued this way with expensive hotel rent," Pat countered. "Move in right away." Karen noted the softening in her persuasion. "Tonight."

"But I feel so awful," Karen stammered. Then on impulse, she made a stipulation. "I'll move in if you'll stay here, too. I couldn't bear the thought of running you out." Karen watched as Pat seemed to digest the suggestion, and she hoped that Pat would accept it. She didn't want to go back to that empty hotel room. She hated the darkness. Childish, yes, but she dreaded being alone in the dark. Some people could live alone; she loathed it. "Would you stay, Pat?" she couldn't bear the silence another moment.

"All right," Pat agreed, smiling. "But I warn you, I'm cranky as the devil in the morning. I can be an awful stinker before I've had my breakfast."

"Simple," Karen said buoyantly. "I'll fix breakfast for you." It was settled then, she thought in a rush of satisfaction; she would stay here at the studio with Pat.

They cleared away the dinner dishes, washed them, and Karen put up a fresh pot of coffee.

"I'll loan you a pair of pajamas for tonight," Pat offered. "No sense in rushing back to the hotel for that. You can pick up your luggage and check out in the morning."

"One suitcase," Karen said with a faint smile. "Whatever I could carry with me, I took."

Karen had thought they would sit up until all hours talking, but the satisfying dinner, the warmth of the room, the aura of relaxation that seemed to overtake both girls set them both to yawning by midnight.

"This is crazy," Pat laughed, trying to stifle a yawn. "Usually, I lie awake till all hours, wishing I could fall asleep." She glanced thoughtfully across the room to the double divan. "We'd better share that until I get more blankets. You'll freeze to death if we split up the blankets between us." The fire was low and Pat moved forward to toss on another log. The steam had long since disappeared, and the winter cold crept in now through the skylight, despite the heavy drapings Pat had provided against the drafts. "You'd better undress here by the fire."

"All right." It was strange, Karen thought, how quickly she had moved from one existence into another. But it was good. It was good to be away from Stan, from his gutter sex.

"Try these." Pat tossed a pair of blue pajamas of some delicate cotton across to Karen. She viewed Karen's smaller dimensions with something like tenderness. "The top will probably be a nightshirt for you."

In the russet glow of the fireplace Karen undressed, for some reason feeling shy. She hadn't felt that way when she had stripped to skin for the modeling bit. Her clothes fell into a heap about her and she struggled to cover herself with the blue pajama top. Pat was right. The top hit her midway down the thighs. She wouldn't bother with the pants. She shivered, yet she wasn't cold, as she watched Pat make up the bed for the night.

"I'll have to wash my face, at least," she laughed self-consciously, and ran in bare feet towards the bathroom.

When Karen returned, Pat was in tailored red pajamas, beneath the blankets already, the other side of the bed neatly turned down in readiness for Karen.

"You don't mind if I smoke in bed, do you?" Pat smiled. "I promise not to fall asleep and burn us to death."

"I don't mind." Karen pulled the blankets high about her neck, grateful for this peace that enveloped her. She felt so *safe*.

Karen drifted into a semi-slumber, aware of the delicate glow of color from the fireplace, the cautious movements of Pat as she smoked and stared at the ceiling. She felt almost like a child again, protected and loved. And then she slept completely, for a while. Coldness crept into the room. Karen pulled her legs up beneath her, seeking warmth. She found another warmth beneath the blankets, and in sleep huddled close. And then the cold white shock of what was happening threw her into utter wakefulness, though she uttered not a word, made no motion.

"Darling, you're so sweet," Pat was crooning. "I was afraid—I couldn't be sure. I didn't dare be sure." Pat's arm pulling her in close, gentle, warm. "I hardly dared hope." A large, tender hand touched her breast, and Karen tried to come to grips with the strangeness of this. The fingers found the buttons, undid them. Fingers caressed her breasts, feather-touched a nipple, and an odd excitement brushed her. "Darling, don't be afraid."

"I'm not afraid," Karen stammered, a white heat touching her. "I just don't know." Shame colored her voice as she made the admission. And yet, this wasn't wrong.

"I'll die if I can't kiss you," Pat said passionately, and her mouth covered Karen's, and her tongue moved eagerly between Karen's teeth and ignited a fire there.

Karen lay breathlessly, waiting, savoring. Fingers roamed about her body, building the desire Karen knew was there, that Stan could only kill. Pat's tongue withdrew from hers, but brought fresh heat to the white mounds of panting satin. Finding a delicate pink nipple, she teasing it into flame. A low sound of excitement escaped Karen and she moved beneath Pat.

"Easy, darling," Pat said, and Karen sensed her pleasure.

And then they both forgot to be easy because Pat's mouth was loving her, building her to a wild impassioned crescendo that was vocal in its demands. Pat's hands caressed and teased, everywhere that desire soared. Pat, so gentle, so sure. Pat's fingers brushing her thighs, Pat's mouth finding the core of her. Oh, God, Karen thought, she couldn't bear it! She couldn't bear this another moment!

"Oh, Pat!" It was a sob of gratitude. She had known there could be something like this! Not with Stan, with his rough, insane jabbings of himself, his brutal passion. But this touching, this reaching. "Oh, Pat! Pat!"

They tangled together, all legs and arms and writhing demanding flesh. And it was marvelous, and it was right, and it was passion fulfilled. She wasn't frigid! She could love. She could be loved!

An intimate story of the third sex, told with tenderness and unblushing honesty!

Chris

by Randy Salem

A young and ardent girl, Chris Hamilton also was an incredibly handsome one. You would hardly have suspected her of harboring perverse hungers, odd desires—unless you knew of her love affair with another woman…named Dizz.

That cruel Dizz! She accepted the advances of Chris yet withheld love. She behaved so coldly, so harshly, that Chris seemed sure to turn to a third girl—sweet little Carol Martin.

Was there any escape for Chris? The answer is disclosed in this delicate yet unblushingly frank novel…

Chris

Chris sat in the back room of Tony's, cupping a shot glass in her palm. She was on her fourth round. She wanted to get very very drunk, drunk enough to forget. But the liquor didn't touch her.

She leaned her fist on her chin and glared across the room at a bull-fight poster on the opposite wall. Under the poster were two long-haired blondes in leotards and trench coats, hunched over a table and gazing deep into each other's eyes, sighing now and then and occasionally touching fingers. They had neither moved nor spoken for an hour. They thought they were in love.

The swinging doors banged open and then shut behind someone. Chris glanced up. It was the fat blonde with the beautiful green eyes. Jennie. She was wearing a tight black dress and no coat, despite the rain. Her hair hung in wet strings.

Jennie spotted Chris and sidled drunkenly across to her table. She looked as though she had never been completely sober in all her life. She pulled out a chair and sat down.

"Hi, big boy," she said. "Who the hell hit you?"

"A truck," Chris said.

"Oh?" Jennie said. "Blonde or brunette?"

"Redhead," Chris answered. She was in no mood for Jennie. She had too much on her mind to bother being charming to a female like this one.

"I've been looking for you, handsome," Jennie said. "Cruising all these crummy queer bars. Where you been hiding?" She moved close to Chris and pressed a thigh against her.

Chris picked up the shot glass and drained it. "I don't spend much time in the bars," she said.

"You married?" Jennie asked.

"Yeah, I'm married," Chris answered. Some hell of a marriage, but she had always thought of the arrangement with Dizz as that.

"Oh," Jennie said. She put her hand on Chris's leg and moved it slowly upward.

Chris grabbed the wrist and pushed the hand away. She wanted to slap the girl, but hesitated to start what would end up as a brawl.

"I live near here," Jennie said.

Chris sighed. "Look, Jennie," she said. "No dice."

"C'mon, handsome," Jennie said. "She'll keep the bed warm."

Chris smiled to herself at the irony of it.

Chris stood up and pushed back the chair. "No good, kid," she said. "I've got things on my mind." She handed the waiter a ten and told him to keep the change.

She left the bar without looking back, stopped a cab at the corner and got in. She felt almost glad for the incident with Jennie. It was the first time in four years that she had turned down an offer, and that felt good.

When she left the cab, Chris went to stand in the rain and look down at the river. She pressed her face close to the wire of the fence. Somewhere out in the darkness was Carol. Somewhere behind her was Dizz. And somewhere in the middle she stood on an island, clinging to a fence. Too sober, too sad, and too lonely.

She walked back to the house and went in. She could hardly move now. Her body was hot with fever and wracked with pain. She felt sick and tired and very old. She hoped Dizz would be good to her tonight. Or, if she was in a foul mood, just ignore her altogether.

Dizz was squatting on the kitchen floor, waggling a scolding finger. In front of her on the linoleum was a very large puddle and a very small dog. She did not bother to look up when Chris opened the door.

Chris closed the door behind her and walked into the living room. She took off her trench coat and threw it into the sling chair. She kicked off her shoes, pulled off her socks, then took off her shirt and dropped it on top of the trench coat.

When she could talk again, she walked back into the kitchen. Dizz and the pup were still glaring at each other defiantly. The puddle had been wiped up, but the pup had not apologized.

"Where did he come from?" Chris asked quietly.

"George left him," Dizz said. "He has to be out of town for about a week. I said we'd take care of Schnitzel." She made it sound like the most natural thing in the world.

"Did you, now?" Chris said. "I thought you weren't going to be seeing George."

Dizz picked up the puppy and stood up. "I'm not seeing him," she said. "But I didn't see anything wrong with baby sitting for a few days. Are you hungry?"

"No," Chris said. "Just nauseous."

Chris turned and limped into the bathroom. She closed the door behind her and turned on the hot water full blast in the tub. She sat down on the john and dragged herself out of the rest of her clothes. She dropped them on the floor, then ripped off the soaked bandage and flushed it down the toilet.

She turned the water off and climbed in. She leaned back against the tub. The hot water felt good on her aching limbs, but it didn't help where she hurt the most.

Completely depressed now, Chris could see no way out. Maybe she was supposed to spend the rest of her life baking in hot tubs and hobbling around the house; maybe she had no right to expect anything good out of the future. She'd had a chance and she had muffed it. Maybe she would never get another one—maybe she wouldn't know one if she saw it.

Dizz opened the door and came in. She sat down on the john with Schnitzel on her lap.

"Christopher," Dizz said, "this has got to stop." She looked decidedly unhappy.

"What has?" Chris said.

"You," Dizz said. "Moping around in a rage. If there's anything wrong, let's get it over."

Chris looked at her sadly and shook her head. "You just don't understand, do you?" she said. And she knew as she said it that Dizz wouldn't even know what she was talking about.

"Understand what?"

Chris sighed. "Did it ever occur to you, my dear," she said, "that we're supposed to be leaving for Tongariva the day after tomorrow?"

"Oh, Chris, don't be an ass," Dizz said with impatience. "You know very well you can't go diving in the condition you're in now."

Chris flushed angrily. "But you didn't bother to ask about my plans," she said.

Schnitzel stood up on Dizz's lap and turned around. He sat down again and yawned. He propped his rump on Dizz's thigh and buried his nose under her wrist. He kept one eye open, staring at Chris.

"Honey," Dizz said, "if it's so damned important to you, I can get Mother to keep Schnitzel."

Chris sighed. She knew this was getting nowhere fast.

"That's not the point," Chris said.

"What's the point?"

"When did you agree to keep Schnitzel?" Chris said. She tried hard to keep her voice low. She wanted to shout at Dizz and make her understand.

Dizz thought for a minute. "I don't know," she said. "Sometime last week. Why?"

"In other words," Chris said, "you never did intend to go to Tongariva." She glared at Dizz accusingly and Dizz averted her eyes.

Dizz hesitated. She looked just slightly uncomfortable. "Well," she said, "I meant it when I said it. But I didn't think you'd take it so seriously."

"Oh, never mind," Chris said. She pulled herself up and climbed out of the tub. She grabbed a towel and began rubbing. "The point is, I need you now. Jonathan wants you to be along to keep me out of trouble. He'll keep me at home if you don't go. And, Dizz, I want to make this trip."

"All right," Dizz said quietly. "I'll go." She stood up and held on to Schnitzel.

"Thanks," Chris said bitterly. She wrapped the towel around her and left the bathroom. She picked up the clothes in the living room and carried them to her room.

In pajamas and a bath robe Chris sprawled out on the bed and propped her bare feet against the wall. She looked out through the door-way and watched Dizz playing with Schnitzel on the floor. She caught herself smiling and knew she was lost. As usual.

There was no help for it, Chris decided. Even when she was hating Dizz, she was still in love with her. She looked adorable now with the little pup. Adorable and beautiful and...

Oh, God, what's to become of me, Chris thought. She's killing me. But I can't give her up. I can't.

Killing me? I'm killing myself. It's not Dizz. It's me. I can't blame her if I'm a failure. And I can't even blame her if my knees turn to water every time I look at her.

Dizz looked up at her from the living room and smiled that crazy delicious smile.

Chris felt herself slipping. She still wanted that smile. And she still wanted Dizz, for all the frustration of it. What the hell. She couldn't go back to a world full of Jennies.

Chris was really too stiff and sore to move, but she wanted to be near Dizz, to let her know things were all right—that they were right. So she heaved herself off the bed and went into the other room to lower herself painfully to the couch. She stuck out a toe for Schnitzel to chew on.

"Honey," Chris said, "how about some coffee? I'm not feeling very well. I think I've got a fever."

Dizz got up and put a palm on Chris's forehead. "You certainly have," she said. "I think I'd better call the doctor."

"No," Chris said. "Just get the coffee."

Chris picked up Schnitzel and sat playing with him until Dizz came back into the room. Then she put him down and took the cup from Dizz and swallowed a gulp of the hot coffee. She set the cup on the end table.

Dizz came and curled up beside her on the couch. She put her head on Chris's shoulder and kissed her on the cheek.

Chris took Dizz's hand and held it in her lap. She wanted to put an arm around her. But her arms were too sore to lift.

"Darling," Dizz said.

"Hmm?"

"How much does this trip mean to you?" Dizz asked.

Chris had been expecting this. She knew Dizz did not want to go. And right at the moment she was far too ill to give a good damn. It did not seem important anymore. All that mattered was that they shouldn't argue anymore. That they should just be quiet for a while and then go to sleep.

"Well," Chris said slowly, "yesterday it was a matter of life and death. At the moment, I'm not so sure. Why?"

"It would make me a lot happier," Dizz said, "if you would call it off."

"Why?" Chris said.

"Because I really don't believe you're in any condition to go," she said. "You're bandaged and stiff and now you've got a fever. How about it?"

Chris sat very still. She couldn't argue with Dizz about her physical condition. She felt lousy. If she were dumped in the ocean now, she would sink like a stone.

But she had to consider something else, at least for a second.

What would happen if she backed out? Jonathan would scream, for one thing. He was counting on her to help finance the deal. And he wanted her to be there, whether he admitted it or not. He knew he could trust her to know a Glory-of-the-Seas when she saw one, even if he couldn't trust her to stay out of the water.

But what would happen to her? If she quit now, would she ever have what it would take to go diving again? Or would she spend the rest of her days regretting that she hadn't gone?

She would have to take that chance. She would have to take that chance because she was just too wretched to think about it anymore.

"OK, honey," she said tiredly. "I'll tell Jonathan in the morning that I won't be going. I have to see him anyhow."

"Good," Dizz said pleasantly. "Now you'd better get yourself off to bed."

"Right," Chris said. She let go of Dizz's hand, put out her feet and tried to stand up. Her head was splitting and the room did a flip in front of her eyes.

She made it to the bedroom door before she passed out.

When Chris awoke, it was well past noon. She lay still in bed, listening to the rain. It was still pouring hard and dripping off the trees.

Gradually she became aware of other sounds and she knew that Dizz was in the kitchen doing something and that Schnitzel was on the floor beside the bed chewing a shoe. And she knew it was Wednesday afternoon and that she had to see Jonathan. And that she was cold and weak and hungry. The fever was gone.

Chris threw back the covers and quietly made a good effort to sit up. She got halfway, then she fell back on the bed. The second try was a little more effective. Her feet touched the floor.

Schnitzel abandoned the shoe and bounded onto Chris's foot. She felt his tiny tongue massaging her toes. She reached down and scratched the top of his head.

She got up from the bed and went to the closet and opened the door, careful not to make a sound. She dressed as quickly as she could in a warm suit and shirt, then sat down on the bed to put on her shoes.

She saw Schnitzel run to the door. She looked up and straight at Dizz who was standing in the doorway with a heavy tray.

"And just where do you think you're going, young lady?" Dizz said.

"I have to talk to Jonathan," Chris said.

"Oh, no," Dizz said. "If you have to talk to Jonathan, you can use the telephone." She set the tray down on the desk. "I'm under doctor's orders to keep you in bed."

"I feel fine," Chris said. She walked to the door, put a finger under Dizz's chin and tilted her face up. She kissed her on the nose. "And no arguments from you."

Dizz breathed a resigned sigh. "Well, at least eat something."

"Right," Chris said. She moved across the desk and sat down.

She did not speak again until she had finished eating. Then she turned to Dizz and said, "I should be back in a couple of hours."

"Shall I come with you?" Dizz said.

"No," Chris answered. "You have to baby sit." She reached down and scratched Schnitzel behind the ears.

"Go," Dizz said. She kissed Chris on the cheek.

By the time she reached the museum, Chris had thought of fifty bad ways to break the news to Jonathan. He didn't give her time to use any of them.

"Chris," he said, jumping up as she came into the office. "Thank heaven, you're here."

"What's wrong?" Chris said.

"Plenty," Jonathan said. "I've been trying for two days to get a good diver. All I've been able to come up with is Nevins."

"And what's wrong with Nevins?"

"Nothing's wrong with him," Jonathan said. "It's just that he's used to doing salvage work. He doesn't know the first thing about spotting shells."

Chris understood. She knew it was a matter of knowing where to look, of knowing what you were looking for and being able to recognize it when you found it. She realized that Nevins had no experience along these lines. He knew more about a blow torch than he would ever know about a Glory-of-the-Seas.

It hurt her to say it, but she had promised Dizz.

"Jonathan," she said slowly, "this will break your heart. But I'm not going."

"What?" he screamed.

"Dizz chickened out on me," Chris said. "You said you wanted her to be along."

Jonathan paused for just one second. "Forget about her," he said. "Do you want to go?"

Chris walked to a chair and sat down. "I promised her I wouldn't," Chris said. "She's worried about my physical condition. I keeled over last night. She's afraid I'm not well enough to make the trip."

"Chris," Jonathan said, "that's not what I asked you. I asked you if you want to go."

Chris flushed red. She knew Jonathan was putting her on the spot for a good reason, and that he knew as well as she did that she wanted desperately to make this trip. He understood that behind all her physical misery and the tortured anguish of the past few days was still the old Chris Hamilton who would risk her neck for a good shell any day. And for this particular shell would risk everything she had.

"Yes, Jonathan," Chris said. "You know damned well I want to go. But—"

"But you promised Sheila," Jonathan said. "Look, Chris. This could be the chance of a lifetime for you." He looked at her pleadingly. "You said so yourself."

"Yes," she said, "I know. It could also mean disaster for you if I don't go."

"That's true," he admitted. "The Board of Directors would hardly approve of my having spent a small fortune on something that turned out to be a total flop."

Chris ran her fingers through her hair. She stood up and walked to the window. She walked back. She looked at Jonathan and shook her head sadly.

"Jonathan," she said, "I'm truly sorry. But I can't."

He sighed. "At least think it over, will you?"

"I'll think it over," she said.

She left Jonathan without saying good-bye.

In the middle room a young man with sandy hair, wearing dirty white bucks and a bright red tie, was busily fussing over a new display. On a twelve-foot table had been laid out a detailed relief map of the Florida Keys, finished in sand-crusted plaster of Paris and sea blue silk. Tidily arranged in the appropriate spots were the best of the specimens Chris had picked up on her last trip. A small white card, meticulously lettered in Carol's fine print, identified each shell. Chris spotted the "Hamilton" in the bottom right corner of each card.

When she had carefully circled the table twice, Chris turned to the young man and said, "That's quite an impressive lay-out."

The young man blinked at her owlishly through thick black-framed lenses.

"I'd like to make one correction though, if I may."

"Well," the young man hesitated, "I don't know, ma'am. I'm not supposed to let anybody touch it till Dr. Brandt says it's all right."

Chris smiled. "It's OK," she said. "I'm Chris Hamilton. I brought these shells in."

"Oh, Miss Hamilton," he said breathlessly, "I'm sorry, I didn't recognize you."

"Forget it," Chris said. "There's no reason why you should have."

She moved along one side of the table. "This," she said, moving a tiny cone shell about three inches and putting it down, "belongs over here." She picked up the marker and put it down by the shell. She stepped back and surveyed the table. "That's better," she said.

"Thanks, Miss Hamilton," the young man said. "I'm Tommy Samson. I just started this morning."

"I'm glad to know you, Tommy," Chris said.

"Miss Hamilton," Tommy said slowly, "I've seen the collection of treasure maps they've got upstairs. All the ones you brought in, I mean."

"Yes?" Chris said.

"Well," he went on, "I've got about fifty old maps that I'm pretty proud of. I picked them up in book stores and second hand shops. I was wondering if maybe you would take a look at them sometime. I don't know if they're worth anything or not, but I'm sure you'd know."

Chris smiled. "I'd be glad to look at them, Tommy. I hope I'll be able to tell you what you want to know."

As she limped into the solarium, Chris was thinking about Tommy and his maps. She chuckled wryly to herself. She could see herself ten years from now, sitting in an arm chair by the fire, giving the final authority on maps and travelogues and the like.

But, damn it, she thought, I didn't pick mine up in book shops. I went out and found them. In Singapore and in Cuba and in a pawn shop in Paris. And I never spent my time setting up displays in a museum either. I went diving for those shells. In every puddle of water big enough to hold me. It's all wrong somehow.

The solarium had changed. Tommy had moved in. A striped chino jacket hung on the back of a chair. A container of orange juice sat where the coffee belonged. There were no signs left of Carol.

Chris sighed, she sat down at the desk and propped her foot on the other chair. She opened the middle drawer and took out the blue drawing pencil. She held it lightly between two fingers and drummed it against the desk.

Dizz, old girl, she thought, you and I are going to have a nice long talk this evening.

Talk about what, Chris? Dizz'll take one look at you and laugh in your face. And she's right. You're so beat up now you can hardly walk.

And just what do you think will happen to you if you try to dive now? You'd better save that for the bathtub, old girl.

But, Dizz, you don't understand. Bathtubs are for baths. I'm not ready to retire yet. I'm not ready to die, Dizz. Sure I'm scared. I'm scared as hell, all over again. I know now what it feels like to be trapped under water and look death straight in the eye. And I know the prettiest sound in the world is the surf on the beach because when you hear it you know you won't drown.

In fact, I was so damned scared and so damned tired that I almost let you convince me that I belonged in dry dock. Almost, Dizz. I let you look at me and smile that crazy smile and hypnotize me like you always do. What for? Oh, no, Dizz darling, not because you're worried about me or what might happen to me. You never worried about anything in your life but good old Dizz. But because you don't like water and sand and sea shells.

Chris bit down hard on the end of the pencil. Maybe she wasn't being fair. Too harsh, maybe. Maybe Dizz really did care what happened to her.

She wondered for the ten millionth time if Dizz loved her. Not that it really mattered. The way she hung on to Dizz was her own sickness, her own pet form of masochism. It had very little to do with love.

Carol had known that. That's why she had pulled out. She'd had sense and strength enough not to get caught in this destructive web.

Chris put her face in her hands and wept without tears. She was feeling terribly, terribly sorry for herself. She felt as though she were running circles around herself. Muddled, muddled brain.

Chris knew that the confusion has started with Carol. Before that she had been miserable, but she had been able to live with it. In just one week, Carol had shown her what it was like to be loved and appreciated, what it was like to share love with somebody. And Carol had made her take a good look at this shabby thing she had with Dizz.

Carol had done everything, in fact, except tell her how—how to pick up and walk out on something that you've thought was your whole life.

Somewhere way in the back of her mind, Chris felt a fact demanding indignantly to be heard. The very simple fact that though Carol had not told her, she had shown her how to do it.

Chris felt a hand on her shoulder.

"Is anything wrong, Miss Hamilton?" Tommy asked. His voice was worried.

Chris looked up. "No," she smiled. "Nothing's wrong." No, Tommy, nothing at all.

Chris stood up tiredly and moved away from the desk. "Bring the maps in any time," she said.

Tommy grinned. "Thanks," he said.

He watched her hobble out of the room and shook his head sadly.

Chris did not see him, but she felt it. And she cringed. To that boy, Chris thought, I must look like a hundred and ten and finished. Sad, he's thinking, to lose Miss Hamilton. She was good in her day.

Chris stood up straight and stopped limping.

It's about time, she decided, for Miss Hamilton to stop feeling sorry for herself.

Chris entered the apartment full of the determination to blast Dizz off the face of the earth, if necessary. She'd be as gentle as she possibly could, but Dizz or no Dizz, Chris Hamilton was going to be on that plane to Tongariva tomorrow morning.

She had her mouth open to make the announcement as she came through the doorway. She didn't get the chance. Dizz was not there.

Chris swore bitterly to herself. Only she knew what it had cost her to work up enough nerve to assert herself with Dizz. And she wasn't at all sure it would last.

She walked into the living room and turned on the lamp at the end of the couch. She took off her shoes and kicked them under a chair, then went to the liquor cabinet and fixed herself a stiff drink from a half empty bottle of scotch. She drank it down quickly and poured another.

She looked at the mail Dizz had left on top of the cabinet. A brown envelope with a telephone bill and an ad for vitamin tablets. She didn't bother to look at the bill and dropped the ad into the waste paper basket.

She went into the kitchen and set the drink on the table. It left a ring of liquid on the polished surface. She took the sponge from the sink, wiped the table and dried the bottom of the glass. She put the drink on the stove and threw the sponge into the sink.

The well-trained spouse, she thought. She wrinkled her nose distastefully.

She opened the refrigerator. She was confronted as usual by neat packages of heaven knew what in aluminum foil. She hated the dullness of it.

She slammed the refrigerator door and turned to the cupboard. A box of crackers, soup, cranberry sauce, more soup, sardines. She took down the can of sardines and stuck it into the opener. She cranked the handle, then took the can on her palm and reached for a fork.

She ate standing up. She drained the glass. Then she dumped soap powder on the fork and scrubbed it hard to get off the fish smell. She rinsed out the glass. She wrung the water out of the sponge.

She sighed.

She went back to the living room and sprawled out on the couch. She closed her eyes, hoping maybe she'd doze off and relax a little, get some of the ache out of that blasted leg and the shakes out of her body.

But she could not sleep. Her ears were straining toward the door, listening for Dizz. She figured Dizz ought to be back soon. She was probably just out doing some shopping, or walking Schnitzel.

She wanted a cigarette. Really wanted one.

A drop of water splashed into the sink. A branch creaked outside the French windows. Somebody upstairs flushed a john. Nobody came in the front door.

Chris lay on the couch listening and wanting a cigarette. Every ten minutes she looked at her watch.

The phone rang at ten minutes and twenty seconds after eight. It was Dizz.

"Chris," Dizz said. "I'm at Mother's. I've decided to stay over."

Chris made a nasty face, but said nothing.

"Chris? What's the matter?"

"I wanted to talk to you," Chris said. "I've been thinking about this Tongariva deal and—"

"It'll wait till morning," Dizz said impatiently. "I'll be back early."

"But—"

"I can't talk now," Dizz said.

Chris hung up the receiver.

It'll wait till morning. You'll wait till morning, Chris. You'll wait until I have time to get around to you. You'll wait, Chris.

Chris went into her bedroom and took a pack of cigarettes out of the dresser. She took the lighter out of a jacket pocket. It was dry. She found some matches in the desk. She went back to the couch.

She finished the third cigarette before she decided to get really angry. Then she fumed. Here she was, tired and sick and needing somebody to take care of her. She had been sick enough to need a doctor last night. And she really didn't feel at all well now. And the person who was supposed to be catering to her, where was she? At Mother's. And Dizz hadn't even bothered to ask how she felt.

The pack of cigarettes was empty before she fell asleep. So was the bottle of scotch.

Her watch showed nine-thirty when the buzzer rang. Chris shook herself awake and got up and went to the kitchen to push the button.

She opened the door.

Dizz entered and walked straight to her bedroom. Schnitzel was not with her.

Chris closed the door and followed Dizz into the room. She was too furious to trust herself to speak.

Dizz was lying on her back on the bed, staring at the ceiling. She did not look at Chris.

Chris sat down on a chair to wait. She made herself comfortable, knowing from experience it might be a long time. This was one of Dizz's favorite poses.

When she could sit still no longer, Chris asked quietly, "What happened this time?"

"Nothing," Dizz said dully. She did not move. She did not bother to look at Chris.

Chris got up and went to stand beside the bed. "Look," she said, "this may sound indelicate of me. But I don't have time for a tantrum this morning. Sit up."

Still Dizz did not move.

Chris put out her hand and grabbed the lapels of Dizz's coat. She pulled her into a sitting position. "I said sit up," she said between her teeth. She pulled the coat tight in her fist and shook Dizz hard.

Dizz looked at her and straight through.

"Where's Schnitzel?" Chris said.

"With George," Dizz said.

"That's what I figured," Chris said. "You'd better have a good story, kid."

Dizz was still looking through her. "He got back early," Dizz said. "He came for Schnitzel."

"And?" Chris said.

"That's all," Dizz said.

"You're lying, Dizz."

Dizz focused. The look was full of hate. "What do you want from me?" she said.

"The truth," Chris said. "If you know how."

"All right," Dizz said. The deep voice was flat and dead. "I knew he'd be back yesterday. I'd promised to see him. He knew how upset I was after that weekend. He wanted a chance to make friends again." There was no expression in her eyes or on her face.

"And you spent another night with him, after the way you felt the other day?" Chris said wonderingly.

"Yes," Dizz said. "I thought I was in love with him. I even thought so after this weekend. I thought we could work out this sex problem."

Chris laughed. "Like we have," she said. "Anyway, are you?"

"What?"

"In love with him," Chris said.

"No," Dizz said.

"That's too bad," Chris said. She let go of Dizz's coat, pushing the girl away from her in disgust, and stood up.

"What do you mean?" Dizz said.

"Never mind," Chris said. She sat down in the chair. She sat back and crossed her legs, coldly self-possessed. "I'm curious," she said. "Why did you bother promising me you wouldn't see George again?"

"I wasn't sure I would."

"You're contradicting yourself, Dizz," Chris said. "You just said—"

"You were yelling at me," Dizz said. "What did you expect me to say?"

Chris shook her head. "No, Dizz," she said. "That won't do at all. You said that to make me get rid of Carol. It wasn't necessary. It will probably please you to know that she dumped me instead."

"Why?" Dizz said.

"Because she thought I was wrapped so tight around your finger that I'd never be able to break loose," Chris said. "And she was almost right."

Chris looked at her watch. Five of eleven. There was still time.

She picked up the phone and dialed the museum.

"Jonathan," she said. "Hold that car. I'll be there in ten minutes. Alone."

To fool the world, they married, for Joan loved women...and Marc preferred men!

The Third Sex
by Artemis Smith

Joan tried to be like other girls...

...And she could not understand why ecstasy remained unattainable. Desperately she sought surcease in the arms of David, of Paul, of a succession of other men. But the satisfactions of love were gained only when at last she found herself passionately involved with another girl—with the blond, enchanting Ruth!

Never before has there been a novel which so compellingly comes to grips with the problems of the third sex...a brilliant convincing book, boldly handled.

The Third Sex

Jay rang, awakening Joan at noon. "Are you still in one piece?" His amused voice, slightly catty, sounded like the tinkle of a raucous alarm in her ear.

"Almost," she groaned and turned over, holding the receiver a little away. "I told you there was nothing to worry about."

"Well, I'm glad you were right," he said. "I suppose I'm inclined to be overly cautious. So many strange sidelines go on in all the bars, you see."

"You're not telling me anything I don't already know," Joan said. She tried to raise herself out of bed but gave up. Her body was limp and tired, painful in every bone, almost as bad as it had been after Paul that first night.

"Shall I pick you up for breakfast?" Jay asked. "I'm going to be in the neighborhood."

"Fine," Joan yawned, "in one hour, at the Positano."

"Right," he said, and hung up.

Joan let the receiver drop back in its cradle heavily, then made another effort to get up. Slowly, painfully, she raised herself out of bed and plodded to the shower.

When Jay met her at the Positano she was fresh and awake again, wearing the same slacks as the night before. She had decided to wear those slacks often, at least for the weekend and her visit to the Sun Dial. She would ask Gig about the Sun Dial later, when they perhaps might meet for a drink.

"Well, you certainly look fine," Jay said when he saw her.

"I feel wonderful," Joan said, taking him up on it.

"How's your F small c this morning?" Jay's words might have confused Joan, except that she remembered that "F small c" was a term used in the Rorschach tests.

"Great," she said. The term referred to the appreciation of furry substances, for one thing.

"As a matter of fact," she added, "I wish my F small c had gotten a better work out last night than actually was the case."

"What's wrong?" Jay teased her. "Inhibited?"

Joan smiled. "No. As a matter of fact, I'm happy to say that I am not. I think that my psyche is in better shape this morning, speaking of psyches, than it has been for some years now."

Jay smiled sympathetically. Joan could see that he understood her feelings; moreover, he approved of her deliberately seeking to become an active Lesbian.

"For some women," he asserted, "repression of homosexual desires is a living hell which can lead them into all sorts of crazy mixed-up scenes. For other women," he emphasized, "these desires are fleeting—in terms of months or years—and disappear as would any other neurotic symptom when satisfied directly or indirectly. The problem with this sort of neurotic woman, of course," he went on, warming up to his subject, "is that her indirect satisfactions may take some mighty strange forms. I'm sure you've probably run into the rabid Lesbian-hater or homosexual hunter among married women you know—or even among some of the young career girls."

Joan felt that she had given him a false idea about herself. Now was the time, she decided, to tell him the truth. She was certain now, and the knowledge gave her a happiness and a feeling of wholeness which she knew would grow as time went on.

"Jay," she hunted for a way of telling him, "I'm afraid I've been giving everyone the wrong impression for a while now. You see, I told Marc that I was a Lesbian. Well, I was. I think I always have been. But I've only really felt strongly since I grew up and came off to college. Of course, the reason I left home was linked with my wanting to know more about myself. But still, I didn't really have anything to do with a woman until last night." She stopped flatly. She had said it. Now Jay and Marc would know that her front was false and that she was a pretender who had only recently worked into the role.

Jay laughed, but his laughter was unexpectedly soft. She hadn't expected such gentleness from a queen, from such a mad camping fairy. He took her hand and held it gently.

"Now you listen to Uncle Jay. There's a first time for all things. I know that you are very experienced as far as men are concerned. This much you've told me. But I know that you are able to evaluate your experience last night in terms of its real values for you. So be it. I'm fairly sure that you are not one of the neurotic women I just mentioned. Professional opinion aside, I think you're gay."

Joan smiled. "Thanks," she said, "I consider that a compliment."

"Good girl," Jay countered. "Most people have little or no insight into what makes them tick. Most of their desires are unconscious—makes for trouble later in life, when they're all wound up in their own knots."

"Are you free tonight?" Joan changed the subject; it was too nice a Saturday to talk shop.

Jay nodded. "Why?"

"I thought we might make a late stop at the Sun Dial," Joan said. "After you give me that Rorschach."

"Haven't had enough, I see," Jay smiled. "All right, it's a date."

Joan took out her books and they sat in the Positano studying together for a few hours. Later they had dinner and then Jay went upstairs with her to give her the psychological test.

Spending the day with Jay was soothing for Joan. He was a good companion. Secretly, she almost wished that she hadn't married Marc, but had married Jay instead. Jay was much more like David.

They were seated side by side on the bed. Joan was going over her last Rorschach card while Jay busily jotted down her impressions. Finally she stopped and Jay glanced quickly at his notes.

"I won't be able to tell you exactly until I score it," he smiled, "but offhand, you've one of the most creative Rorschachs I've seen. You're a fascinating creature, Joan." He turned to her and took her hand.

Joan wore a sphinxish expression. She was pleased to have charmed Jay; she had never been able to charm David that way. Impulsively, she brought her face forward and kissed Jay on the lips. She kissed him as a man might first kiss a woman, sweetly, but taking the lead. Jay let himself be kissed, responding like a woman, almost in fun.

"Do you still think I'm fascinating?" she asked when she stopped. She looked at him, teasing.

"What made you do that?" Jay laughed awkwardly. He was blushing now, taken by surprise.

"Kicks," she said with a sophistication that was only recent with her. She got up and walked around a bit, feeling the smallness of her apartment. "You know, lately I've been fighting a strange compulsion," she said. "It's as if I wanted to be a man—so much a man that I want to prove how much more I am a man than men—prove it to men, that is. I want to be a man with a man. Can you explain that?" She looked at him, concerned with her problem. She was fighting an attraction that she felt for Jay because she knew she could be masculine with him, could take the lead.

"That's odd," he smiled. "I don't know if I can explain it. It sounds as if you're terribly angry at someone."

"Perhaps that's it." She laughed embarrassedly. "Perhaps I'm just angry at David." This thought relieved her and she came to sit on the bed again. But Jay was handsome, sitting there so helplessly, and she decided to let herself do what she wanted to do—seduce him.

"Do gay men often sleep with women?" Joan asked.

"Some do," Jay said. "It depends—also, there's always a first and only time for some, before they decide they're gay."

"I suppose you know why I asked," Joan said. "Have you ever slept with a woman?" She was studying his face now, catching every change in his expression in an effort to understand him. Jay was fidgety, but he wasn't exactly running away from her stare.

"I'm not mixed up, Joan," he said, ignoring her question.

"I didn't think you were," she said. She sat back and stopped trying to be a vamp, conscious of Jay's discomfort. By retreating she succeeded in interesting Jay. He sat forward and took her hand.

"Joanie girl, you're a card!" he laughed. "God, what a triangle that would be—you, me and Marc."

"It might be fun," she smiled. "I've always wondered what a threesome was like."

"It doesn't work, Joan," Jay's face twisted in experienced distaste. "There's always one of the three left out. I'd hate it to be you."

"That would be all right," she laughed embarrassedly. "I don't care for men for very long anyway." She looked at him seriously and took his head, brought it to her and, kissed him again. This time her kiss was more forward, her hands ran over the pleats of his jacket and to his shirt, stopping finally when they reached his belt buckle. Joan felt the buckle with her fingers and began gently to open it, almost too gently for Jay to notice.

It was like undressing a girl. Jay made no effort to stop her. Patiently, she undid the buttons of his shirt, feeling his smooth hard chest beneath it. Jay's chest was sculptured, his entire body handsome and strong; for the first time Joan felt desire for a man. For the first time she really wanted to go on. But then the mood was broken. Jay had become aroused, and was responding now just like all the others, not allowing himself to be passive. He sat up and took Joan's arms with his strong hands and pressed his body to hers, finding her lips hungrily with his, and the same repulsion she had felt with other men, the same feeling of withdrawal began to take her. Detachedly, like so many times before, she waited for him to remove her clothes, allowing his mouth to find her breasts, allowing his hands to do what they wanted with her body, feeling nothing but a familiar sense of discomfort and distaste.

So that's what it would have been like with David, Joan thought again and again. Jay was lying naked next to her, a cigarette in his mouth, staring at the ceiling. She could not help admiring his body. In fact, she wished she had his body instead of her own. Her own body felt soiled with acrid sweat and her lungs were sick with cigarette smoke. It was nearly midnight and she wanted Jay to leave. She wanted to take a shower, and then find the Sun Dial, alone. Gig, with all her coarseness, had been a woman, had really pleased her; Joan wanted to find other women. Not even Jay would be a substitute.

"What are you thinking?" Jay asked, noticing her silence.

"I'm secretly trying to get rid of you," she smiled. She played with the hairs on his leg, her hands unable to keep still. "I was hoping to make the Sun Dial for an hour or so tonight."

"*Cherchez la femme,*" Jay sighed with a slight bit of humor. "Doll, didn't I tell you you were gay?"

"What about you? You certainly weren't gay a while ago," Joan countered. "Are all homosexuals that good in bed with women?"

"We all have our ups and downs," Jay replied mockingly. He swung his legs off the bed. "I'm going to use your shower," he said, "then maybe I'll go cruise the bars. I'll walk you to the Sun Dial if you like."

"Thanks," Joan said.

It was odd, the way they were still friends on some other level, as if nothing had happened between them. She was glad, because she enjoyed Jay's friendship.

Jay sang in the shower and when he was through, Joan used it. And then they dressed, Joan in slacks and Jay in his smartly styled suit. They walked out into the street together like brother and sister, but a little more familiar than that now, as if their friendship had taken on a new dimension. Joan knew that at some time or other, for lack of something better to do, they would repeat that strange scene all over again, and it would mean just as little to both of them then.

Jay walked her to the Sun Dial, which was across the park, and left her at the door. Joan felt safe as soon as she walked in. The customers looked like part of a college sorority shindig, like healthy all-American girls in slacks or in shirts; not the way Gig had looked—not strange and grotesque like Gig.

The Sun Dial was noisy and smoke-filled, but with happy noise and smoke. A great feeling of relief came over Joan as she looked around.

Not all Lesbians were like Gig. There were attractive women here like herself, some very feminine, and most of them her own age. The bartender and the waiters were men, clean cut and not seedy-looking like the ones at the Daisy. She felt secure as she walked to the bar. It was very crowded, but only with women.

She found a clear spot at the far end near a young couple who seemed happily involved with each other and deaf to the noise around them. Joan studied them for a moment. The more masculine girl wore a broad smile. She was wearing a college blazer and her hair was cut short, but not short enough to make her look like a boy. She had a large and interesting profile, not pretty, but appealing. Her partner was blonde and also wore a blazer, but her features were more feminine. They both were about twenty-two. Joan noticed that particularly. Unlike the Daisy, the crowd here was not in their teens. This was a clean bar. And then, as if to echo her thoughts, the bouncer walked toward her. He was small for a bouncer, but with the shapeless ears of a boxer. Joan wondered why he was approaching her; for a moment she felt afraid. Perhaps he wanted to throw her out because he had never seen her before.

"Hey, you," he motioned to her. "Yeah, you, miss.""

Joan did not know what to make of his tone. She hoped it was just natural coarseness. "Are you calling me?" she said.

"Yeah," he said, coming nearer. "Can you prove your age? I don't want any minors drinking here," he growled.

Joan took out her birth certificate; she always carried it in her wallet, because she knew she looked too young to be drinking.

It satisfied him but he took hold of her arm briefly. "Who you looking for?" he said.

Joan, confused for a moment, mentioned Gig. It was the wrong name.

"Look, I want this place kept clean," he said. "I know you're new and you've been to them other places, but here it's different. Here we got rules. I want none of them characters in here—and no men! Now I tell all the girls when they first come in—no men, no characters. One slip, and you're out."

Joan held her temper, reminding herself that it was just his coarse manner that made her angry. Those rules were good ones; she wished they were applied at the Daisy and the Yellow Page. It was the prostitution and the other traffic that made those places unsafe, not the Lesbians.

She went back to the bar and ordered a beer. The evening had turned very hot, especially here in the crowd.

Joan looked around her more freely. The table directly opposite her was taken up by a jolly crowd of Irish-looking girls who might all have been student nurses. They reminded her of something Paul had said about most homosexuals being blonde. She had to laugh, because there were more than blondes here—all races seemed to be comfortable in this place, without any sort of segregation, black next to white, sometimes coupled and each shade attractive. On the whole, there were more attractive women here than one would find in an ordinary bar or at any of the Bohemian spots that Joan had frequented. She noticed especially one girl at the bar, a very blonde and small girl with sensitive eyes and lips. She was talking to a taller and more masculine woman, but they didn't seem to be together. Joan decided to wait until the two finished talking and then go over to the blonde. She had forced herself through necessity to be rid of her shyness—for she knew she would have to be aggressive if she wanted to be butch. But another girl had the same idea and before Joan could move, a tall and attractive butch had already asked the blonde to dance and escorted her out to the floor.

Joan sighed and sipped her beer. The juke box was playing a rock; as the beat blared, Joan went over in her mind what had happened a while ago and what had happened with Gig. Half-memories of the night before kept repeating themselves in her mind—little images of lips and eyes and the feeling of soft breasts pressed against hers, Gig's tender embraces that seemed to reach far beneath Joan's skin into the parts of her that needed most the feeling of being touched, of being caressed, of being ordered to and fro without the presence of a hungry, excited partner, who would leave her naked and degraded, corrupted and sore—like Paul, and yes, even Jay. Not even Jay, who was so much like David, had come near Gig in tenderness—and Gig was by no means one of the most attractive Lesbians available.

As Joan thought about all this, she suddenly became aware that she was being watched. She raised her eyes and saw a mustache, and, behind it, a bald-headed man who seemed about thirty, dressed in a sloppy brown suit.

"Hello." He smiled pathetically.

Joan turned around, ignoring him. She wondered why the bouncer had let him in at all. Most of all, she wondered why the man had wanted to come here—to a place filled with women who would have nothing do with him.

She tolerated the mustached-man's stare for a while longer and then took her beer and moved to the other side of the bar, noticing a well-tailored girl sitting there with a drink in her hand. She seemed to be alone. Joan decided to practice at being butch.

"Would you like to dance?" Joan said, perhaps more awkwardly than she had intended.

The girl looked at Joan and smiled. It was an odd smile, one attractive with age and maturity; the woman seemed about thirty—not exactly feminine but not overly butch either.

"Why not?" the woman answered, putting her glass on the bar. "The name's Kim. What's yours?"

"Joan," Joan said. She smiled in return, feeling more confident.

They walked together to the back of the bar where the couples were dancing and fell into a fox trot despite the rock music.

"What do you do, Joan?" Kim said as they danced. They were dancing closely but not the way Gig had danced, not with all their bodies.

"I'm a student," Joan said. "And you?"

"I'm a WAC," Kim replied reluctantly. They danced cheek to cheek for a while without speaking; then the record changed.

"Let's sit," Joan said. They found an empty table nearby and Kim went back for their drinks.

"God," Kim said when she returned, "what a bore—not you—I mean this dive."

"We could take a walk in a while," Joan suggested. The idea appealed to both of them.

"Are you on leave?" Joan asked.

Kim nodded. "Forty-eight hours—half spent already." She lit a cigarette and bobbed her head to the rhythm of the music. "You from New York?"

Joan nodded. There was something dreadfully restless about Kim and it was catching. They drank more beer and danced again and this time Kim held Joan tight. There was something very strong about Kim, but it wasn't an unpleasant strength—like a man's strength was; it was an assurance and a protectiveness that seemed very natural and soothing to Joan. She closed her eyes and let her lungs fill themselves with the odor of Kim's cologne. Kim's cheek was very soft against hers and Kim's breasts were warm and comfortable. They danced without speaking until arousal grew too strong. Then they picked up their cigarettes from the table and walked out of the bar into the fresh night air. It was drizzling slightly, cutting the heaviness of the warm night; holding hands, they walked slowly to the corner.

"Want some coffee?" Kim suggested, seeing the drugstore still open.

Joan nodded and they went inside.

The quietness of the drugstore was a relief after the noise of the Dial and in the stronger light Joan had a chance to study Kim's features more closely. Kim's face was beautiful, but in a hard, quiet way. Her eyes were colder than Gig's—they had a look of someone who had lost interest in people and things—yet their hardness was attractive. It was a hardness that went with a trim, muscular body and a self-sufficient personality. In Kim there was also a bitterness that can come with age, but also a rare wisdom and understanding. Joan reminded herself that she had just met Kim; she would hold off judgment until later. In the meantime, she wondered why Kim was so serious and distant.

"Just lost your friend?" she asked Kim. The counter man was far on the other side of the store and they could talk without his hearing them.

Kim gave a short laugh. "Months ago. And you?"

"No, just looking to find one," Joan said. This left them silent for a long time and they drank their coffee slowly.

"When do you have to be back on base?" Joan asked finally.

"I have to leave by three o'clock tomorrow," Kim said. There was another long pause and Kim seemed to be thinking something over. At last she said, "I've got a room in the hotel across the street. Want to come upstairs a while?"

Joan hesitated for a moment. The question had taken her by surprise. She hadn't been prepared for such a quick invitation. She almost didn't want to go—she had been with Jay not long ago and she didn't yet feel clean. She didn't want Kim to touch her tonight. But she did want to love Kim. In the bright light of the drugstore Kim was even more attractive than she had been at the Dial.

"All right—for a while," Joan said, rubbing her finger on the counter, tracing a line of water nervously with her hands.

Kim reached into her pocket and threw money on the counter and they both got up lazily and walked across the street. The lobby was dark and an old Negro porter who was at the desk got up and took them up in the elevator.

Joan knew the hotel. It wasn't a cheap hotel but it was shabby nonetheless, as the management found a certain pride in the tradition of old upholstery and threadbare rugs. Kim had a double on the eighth floor with a private bath and a comfortable bed. They waited until the porter had left before Kim closed the door and latched it.

Joan threw her light jacket on a chair and looked around the room. The blinds were down, hiding the view across the courtyard to the other rooms, rooms just like this, where men or women, and men and women, were putting them to the same use. Joan had always hated hotels. For a moment she was sorry she had not brought Kim to her apartment, but laziness made her dismiss the thought.

Kim also threw her jacket down, reached into a drawer, took out a bottle of scotch and two glasses and offered Joan a drink. Joan accepted the offer and stood, watching Kim pour. Kim seemed to be quite tired, using liquor to wake herself up. Joan too felt the strain of the evening and sat at the foot of the bed, waiting for Kim to speak. They both took a swallow of the scotch before Kim broke the silence.

"I'm sorry there's no radio or anything," she said.

"I like the silence," Joan countered. She let her eyes meet Kim's. They were finally alone and she wanted very much to be kissed. Kim seemed to read her mind. She came nearer and put her mouth on Joan's. It was intended to be slow and casual, but they couldn't be casual. Joan felt as if she had been thirsty for months, and finally her mouth was being cooled by the refreshing sweetness of Kim's, finally her burning body was being soothed.

It turned into more than a kiss and they both lay back on the bed, each caressing the other simultaneously, lost in a hunger both had for the body of a woman. Joan felt that this wasn't the same as it had been with Gig. Kim was more her type, was even a potential lover, and so there was more than animal passion here, there was a beginning, a beginning of a good, clean feeling, a beginning of love. And Joan felt very butch. She forgot Jay, forgot about everything except making love to Kim.

Joan's lips and hands seemed to be electric with awareness as she gently opened Kim's blouse and slipped off her bra; and then she let Kim undo her own blouse and bra. They were both half naked on the bed and they paused for a word or two in order to establish some feeling of contact on another plane. They were both embarrassed at having skipped the preliminaries of love.

"Let's have more scotch," Kim said. She broke away from Joan a little and poured some liquor in each glass. But Joan shook her head; she didn't want any. Kim drank hers down, looking at Joan from a distance.

Her eyes seemed disturbed; they were still hard, as before, but they were uncomfortable now.

"What are you thinking?" Joan asked. She was sitting up by the side of the bed, herself upset by the suddenness of their contact. But mostly she was disturbed because Kim was bothered by it. She knew instinctively that this sort of thing was new for Kim—that Joan might have been the first girl Kim had kissed since months ago, when she had lost her friend.

"I'm thinking there's a shower that goes with this room," Kim said, making a good recovery into a careless mood. She looked at Joan with an air of What next? as if the scotch had reminded Kim that her standards were supposed to be those of men, not of women, and that a soldier couldn't turn down a beautiful girl who wanted to go to bed.

Kim moved suddenly and took her overnight bag with her. She was in the shower only a few minutes and she came out wearing pajamas. She tossed a towel to Joan and then got under the covers, preparing to read an old issue of *Life*.

The hot water relaxed Joan's muscles and awakened them at the same time; she was washing off Jay a second time. She had taken another shower earlier, but now she wanted to be cleaner than surface—for Kim.

When Joan came out, Kim was in bed blowing smoke rings up to the ceiling. Only the bed lamp was lit and Kim closed that also, moving over on the bed.

Joan put her clothes on the chair with the jackets and lay down beside her. The only light came dimly through the white blinds on the window and the two lay there, letting their eyes become accustomed to the near-darkness. Then Kim put out her cigarette. There was a long silence. There was only the feeling of fear and even slight repulsion that always comes when strange bodies prepare to meet.

And then Kim's hands took hold of Joan's, and there was Kim's warm breath as her lips touched Joan's—and then the fear and repulsion were gone. They became a strange familiarity and joy.

The maid's knock woke them early the next morning. "It's occupied!" Kim shouted through the door and the maid went away, apologizing, to another room. But it was too late. They were both awake now and didn't want to go back to sleep. Kim had only until three o'clock before the last train back to the base. She lit a cigarette, came back to bed and fondly took hold of Joan's hand. Kim bent down and kissed her sweetly on the lips.

"Ready for breakfast?"

Joan nodded, yawning one last time. She was very sleepy, but the beautiful Sunday morning kept her awake. She tightened her grasp on Kim's hand and brought it to her lips. Somehow they were not strangers this morning. They had become used to each other's presence and it was as if they had been living together a long time.

"I want a great big breakfast," Joan said, "and then let's walk together. We might go somewhere, like the zoo."

Kim laughed and bent over Joan once more, warming her cheek with her own. It reminded Joan of their lovemaking and she pressed Kim to her with both arms. It was almost too soon to say it, but that didn't matter now. Joan said—"I love you."

Kim laughed again and nibbled Joan's ear. Joan waited for her to say something in answer, but Kim did not. Instead, she sat beside Joan and said, "Do I see you again?"

"As often as you like," Joan answered. She felt happy. At least Kim liked her. "When are you coming back?"

"I can't get another leave for two weeks," Kim said. She seemed disturbed at this, as if she hated being in the Army. "There's a year left on my enlistment," she added, as if she wanted Joan to know all the disadvantages.

"And then what?" Joan asked.

"Then I can quit and go to school on the G.I. Bill," Kim said. That had been her reason for enlisting. That was the most usual reason in peacetime, not the fact that she was a Lesbian. There was no advantage to being a Lesbian in the Services.

Joan sat up and kissed Kim tenderly and they held the kiss a long time, almost starting all over again, their bodies beginning to remember the night before.

"Let's get dressed," Kim said finally, pulling herself away from Joan with great effort. They both felt that they needed some time simply to talk. Getting to know each other now was very important—important because it would carry the memory of this weekend along in the following awful days of separation.

They got up and dressed and groomed themselves and then left the room. Kim checked out and then they were free of the hotel, free of the stifling upholstery and tattered rugs, free to go out into the late May sun.

They walked with Kim's overnight bag between them, each with one hand on the handle and sharing the case's weight—almost like walking hand in hand. There was a large and modernly decorated restaurant on the corner, the kind that serves charcoal broiled hamburgers and eggs in the skillet. They stopped at the window and decided this was the place for breakfast. It was not crowded at this hour on Sunday morning.

They took one of the large booths next to the wall-length window that let the sun shine directly on them, filling them with the warmth of a comfortable spring day. Their order was taken quickly and then they had nothing to do but sit and look at each other, sit and study each other's faces.

Kim's face was beautiful, Joan noticed again. It had the inner glow of someone who liked the outdoors. Kim didn't look thirty in daylight. "How old are you?" Joan asked.

"Twenty-eight," Kim said. "And you?"

"Just twenty," Joan said.

This came as a shock to Kim and for a moment she was plainly disturbed. "You mean I've been corrupting a minor?"

Joan smiled. "This minor was corrupted long ago and not by women." She touched Kim's hand. "It can't matter that much to you, can it?"

Kim squeezed Joan's hand for a moment and then let go. "I guess it's too late to worry about that now." She looked down and played with her fork. "I'm very glad we met."

"So am I," Joan said. She leaned forward. "Tell me about yourself. Where do you come from? I want to know all about you."

Kim smiled. "I'm from Chicago." Not freely, but under Joan's prying questions, she began to talk about herself—about her family and the Army and the friend she had lost six months ago. "It's hell in the Service," she finished. "You're always watched. Gay couples don't have a chance. If they can't get something on you, they transfer you to a different outfit. That's what happened with Bea and me. Bea's in Frisco now. They were close to kicking us out but they had no proof."

"And you don't even dare write her?" Joan had listened to Kim's story with horror. The Army's attitude toward homosexuals seemed close to Gestapo tactics, not at all what one expected in a free country. Why persecute two consenting adults for what they did in private?

"She has a new friend there," Kim finished. "I guess it's better for both of us that way."

"How can you say that?" Joan said, forgetting her own interest in Kim for the moment. "How can you let them beat you?"

"Time does things to people," Kim answered simply. She looked at Joan and smiled a little sadly. "That's why I'm somewhat cynical about last night. I don't dare hope that anything can last a year. It wouldn't be fair to expect you to wait that long just on the basis of a few weekends we can have together."

Joan thought about this for a moment. Seeing Kim briefly after long intervals would be difficult. Joan's body was young and alive and needed satisfaction—and her mind needed a friend, someone to share her daily life. It would be difficult to save herself for Kim. "We can give it a try," she said at last. And then she added, "I can't promise to be faithful, but at least we can keep on seeing each other."

Kim nodded and quietly finished her scrambled eggs.

After breakfast they walked to Washington Square and fed the pigeons. Suddenly, they realized how little time they had left before Kim's train.

"Let's go to my apartment," Joan said, and her words made them quicken their steps out of the park, made them anxious to return to each other's arms, anxious to spend the last hurried hours satisfying a need that would torture their bodies for two long and vacant weeks.

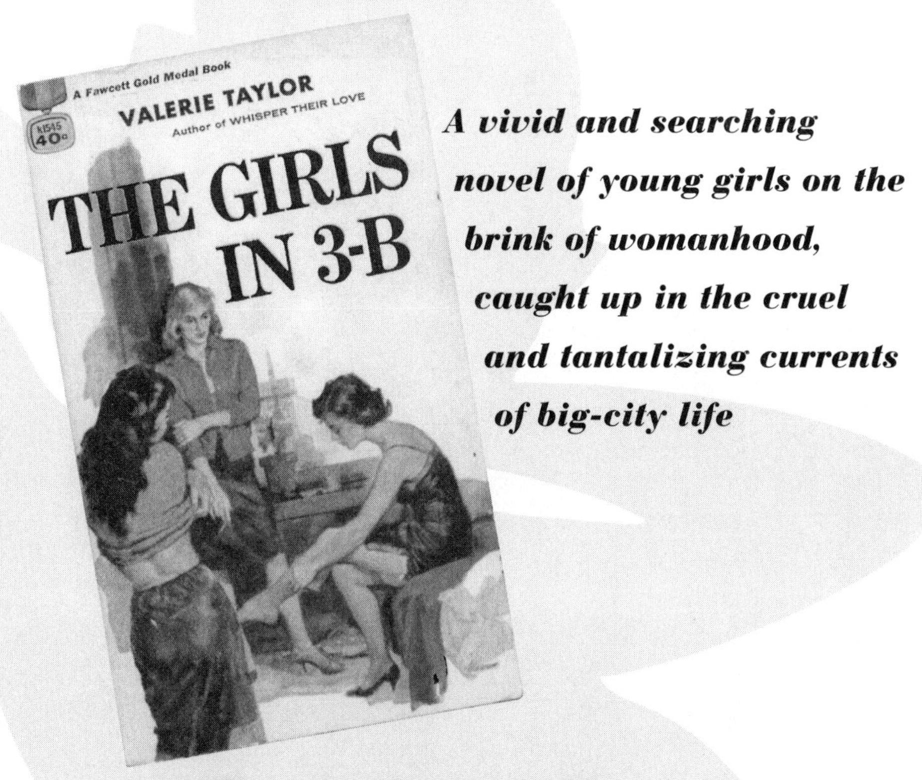

A vivid and searching novel of young girls on the brink of womanhood, caught up in the cruel and tantalizing currents of big-city life

The Girls in 3-B

by Valerie Taylor

They came to the city fascinated, frightened…

There was Annice…Bright, curious, full of untried passion, she let Alan drag her into his beat-generation world of parties, jazz, booze, marijuana and sex.

And Pat…She was big and blonde and built for love, but she was saving herself for marriage. Until she met her boss. Right from the beginning Pat knew she'd do anything for him—anything.

And Barby…She was the most vulnerable. Men terrified her and for a good reason. When she finally fell in love it was with a woman.

The Girls in 3-B

"Good-looking?" Betty Pelecek said. She looked at Barby over the rim of her coke glass, her lips twisted scornfully. "I guess she's all right—if you like that kind. I like normal people myself."

Through Barby's mind there flashed the names of half a dozen hidden disabilities—TB, cancer, leukemia, all the names that flashed at you from billboards and magazine pages. She said weakly, "Normal?"

"Sure, she's a Lesbian." Barby's puzzled expression was all the answer she needed. "Don't you know what a Lesbian is? It's a woman who likes other women."

"Well, I like other women. Don't you?"

"To go to bed with, stupid. Instead of men."

"But I don't see how—" She ran through her considerable knowledge of the relationship between men and women. "I mean, what do they *do?*"

Betty shrugged. Either she didn't know, or, more likely, she considered it an unfit subject to discuss at a drugstore counter. "They find ways," she said darkly. "They're not like other people." She gathered up her handbag, gloves and packages, preparatory to getting down from the high stool. "We better get back. She'll give us both hell if we're late. Unless," she said maliciously, "you're teacher's pet or something."

Barby frowned. Betty sounded so positive; surely you couldn't make up a thing like that, and yet she didn't see how it could be possible. Fragments of talk, ignored at the time; allusions in books; clinical-sounding magazine articles—this might explain a great deal she had ignored or dimly wondered about. "Anyway," she said, "I don't think Miss Gordon could be one. She looks like anybody else."

"You can't always tell. Sometimes they dress in men's clothes. But other times you can't tell them from ordinary people."

"Well, but—what people do is their own business." She fell silent, knowing that Betty didn't agree. When someone in the department got married it was Betty who made a note of the date, to compare it later with the arrival of the first baby; she seemed to know what every girl in Blouses and Sportswear did over the week end and which ones were sleeping around, what married employees were two-timing their husbands and which of the floor managers and department heads got fresh with the girls. Her gimlet gaze frightened Barby, conscious as she was of all she had to hide. She tried to avoid Betty, and when there was no way to avoid a coke break or lunch hour with her, she breathed easier when it was time to get back to work.

She looked at Miss Gordon with new curiosity when they reached the Store, half expecting to discover some disfigurement she hadn't noticed before. But Miss Gordon looked quite ordinary: neat, attractive, with a pleasant smile. In her dealings with the other supervisors and the salespeople she was both relaxed and capable, as if she knew her value to the company and, at the same time, recognized an obligation to do her best. Her girls didn't loaf when she was around, didn't sneak off to the washroom for a smoke or spend their time visiting, but Barby had never heard her reprimand anyone. She didn't have to. *If she's a—if she's one of those,* Barby thought confusedly, feeling Miss Gordon's eyes on her and blushing, *they can't be so terrible. Anything she did would have to be all right.*

She thought about it a great deal, and suddenly it seemed to her that Miss Gordon was everywhere she went—in the elevator before and after work, in the third-floor washroom, in the corner drugstore when she stopped for a box of Kleenex. She stopped at the long worktable where the girls were sewing tags in the $3.98 blouses, and stood for a long time looking at Barby. The look went through her like a ray of sunshine and left her feeling warm and shaky so that she sat for a while doing nothing. Then, catching Betty's eyes on her, she got briskly to work. But she couldn't shake off the memory of that deep, questioning look.

They fell into step at lunchtime the next day, reaching the street together; Barby stood back to let Miss Gordon go through the revolving door first, and was glad but somehow not surprised that she waited. "Alone? Then why don't you have lunch with me? My treat, of course." She looked at Barby, thoughtfully. "You needn't mention it to the other girls, though."

Barby nodded. Nobody is lower in the department-store hierarchy than a stock girl, unless it's the man who sweeps out or the drabbled women who come in at night to scrub. A stock girl is nobody. Even if she is the owner's daughter, learning the business from the ground up, within the walls of the Store she is without status. Barby knew and accepted this. Dimly, though, she realized that something more underlay Miss Gordon's admonition. She walked silently, excited and a little frightened.

They went to a little restaurant tucked away between two taller buildings, a dark little cubbyhole lighted by candles and frequented by couples who looked ardently at each other across the small linen-draped tables. Some of the couples, Barby noticed, were women. Miss Gordon ran a hand through her hair, ruffling it, and smiled. "I love this place," she said softly. "Glass of wine while you're waiting?"

"Well—"

The wine sent a glow through her, making her feel at once relaxed and alert. She looked around curiously. This was a different world from any she had seen—as unlike the expensive hard-surfaced world of the big hotels and department stores as the small-town streets and tree-shaded lawns of her childhood. It was, somehow, more personal. The flicker of candlelight on intent faces, the silence of the deferential waiters, the soft lilting and wailing of violin music that seemed to come out of nowhere—all of these evoked a mood of nostalgia and romantic yearning.

Surrounded by a rosy haze, she realized that she was answering Miss Gordon's questions without self-consciousness. Yes, she lived with two other girls—they had been friends in school, that was how they happened to be together, but they seemed to be making separate friends and doing different things. One was in school and the other had a job with a book publisher. Yes, she liked working in the Store. "Only I don't want to be a stock girl all my life. I don't know just what I want to do, yet."

"Perhaps get married and have a couple of nice children?" Miss Gordon's lips quirked.

"No, I'll never get married."

"Don't you have a sweetheart?"

"I hate men," Barby said fiercely.

Miss Gordon turned her wine glass between slender fingers. "You don't look like a girl who hates men."

"Oh, I hate the way I look, too. If I were a Catholic I think I'd go into a convent. I really mean that, Miss Gordon."

"Ilene."

"Ilene." She blushed. "All men want to do is get their hands on you all the time. They just go by the way you look, they don't care how you really are."

"And how are you really?"

"I don't know," Barby said slowly. "It's like I'm waiting to find out."

"Yes," Ilene Gordon said, "that's the hardest part of growing up, waiting for someone else to show you your own possibilities. So often the right person doesn't come along."

The waiter refilled Barby's glass, setting a plate down in front of her. The food smelled wonderful, but she wasn't hungry. "I'm doing a lot of talking," she said shyly. "What I'm really interested in is you."

It was a simple story, Ilene Gordon said laughing. She lived in an apartment on the North Side—she named the neighborhood, and Barby recognized it as a very good neighborhood indeed, far better than her own. She had been sharing it with another girl, who was moving out in a few weeks. "She's being married. I'm not sure what I'll do then, but anyway, it will work out."

Barby tried to imagine a marriage that would be better than sharing an apartment with Ilene Gordon, seeing her every evening, talking things over with her. She said, "Your friend will be sorry," and was rewarded by another of those long, searching looks. They left the subject there, as if it were not time to develop it further.

Miss Gordon picked up the check which the waiter presented deferentially, and tucked a bill under the edge of her plate. None of the nickel counting exactitude Barby was used to when she went out with the girls. "We must do this again. It's been fun."

How nice she is, Barby thought, glowing with wine and talk. *How nice and understanding.*

For some reason, she didn't mention the lunch to Annice and Pat.

The book was on her end of the worktable a couple of days later, tucked under a box of tags as though someone had slipped it there, hastily, while she was out. There was no note with it, and nobody mentioned it, but when she opened it she found Ilene Gordon's name on the flyleaf in a clear, small hand, and she knew that it had been left for her with a special purpose. She took it out to lunch, choosing a small cheap restaurant where she was unlikely to meet anyone from the Store. Without paying attention to the young sailor who was ogling her from the next table or to the mediocre food, she plunged into the pages of such a story as she had never read before.

It was the story of a young woman who, growing up, rejected the love of men and was lost in loneliness for the years of her girlhood, only to find a kind of love she had never known existed—the passionate unselfish love of another woman. Barby was fascinated. There was a relationship, then, without force or fear. Tenderness was in it, and compassion. There was a love between two individuals who understood and cherished each other because they shared the same nature. They could even pledge themselves to each other—perhaps not for a lifetime, but then, how many wives could count on their husbands to be faithful after the first weeks of marriage? For the last five years Barby had looked wonderingly at all the serious, respectable married men she knew, wondering what fearful secret lives were hidden by their everyday faces.

She read on, overstaying her lunch hour and not caring, though the time clock was as relentless as death or taxes and her tardiness would mean a deduction. It didn't matter. She was like an explorer who, long drifting on an unfriendly sea, finally sights land and dares to hope he will make it to shore, after all.

She carried the book home with her that afternoon, reading a few pages in the station, a chapter on the train, propping it on the kitchen table while she opened cans and threw together some kind of a supper. Annice was out, doing God knew what—the thought of what Annice was probably doing made her feel a little sick—and Pat was too absorbed in shortening another new dress to have time for food. This concern of Pat's for her looks bothered Barby, who had always been well-dressed with very little effort on her own part; she might have expected it in Annice, but Annice was getting downright careless since she no longer went to school. Pat was all wrapped up in clothes—insane about clothes, in fact. She had thrown away the skirts, sweaters and flats that went so well with her wholesome chubby appearance and was slinking around in a series of glamorous outfits that looked a little bit funny on her. Well, that was another problem to straighten out when she had time to think about it. Tonight there was something more urgent. She filled a plate with canned vegetables, not so very well seasoned, and took it to the davenport, where she sat down with the book. Long after Pat finished her pinning and hemming and went to bed she was still sitting there, the empty plate still on the floor. It was like stepping into a new world, a world where secret hidden emotions ruled people's lives.

Was it possible that she belonged in that world, too? She was shy about facing Ilene Gordon at work the next morning. She need not have been. Everything went smoothly. She was on time. Her face in the washroom mirror looked the same as always, a pretty girl's face made up in the current style. Only everything in the Store looked brighter and sharper than usual. The stock shimmered with newness and color; the faces of clerks and customers held a depth of feeling she hadn't noticed before. She saw a young mother with two whining children, tired, hungry for some of the pretty clothes the household budget wouldn't cover; she looked at the older saleswomen and saw their ugly comfort shoes at variance with their smart dresses and modish hair styling, and her heart swelled with pity for them. How hard it must be to get older and have nobody to love you, nothing to look forward to except a skimpy existence on Social Security!

But she was young. Her best years were ahead.

She had never felt this identification with other people before. She had always been alone. She wasn't sure whether she liked it or not. When Ilene Gordon showed up, looking as she always did, Barby was conscious of an intense pleasure at the sight of her. That was all. No anxiety. She was sure everything would work out all right. Nothing in her life had ever worked out right before. But then, nothing like this had ever come her way.

Barby had known this would be the day, even before she was out of bed. She woke with a feeling of bright anticipation, like the expectant tingle a child feels on Christmas morning—a feeling of happy, calm assurance that was not excitement, but pure joy. Pouring coffee, too pleased to be hungry, she thought, *It has to happen today, it simply has to. I'm ready for it.*

It was the first time in her life she had ever been sure of anything good.

They had lunch together in the candle-lighted hideaway that had become their special secret place. It warmed Barby to enter the small, smoky room, dim after the sunshiny street, and cross to the corner table where they had sat the first day. When someone else was there first, her pleasure was flawed. Today the table was empty, as she had known it would be, and she hung her coat and Ilene's on the old-fashioned rack in the corner and sat down, smiling across the checkered cloth. "I love this place."

"The trouble is that we haven't long enough to talk." Ilene moved the silver at her place, then moved it back again. "I've been wondering. Would you like to come up to my apartment this evening? It's rather nice—and I do have a fireplace, and we'd be free from interruptions." She bent her head to examine the spoon. "We could have a real visit."

"I'd like to."

"Do your roommates ask questions if you're late?"

"No. They quite often stay out late themselves. It's funny," Barby said thoughtfully, "but the longer we live together, the less we seem to have in common. I suppose eventually we'll all know different people."

"I suppose it's cheaper, sharing a place?"

"Partly. And then partly, our families all know each other. That's one reason they let us come, because we were going to live together and they thought we'd sort of check up on each other. That shows how much parents know."

"But you don't have to stay together."

"Oh no. We'll split up, sooner or later. Annice is sure to get tired of running around and get married, one of these days. Pat, too. She's the kind to settle down and have one of those big Catholic families."

"You're not thinking of marriage?"

Barby said low, "No. Never. I told you before, I hate men."

"I'm not going to ask you any questions, who hurt you or how," Ilene Gordon said. She reached across the table and laid her slender, well-manicured hand on Barby's. The touch tingled up her arm. "I've learned not to ask questions. The past doesn't matter for people like you—and me."

"No."

Ilene straightened up. She smiled. "Well then, you will come up this evening, won't you? Around seven, maybe? It's better if we don't go home together."

"Of course. I can take the subway."

"Take a taxi. Here, I'll give you the money for it."

Barby took the dollar slowly, folded it differently from her other money and put it in the back of her billfold. It was good to feel provided and cared for. When she went back to the Store, too well-nourished on happiness to know or care what she had eaten, she removed the bill to an envelope and sealed it shut. *I'll keep it,* she thought, *and when I'm old it will remind me.* She knew she was being young and silly, and romantic; but it didn't matter. She felt that she had never been really happy before, in her whole life. It was like feeling well and light-bodied after a long illness.

She called to tell the girls that she would be late, not because they would be concerned even if she stayed out all night—a thought that made her dizzy with anticipation—but because she passionately wanted everything about this to be just right, to be perfect. Annice was at home, as she had expected. She sounded tearful. Damn the girl, Barby thought, she used to be so steady and reliable, and eves since she quit going to school she hasn't cared about anything. Half the time she doesn't even show up for that crummy two-bit job. It's that bearded Bohemian character she runs around with, that comic-book character. I wouldn't trust him around the corner. She turned away from the telephone, her good mood shattered.

Forget about it. Forget everything, she told herself, except the work you're doing. She couldn't think about the evening ahead; it was too bright; it dazzled her inner sight.

The twilight street was delicately dusky when she emerged into it, and a light snow was falling. It blurred the outlines of the tall buildings and put halos around the street lights. The first snow of winter. She smiled self-consciously, knowing it would turn to a dirty mush as soon as it reached the sidewalk, knowing she would have more than enough snow before the winter was over. She could see herself standing on a bus corner with the icy prairie wind whipping her skirts and piercing through her heavy coat; slipping on the frozen sidewalks, begging the landlord for more steam in the lukewarm radiators. This was Illinois winter, worse here than at home because of the Lake. But for a few minutes, she lingered in the muffled streets, recapturing the magic of childhood mornings when, after the dull tan monotony of autumn, she looked out at a world of pearl and crystal.

She wasn't hungry. It seemed unnecessary to eat, but she had to do something for an hour. She went into a drugstore and had coffee, drinking it slowly, watching the clock over the door. From the long mirror behind the counter her reflection looked back at her, wide-eyed and pink-cheeked.

I want to remember every detail of this, she thought, hailing a cab. *The feel of the upholstery and the driver's face and the way the store windows look through the falling snow. I want to remember it as long as I live.*

Ilene's neighborhood was expensive-looking. The strips of lawn between sidewalk and apartment buildings were manicured; the cars at the curb were of two kinds—small, smart and foreign, or large, smart and impressive. She walked across the lobby, heels clattering on the marble flooring, and was wafted up by a sallow elevator boy in a skintight uniform and a chestful of ribbons. Then she forgot to be impressed with the aura of money and splendor, because Ilene was at the door, waiting for her.

She wore Bermuda shorts, with knee socks and sandals; her short hair was ruffled, and she held a thin-stemmed glass. Her hands were warm on Barby's. "I'm glad you could come. Come in and see my place."

It was the sort of apartment Barby had learned to appreciate during her noonday prowlings through department stores and specialty shops. A step led up to the living room, which was long and narrow, decorated all in white and warmed by the jackets of books and the soft glow of a blaze in the fireplace. She stood before it, hands spread wide. "A real fireplace, imagine," she said, and Ilene laid a light hand on her shoulder and said, "Yes, it's marvelous for conversation." The sofa was wide enough for five people and the coffee table that stood in front of it held an elegant service in crystal and silver, glittering in the firelight. The shelves held books, Wedgewood and Spode plates, odd bits of silver. Two china dogs sat at the ends of the mantel. "Staffordshire," Ilene said, turning one of them over in thin, nervous fingers. "See the marking?"

"Is it all yours? I mean, did it come this way?"

A shadow crossed Ilene's face. "I furnished it six years ago with the girl who left to get married."

"I'm sorry."

"Never look back," Ilene said. She replaced the china dog. "Six years is a long time; keep looking ahead."

Barby could accept that. *If I could cut off the past right now,* she thought, *and be born fresh!* Ilene smiled. "You learn to remember the good things, but that takes time. Come on, I'll show you the rest."

There was a tiny dining room. "Silly, because it's too small for guests and we hardly ever used it when we were alone. I like it, though. Leila made the chair seats." She touched the petit point caressingly, and Barby felt a pang of jealousy for the unknown Leila. They moved into the bedrooms, one large, decorated in blue and pale green, with a handful of detective stories on the bedside stand and a row of tailored clothes in the closet; one small, bare, with a single bed. The immaculate bathroom, with a blue and green dressing table. And the small kitchen, best of all, with copper pans hanging on the wall and a shelf of spices in decorated jars. "Best room in the house," Ilene said. She measured coffee into the drip pot, set out a coffeecake, and then, hesitantly, took down a small squat bottle. "Kümmel. Ever drink any? It tastes like hell, but it makes you feel all warm and cozy inside."

The drink relaxed Barby, took away the last lingering bit of self-consciousness. They sat at opposite sides of the linen-covered table. "This is a wonderful room."

"It's the main reason I don't want to sublet. But this place is too big for me alone."

"Can't you find someone to share it?"

"It would have to be someone special—who meant a lot to me, personally. I don't believe in grieving for the past. One has to move ahead." She poured coffee into a heavy pottery cup, set it in front of Barby. Her hand trembled a little.

"I'm a very direct person," Ilene said. "I don't finagle around and try to put over a deal—not where my personal life is concerned." She looked at Barby, the long straight look that had melted her heart the first day, as if she could see through her eyes and into her mind. "You're very young."

"Not that young," Barby said low.

"I don't know if you even know what I'm talking about."

"I've known for a long time."

"You don't have to commit yourself to anything. I want you to think it over. But—will you stay here with me tonight?"

Barby's heart missed a beat, then righted itself. She waited a moment, to be sure her voice was steady. "Yes," she said. She reached across the table and laid her hand on Ilene's. "Yes. I've been wanting you to ask me that."

Much later, when they stood together at the bedroom window, watching the soft flakes of snow drive against the glass and shatter, she said, "It's what I've wanted, all my life. How can anybody want a man, when there's this?"

Ilene held her close. "Don't be sorry."

Just before she fell asleep she thought about Rocco and the basement room; and then, dimly of something farther back and more dreadful. But it was all far away, like a dream already dissolving. The experience of this night had washed away all the hurt and terror of it. Nothing could hurt her anymore. She fell asleep in the circle of Ilene's arms, safe.

Breakfast was the best part of the day. They never had it in the bijou dining room, but in the kitchen, with electric light winking off the hanging copper saucepans and the coffeepot within easy reach of the pilot light. Barby had never wanted a home of her own, thinking of it as a by-product of marriage—husband, home, and children. But now she had one, and it was wonderful.

I have everything, she thought. *A home, and love, and the chance of a raise at the Store*. More would be too much.

"I'm so happy."

Ilene said softly, "Are you, baby?"

"Yes." She turned from the stove. Ilene had on her favorite lounging pajamas, blue and gold; her eyes were sleepy and her hair tousled. Love rose in Barby. She crossed the kitchen floor and laid her head against Ilene's shoulder, too full of contentment to need words.

"Really happy?" Ilene persisted.

"I think it's the first time in my life I was ever really happy."

Ilene's arms closed around her.

Barby shut her eyes. "I love you so much," she whispered. She had never said that to anyone before. The words, hanging on the still morning air, had a perfect rightness that nothing else in her life had ever possessed.

"I love you too. All the time, not just at night. But the toast is burning." She reached to shut it off, keeping one arm around Barby. "You might rumple your bed a little. This is the cleaning woman's day."

Barby blushed. Technically, the small bedroom was hers. Her clothes hung in the closet and her cosmetics stood in tidy rows on the mirrored dressing table. But she had yet to spend a night in the single bed. She said, to cover her confusion, "We're going to be late for work."

Ilene buttered her slice of toast and sat down, pushing her cup and plate into easier reach. "We can take cabs. You can't afford to be late when you're bucking for a raise."

"Do you think anybody suspects?"

"They always do. As long as nobody can actually prove anything it's all right." Ilene tasted her coffee, added cream. "You need spring clothes. The best will come in around the middle of this month—by February everything's picked over. I'll have a couple of outfits laid away for you."

"But I want to start paying board."

"Don't worry about that "

The telephone rang. Barby jumped. "Who on earth—"

"Answer it and find out."

"I'm afraid to."

"Don't be silly. It's probably for me anyway. You didn't change your address on the payroll records, did you?"

"Then you answer."

Ilene raised her eyebrows and stepped into the living room, toast in hand. The shrilling stopped. Her voice, low-pitched and calm, reached Barby. "Hello. Oh, hello. Yes, she's right here. Just a minute, please." She put the handset down quietly. "It's your father."

The color drained from Barby's face. Her eyes widened. She put her hands behind her back, a childish gesture of refusal. "Do I have to?"

"Afraid so." Ilene made a gesture indicating, *We'll talk about it later.* She picked up the phone and handed it to Barby, who took it unwillingly.

"Don't go away."

Ilene came to stand behind her, both hands on her shoulders.

"Hello." At a standstill, she listened, looking at Ilene's fingertips for courage. "Why, I don't know. I'll ask her." She put a hand over the mouthpiece. "He wants to take us to lunch. Do we have to?"

Ilene nodded.

"Sure, but— Well, all right, what time? No, it's against the rules. We'll meet you somewhere." She listened again, her head bent, her hair touching Ilene's right hand. "All right, we'll be there at one. I have to go to work now."

Ilene said, "You could have been politer."

"He wants us to meet him at the Brevoort, one o'clock. Some salesman took him there once and he thinks it's the absolute end."

Ilene said reasonably, "Well, it is nice. Expensive, too."

"Do we have to go?"

"You can leave five minutes early. I'll follow." Automatic caution, necessary to keep private affairs from the public. "It could be worse, you know. He could have wanted to come up here."

Barby looked around, horrified. Their home, the place where they were together with the rest of the world shut out. "You wouldn't let him, would you?"

"No." It was a complete promise. Ilene asked curiously, "Do you hate him so much?"

Barby's eyes widened. "I don't know. I've never thought about it like that." She considered. "I've been afraid of him. Because he's the only one that knows—"

"What?"

"Nothing"

Ilene patted her cheek, moved away. "OK. Now hurry up, or you will be late."

Barby's glance at the clock was perfunctory. It struck her, however, that ten short minutes ago she had been looking at Ilene across the breakfast table, happier than she had ever been in her life—happy for the first time in her life. She thought, *I wish I could die. No, I wish he'd die. I do hate him. Why didn't I ever think about it before?*

Because you were never a real person before, a small inner voice suggested.

"You know something? I haven't had migraine since I left home. Except once."

Ilene's voice drifted back from the bedroom. "Then you better stay away."

She dressed carefully, to look older and more sophisticated than she was. The good black dress Ilene had given her, hand-hammered earrings from a little shop on Michigan Avenue, dark lipstick. Betty Pelecek took it in with one jealous look. "Man?" "A special date," Barby lied, not caring. Ilene was always mentioning that she ought to date, or pretend to date men, in order to avoid suspicion of being queer or different. Barby saw Betty's eyes widen with respect, and a feeling of cool self-assurance filled her.

Ilene passed, murmuring, "Remember, leave early. Take a cab. I'll meet you there."

Her father, waiting in the lounge at the Brevoort, looked familiar and yet strange in this setting. He stood up when he saw her, and she saw that he looked nervous. She had never seen him less than self-contained, and it gave her a feeling of mastery. She smiled at him, seeing the two of them as the onlookers must—charming young girl, attractive older man.

"I thought you girls might like a steak."

"That sounds good."

"Bet you don't get one very often."

"No, we go in more for hamburgers."

She didn't know how to tell him that Ilene wasn't a girl. A moment later the door swung open again and Ilene was there, trim and composed as always. Barby analyzed her father's expression—surprise, approval, and the fatuous wish to please of the middle-aged married man. "Well, this is mighty nice."

Ilene's glance at Barby evidently reassured her. "It's a pleasure to meet Barby's father. We think she has a real future at the Store, you know. I'm quite proud of her."

His gun knocked out of his hands, as it were, Robert Morrison was silent for a moment. Barby looked from one to the other, aware that something she couldn't follow was happening. Ilene wore her Store face—determined, thoughtful—with a social smile on top. Whatever it was, she was in there fighting.

Robert Morrison said, "Her mother and I were kind of surprised when she left the other girls. They were chums through school, pretty much."

Ilene shrugged. "Barby's outgrown them. She has a real talent for merchandising. Inherited, maybe. She's told me what a fine business you've built up."

"Well—" Robert said. The arrival of the headwaiter saved him from having to sound modest. Barby followed him to the table, relaxing almost visibly. *It won't last much longer,* she promised herself. *One hour. You can stand anything for an hour.*

Morrison said, when he had seated them, "We've never taken Barby's job very seriously. I thought maybe she was getting enough of it, by this time."

Ilene leaned forward, smiling. "Oh, it would be a pity if she quit now. She's lucky to have such understanding parents. Such an up-to-date father." Barby ventured a look over her menu; could Ilene possibly get away with this? But his expression was pleased. "She has a real future. You're going to be proud of her."

"Her mother can't see that."

"Some women can't."

His thoughts were as plain as if they had been printed on his face in large type. This was a damned attractive woman, and she seemed to like him. Older than he'd expected, with enough experience of life and men to know a winner when she saw one. Barby turned away to hide a small smile, remembering some of Ilene's comments on the male sex. She had a good job in a Loop store, so she was smart as well as good-looking. He shifted his gaze from her face to his daughter's, and Barby gave him back a facsimile of Ilene's bright courteous smile.

You take a bunch of young kids in an apartment, away from grownups, Robert Morrison was thinking, *and the first thing you know they're running around with boys, staying out late at night and eating all kinds of crazy stuff in drugstores. But a woman like this—even if she was young enough to speed up a man's reactions—had more sense.* He smiled at her. "I feel better about Barby with you looking after her."

"Believe me, I'll take care of her as well as I can."

Barby, surveying a small bruise at the edge of her sleeve, said nothing.

He said cagily, "I suppose you two go out in the evening, now and then? Both too good-looking to stay at home."

Ilene's eyes met his candidly, "Not very often, I'm afraid. Both of us keep pretty busy. Then too, most of the men you meet in merchandising are married—all of the nice ones are." She made it sound like a compliment to him. "I'm afraid Barby hasn't done much dating since she began work."

"Well, that's all right too. She shouldn't run around nights, wear herself out."

"How right you are."

The waiter set down their drinks. Barby seized hers and took a deep swallow, thinking, *If I can get just a little fuzzy it won't be so bad. Ilene will fix everything.*

She had never trusted anyone before.

She wasn't sure, listening to the give and take between the other two and watching her father melt into acquiescence, what she ate. The empty plate was whisked away and a dessert, sugary and elaborate, set down before her. She dabbed at it with a spoon. Through the gentle warm haze that liquor always induced in her she heard her father—like any other man, being flattered by a woman—telling Ilene in boring detail how he had built up his store, while she listened with parted lips and shining eyes. The question of her going home dropped out of sight somewhere along the way; and while she knew it would come up again, sooner or later, she felt sure that it was settled for this time.

He shook hands with them at the door. "I wish you girls would let me give you a lift back, if you really have to work this afternoon."

Ilene smiled at him. Her face must be tired, Barby thought. "Thank you so much, but I have an errand in the neighborhood."

"What errand?" Barby asked curiously when they were free again, walking arm-in-arm down the street.

"I want to buy you a flower. Not an orchid this time. Something different." A look like a caress passed between them.

Robert Morrison, looking out at the rushing streets as his car sped back to Union Station, was wondering how he had been made to change his mind so deftly. *That damn woman,* he thought, smiling pleasantly at the recollection of her admiring look. There was no question about it, he'd made a hit with her. He would have to come back soon, see how Barby was getting along. Although she'd be all right with a woman like that keeping an eye on her.

I don't suppose she sees many men, he thought. *Too busy making a career. Well, that's all right. I don't want Barby running around with fellows.*

He hummed a little, the nameless tune that indicated he was contented.

Trapped in a web of her own making, drawn to the world she married to escape

Return to Lesbos

by Valerie Taylor

A haunting story of a beautiful and mature woman, trapped in a web of her own making, drawn to the world she had married to escape… and of her quest for emotional tranquility, her struggle with a physical hunger condemned by society even in this free-living and free-loving age.

In this absorbing sequel to her best-selling novel, *Stranger on Lesbos*, novelist Valerie Taylor justifies her position as a fore-most writer of lesbian love. Certainly few can match her dramatic realism and artistic sensitivity when treating this most elusive of all subjects.

Return to Lesbos

She lay awake for a long time after Bill rolled over to his own side of the bed, turned his face to the wall and began to snore. The male smell was on her, the events of the last half hour were clear in her mind, yet it all seemed unreal, like something seen in the movies. She thought, *I really am a whore.* And she didn't care.

At last she got up, too restless to lie still anymore and afraid that her turning would wake Bill. She showered, put on her old terry robe and went downstairs, feeling her way along stair railings and groping for doorknobs in the still-unfamiliar house. Under the bright overhead light of the kitchen she made coffee and sat writing shopping lists while it perked. Things she needed for the house: a sofa, rugs, curtains, a telephone stand. Things she needed for herself: a light jacket, gloves, shampoo. In the morning she would read it all over and decide how much of it made sense; she always felt wide-awake and alert at this hour, but in the light of day her ideas sometimes looked quite different.

She knew, in the back of her mind, why she was doing all this. With a handful of lists she had a valid reason for going downtown in the morning, and while she was there she would visit the bookstore. That was what she had been waiting for all through Friday night, Saturday and Sunday—might as well admit it. She set down her empty cup and looked blindly out of the window.

She was setting out to look for a girl she had seen only once, a girl who had no reason to be interested in her; who might even, if they met again, actively dislike her. No reason she shouldn't.

She put all the lists in her purse and picked her way back to bed. The radium dial of her clock said one-twenty. She lay thinking about Erika's greenish-gray eyes. Did they slant a little or didn't they? Something gave her a slightly exotic look, piquant with that fair hair. She fell asleep trying to make up her mind.

Bill looked a little guilty at breakfast and a little resentful too, like a man who has been accused of something he didn't do but would have liked to. He said, "It's going to be a hot day," and she said, scorning the weather, "I'm going downtown to look at some furniture. All right?"

"Better fix yourself some breakfast then."

"I'm not hungry."

"You don't need to diet. You women are all crazy when it comes to weight."

"That's right."

He looked at her, unsatisfied but finding nothing to argue with.

She put on an old cotton skirt, plain shirt and loafers, office clothes left over from the days when she was Bake's girl—not to be confused with Mrs. William Ollenfield. Pushing the hangers along her closet bar and looking with distaste at her wardrobe, she wondered what had ever possessed her to buy so many clothes she didn't like. Mrs. William Ollenfield seemed to be the sort of woman who goes shopping in a hat and gloves, who wears little printed silks and puts scatter pins on the lapel of a suit. Sooner or later, she would want and get a fur coat. Frances faced herself in the long mirror.

She was no longer certain who she was or what she might hope to become, but she certainly didn't intend to spend the rest of her life pretending to be Mrs. William Ollenfield, that smug little housewife. She didn't even like the way the woman did her hair. She ran a wet comb through the lacquered curls, smacked down the resulting fuzz with a brush dipped in Bill's hair stuff, and caught the subdued ends in a barrette. The plain styling brought out the oval shape of her face and the winged eyebrows, her only beauty. (Not quite the only one, Bake had argued, touching her lightly to remind her.) Now she was beginning to look like herself again.

She ran downstairs, relishing the freedom of bare legs and old shapeless loafers.

It was one of those lazy summer days that seem endless, with sunlight clear and golden over the world and great patches of shade under arching branches. Grass and trees still wore the bright green of early summer. People moved along with open, friendly faces, looking washed and ironed. She climbed aboard a fat yellow bus and handed the driver a dollar, not wanting to admit that she didn't know what the fare was. He gave back eighty-five cents.

She saw now that at some point during the weekend she had ceased to take for granted the continued backing of the Ollenfield income. She felt free and self-reliant. She wasn't sure why, but no doubt she would find out in time.

In front of the bookstore, however, she lost her courage. She stood looking into the display window, which was just as it had been on Friday except for a small ivory madonna where her wooden cat had been. As long as she didn't go in, anything was possible. But if she went in and Vince wasn't there, or if he was cool to her or refused to tell her about Erika—*well,* she reminded herself, *I won't be any worse off than I was this time last week. Back where I started from.*

But she knew she would have lost something important. A hope so new and fragile she dared not examine it.

She turned the knob and went in.

The fair girl was sitting on a folding chair at the back of the room, writing on a clipboard. She looked up as Frances came in, heralded by the little silvery bell. Several expressions crossed her face—recognition, surprise, terror. She stood up, holding the clipboard stiffly at her side. "Vince. Customer."

A voice from somewhere in the back. "Don't forget what I said."

"Vince says that I owe you an apology. I'm sorry I was rude."

"But you weren't rude. You were terribly polite."

"That's what Vince said. There is a rude kind of politeness."

"I know, you use it on people you don't like. But there's no reason you should like me," Frances admitted. "You don't even know me. I have no business going around asking strangers out for drinks—"

"I keep telling her," Vince said, coming in elegantly from a back room, dirty hands held out in front of him, "you either like people or you don't, and why wait for a formal introduction? Personally," he said airily, "I always know the first time I meet somebody, and I hardly ever change my mind. I must say this is an improvement over that terrible dress you had on the other time, though."

Frances was too embarrassed to answer. Vince came to a graceful stop between her and Erika. "It's my day for apologies too," he said nicely. "I didn't get your name and address when you were here, or ask you what kind of books you were interested in. You left your packages, too."

"Frances Ollenfield."

"This is Erika Frohmann. Now you've been introduced. You can be rude to each other if you want to."

He retreated into the back again. There was the sound of running water. Erika Frohmann seemed to be gathering up her courage. "I'm not very good at meeting people," she said, looking not at Frances but at the floor. "And you reminded me of someone too. Not a parent."

"I look like a million other people."

Vince emerged again, drying his hands on a small grimy towel. "Don't be modest, my dear. You have a lovely profile—now you've done away with those dreadful, horrible curls. If I didn't give my customers a little shove they might never get acquainted. They're such a small group I feel they ought to know one another."

Frances said, "I like small groups." Take off your mask, let me see if you know. They wouldn't, of course. Even if they wondered, caution was an hourly habit. She asked, hot-faced, "Is it all right if I look at the books?"

"Sure, go ahead. You can wash your hands when you get through."

Erika Frohmann said defensively, "Paper gets so dirty." She sat down again, but tentatively, propping her clipboard against the edge of a counter and plainly trying to think of something to write. Her apology made and accepted, if only tacitly, the conversation was apparently over as far as she was concerned.

Frances walked slowly to the shelves, conscious of the silent figure behind her. But the fascination of print took over. Bake had long ago introduced her to the second-hand bookstores on Clark Street and Dearborn, a wonderful clutter of junk and treasure, with the three-for-a-dollar bins just outside their doors and tables of old tattered paper-backs just inside. She was still unable to pass a second-hand bookstore.

This place was small, but there was enough to keep her here all day. She walked slowly, picking up volumes as she went along, now and then putting one back, scrupulously, where it had been in the first place.

Here were the Ann Bannon books side-by-side with Jeanette Foster's *Sex Variant Women in Literature*; *North Beach Girl* and *Take Me Home* next to the Covici-Friede edition of *The Well of Loneliness*, dated 1928. Here, huddled together as though for warmth in an unfriendly world, were Gore Vidal and a tall thin volume of Baudelaire, translated by someone she had never heard of. Here were books in the field, for people with a special interest, a special orientation.

Her voice came out shrill with self-consciousness. "Are these for sale?"

Vince came to see what she was talking about. "That depends. Why do you want them?"

Now. Tell him. But she could only say, "I've read most of them, but there are some I don't know."

He looked at her. The right answer evidently showed on her face; he nodded. "I'll ask Erika. A lot of them belong to her. She may want them back."

Erika stood up, soundless in flat canvas shoes. He said, indicating Frances with his thumb, "Can she have your books?"

"What for?"

"I thought you wanted to get rid of them. That was the general idea of bringing them here, wasn't it?"

"But not to just anybody."

Frances waited. The books are here to be sold, she thought, this is a bookstore. Why are they on display if they're not for sale? But she said nothing. Something more was involved—this was a matter with deep emotional implications, and anything she said was likely to be wrong. It was the boy, Vince, who said with an impatient edge to his voice, "You can have them back if you've changed your mind. Go on, take them home with you."

Erika's face was hard and cold. She looked at Frances. "Let her take them if she wants. But not for money."

"Look, we went through this with the insurance money."

"It's the same thing."

Vince said to Frances, "It's not just curiosity, is it? You won't pass them around for your friends to laugh at?"

Frances said steadily, daring everything now, "If I had any friends here, they'd be interested for different reasons."

Vince smiled. "OK, they're yours. No charge. Get them out of Erika's way. She likes to come here and brood."

Erika put the clipboard down on the counter, carefully, as though it might shatter. She walked soundlessly out of the store. The chimes over the door jingled. A streak of sunlight flashed across the floor and was gone.

Vince took the half dozen assorted books Frances was holding, since she seemed unable to put them down. "Don't look that way. I wasn't trying to hurt your feelings."

"It's her feelings."

"Her best friend was killed. I told you." The graceful shrug was as much a part of him as his clear brown eyes. "Girls are so sentimental. You have to go on living, and sooner or later you find someone else. It's a little soon for her, that's all."

Frances said in a whisper, "I like her."

"Sure. She's had a bad time. She's an Austrian, she was in a concentration camp when she was eleven, twelve-years-old, I don't know exactly. Her whole family was murdered. I think it took all the courage she had to really love anyone—I think Kate was the only person she ever gave a damn about. If Kate had lived they would have stayed together forever like an old married couple. She's a monogamous type," Vince said, apparently not considering monogamy much of a virtue.

Frances opened one of the paperbacks to hide her confusion. The name, Kate Wood, was written strongly across the top of the title page in black ink. She said, "Some people would have kept these, and grieved over them."

"Erika's very strong. It would be better if she yelled and fainted," Vince said sadly. "I love her. Not in an erotic way, of course."

Frances said, "I think I could love her, period."

"You're gay."

"Yes."

"Doing anything about it?"

"Not right now."

"You should never admit you're gay," Vince said quietly, "people have such fantastic ideas. You have to wear a disguise most of the time—if somebody finds out!" He drew a forger across his throat. "It's worse for us, though."

"I believe you."

He lifted graceful shoulders. "So keep the books. Erika won't take money for them. It's a superstition, like the women who won't cash their children's insurance policies. We went through that, too. Kate had a group policy where she worked, made out to Erika as the beneficiary. Erika paid the funeral expenses out of it and gave the rest away. She's terribly hard up, she never has any money, but that's what she wanted to do."

"I can see how she felt."

"Yeah, but couldn't she see that Kate wanted to leave her provided for? She hasn't got a nickel saved. What happens if she gets sick and can't work?"

I'd take care of her, Frances thought, warming. *I'd work my hands off to take care of her.*

"She gave away all Kate's clothes and all the furniture and stuff they had and moved into a furnished room. I don't know what it's like, I've never been there. As far as I know nobody has. I've got a key, she gave it to me when she got out of the hospital—she was afraid of dying in her sleep," Vince said matter-of-factly. "She was supposed to call me up every day, and if she missed a day I was supposed to check. But she never missed. You don't just walk in on Erika."

Frances wondered if it were a warning. She said, "I'll take care of the books. Maybe she'll want them back some time."

"I don't know why she didn't keep them."

Frances knew. Books have a life of their own. She felt warm and tender, as though she were melting with compassion. She said with some difficulty, "Tell her I took them, will you? And tell her—"

"With some things, you have to do your own telling."

"Yes. Of course. Can I take some of these now and come back for the rest?"

"Any time, sure. Wash your hands before you go." Out in the street, she looked around with some surprise. For a while she had forgotten where she was—and who she was supposed to be. Maybe, she thought, I can start being myself again. She stood uncertainly in the middle of the sidewalk, holding the heavy package Vince had tied for her: ten, and she could pick up the rest a few at a time. She had a good reason to go back.

Furniture, she thought dimly, finding her crumpled lists as she hunted for tissues in her handbag. She didn't want to shop. She wanted to go somewhere and think about Erika Frohmann. She wanted to talk to Kay, who was in Iran by this time and out of her reach since there are some things you can't say in letters.

Vaguely, with nothing better to do, she made her way to Shapiro's and roamed through the furniture department on the top floor, looking at things without seeing them, until her package became too heavy.

What difference did it make how she furnished the house? It wasn't her house, never would be. She wasn't going to stay in it. But she realized that she would have to account for the day to Bill.

She had forgotten Bill, too. For a couple of hours he had stopped existing.

She stood in front of a French Provincial chest, looking beyond it, holding her packet of books as though it were a child.

In the days when Frances was still Frankie Kirby, the pindling half-fed child of a soft-coal miner, the district school was the heart of her small world, not the company house where her ailing mother dragged from washtub to dishpan to cookstove, or the mine where her father disappeared every morning, to emerge grimed and sullen at night. For Frances Ollenfield, married to a young man more and more absorbed in business, it lay inside the covers of books—a vicarious life that ranged from Jane Austen to Kerouac. And later, everything important was concentrated in the apartment where she and Bake had so much happiness—and then, at the end, so much bitterness.

Now she had no center, and she was incomplete and fragmented. More and more, as the days passed, she found herself thinking about Erika Frohmann. The girl was becoming an obsession, the focal point in a life that had grown increasingly meaningless. She longed to take Erika in her arms and comfort her for all the evil which life had brought her. Her arms ached, her breasts ached for the pressure of Erika's body.

To a bystander, the life of Mrs. William Ollenfield at this time was centered in the big square layer-cake house on Regent Street. She threw herself into the furnishing and decorating of the rooms, drowning her needs in work. She bought a table and sofa, three chairs, rugs and curtains and numerous small things for the living room, ending with something that looked like an illustration from *Home Beautiful*. It wasn't a decor that encouraged blue jeans and bare feet—but of course Mrs. William Ollenfield wore shoes even when she was alone in the house.

She even talked to Bill about fixing up the basement for parties, a step that seemed to have special meaning for him—a status symbol, she thought scornfully, like the backyard barbecue and the car with tail fins. A place to give parties. That she disliked parties didn't make any difference, people gave them anyway, and probably the guests disliked them too. But one had to go.

She fitted up one of the bedrooms as a guest room, with light functional furniture and flowered curtains; the effect pleased her. It occurred to her that she would like to move into it herself, away from Bill's nightly tossings and his twice-a-week fumbling and the male smell of him. It would be a place where she could sleep deeply, not intruded upon, not violated. But if she left Bill's bed she would have to leave his house as well, and she wasn't ready for that decisive step. Not just yet.

She didn't know where the idea of leaving had come from. It seemed to spring up in her mind from some long-dormant root, putting out leaves and blossoms at an astonishing rate. She waited to see what the fruit might be.

In the meanwhile, to pass the time and keep herself from becoming tense with wondering, she went on buying things and putting them in place, creating an effect of comfort not like a housewife building her own nest, but like the manager of a hotel, paid to do what she did. She felt no involvement. She would never live here, or not long enough to make any difference. It was no home of hers.

She thought about it, soaking in the bathtub an hour before the Wives were due for cards and coffee. It was the feeling that goes with working out two weeks' notice on a job, already emotionally separated and impatient to leave. Between two worlds and accountable to neither. In this frame of mind she had called up the Wives, putting an end to Bill's nagging; she faced their arrival calmly because they were not and never would be a part of her life. It cost nothing to be polite to them.

She dressed for the Wives with great care, put on a dress with flowers on it, did her hair the way Bill liked it. Going downstairs, she felt a flash of proud pleasure. The house was spotless. She had made a date torte, more impressive than a layer cake and really no more difficult. She was safe.

The night before she had lain awake sick to her stomach with fright, hoping she might be coming down with something spotty and contagious so she could call off the party. But when the doorbell rang, she went calmly to let the first two in, the freckled redhead and a small blonde who kept throwing bits of babytalk French into the conversation. They were laughing, but in a nice way, a social way. The redhead said, "I adore the way you've fixed this place up. I want to do my living room over but Joe keeps saying not this year—"

It was easy. She was one of them, for the time being. If you were married to an executive and had your hair done professionally and never, never said anything you really thought, you were in. For what it was worth. I can be charming as all hell when I want to, she thought, hiding a giggle.

Four hours later, standing at the front door to let them out, she wondered why she had worried. It had been easy—knowing that it wasn't going to last, it had even been fun. Things are only difficult when you care, she thought, pleased. She could play it cool with these pleasant women because she wasn't going to be doing it forever. She was going to get out.

The conviction lingered in the days that followed, even though events seemed to stand still. July deepened into hotter sunshine and richer growth, the grass in the back yard darkened and thickened, the humming of insects filled the late afternoons. Frances discovered a simple pleasure she had forgotten since the first years of her marriage: sitting outdoors alone after nightfall, breathing the cool grassy fragrance that follows a hot humid day. Bill was often out, as he had been on the other job; his busyness gave her a chance to breathe. She took an old leather cushion out on the grass and sat relaxed, idle yet aware, breathing in the summer nights.

The old couple next door sat on their front porch, in a plastic glider with creaking joints. When they went in she usually sat for a while relishing her aloneness, looking at the moon and the little drifting clouds and listening to the tree branches making the same gentle sighing they had made in Shakespeare's England. "On such a night as this," she thought, standing up, cushion in hand, as the next-door television came to life. No soft summer evening would keep the old people from going in to listen to Floyd Dalber's newscast on channel five, after which they would go placidly to bed.

It didn't seem to her that the news could be regarded as soporific, but at least it made a break in the day. She usually drank a last cup of coffee and went to bed around half past ten because there was nothing else to do.

Going to bed didn't necessarily mean going to sleep, however. Bill had installed a window air conditioner in the bedroom; next year, if he took over the house, he would have the whole place air-conditioned, sealed away from the living, breathing outdoors. The unit made a hypnotic whirring whisper that sent her into a half-drowse for an hour or so. Then she was awake, sweating with tension in the artificial coolness, and lonely to desolation.

Bake, she thought, turning and moving on the bed as though her hungry body might touch another in its need. But Bake was part of a past that was irretrievably gone. She didn't want to think about Bake in terms of the present, driving swiftly with Jane beside her in the car, waking on Sunday mornings to hear Jane moving around quietly in the kitchen, or—Frances drew a sharp breath—peeling off her shirt and slacks in the white moonlight that flowed through the bedroom window, while Jane lay in bed watching her with wide eyes and a waiting smile. That hurt.

It was better to think about the future. At least, it would have been better if she could have foreseen any future. There was no predictable end to the hunger for love that tore her in pieces, these hot summer nights.

In the daytime she was hungry for two things: something to do that had meaning, someone who offered companionship. At night she was kept awake by a craving that only one thing would satisfy. There were things she could do for herself, but which filled no real need, which only eased the physical tensions for a while. She scorned them as childish. *I need someone to love,* she thought in misery.

It was worse when Bill felt amorous. After he fell asleep she got up and bathed, brushed her teeth and shampooed her hair as though hot water could dissolve his touch. She didn't hate him; sitting on the edge of the tub, rubbing her head with a thick towel, she wondered why that realization made her feel worse instead of better. *Hell, I don't even dislike him. He's a nice guy. I wouldn't mind being his secretary; he'd be a nice boss, kind about days off and small raises. I just don't want him to touch me. I don't want any man to touch me.*

That's what marriage is, though. It makes an obligation out of a free gift. *I want—*

I want a lot of things, she concluded, pulling a fresh nightgown over her head. (Bill liked her in nightgowns, preferably sheer nylon ones with lace. Left to herself she slept in cotton pajamas. Bake had wanted her naked.) *A lot of things I'm not going to get in a hurry.*

She smoothed the sheets and got decorously back into bed, lying well away from Bill and pulling her gown down as far as she could. Bill was sleeping out loud, his mouth open a little. The top sheet was pushed down around his legs, and the chest and groin hairs were beaded with sweat. She felt repulsed and pitying at the same time. A nice guy, as far as he knew how to be. He had taken her back and been kind to her—as far as he knew how to be. He even wanted to buy her a fur coat, she reminded herself, closing her eyes and composing her face for sleep, although she knew she wasn't going to get any sleep for the next few hours.

The problem was that she didn't want a fur coat, or a new sofa and wall-to-wall broadloom, or even (smothering a nervous snicker) the pure love of a good man. No, nor fifteen minutes of his valuable attention twice a week. She wanted someone to love. It wouldn't be a man, no matter how kind and generous he was. To make love with a man seemed to her a kind of perversion.

Bill stirred in his sleep. She lay still on the front edge of the bed, watching the shadows move along the wall as late cars rolled down the street.

It was almost morning when she fell into an uneasy half-sleep broken by street sounds and the heat of Bill's body so close to hers. She dreamed of Erika.

The alarm clock woke her, not tired now but strangely rested and clear in her mind. It was a fine, hot, sunny day. She got up and stood, looking out of the bedroom window, hearing Bill thumping around in the bathroom; he was the kind of man who jumps out of bed at the first buzz and goes into high gear immediately. The old man next door was already out, placing the sprinkler so his flowers would get the good of the water before the sun was high. He looked busy and contented. She beamed at him from behind her curtain.

She was going to find Erika Frohmann.

She didn't know what would happen after that, but anything would be better than these long nights full of needing.

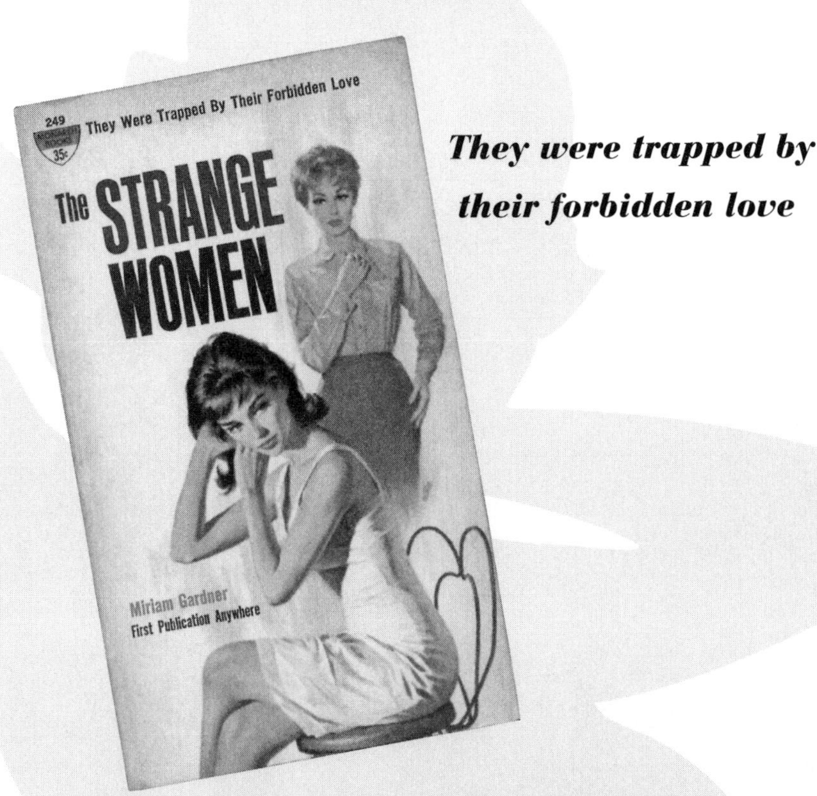

They were trapped by their forbidden love

The Strange Women

by Miriam Gardner

"I'm not that sort of freak!"

Precise and scientific...Nora was still a woman—passionate and longing to love and be loved.

She thought of Kit, her husband...and felt a pang of remorse and pain. Yet, here was Jill, a tempting child-woman whose elfin beauty and sexuality were luring Nora away from her husband. And to complicate things further, there was Mack...who was Nora's stepbrother and Jill's lover.

These four people caught in their own private purgatory, struggled against overwhelming odds in their frenzied search for emotional happiness.

The Strange Women

Nora had been kept all morning by one crisis after another, and by the time she got downstairs, dinner had long been cleared away in the staff dining room. As she carried a tray between rows of empty tables, she saw Vic Demorino, still in the glareless green jacket of the operating room.

"Hello, Vic. I didn't know you were in."

He did not rise, only nodded tiredly as she set her tray down. "I'm having a run like a bank in a market crash. The drugstores must be clean out of castor oil. Every unprintable pregnant female in Albany, Troy and Schenectady must have decided to give birth. The astrology magazines must have told them it's a lucky day. Do you know how many little squallers I've delivered since two A.M.? Go on, make a guess!"

"Three?"

"Oh, hell, girl, I delivered three before I got breakfast, including one classic breech. Seven's the score so far, and another coming on. Sister Gabrielle was parking them in the elevator. The fifth and sixth came on almost simultaneously, and DiLuccio was having a bad time, so Quentin took over the sixth for me, and by the time I got through, and went to check on the little details, Mrs. Reski was out of the ether already and giving me blue flaming hell. No young snip of a girl doctor was going to learn how—get that, learn how, and Barbara Quentin's been on maternity for three years—on *her!* And the Reski female could have dropped her kid in a potato patch."

Nora found herself laughing. "Poor Barbara. But we are used to that. You *do* look beat."

"The original beatnik. Can I cadge a cigarette?" He indicated his pocketless operating trousers. "I've got another gal working upstairs, but she's a primapara and thank God, she won't need me for a couple of hours." He took a deep pull at the cigarette. "You have it soft. Your patients make appointments *before* they hit the hospital."

This was a ritual and she made the expected answer. "You have nine months to get ready for yours."

"I'm going to grab a nap in the doctor's lounge. Will you tell Ramona to cancel my appointments, and you see anyone who looks like an emergency?"

"Sure."

"I ought to be finished with the population explosion by four. Dinner?"

"We had that all out last fall, Vic," she said, smiling.

"I don't take no for an answer that easy. You're eating dinner with me now. Does it make that much difference if I'm wearing a tie and picking up the check?"

"Not if it stopped there. It wouldn't, Vic."

"Damn right." He reached for her hand. "We went good together, didn't we?"

"Very. That was a long time ago, though."

"We still could, Nora."

She said it carefully, for this man was a friend she valued. "You're forgetting, Vic. Things have changed. I'm married."

"Don't you forget it yourself?"

"I'd rather not discuss that. Do you mind?"

"Yes, I do. Pity is a damnably poor foundation for faithfulness in marriage," he said. She sat very straight, the Spartan who has had and must conceal his death-wound. He put his elbows on the table, not smiling.

"Truth hurts, doesn't it? So you're married. What good has it done you? This year has taken it out of you, you know. You look like hell. You're a woman, and you need loving—as who should know better than I?"

"That's a caddish thing to say," said Nora, coloring.

"So I'm a cad. I'm also a doctor, and a friend. The life you're living simply isn't normal."

Nora slammed the table impatiently, shoving back her chair. "Christ! If I can't even eat dinner in peace—"

Vic caught her wrist. "Sit still. See?" he said, without heat, "you can't live this way, your nerves won't take it."

Why should I be angry with Vic, she wondered. *He's only saying what I've been thinking*. But she was angry.

"What is this, Vic? Offering to sleep with me as a favor to a nervous wreck? Dr. Demorino's old reliable prescription for frazzled females? Vic, if I were a man I'd smash your teeth down your throat."

He chortled. "If you were a man and I made you that kind of proposition, I'd expect you to!"

Her anger dissolved and she laughed. "Thanks, Vic. But—no thanks."

"Now look. Suppose the shoe were on the other foot. Suppose you were in the hospital a year, and your husband going through all that—"

"It's not the same and you know it. For God's sake, you make me feel as if I were going around like a bitch in heat!"

"Oh, come—" but the drone of the paging system cut him off. "Sister Amy, wanted in Ward Fi-yuv. Doc-tor De-morino, wan-ted in Delivery Room. Sis-ter Amy—"

He scowled, dumping his cigarette. "Well, here we go again. I'd hoped Pizzetti would take another hour—"

"Let Quentin handle it. That's what she's for."

Vic shook his head wearily. "Can't. I don't think the Pizzetti kid speaks more than twenty words of English, and it's her first baby. I kind of promised I'd show up and hold her hand." He put his own hand momentarily on Nora's shoulder. "See you later, girl."

She sat watching him, poking idly at her congealed lunch. For the first time she was brought smash against a new fact; after sixteen years of total freedom, the habits and attitudes of a married woman are not acquired overnight.

She could still feel, like a speck of heat, Vic's firm hand on her shoulder; it brought back, with a physical vividness that made her gasp, the memory of his hot mouth; the feel of his thick-set hairy body against hers. She cursed, humiliated, under her breath, but the memory went on; an inexorable playback on some mental recorder whose cutoff switch was out of order. That first, perfect time in her apartment, in broad daylight....

She had come to Albany four years ago, at the end of her residency in a large Chicago hospital. Vic sent all his patients to St. Margaret's; he and Nora ran across each other frequently. It seemed natural to date him—the snatched, time-pressed casual dates of overworked people who can't call their lives their own; coffee in the lounge, spaghetti in an Italian restaurant owned by an uncle of Vic's, who gave them special food and wine and a flow of talk not too subtly aimed at urging Vic to settle down. But he was still a colleague, a casual friend.

Things had changed suddenly. One cool spring day he had suggested a game of tennis and driven her to the park. Nora, who had only changed her shoes for canvas-soled sneakers, was startled to see him in shorts and an armless singlet. Dressed, he simply looked thick-set; stripped, he was strong and smoothly tanned, with the muscles of an acrobat, legs like shafts of bronze covered with fine, soft reddish down.

Nora, on her mettle with his first serve, played her best, but his every move had an almost professional grace. When he had won two sets out of three, she took him back to the apartment for a drink—already half knowing what would happen. Dressed again in slacks and shirt, he looked like the man she knew—grave and stern, with kind eyes and good hands—but behind the mask Nora still saw the muscular athlete's body, the boyish grace with which he ran and dodged across the court.

Confused under his eyes, she put up her hands to her still-disheveled hair; but Vic moved swiftly to her side, put down his glass and held out his arms. His arms were crushingly strong and his mouth vigorous. Then he held her at arm's length, and she heard his roughened breathing.

"Girl, all day long I watch women taking their clothes on and off, and it doesn't do a damn thing to me. You take down your hair—" he pulled out a pin, sending the copper weight of it tumbling—"and unbutton your blouse button, and I could knock you over the head and rape you."

She leaned forward deliberately and kissed him. She said clearly, "Don't bother knocking me over the head."

The sun in the bedroom came in bright and clear green through the leaves outside the window. Vic stood in the sunlight, unaffectedly flexing his arms as he cast aside his clothes. He was unashamed of his strong bronzed nakedness, vigorous and virile; his hot eyes made her a little shy, and when she hesitated, he sprang at her, laughing, pretending a Tarzan growl, and she felt her brief panties tear away; she laughed breathlessly and sank under his weight. Though she was taller than he, she felt fragile in his muscular arms.

It was as wholesome as sunlight—that fierce mating in the glow of day, Vic's hearty strength bearing down on her until she gasped and cried out with the delight of it; then stronger and stronger, the rhythm of elemental need beating up in them both, until a toppling crest of violence swept away all awareness of time or place, daylight or dark. She heard herself cry out without shame or reserve.

Afterward, lying cool and relaxed in the strong circle of his arms, she had felt the rough touch of his mouth and heard him say softly, "So there's a hell of a lot of woman going to waste under that marble front. I thought so. We won't let it go to waste—will we, girl?"

They hadn't. Nora knew now—sitting in the deserted hospital cafeteria—that if things had gone on much longer, she and Vic would have drifted into marriage; not love—it never entered her mind, to connect romantic passion with Vic Demorino—but still, a good marriage, born of shared work, compatible interests, and the high flare of intense sexual attraction.

And then a thin, insolent man on crutches, with the flaming eyes of a caged falcon, had crossed words like swords; she had seen Vic, briefly, at his dictatorial worst, and Kit's high-tension-wire of veiled sensuality had made Vic's hearty lust seem schoolboyish. Vic had not taken her marriage seriously at first, then had been outraged, almost pitying. She had not tried to make him understand....

She realized, with a start, that she was due at her office in ten minutes. She could just about make it.

She sent Ramona home when the last patient had gone, but lingered herself; and she did not pretend surprise when Vic came in.

"Still here, Nora?"

"Come in, Vic. I saw Mrs. Kerraday for you. She's convinced she's going to have twins or a two-headed freak, and wants an X-ray."

"Anyone who says twins to me for at least six weeks gets murdered," he groaned. "Kerraday, Kerraday—let me think—oh, *her*. If she's pregnant with twins, they only have one heart between 'em."

He sank wearily in the padded chair. "I could go to sleep right here. They wheeled another one upstairs just as I finished up with Pizzetti—emergency Caesarean. Premature twins. Two pounds, odd, apiece. I thought we'd lose one of them, but they're still breathing." He chuckled, his eyes blinking open. "Hey, you know what? That leaves me with no patient expecting to deliver for—" he considered briefly, then rapped his knuckles on the wooden desk-top, "two weeks. Give me a lift home, Nora? My car's in the shop."

He settled into the car cushions a few minutes later. "God, I *am* tired. Consider the invitation this afternoon withdrawn. I need *sleep*—and alone, thanks. Kinsey or somebody ought to write a report on the sex life of the overworked obstetrician."

She laughed. "Do you really think it would even fill up a pamphlet?"

She braked at his apartment house, and he turned before getting out. "Want a drink or something?" he asked suggestively.

Nora hesitated, knowing she walked along a knife-edge which would alter her future. But before she managed to speak he reached for his bag.

"Not on an empty stomach, huh? You might lose control and rape me, and I'm too tired to fight you off. OK, Nora." He gave her shoulder a quick pat as he got out. "You won't have any more trouble from this quarter. I hope Ellersen deserves what he's getting. If he doesn't, damn it, he'll have a fist fight on his hands." He went quickly up the steps without looking back, and Nora was not sure whether she looked after him with relief—or regret.

Her own apartment was dark and empty and a little too hot. Nora said "Jill?" switched on the light and went, startled, from room to room. The cat mewed in the kitchen, and Nora went and picked him up.

Oh come, she told herself, this is ridiculous, *Jill doesn't have to tell you when she's going out.*

She lighted the oven, made a salad, carefully laid a single place; but though she was hungry after her sketchy lunch, she found she had no appetite.

Careless for once of the polished and waxed floor, she handed a generous morsel of ham down to Archy, watching him bat it back and forth with languid grace.

"Are you frustrated, Archy? Do you wish you could go out tom-catting in alleys?" she asked aloud. *You old maid. Talking to a cat.*

The silence was oppressive, and she found herself turning over in her mind words that had to be said between herself and Jill.

Jill, about the other night...

Jill, we were both upset, I acted like an idiot...

Jill, you know perfectly well I'm no lesbian...

The word had finally escaped her. *Lesbian.* Was Pammy's father right after all? Am I the sort of person who goes around corrupting little girls?

The hall door banged; Jill came through to the kitchen, wind-flushed, arms full of packages. "Is there some coffee left? Oh, good." She got herself a cup.

"Why didn't you have supper before you left, Jill? Everything was all ready. Next time I'm late, do have a proper meal, I might be out all night."

"I wasn't hungry." Jill paused, cup in mid-air. "And if you tell me I'm eating for two, I'll throw my cup at you."

Later in the bedroom she watched Jill unwrap her packages. "I thought you didn't wear brassieres," she said idly.

"I don't, but now I think I should."

"What's this? Lace panties?"

Jill spread them on the bed. "Sinful britches."

"Wha-at?"

"Family joke. One Christmas—I was about fifteen—Pam gave me a set of black lace underwear, very flimsy and naughty-looking. Mama said it was in very poor taste for young girls, but I think Pam meant it as a joke. She was always like that. *You* know."

Nora positively had to remind herself that Jill could not read her mind.

"Great-Aunt Harriet was shocked. Not just disapproving like Mama, but—oh, horrified, as if—as if—"

"As if she expected you to do a Gypsy Rose Lee in them?"

"I guess. Jackie asked why it was indecent if nobody ever saw it. After all, nobody sees your underwear, and Jackie said black lace was just the same as flannel bloomers." Jill giggled again, mimicking a thin, rasping old voice. "A nice young girl who wears fantastical underclothing is always looking for an excuse to display it. Unbecoming undergarments are the surest guarantee of modesty."

"Oh, no, Jill!"

"Oh, yes, Nor! So every time I wore them, Pammy asked if I could be good in my sinful britches."

"Jill, where is Pammy living now?"

Jill dropped the "sinful britches," startled. "Why, Nora, Pammy's dead. Didn't you know?"

"Oh, no, Jill, I never heard anything. What—how—"

"She died in childbirth. She married Ken Rainsbury and she lost the baby and she died."

"No, I never knew. I'm so sorry!" She had thought of Pamela living and warm, surrounded by hearty children. It had seemed necessary to think of her that way. She was too shocked and distressed to speak.

After her bath, toweling her spare body, she found herself thinking again, with muted grief and tenderness, of Pammy. Her father had feared a lesbian might corrupt his daughter. Yet it was normal married life that had destroyed Pam—

That is absolutely the most neurotic...if a patient said that, I'd tell her to run, not walk, to a psychiatrist!

Jill was buffing her nails before the mirror. She said, without looking up, "Nora, I—I wrote Mack today and told him about the baby."

"Good," Nora said affirmatively, and realizing this meant surrender, she did not dwell on the point.

"The baby ought to be born early in August. Will you—make an appointment with Dr. Demorino for me?"

"Oh, Jill, of course!" Nora held out her arms and they hugged each other.

"Nora, I—last night I behaved like a spoiled brat."

Nora was breathless at the complete capitulation in this. They clung together; Jill smiled up at her shakily.

"How long will it be before I start to—to get big?"

"Oh, there won't be much gross change before March. Maybe April. Let me see—" she put her hands around the slender waist. Her heart was pounding. Then, without word, she unfastened the robe at the throat and slipped her hand into the neck of Jill's nightgown, cradling the small breast in her hand. It felt very warm.

Jill laughed nervously. "See? I do need a brassiere now, don't I?" Suddenly she flung her arms around Nora again, with such violence that Nora fell back on the bed. Nora pulled Jill down to her.

"Jill—Jill, I've been hateful, for weeks I've been pretending—"

Jill stopped the murmured words by kissing her. They lay close together for minutes, holding each other; then Jill, her hands shaking, untied the belt of Nora's robe and flung it toward the foot of the bed.

Nora had not moved. Jill came back to her mouth, and their lips fastened and fused together. Her hands, small and soft and gentle, moved caressingly down Nora's shoulders. Nora heard herself gasp aloud with an almost painful delight, as Jill shyly repeated her own gesture, cupping her hand around Nora's breast. She caught Jill close, pulling the girl down heavily across her, feeling the sudden, sweet, savage ache all through her body.

Their feet were still tangled in Nora's robe. Nora said in a roughened voice, "Wait, darling," and reached to snap out the light. With her other hand she swept down and pulled away the tangled clothes, flinging them off on the floor. Then with impatient fingers she jerked off the coat of her pajamas and threw it after them.

The room was flooded with the pale, lustrous light of the moonlight outside, reflected from snow. Nora heard Jill make a strange little sound, halfway between a sigh and a sob. Then Jill's bare arms closed around her, and the ache and tension of anticipation suddenly melted and flowed. She went limp all over with the anguish and delight of surrender.

Her hands, instinctively seeking softnesses, seemed to have a life of their own. She pressed Jill's head to her breast, feeling the soft lips close over the hardening nipple with strangely pleasant pain. And then she lost track of separate sensations, conscious only of softness, of sweetness, of wave after wave of spreading small shivers that carried her along on their crest.

Through it all she was conscious of immense surprise, of growing tenderness like a counterbass chord pattern to the singing in her nerves. As the diffuse patterns swept to their summit, she heard her own cry, hardly more than a whisper, like a final, explosive cadence; then silence.

It was a long time before either of them moved again. At last Nora turned and reached across Jill for a cigarette. She lay on her back, smoking, the confusion of thought and feeling slowly clearing. But the tenderness, and the surprise remained.

She had always clung, down deep, to a half-formed notion that no woman could possibly give another woman genuine sexual satisfaction. In spite of Kinsey, she had believed the alleged pleasure felt by homosexuals to be a childish delight in kisses, a schoolgirlish shivering because they had never known real sex. But this had been real enough. She felt almost amused at the collapse of the illusion, but also troubled, and humiliated.

Jill was laying face down, her nightgown crumpled beneath her. Nora put out her cigarette and bent to kiss the bare shoulder.

"Aren't you cold, darling?" She pulled up the blanket; then, trembling, circled the narrow waist with her hands. "Jill, what on earth have we been doing?"

"I don't know, but whatever it is, I'm in favor of it. Why aren't men—" she hid her face against Nora's bare breast, "why aren't men this—comfy?"

Nora was glad the girl could not see her burning face. "Men aren't especially emotional, I guess. Or if they are, it doesn't express itself physically. In short, my darling—" she broke off, then went on steadily, "men have an unconquerable itch to get it inside, and when they've done that, whatever their good intentions, that's that. Erotic play is something we decadent females invented because we didn't like being dragged by the hair to the cave."

She was betraying herself, she knew—betraying men she had known who were gentler, more emotional than she was herself. But she went on, using the words as whips to lash herself: "So I fail to see why it should be socially or morally taboo for women to enjoy it together; since men neither need nor want it."

There was a short, stricken silence. Jill lay so still Nora could hardly hear her breathing. Nora said, "And speaking of social and moral taboo, pet, one of us had better go and finish the night in that other bed. Or at least muss it up a little."

Jill put up her face to be kissed. "Nora. Are you—*ashamed* of this? Listen, this was my fault, don't think I don't realize—"

"I wasn't blaming—"

"If you're ashamed, or anything, I'll never forgive myself. I thought we both wanted it."

"I did," Nora said very quietly. "Surely you could tell. The clock ticked in the silence and a little ruffle of wind flung a branch against the window. "Jill, may I ask you—a terribly personal question?"

"Ask me anything you want to."

But with this license Nora could not frame her question. She had been thinking of Pammy; but at last she asked, "Were you and Mack—physically compatible?"

"If you mean did I enjoy going to bed with him, the answer is yes, doctor. At least after the first couple of times." Jill sat up abruptly, pulling the fallen robe around her bare shoulders.

"Where are you going?"

"Back to my own bed" she snapped haughtily, "can't forget all the social and moral taboos, can we?"

Ill at ease, Nora switched on the light. Tears were raining down Jill's cheeks, and the thin arms were shaking as she fumbled with the buttons.

Nora went after Jill, picked her up like a child and carried her back to bed. She climbed in beside her and took the girl in her arms, kissing the wet eyes and the little feathers of hair at the temples.

The only thing that mattered in the world was to banish the shadows from those wet gray eyes.

Nora sat in her office, thinking vaguely about the patient she had just seen, then discarding the thought, deliberately, until the next day.

She had a curiously compartmented mind. A doctor cannot afford to be preoccupied with personal problems; and only by this rigid division of her life had she managed to keep the disaster of her first marriage, and now the tension of her second, from affecting her work.

She had managed likewise to keep her feelings for Jill in an air-tight, light-proof portion of her mind. But in these transitory moments, crossing the bridge that separated doctor from woman, she found herself surveying both with sharp perspective.

She had dismissed Pammy as childish nonsense. She had expected to dismiss this business with Jill as loneliness and sexual starvation. She had expected to say to herself; *well, now you know*. Most women were curious about lesbian practices, and, whether they would admit it or not, wanted to experiment. Jill had taken her off her guard, at a low point of physical need.

She knew the clinical phrases. Frustration. Substitute satisfaction. Mutual masturbation. The sort of thing that flares up on board ship or in girls' schools. A *faute de mieux*.

But she found she could not dismiss it so easily. Next morning, looking into Jill's flushed face, she had smiled and kissed her reassuringly; and that night when Jill held out her arms, she had gone to them as if compelled.

Wearily, Nora laid her face on the desk, almost grateful for the consultation that had held her here—away from Kit—this afternoon.

Ramona came to the office door, and Nora looked up at her with newly perceptive eyes. "Are we through?"

"Just about—no, someone's on the stairs."

Nora went to the hall door and looked out, then smiled; it was Jill, her small white cap jaunty on her curls.

"Am I butting in, Nora?"

"No, I'm through for the day." There was a smudge on Jill's bright face and her curls were badly in need of a comb, and Nora felt an unruly lift in her voice as she said, "Let's hurry up and get out of here before somebody comes along. Ramona, can we give you a lift home? We might be able to catch Margaret at the library—I've been wanting Jill to meet her." She added, to Jill, "It's time you met a few of my friends."

As they pulled up before the library, they saw a tall, slender girl coming down the steps. "Success. We did catch her," said Nora.

The girl saw them, waved, and came hurrying toward the car. She was tall, with a wide and flexible mouth and pale-green eyes behind thick glasses. Light hair, carelessly brushed, swung loose around her coat collar, and her hands, large and heavy-knuckled, had the librarian's occupational grime embedded in the knuckles; yet the effect was not shabbiness but careless grace. She got in beside Ramona.

"This is Jill," Nora said, "she's living with me now. Jill, Margaret Sheppard."

"It's nice to know you." Margaret's voice was huskily sweet. She leaned forward as Nora started the car; "Jill—have you any name besides Jill?"

Nora said quickly, not giving Jill the chance, "She's Mrs. Roger MacLellan, my—stepbrother's wife. Mack's in Peru now with an archaeological expedition." She brought the car to a stop before an enormous frowsy house which had once been a mansion. Now it bore the painted sign LENOX APARTMENTS.

Ramona got out and stood on the sidewalk. "Blossom and Melinda have had their kittens, Nora," she said. In the office it was always, correctly, Dr. Caine. "Won't you come up and have a peek?"

Nora looked questioningly at Jill.

"Love to."

The apartment was up two flights of stairs that smelled of floor-sweep and, faintly, of mice; but the rooms were freshly painted and tastefully furnished. On the sofa a package of laundry was spilling blouses and pressed white uniforms from torn brown paper. Margaret frowned and began to gather it up.

Ramona opened a door leading to a glassed-in porch, empty except for a narrow single bed covered with a faded blanket. Two cats were curled on the blanket; Ramona bent over them scooping up a kitten in each hand. The cats purred, but did not protest. Ramona turned, dangling the kittens between loosely competent fingers. She was rather like a kitten herself with her triangular face and furry eyebrows.

"We'll make money on this batch. They have perfect points. But then, we've never had one left on our hands."

Margaret, hunched over to look into a mirror too low for her, was running a comb through her untidy hair. "No—only in our clean laundry and all over the beds," she said dryly, pointing with her comb at the burst package.

"May I hold one?" Jill asked. Ramona put a kitten into her outstretched palm and Jill snuggled the fragile, fluff-coated bones against her sweater. Margaret took Nora's hat and gloves. "Let me put these up. Nothing's really safe with the cats around."

Ramona was fiddling with a record player. Dance music, smooth and bright, filled the room.

"Jill, do you like Dave Brubeck?"

"Who's he?" Jill asked blankly, and Ramona stared.

"You don't like music?" She held up the record envelope.

"Not jazz, especially."

Ramona sniffed, a very tiny sniff. "Then you and Marg ought to get along. She is strictly square and longhair. She even likes opera!"

"If you're going to fight that one out again," Nora said, putting down an empty record sleeve, "let me pick out a neutral corner."

Jill said shyly, "With a name like Barbieri, I'd think you'd be a real opera fan."

"Well, I'm not," replied Ramona shortly.

Margaret said with a crooked smile, "Careful, Jill, you've hit her sorest spot. She's afraid someone will call it a low Wop taste. She won't admit she knows Toscanini from Rocky Marciano. Come and see *my* records."

Jill was already kneeling beside Margaret before the record cabinet, "Oh, I see you have the new Turandot. Is it better than the old Cetra set?"

Ramona laughed and made an "I give up" gesture at Nora. "Well, Marg is in her element. You come along and see my kittens."

The porch was empty except for the cats' boxes and sandboxes; two half-grown kittens scuffling softly over a length of ribbon, the two queens suckling their litters. Nora looked down at the tangled, tumbling balls of fur, listening with half an ear as Ramona analyzed their perfection of points and eye color. She was not an animal lover, nor—usually—sentimental about baby creatures. But the curious, aloof maternity of the queens, the blind helplessness of the kittens, struck some new, deep-down emotion she could not reach.

Jill and Margaret came out after a while. While Jill crooned over the kittens, Nora asked, "How is Skippy, Marg?"

"I saw him at Christmas. He seems healthy and happy." Margaret looked out the window. "It's going to drag on for years. A child custody suit is like a perpetual motion machine. Once you get it started, you can't shut it off again."

Jill asked, "Which cat is the mother of which kittens?" and Ramona laughed.

"I wouldn't know. Cats do the nuttiest things. These two wouldn't even eat from the same dish, but a few weeks before the kittens came, they began snuggling up to each other, and—this is the craziest thing ever—when Blossom started to deliver, Melinda—the one with the dark patches, there—crawled in with her and did likewise, just to keep her company. I lifted her into her own box a dozen times, but she had her mind made up. I had to go to work, and Marg never notices, so when I came home, here they were, five kittens between them, licking them all indiscriminately. And they've made a regular community project of bringing up the babies."

"Communists," Nora said. "Collective nurseries."

"Early Christians," said Margaret.

"Lesbians," said Jill.

Ramona straightened, with a curious sharp look at Jill. Then she laughed. "Exactly; crazy, mixed-up kittens." But there was a silence around the laughter.

Nora picked up a kitten, then put it gently down, and dug in her pocket for a cigarette. "Marg, Ramona, are you doing anything tonight? Jill hasn't been out since we came to Albany. We could go for a drink. I thought—" she crushed out the cigarette, though she had taken only two puffs, "we might take her to Flora's."

Margaret said sharply, "You're not serious."

"I am. I haven't been there for months."

"Why not?" Ramona's dark eyes twinkled. "Don't be a wet blanket, Marg."

Margaret frowned a little at Jill, but finally said, "All right. Why not? You can pick us up at seven."

Inside their own apartment, Jill turned on Nora angrily. "What possessed you to introduce me as Mrs. MacLellan?"

Nora stared. "What else? In a few weeks you will be very obviously pregnant. I thought it would save embarrassment."

"I'm embarrassed enough, right now! I gave in my name to Dr. Demorino as Mrs. Bristol—to Ramona!"

"I never thought of that," said Nora, startled and angry. What a stupid thing to do! All of a piece, of course, with Jill's self-punishing actions. "I thought you'd feel awkward."

"You sound like my mother," Jill said, cheeks flaming, "Regard for appearances! Lie, cheat, steal, as long as the neighbors don't know!"

"Nonsense." Nora went through into the kitchen. "We'd better get supper, and I've got to check with the answering service. Jill, you're not on the witness stand. For that matter, at common law, Mack's baby has a right to his name—legitimate or not—and you have a right to call yourself his wife."

"Who's talking about *rights?* That's just the sort of thing I won't do. I haven't any *claim* on Mack—"

Nora turned away impatiently. "Oh, you're hopeless. All right, you can tell Marg what a liar I am, and set the record straight by confessing all your sins. Why not wear a big scarlet letter while you're at it? Will you set the table please, or do you want to eat out of the sink?"

Jill did not move. She said thinly, "Nora, are you ashamed to introduce me to your friends because I'm going to have a baby and—and not married?"

"For God's sake, *stop* it," said Nora. Then it dawned on her; Jill had meant it. She was actually fighting back tears. Nora came swiftly and put her hands on the shaking shoulders. "My dear, don't you know me better than that?" But through her dismay, exasperation surged up, so that she felt conflicting impulses—to hug Jill and to shake sense into her.

"But, dear, you're too sensitive. If we want to live in this world, we do have to accept a certain amount of—"

"Hypocrisy."

"Exactly." Nora let her arm drop and began dishing up the chops. "There are more polite words. Look, let's turn it around. After my divorce I lived alone ten years. The world subscribes to the notion that, being legally unmarried, I have no physical, psychological, emotional or spiritual need for sex. If I want to keep on practicing medicine, I have to subscribe too—or make people think I do. Rightly or wrongly, our society is dedicated to the proposition that I couldn't possibly be a tramp and a good competent doctor at the same time. The way it works out is that anyone who wants to leave the paths of so-called virtue shows a little—not hypocrisy—a little decent discretion."

"Decent! I don't think it's indecent for a woman to have lovers, if she wants to. But sneaking around to do it—that's dirty!"

"Well, you're outvoted," said Nora wearily, unfolding her napkin. "Be honest and a martyr, or be a mild hypocrite and do as you damn please. It's your life."

I'm angry, she thought, *because Jill's more honest than I am....* There was something else she had to say, and she didn't know where to start. "More tea? Jill, by the way—no more cracks about lesbians in front of Marg."

Suddenly she realized; Jill might interpret this like her lie about Jill's marriage; a hint that she was ashamed of the true state of affairs. "But you couldn't know—Marg left her husband and baby to live with Ramona."

"Husband? I thought real lesbians never married."

"Whatever you mean by a real lesbian," Nora said dryly. "Since I've said so much—Frank Sheppard is a heel. He never did a decent thing in his life. When Skip was a month old, Marg packed up and walked out. For a while, she lived here with me."

Nora thought of the weeks when Margaret and Skippy had lived here; the force of her own self-deception now became clear to her. She had thought she was simply doing a down-and-out girl a favor.

"I mean; she kept house for me, before she got the library job. Later she moved in with Ramona. She had watched them with detachment which now seemed wholly false, hiding from herself.

"In another state, Marg could have a divorce for non-support, abusive treatment, what have you. But in this one you need proof of adultery, and no sane woman would mess with Sheppard. Then he dragged it all into court—demanded custody of Skippy, called Marg an unfit mother—it was all bluff, he wouldn't be bothered supporting a child, not him. But then Frank's mother got into the act—she has Skippy now. You've got to say one thing for Ramona," she added with scrupulous fairness, "she stuck to Marg, through all the hell."

The words were self-reproach; she was remembering others. *Of course, Margaret, if you ask me, I shall testify that you have always been a good mother and led a quiet and respectable life in my house, and that I know nothing to the contrary.* But had Margaret wanted only a character witness?

Had Margaret's refusal to endure a bad marriage been a reproach to Nora's own failure with what might have been a good one with Les Rannock? Margaret, who had been willing to bring up a child alone if need be?

Had she thrown Margaret and Ramona together, fearing to be involved herself?

Impatiently, she rose. "Let's go. It's almost seven."

Jill asked in an undertone, as the car pulled away from the Lenox Apartments, "What sort of place is this—Flora's?"

"It's a bar," Nora said slowly. "Men—aren't admitted."

"One of—those?"

Nora shrugged. "It's respectable. It's about the only place I know where a woman can have a drink alone without being molested by drunks and sailors. Most places, an unescorted woman is treated like a prostitute looking for a pickup."

The streets of the South End were cavernous and dark, between the neon signs brightening every corner; lurid orange, poison-fruit red, electric blue and green. The street-lamps flickered a sickly yellow by contrast.

Nora pulled the car to the curb and, when they got out, locked it. The door, modestly glassed, announced in a small neon voice FLORA'S. Holding the door for Jill, she blinked at the splotched brightness. A juke box was playing, a little too loud.

Soon they were seated around a table covered with white oilcloth. There were about twenty women, in couples or small groups, at the tables. At one end was a small bar with half a dozen stools. A few of the women were wearing slacks; but in this weather, that was nothing unusual.

Nora leaned over and whispered to Jill, "See? Bet you a dollar to a dishrag you can't tell the gay girls from the others. What would you like to drink?"

Jill shrugged. "Ginger ale, I guess."

"Jill, if you really don't drink, I won't persuade you. But if you ever do, this is both the time and the place."

"Well, if I get drunk, it's your fault, remember. Rum and coke, then."

Ramona made a disapproving face and, like Nora, ordered scotch. Margaret smiled. "The usual for me."

"Wet blanket," Ramona muttered.

"If you were smart, you'd stick to beer yourself. You know perfectly well—"

"Listen, I don't need you to tell me—"

"Ease off," said Margaret, "this is a party. Remember?"

Ramona leaned toward Jill. "That's Flora Danbury at the bar. She owns the place." She indicated the tall, very thin woman in a fashionably cut business suit, graying hair touched up with chic blue. Jill smiled:

"She looks more like a Dean of Women."

The woman swiveled suddenly and her sharp eyes raked their table; then she walked with long strides toward them. "Good evening," she said, in a crisp low voice. Her face was deeply lined; her eyes, dark behind thick horn-rims, met Nora's briefly, with cool recognition; then, came to rest on Jill.

"You haven't been here before. How old are you?"

"Twenty-two."

"No offense, young woman. But we can't endanger our license by serving to minors."

Jill extended her driver's license, with a demure smile. Flora Danbury barely glanced at it, putting a familiar hand on Jill's shoulder.

"It's all right, kid, I just have to be sure."

Jill glanced at the hand on her shoulder and suddenly giggled. Nora could almost read her thoughts; this was an exciting adventure, to be sitting in a slum bar—a queer joint.

Flora was older than she looked; and the hands, as finely kept as Nora's own, were not young hands. Jill smiled up brightly at Flora, and the hand on her shoulder moved slowly up to rumple Jill's curly hair before she said, "Well, dearie, I hope I'll see you often. You come in any time."

Nora, noting the contracted pupils, thought: she's mainlining now. She sighed, the reminder of the world's ceaseless misery striking through the juke box noise.

Ramona giggled as Flora moved away. "Whew! Jill, my pet, you're playing with fire!"

"What do you mean?"

"Flora never bothers couples. It's bad for business. But when a new girl starts cruising her—"

"What do you mean?"

"Oh, come off it. Cruising. Making eyes. *Flirting!*"

"I wasn't!" Jill protested.

Nora was wondering why on earth she had come. This place was harmless enough—she had been here a dozen or more times—but it was no place for Jill. She-put down her second drink untasted. "Want to powder your nose Jill?"

In the ladies room, which was cleaner than Nora expected, she glanced randomly into the mirror.

"Do you want to leave, Jill?"

Jill smiled with mischievous stubbornness. "Why, no, I've always wanted to visit a place like this—I hadn't the least notion *you'd* know a lesbian bar!"

Nora sat down on the painted bench before the mirror. "This isn't, quite. It's borderline—the so-called gay world calls it square. It doesn't cater exclusively to homosexuals and mostly it attracts the ones like Marg and Ramona who try not to attract attention to themselves."

"And you?"

"Exactly," said Nora: smoothly, though the barb had hurt, "Otherwise it's very conservative; no men in drag, very few cruising butches."

"Darn! I thought that would be the interesting part!"

"I'm very sorry I can't accommodate you," Nora said stiffly, "but Flora doesn't want the police—or a lot of rubbernecking tourists who come to stare at the queers."

When they returned, Margaret and Ramona were dancing together, and Jill touched Nora's arm. "Dance with me?"

Nora had already stiffened to shove back her chair when the enormity of it struck her; and the memory...Pammy, teaching her to dance on the cool parquet floor of the library. She could not—she *could not* stand up here and take Jill in her arms.

"I'd rather not, Jill. I'm not much of a dancer."

"Please? Just once?"

"I really would rather not. Not here."

"You mean—" Jill's voice was almost shrill, "you'll dance with me—but not *here,* where people might *think*—"

"I will not. My reasons are none of your business." Nora was angry now.

"Of course not!" Jill was breathing raggedly, two red spots on her cheek. "I didn't ask to come here, Nor. You brought me. But now that we're here, you turn prissy—"

The word, Pammy's word, repeated the lash on the sore spot. "Jill, lower your voice, people are looking."

"Let them look! *I* don't spend my whole life worrying about what people will think—"

Nora clenched her hand over Jill's bony wrist, her strong fingers crushing down, hard. Part of her confused cruelty was guilt—for Jill had only voiced what she herself had been thinking.

"Jill, I've taken a lot from you, but this I won't take. I'm damned fond of you," she added, in a voice that shook, "but not fond enough to let you make scenes in a bar and get away with it." She had to force herself to unlock her grip before she broke Jill's wrist. "Flora's on her way over. Pull yourself together."

Flora was apparently unaware of the contretemps, but Nora, remembering other occasions on which Flora had turned up—as if by magic—just in time for a brewing storm, could not face her.

Flora smiled blurrily at Jill. "I noticed you're not dancing, dearie. Would you dance with me?"

Jill, covertly rubbing her abused wrist, pushed back her chair. "I'd love to," she said quietly. "Nora doesn't feel like dancing. I was just trying to persuade her." And she moved away, Flora's arm around her waist.

Slowly, Nora became aware that Margaret and Ramona had returned to the table. Ramona giggled, and Margaret said viciously, "That little bitch!"

"It's my fault," Nora muttered. "She went to a girls' school, she's used to seeing women dance together:" She realized too late that her words must offend her friends, but she felt constrained to defend Jill. She watched them, feeling a little sick at the sight of Jill encircled by Flora's craggy arms.

How do I get this way? It turns my stomach to see Jill with that old pervert—but who am I to call anyone a pervert?

As Flora and Jill passed their table, Ramona rose, touching Flora's shoulder lightly. "We'll be leaving soon. I'd like to dance with Jill first, do you mind?"

Flora relinquished Jill graciously; as the two girls spun away from the table, Ramona's wide skirt swinging out in time to the music, Margaret leaned across the table.

"Nora, when they get back, let's cut out of here. It's no good. Ramona's half drunk."

"Jill isn't any too sober. You were right, Marg, this was a nitwit idea and I apologize for it."

Margaret propped her chin in her hands, her loose fair hair spilling over the collar of her striped shirt. "Nor, it's none of my business, but—what the hell are you playing at with that kid?"

"She's no kid, Marg, she's older than you are."

"Whatever she is, it doesn't make sense. When she looks at you, her eyes light up—you've no business—you're on the wrong side of the street for that game."

"Pot calling the kettle black?"

"Nor, I had some reason, some excuse. You—you've got everything. A top professional reputation. Work that means something. The Major—"

Nora pleaded, "I thought you of all people would understand—"

"No. For you it's the last thing I could ever understand. As for Jill—well, hell, she's married, she's pregnant—what the devil is she doing in this galley? She doesn't look like a thrill-seeker, so what is it?"

"I only wish I knew! Maybe if I rub her nose in it, good and hard—believe me, Marg, I'm not playing around for kicks!"

"If she hurts you," said Margaret with unexpected violence, "I'll break her goddamn neck!"

Nora said, not looking up, "It's more apt to be the other way around."

"Are you sure of that?"

Jill and Ramona almost collapsed into their chairs.

"Oooh, I'm dizzy," Ramona squealed, and picked up her glass, drinking fast, and coughing. Jill's lipstick was smeared, and Nora refused to think about that.

"I hate to break the party up, but we're all working women. Let's go somewhere for some solid food."

She saw Ramona's guarded attempt to draw Jill aside, and briefly considered leaving her to it—rub her nose in it...but Margaret's drawn face decided her.

In the car she let Jill nestle against her like a sleepy, somewhat drunken child. She found a favorite crossroads restaurant; they gathered in a booth, silent, the effects of the drinks wearing off. Nora was surprised to see that it was barely ten. It seemed they had been sitting in Flora's half the night.

A gust of icy air blew around them; a man came in and plunked himself at the counter. "Coffee," he said with weary incisiveness, "black."

Nora straightened and stared. "You're out late, Vic."

He spun the counter stool to face them. "What are you doing here?"

"Out for a night on the town." Nora remembered; this had been a favorite hangout when she and Vic had snatched their crumbs of leisure together. Jill withdrew her hand.

"Come and sit with us, Vic."

He nodded pleasantly to Jill, politely to Margaret, and his eyes lingered on Ramona in surprise and discovery. My God, Barbieri, I didn't know you out of uniform!"

"I'll take that for a compliment," the dark girl said gaily as Vic slid into the booth. Margaret drew herself ungraciously against the wall. Nora met Margaret's cornered eyes, and sighed, remembering that Margaret had the unhappy quality of freezing up, silent, in a crowd. Jill, too, sat silent, making no effort to join in the fast repartee of Vic and Ramona. It was partly their quiet which made Nora say presently, "Vic, we were just leaving."

"Oh, it's early yet. I'm going to have more coffee. Who's with me?"

Ramona disregarded Margaret's mute headshake.

"Please."

Nora shrugged. "Me too, then. Jill? Marg?" The waitress flicked away and replaced cups. Vic rose and went to the juke box; the fluid colors shifted, spraying juicy green, sensual orange on his dark face. Ramona slid from her seat and joined him, leaning so close that her loose curls touched the man's shoulder. Margaret looked cold and wretched. Coins clattered; the bleat of a popular crooner filled the steamy air with the sweet strains of "Ramona."

"I prefer my own version," Margaret muttered after the song had ended. "Ramona, I'd like to break your little neck, Ramona, I'll do it yet someday by heck..."

Jill giggled nervously as Vic and Ramona came back.

"Ramona, Nora really wants to get back," Margaret said.

"Must you?" Vic asked.

"I'm afraid we must, Vic."

The man glanced at Ramona. "Well, if you others must run along, I'll bring Ramona later."

"You don't mind?" Ramona dimpled.

Vic's eyes crossed Nora's for a split second, with a rapier flick of something like triumph. As they crowded into Nora's car they saw Vic and Ramona walking toward his gray Chrysler; Nora slammed in the clutch violently.

"Did I hear somebody call somebody a bitch?"

Before the Lenox Apartments Margaret paused before getting out, her hand on the doorframe. "Jill, come over some time. We can play some records."

"Love to. And some night when Nora's working, we could go to a movie, too."

Nora leaned past Jill. "Marg," she said, "don't be too damned stoic this time, the kid's not worth it."

Margaret smiled, without amusement. "Physician," she said gently, "heal thyself."

Nora did not speak again until the door of their own apartment had closed behind them; then she exploded.

"That—little—whore!"

"Margaret? I liked her!"

"Ramona!" Nora pitched her coat at the divan; it missed but she let it lie there, and Jill stared. "Are you drunk?"

"No, but I'd like to be." Nora went to the kitchen and took down the almost full bottle of whisky. She poured a little in the bottom of a glass. "Nightcap, Jill?"

"A little. I don't understand—you said—she's a lesbian—"

"Ramona is a consummate bitch. Lesbian? Sure—or anything else that suits her at the moment." She had, Nora thought, confirmed Margaret's turning into that path; when Margaret was disillusioned and alone. "I'm no Puritan. But, damn it, Ramona doesn't have to flaunt her affairs under Marg's nose." She put the glass down. "Just because she stuck by Marg before, she thinks she can put her through hoops forever—I won't offer you another drink, Jill. It might be bad for the baby."

"I'd forgotten all about the baby." Jill went into the bedroom and took off her shoes. "Why did you take me to Flora's?"

"I thought it would interest you, maybe."

"But when we were there—just like Marg and Ramona, but you wouldn't dance with me—"

"Why, Jill—" she held out her hand, but Jill jerked away.

"Don't worry about my feelings, it's too late for that! Treating me all evening like—like—" Jill's voice broke.

Nora put her arms around Jill and by main force pulled her down on the bed. She sat there holding Jill till the shaking quieted. Her own mind was almost a blank. At last she said, "Jill, we've never really talked about all this. Do you want to?"

Jill blew her nose. "Not if you don't want to. But—if you didn't want—why did you take me there anyhow?"

"Quite apart from the fact that Marg is my friend," she said, slowly, "I suppose I felt they'd accept our—situation, and that might make it easier for me to—to look it in the face." She clasped her hands, staring at an acid burn near one nail.

"But why is that necessary?" Jill asked. "I love you. Why is that something you have to accept, or not accept, or make it look and sound good? Why can't you take it for what it is? I love you."

Nora finally looked up. "But—you love Mack, don't you?"

"Oh, God, I don't know! I—I was lonesome, and I felt funny about being a virgin at my age, and I was wondering if there was something wrong with me because I'd never wanted any man. But now—now I feel as if I'd started an avalanche rolling, and I couldn't get out of the way!"

"Nobody can," Nora said, but Jill collapsed on the bedspread, digging her head into the pillow in silent, agonized sobs; so convulsive that Nora was alarmed.

"Jill, you mustn't cry like that, it's very bad for the baby."

"I hate the baby," Jill screamed, "I wish it would die, I wish it would die, die, *die!*" She pounded the pillow frantically with her fists.

Nora bent and gripped Jill's shoulders. Her voice trembled as much as Jill's.

"Stop this damned nonsense, or I'll phone Vic and have him put you in the hospital! You'll work yourself up into a miscarriage!"

"I only wish I could!" Jill struggled; went limp under Nora's hands, crying. "I'm—I'm sorry, Nor. I'll be good."

Nora straightened, ragged with the ache of pity. "Honey, you're overtired, and you've been drinking—which I shouldn't have allowed. You lie down and let get me get you something to make you sleep." *This was her fault, too.*

When she came back with two phenobarbital capsules, Jill was undressed, lying on Nora's bed, her face scrubbed and penitent. Nora sat down beside her.

"Jill, you're pregnant, you've got to learn to expect these silly moods—not let them throw you."

"I don't want the baby to die. God forgive me for saying it. But I don't want a baby. I'll be an awful mother."

"You mustn't talk that way. Jill, the real reason you feel like this is because you're alone, when Mack should be sharing this with you. It's natural, to want your baby's father."

"But I don't," Jill said miserably, and laid her head in Nora's lap. Nora sighed and stroked her hair.

"Most pregnant women go through moods like that. You'll get over it," she said.

At least I hope you will. I hope I will. Hell, I'm only giving her the emotional support she ought to be getting from Mack. No girl ought to be alone at a time like this. Someone has to need her, love her, comfort her, make her feel wanted...

Then as she drew Jill closer, her hands going almost without volition to the fastenings at Jill's throat, a satirical self-knowledge knifed through her real concern.

She had known, of course, that there would be only one way to comfort Jill. Had Jill thrown her tantrum for this reason?

Or—had she herself goaded Jill into it? For an excuse to do just this?

Unnecessarily rough, she pulled away Jill's pajamas and switched out the light.

Jill's face tasted of salt under her kisses; the trembling mouth was still soft and pliant as if with tears. Nora closed her hands over the taut breasts until Jill moaned—with pain or pleasure Nora could not tell and did not much care.

Jill's body was still slim beneath Nora's; but the thought knifed Nora with an anger and frustration she could not understand; soon it would be swollen, promising, fruitful...*he was first. It has nothing to do with me.* The fantasy spun through her mind dizzily as she strained Jill into her arms with a violence new to them both, *if I had been the one to make her pregnant,* and reeled away before she was fully aware of the thought.

In a sort of frantic hunger she gripped Jill close; as if her lips, moving from the soft mouth down to the white throat, down to the small swelling breasts and avidly over every inch of the softness, could obliterate every former touch. Jill cried out softly in the grip of passion and sudden release, and Nora, as the storm center swept her too, felt a savage exaltation. *Mine,* she thought, *mine now, at least.* She fell asleep with Jill locked tightly in her arms.

Different...she searched for a woman who was willing to love her

The Flesh Is Willing

by Dorcas Knight

At first she didn't understand what was wrong with her. Why was she different from other women? Why was she attracted to Ellen? Why did she reject Matt's proposals?

Then Cori discovered she was not alone in her feelings. There were others like herself who preferred to love and be loved by women. But would Ellen leave her husband and children for her? Or would she find another love as deep and as wonderful?

The Flesh Is Willing

Dinner was marvelous and they both ate heartily. Ellen had ordered steak of a kind almost unobtainable in Camsburg, big, two-inch-thick Porterhouse.

All finished, Ellen leaned back, gave Cori a mischievous look and said, "What would you like to do tomorrow, darling? See the Statue of Liberty, Radio City, Central Park? It's up to you."

"What I'd really like to do is get all the sight-seeing and shopping done in one day and spend the rest of the time closeted in this room with you."

"Honey," said Ellen, laughing, "you've got to remember that I'm not as young as you and all this boundless energy is making me feel even older than my years. Seriously, what do you particularly want to do or see? You must have given it some thought." She picked up her coffee, took it to the bedside table and lay down.

"Well, if you're going to be serious, I'd like to see the Guggenheim Museum. We've heard about it even in Camsburg. Frankly, I'm not too interested in batting around all over the place seeing the usual tourist sights. I've seen enough pictures of most of them to give a pretty accurate description. Night life doesn't appeal to me much and, besides, we need escorts for that."

"Generally, yes, but there are a few places where they aren't necessary. I know some nice restaurants where they serve wonderful food and have a good piano on the side. Do you have a cigarette handy? I can't seem to locate mine."

Cori crossed over, took her cigarettes from her pocket, lit one and handed it to Ellen. Then she sat at the foot of the bed, arms wrapped around her knees.

"There's one thing I'd like very much, Ellen, and I hope you'll understand. You've lived here practically all your life and there must be hundreds of places that recall memories of your past. I'd rather not try to fit into your past. Maybe I have no place in your future but, at least for these ten days, let me have and be your present. I know it's a form of jealousy but please humor me in this."

"Why, Cori, darling, I love your sentimentality and I don't blame you. This is really your trip and I want it to be perfect." Ellen frowned. "I had planned to have you meet a few of my friends but if you'd rather not...."

"That's different," said Cori. "As long as they don't consume too much of our time." Cori moved up beside Ellen, placing her head on the soft, inviting shoulder. "I feel like a very contented, fat cat."

"Are you sleepy?" asked Ellen, running her fingers through Cori's still slightly damp hair.

"I'm getting that way fast," mumbled Cori, snuggling against Ellen.

"What happened to all that energy?"

"I just got too comfortable. Do you mind, darling?"

"Mind! My sweet, I'm ten years more tired than you are. It'll be heavenly just sleeping together all night. Let me up for a moment while I wheel that table out in the hall." She got up, collected their cups and put everything on the table and pushed it into the hall.

"There," she said, crawling back into bed, "we won't be disturbed. Hold me close, Cori, very close."

Cori gathered Ellen in her arms and said quietly, "Promise me that it's safe to go to sleep. Promise me that I won't wake up alone."

"It's a promise, dearest. When you wake up, I'll be right here in your arms. I don't expect to even turn over. Kiss me goodnight."

Cori did and, deserving or not, they slept the sleep of the innocent. If they dreamed this night, they dreamed together.

At eight the next morning, they woke simultaneously, arms and legs together. The excitement of waking together for the first time, a few significant words, a certain touch rekindled the fire of yesterday and it was ten o'clock when Ellen breathed a long sign and said, "My God, Cori, we must be insatiable!"

"Why, naturally, I thought you knew it!" Cori rolled over Ellen, off the other side of the bed and struggled into the bathroom. A moment later, she was in the shower, singing at the top of her voice. Never had she known such complete happiness. Out of the shower, she stood before the mirror and studied herself.

You're different, Cori Hadley. You don't even resemble the Cori Hadley I knew a couple of months ago.

She tried to identify the difference but couldn't. It wasn't any one thing. It was *everything* about her.

She dried herself and sailed back into the room with Ellen.

"Did you order breakfast, m'love?"

"Eggs, bacon, toast, and coffee," answered Ellen. "Don't I take good care of you at every opportunity?"

"You certainly do. I only wish the opportunities were more frequent."

While Ellen bathed, Cori began to dress, humming and whistling. Vaguely, she wondered what friends Ellen wanted her to meet but breakfast arrived, Ellen appeared looking radiant, and the thought left her.

They finally got out of the hotel about noon.

"Could we walk for a few blocks?" asked Cori. "I'd just like to move slowly and get used to the place. The buildings are so damned tall, it's like being in the bottom of a canyon," she added, looking up.

"New Yorkers aren't aware of that. Very few of them ever look up unless someone is threatening to leap from the heights. Now *that* can draw quite a crowd!"

"Oh, Ellen," said Cori, squeezing Ellen's arm, "do I see lots of trees over there?"

"That, my dear, is Central Park. I thought we'd walk over there and then down Fifth Avenue. That suit you?"

"Fine with me. By the way, did I tell you how absolutely glorious you look today?"

"You flatter me. It's just a reflection of the way I feel." Ellen smiled.

It was a perfect day, topped off with a Broadway musical, followed by another session of love and Cori went to sleep thankful for another day completely theirs.

Tuesday morning Ellen was awake first and had ordered breakfast while Cori still slept. She didn't get out of bed, however, knowing how Cori would feel if she woke up to find herself alone.

She kissed Cori awake and said, "Don't get any ideas, darling. I've already ordered breakfast. Today I thought we'd try to do all our shopping. After breakfast, I'm going to make a call and arrange for us to meet some people. We can do that early this week and for the rest of our stay, we'll keep to ourselves."

Cori groaned and tried to keep Ellen from getting up. After a playful scuffle, Cori let her slip away and fell back on the pillows.

"Promise you won't get us all involved?"

"I promise. In fact, I've been thinking of letting them think that this is the end of our stay. That way we'll really be safe."

Over breakfast, they planned the day's shopping. There was a lot to do since, to the girls back home, it would have to look like at least a week's work.

While having her coffee, Ellen placed her call. She gave a number to the operator and waited.

"Miss Marston, please."

Another pause and Cori went to the window. *Leta Marston! Ellen didn't tell me she was calling her!*

"Hello, Leta. It's Ellen. Remember me?"

Cori wished that she could hear both sides of this conversation.

"I'm at the Lenox, dear, but only until Thursday." Ellen smiled at Cori and signaled for a cigarette.

"No, Leta, Walter isn't with me. I brought a girl friend. We came up on a quick shopping trip. I thought it might be nice to get together."

Cori lit a cigarette for Ellen, took it to her and went back to stare out the window.

It's ridiculous to be jealous of the past but she should have warned me that she was calling Leta. I'm not sure I want to meet Leta. I'm not so sure I want Ellen to see her, either!

"Tonight? Wonderful, we'll be there at six. See if Jean and Edna can make it, too. I'd love to see them. Tomorrow is shot for us what with finishing our shopping and the theatre in the evening. Sorry for the short notice but it was short for us too. See you at six. Bye."

She put the receiver down, looked over at Cori and half-whispered, "Please come over here to me."

Cori turned but, instead of going to Ellen, she sat in the big chair by the windows.

"So you're going to make me come to you, are you? I don't mind, darling." She got up, crossed the room and cuddled in Cori's lap, draping her arms around Cori's neck.

"Cori," she was serious now, "I know you're hurt and I know why you're hurt. I don't blame you but I did think this out carefully. If I'd told you I was calling Leta, we'd have argued and you might have won. This way, we're committed. I have good reason for wanting you to meet these people. Please, honey, don't think I'm trying to hurt you!" she rested her head on Cori's shoulder and pulled Cori's mouth down to meet hers.

Taking her lips from Ellen's mouth, Cori grumbled, "All right, but what reason do you have for wanting me to meet these people, whoever they are?"

Ellen leaped from Cori's lap and affected a senatorial pose. "I was hoping you'd ask me that question! Honestly, darling, there's the best reason in the world and it's all for your sake. For my own part, I wouldn't care if we didn't see anyone on this whole trip but I think this is important to you."

"All right, cut the build-up and let's have it."

"OK. Look, honey, you've lived in that provincial little town all your life except when you went to college in another little provincial town just like Camsburg. You've wasted years, suffering all alone, thinking you were some sort of horrible mistake. I want to show you that you're not, that there are plenty of people like you, and a good majority of them leading ordinary, everyday, useful lives. Women, and men, too, like you who 'pass for white' every working day of their lives but who go home to what they really want, who go home to a way of life that is natural and, for them, perfectly normal. This is what I want you to see for yourself. You'll never stop feeling alone if you don't!"

"OK, OK, you can get off the soapbox now, I've got your message. I'll meet the ladies, assuming they're ladies."

"Now, Cori, that was nasty. What kind of people do you think I know?"

"I'm sorry, Ellen, I didn't mean that the way it sounded. Forgive me."

"I know you didn't and I'm sorry I snapped. I care so very much for you, Cori. I don't think you really know how much. I want more than anything else in the world to do what's best for you. You don't realize how well I understand you. So well I can often even read your thoughts. You wonder sometimes how I can love you as I do and then go home to Walter. It isn't always easy. My heart wants to stay with you but my head keeps me sensible. It's sometimes called a sense of duty. My God, how I digress! We should be shopping right now. Don't come near me, Cori, or we won't even make our six o'clock date!"

From eleven to five they shopped. Ellen chose only the best stores where everything was good so that they didn't have to waste too much time in selection.

They went back to the hotel to freshen up and change and left in a taxi at six.

"We're late," Cori said.

"Not for New Yorkers," Ellen laughed. "New Yorkers hate people who arrive exactly on the dot. They're never ready on time themselves."

The cab raced uptown to the east seventies.

"Maybe I won't fit in with these people. I'm just a small-town hick, you know."

"Stop that, Cori. I spotted you for something else the first time I saw you and you know it. All I hope is that everyone here tonight is attached. I'd hate like hell to bring you all the way to New York just to lose you."

"You don't really believe that's possible, do you?" Cori became serious. "You know that when you're around, I'm not even aware of other people, male or female."

"Please be a little aware tonight, dear. Remember I'm bringing you here for a purpose not just for the sake of a party."

The cab pulled up before an elegant apartment house and a robot-like doorman popped out. He ushered them into a plush lobby at the opposite side of which was a bank of elevators.

Once inside the elevator Cori asked, "Do I look all right? I'd hate to have you ashamed of me. Will these people know about us?"

"You've waited a little late to ask that last question. About us, yes, they'll sense it but they won't discuss it openly unless we bring it up. And, yes, you look marvelous. I just hope you won't see something you prefer to me."

The door slid open and Ellen led Cori down a corridor.

"I take it you've been here before," said Cori with a slight snap.

"None of that, now. We've been all through that and you know it's only a part of my dim past. Please, darling, try not to think of that every time you look at Leta. She's really a nice person."

Ellen pushed a bell and, after a short wait, the door opened.

"Ellen! My God, it seems years! Come on in. Thank goodness you're the first to arrive. At least we'll have a chance to say hello." This tall, chic, Scandinavian looking woman turned to Cori and said, "And this is your shopping friend from the Deep South." She extended a hand, which Cori gripped, and smiled.

"I'm Leta Marston and I'm so glad that you and Ellen could spare a little of your time for us natives. Come on in and let's settle down with a drink before anyone else gets here."

Ellen, between them, said, "Leta, you never change. If you'll let me get a word in, I'd like you to meet Cori Hadley." Ellen preceded them into a tastefully decorated modern living room.

"Still scotch for you, Ellen?"

"Yes, and for Cori, too. It was marvelous to meet some southerners who drink scotch. I went down there thinking that bourbon was the only liquor they were familiar with."

Cori smiled. "You make us sound rather primitive, Ellen, but I'm afraid you're right about the bourbon, anyway. Our little crowd just happens to be an exception."

Cori watched Leta as she made the drinks. This woman's sophisticated manner made her feel naïve and uncomfortable but she had to admit that Leta was certainly attractive. And Leta preferred women to men!

Leta brought their drinks, raised her own glass and said, "Cheers."

"Cheers," Ellen and Cori echoed simultaneously.

"Who else is coming?" asked Ellen.

"Jean, Edna and—now don't get upset, Ellen—Eunice is coming with them."

"Oh, dammit, Leta," Ellen groaned, "you know how I feel about her!"

"I know, darling, but you said you wanted to see Jean and Edna and they were already tied up with Eunice. What could I do? Tell them not to come?"

"Of course not," Ellen sighed, "but I do hope she behaves herself."

"I'll see to that," said Leta, smiling.

Leta crossed the room to an elaborate hi-fi set, selected a stack of records and put them on. Music filled the room.

The three of them sat around the coffee table and Cori felt awkward, nervous and didn't know what to say. While Ellen and Leta made small talk, she made great headway with her drink. It was strong, much stronger than she was accustomed to and, as soon as she reached the bottom, Leta was on her feet getting a refill.

"A little lighter this time, please," requested Cori. "I wouldn't want to embarrass Ellen by getting drunk in front of her friends."

Leta laughed and said, "Don't try to kid me, honey. I've heard all about how you southerners can hold your liquor."

Just as she set Cori's fresh drink on the table, the doorbell rang and, as she ran to the foyer, Cori was conscious of her long, lean, boyish body, which was accentuated by tight, black toreador pants. Suddenly she was beset by a mental picture of Ellen and Leta in bed, a picture which she attempted to drown in a large swallow of scotch.

"Easy, honey," cautioned Ellen, beside her. "I'd like you to be able to see these people."

"I'll be all right," muttered Cori.

A babble of voices drifted in from the foyer and Leta floated into the room, followed by three other women. She made the introductions and Cori wasn't surprised to learn that they were Jean, Edna and Eunice.

Jean and Edna fluttered around Ellen, talking excitedly.

"When we gave you that farewell party in May, darling, we certainly didn't expect to see you again so soon." Jean's voice was soft with an intimate touch. She was a nice looking woman, not beautiful, but feminine and well-groomed.

"It's good to see you gain, Ellen," said Edna, an altogether different type from Jean. She was tall, heavily built, dressed in a severely tailored, gray suit and her hair was quite short.

From the bar, a new voice, low and vibrant but with a rather nasty inflection, said. "You look marvelous, Ellen, dear. Small town life must agree with you."

"It does, Eunice, it does," replied Ellen, sweetly.

Cori looked toward the bar where Eunice had draped herself while Leta was tending bar. Now here's a completely new type, Cori said to herself. Eunice was such a femme fatale that Cori couldn't believe she was anything but a man's woman. Her long, tapering fingers, tipped with red, made anxious, possessive little gestures in Leta's direction. Her generously made-up eyes wandered about the room, stopping a moment here, a moment there. She reminded Cori of an animal that feels itself in danger of attack from all sides.

Eunice's eyes rested on Cori, and then moved on to Ellen.

"I see you didn't waste any time, dear," she said to Ellen. "Are you planning to revolutionize the ways of southern womanhood?" She showed her teeth in what failed to pass for a smile.

Ellen's eyes widened and she opened her mouth to speak but Leta cut in with, "Drinks everyone," and shot a withering glance at Eunice, along with a menacing shake of her head.

Cori felt herself blush and the blood began to pound in her ears. She just had to say something to put that bitch in her place!

"Just what makes you think that we southern women are so different from you yankee girls?" was the first think that came into her mind. "It's quite possible that we could revolutionize your ways, you know."

"Bravo! Bravo!" cried Edna, clapping her hands. "How do you like that, Eunice? I think you have a worthy opponent in our new friend but why don't we call it a draw and let that last question be a rhetorical one? If we start discussing the differences between southern and northern women, we may be here all night."

"You should know, honey," teased Jean. "You've had your share of both."

The silence that followed was broken by the ringing of the doorbell.

"Oh, my God," said Leta, "I forgot about John and Tony. I thought you'd enjoy seeing them too, Ellen." She dashed to the door.

In the meantime, Cori fixed her eyes on Eunice who was still standing at the bar and, when their eyes met, Cori's didn't waver. Eunice used the entrance of the boys as an excuse to turn away. She slithered across the room and grabbed one of them by the hand.

"Oh, John, darling," she simpered, "it's been ages! Why haven't you called?"

It was obvious to everyone that John was embarrassed by this insincere performance but it was also obvious that he was a gentleman. He held Eunice's hand and smiled.

"It's good to see you, Eunice. I'm sorry not to have called but Tony and I have been on a treadmill for months."

"And we're still on it," added Tony, "but we just couldn't miss the chance to see Ellen."

Tony strode to the couch, pulled Ellen up and swung her around in his arms. He put her down and they stood at arms' length, both laughing.

"Oh, Tony, I can't tell you how glad I am that Leta called you!" Ellen was beaming at him. "Come here, I want you to meet a very special friend of mine."

She pulled him over to Cori and said, "Cori Hadley, this is Tony Walling, one of my favorite people."

"And John, do come here and meet Cori," she called to the other young man, who was still cornered by Eunice. This action brought a venomous look from Eunice but Ellen ignored it.

She introduced John to Cori and the four of them made a little group.

"You seem to have found a measure of happiness in the South," John said, without a trace of sarcasm.

"I have," responded Ellen, "but does it show so much?"

"Only to one who knows you well," answered John, smiling. "Your taste hasn't changed either."

Cori smiled. "Hope that's a compliment."

"It is, honey," John assured her, putting his arm around Ellen. "Ellen's taste has always been exquisite."

"I gather that you haven't been seeing much of Eunice," Ellen grinned slyly.

"Are you kidding?" Tony came in with this remark. "Listen, if I want to socialize with a cobra, I'll go up to the Bronx Zoo where they keep 'em behind glass. I'm damned if I know what's wrong with that girl. She's not happy unless she's making trouble for somebody."

"I see she's still hot after Leta. Doesn't she know when to let go?" Ellen sipped her drink.

"Only if she's the one to let go first—and that was Leta's mistake. If she'd held out a little longer, Eunice would have dumped her and there wouldn't be any problem," John explained.

Leta came around with drinks for John and Tony.

"Are you four talking about what I think you're talking about?"

"I wouldn't be at all surprised." John smiled and raised his glass.

Leta groaned. "All I can say is I hope you appreciate this, Ellen. I haven't been so nice to her for weeks. In fact, this is going to set me back about a month in my campaign to get rid of her."

"Why don't you just tell her off?" asked Cori, naïvely.

They all chuckled, but Leta answered, "My dear, I can tell you haven't had much experience with women of this type, and you'll be wise to avoid them. This kind of experience you don't need. I must admit that before a woman's fury, especially Eunice's, I become a craven coward. You've no idea what scenes she can make."

Leta left them to attend her other guests. Jean, Edna, and Eunice were near the bar and Eunice was talking animatedly. She was looking in Ellen's direction with fire in her eyes. Leta got to her and must have said something soothing for the two of them left the room together, hand in hand. When they had gone, Jean and Edna joined the remaining group.

"Poor Leta," Jean smiled at them all. "She's making the supreme sacrifice to keep the party peaceful."

"Frankly," said Cori, "I'd give that girl a good hard spanking and then, if she couldn't behave like a lady, I'd send her home."

"Listen to that," laughed Tony. "Does she treat you rough, Ellen?"

"So far, I haven't had to," Cori answered for Ellen.

"Why Cori," said Ellen, possessively slipping her arm through Cori's. "You're showing me a new side of you!"

Cori drew Ellen within the circle of her arm and the others smiled approvingly.

They all sat down, with Jean on Cori's left. Cori soon learned that Jean was head of personnel for one of the larger Madison Avenue agencies and that Edna had her own law practice. Cori was amazed and impressed.

"And John and Tony?" she asked.

"John has an antique shop and Tony is an engineer," was the answer.

The bedroom door opened and out came Leta, with a triumphant look. She checked glasses, picked up the empties and went to the bar. Cori got up and joined her there.

"I hope everything is all right," she said.

"It is now," replied Leta. "Eunice has always been jealous of Ellen. She'll watch her tongue for the remainder of this party, anyway. I gave her quite a reading off. As soon as she fixes her face she'll be in, and she'd better be as meek as a lamb."

"And I thought you said you were a coward," laughed Cori.

"I am until I get angry enough not to be," Leta said, and continued, "I wish that you and Ellen were going to be here longer. I'd throw a real shindig. It must be difficult for you in that small town."

"It is a bit," said Cori. "I wish we had more time too, but as you know, Ellen has a husband to get back to and I have a job."

"Well, maybe you can make it again soon. Fall is the best time to be in New York. Why don't you talk to Ellen about it? We could have a ball."

"Sounds like fun to me. I'll mention it to Ellen. Of course a lot depends upon whether the boys go to boarding school or not." Cori picked up the glass that Leta had filled for her.

"Oh no," moaned Leta, slapping her forehead with her hand. "Don't tell me they're considering public school!"

"Is that such a horrible thing?" inquired Cori, raising her eyebrows.

"Certainly not. I wasn't thinking of the educational aspect. I was thinking of the problem for you and Ellen."

"Well," said Cori, "at least we have two things in our favor. We live almost across the street from each other and my job is not a strictly nine-to-five one." Cori was amazed at her ability to discuss this so freely with Leta, whom she'd met less than two hours ago. How wonderful it must be, she thought, to have friends like this, with whom one wouldn't have to pretend. She thought of the folks in Camsburg and, fond as she was of them, she dreaded returning.

"That's a help I imagine, but New York is really the easiest place for people like us. I have to pretend for an average of eight hours a day, more than that I couldn't take. I'm awfully glad that Ellen found you, though. I was worried about her moving out into the provinces." Leta reached for a cigarette and lit it.

"I've an idea that Camsburg is a little less provincial than you imagine, Leta," Cori retorted. "It's a pretty heavy-drinking, hard-living town and the people aren't quite so unsophisticated as you might suppose." In spite of herself, Cori was beginning to like Leta whom she'd been prepared to hate. There was a warmth, a magnetism about her that Cori couldn't define.

"I wouldn't dare argue with you on that subject," Leta said. "I'm a native New Yorker and therefore no authority on small towns."

Leta moved from behind the bar to serve the other refills.

Cori rejoined Ellen and, as the others were talking, said in a low whisper, "What are we doing about dinner?"

Ellen whispered back, "I think it might be nice to go back to the hotel and be alone, don't you?"

Cori sighed in relief. "I was hoping you'd say that, honey. This has been a bit of a strain, you know. Can we go when we finish this round?"

Ellen nodded in reply.

At that moment, Eunice emerged from the bedroom, bag and gloves in hand.

"Leta," she called, and Leta crossed the room to her side.

They confided in low tones and then approached the group.

Leta explained, "Eunice isn't feeling very well and thinks she'd better go along home."

"But Eunice," Edna said, standing up, "you were supposed to have dinner with us. We're leaving after this drink. Don't you want to wait?"

Eunice shook her head. "Thanks Edna, but I do have a splitting headache and don't feel like eating. The best place for me is home."

The boys stood up as she started for the door.

John asked, "Would you like me to see you to a cab, Eunice?"

"No dear, don't bother. The doorman can take care of me. Goodnight everyone."

The door closed behind her and a general sigh of relief swept the room.

"What did you do to her?" asked Tony of Leta.

"For once, I just told her off. I think I got the courage from Cori. She'll find some way to make me pay for this though." Leta went to the hi-fi set to change the records.

John looked at Jean and Edna. "You two are absolute saints, you know. I don't understand how you tolerate her as often as you do."

Jean smiled. "We can't help feeling sorry for her. She always manages to alienate people and has no friends to speak of, except us. When she's with just the two of us, she can be a reasonably nice person."

"It's because we don't represent any sort of threat to her," Edna put in.

"In other words, I do," said Ellen.

"Of course you do," responded Edna. "You were one of the biggest affairs in Leta's life and Eunice is so neurotic and immature than even the past makes her insecure."

Cori winced inside at the mention of Leta's affair with Ellen, but mentally she slapped her own wrist. She certainly wanted to be more mature than Eunice.

Everyone was reaching the end of the last round of drinks and they all stood around saying good-bye.

"Next time, do make it for a longer time," Leta said. Turning to Cori, she added, "If you ever come up alone, please call me. I'm sure Ellen wouldn't mind."

They kissed Ellen good-bye and Cori shook hands all around.

It was heavenly to be alone again, even in the taxi. It was heavenly to contemplate the evening and the following days that stretched before them as they raced back to their little shell of anonymity.

"I love you, my darling," were the first words Cori spoke on Wednesday morning when she awakened from the deep coma-like sleep that is so often the result of physical fulfillment.

She ran a finger down Ellen's spine, across the little valley that was her waist, then enclosing the warm breast that fit her hand so well, she gently rolled Ellen over on her back.

Ellen let out a little groan of protest at first. Then, as Cori's hand continued to explore the hollows and curves of her body, the groan was gradually transposed into murmurs of delight. Her hands moved in frenzied gestures until they found Cori's hair which she held in a vise-like grip, pulling Cori's mouth to her own.

As usual, it was an ascent to the clouds, and with the last exhausted moan of pleasure, they lay entangled in each other's arms.

"You, my darling, are the most marvelous improvement on the alarm clock that I've ever encountered," gasped Ellen, with a satisfied smile.

"I'm cheaper, too," Cori said smiling back. "You don't have to wind me up, either."

"You can say that again," laughed Ellen. "I don't think you ever run down."

"Not with you around m'dear. I'm operated by electricity for which you supply the current." Cori reached for her cigarettes, lit two and gave one to Ellen.

"At what ungodly hour have you waked me up?"

Cori groped for her watch on the night table, "It's exactly eight-ten. Too early for you?"

"No. In fact, I'm glad. I don't want to waste too much of our precious time sleeping. Shall we order breakfast?"

"Might as well. After all the athletics last night and this morning too, I'm quite ravenous." Cori picked up the phone and ordered.

"Let's not dress yet," said Ellen. "Right now, I couldn't care less about leaving this room again before it's time to go to the airport."

"That's a whole week, Ellen! It sounds marvelous, but by the end of it I think we'll both be ready for the hospital."

"You're probably right," Ellen sighed. "But we don't have to do too much running around do we? I know that when we get back, I'll regret every minute that we weren't alone."

"No, honey, we don't have to do much more than step out for a breath of fresh air occasionally." Cori frowned and continued, "There's not much chance of bumping into any of your friends, is there?"

"Very slight," answered Ellen. "I know the places to avoid. Of course, I think Leta might have known we were lying about going back but I'm sure she knows why and understands."

"Speaking of Leta, I must admit I rather liked her. I was prepared not to, you know."

"I thought you would. She's really quite nice and I'm glad you sensed it. A lot of people don't at first." Ellen got up and put on her housecoat.

"What about John and Tony? Are they lovers?"

"Of course. They've lived together for years," called Ellen from the bathroom.

"They're the first gay men I've met."

Ellen came out of the bathroom laughing. "I see you picked up that word last night."

"Yes, I did," said Cori, "and 'straight' is the opposite of 'gay.' You never told me."

"I guess it never occurred to me. They aren't exactly a part of the Camsburg vernacular."

"I liked John and Tony. Are there many men like them?"

"In one sense, yes. In another, no. There are more gay men around than the average person realizes, but there aren't too many like John and Tony. Men don't seem to form lasting relationships as frequently as women."

"Oh," said Cori, pensively. "What about Leta? She doesn't seem to stick with any one person very long."

"Leta's different. I don't think she wants anything to last. She likes her freedom too much. But look at Jean and Edna. They've been together about fifteen years and I could introduce you to a number of couples like them. Put on your housecoat, darling. Breakfast will be here any minute."

Cori leaped out of bed and got into her robe.

As the knock sounded at the door, Ellen whispered frantically, "Quick! Mess up the other bed! We forgot to turn it down last night!"

Cori bounded across the room, turned down the spread and dived into the bed, scrambling the sheets and punching at the pillow.

"There, that should do it," she said, sitting up in the middle of the mess. "You can let him in now."

Over breakfast, they continued their discussion.

"What's wrong with Eunice?" Cori wanted to know.

"Frankly, Eunice is a real bitch, although in all fairness I must add that she can't help it. She's terribly mixed up. Leta finally talked her into going to a psychiatrist but it's going to take a long time to unravel her problems."

"Is she really gay?"

"I don't think she knows for sure. Leta was her first affair and she fell hard. When Leta grew tired, as she always does, Eunice went to pieces and all her neuroses came to the fore. Until Leta, she'd always been a man's woman and she hasn't learned to cope with gay women. There's quite a difference you know, and Eunice doesn't understand it. I doubt that she ever will."

"I see why she dislikes you so," said Cori. "It's more than your affair with Leta, isn't it?"

"Yes," Ellen replied. "She resents my ability to move from one world to another with no apparent difficulty. Although she can't admit it to herself, she'd like to be able to do the same, but unless analysis were to bring about some drastic changes, it wouldn't work for her."

"Why not?" asked Cori, finishing her coffee and lighting a cigarette.

Ellen took a deep breath and thought for a moment.

"Because her motives would be different. You see Cori, I didn't marry Walter for security alone, knowing that I'd continue to have affairs with women. And even though I've had two affairs, I've kept my bargain with Walter. I've been a good wife and mother. This is what Eunice couldn't do. She'd marry some poor guy for security and position in the conventional community and then proceed to make him miserable. She'd never be willing to make any sacrifices in return for her security."

"Have you made many, Ellen?"

"Until I met you, I don't think so," answered Ellen, seeking Cori's hand across the table. "Sure, I missed a few good parties, broke some dates with Leta, but I couldn't call those sacrifices. It's different now. Every time I leave you, I feel like the original Christian martyr. I love you so, Cori, that whatever feelings I've had for anyone else are completely eclipsed by it."

"It's the same with me, darling. Are you feeling a little guilty about it?"

"I'm afraid I am, a little." She gripped Cori's hand and gazed at her intently.

"Cori, would you be terribly upset if I let Walter have his way about sending the boys to school in Camsburg? If I insist on their going to boarding school, I'll never be sure that I didn't do it selfishly, for my own convenience. I'm not at all sure I could live with it."

"I understand, honey," Cori answered gently. "I rather thought you'd come around to it. And don't worry—we'll manage. It'll be easier than coping with your guilt feelings."

Ellen got up, walked around the table and sat in Cori's lap.

She smiled and said, "If you don't mind my saying so, darling, I think you're growing up."

"I'm trying like the very devil," Cori responded, kissing Ellen on the neck. "It isn't always easy, though," she continued. "So please have patience with me."

"Of course I will," said Ellen as she bit Cori's ear. "Shall we try the other bed?"

And they did.

The ensuing days sped past with increasing rapidity until Wednesday, the day of their departure, was upon them.

With a certain sadness, they said good-bye to their room, but they both knew that what had developed between them there could never be destroyed.

The flight to Atlanta was a normal one and everything else went according to routine until, upon entering the terminal waiting room, they heard a familiar voice.

"Hi Ellen, Cori! Over here!"

They turned in the direction of the voice and there, hurrying toward them with her usual awkward gait, was Sara Leggett.

"Am I glad I didn't miss you!" she panted. "Had to come in for some shopping so I called Walter and got your flight number. Thought we might have dinner together before driving home."

"Why, that's wonderful, Sara," said Ellen, recovering beautifully. "Such a nice surprise to be met, isn't it, Cori?"

"You said it," agreed Cori, trying to smile sincerely to hide her sinking feeling of disappointment. "Where would you like to go?"

"I thought the Shack might be nice. It's the most convenient, too, since it's on the way out of town."

"Sounds good. I don't think Ellen's ever been there."

"No, I haven't, but I've heard of it. All we have to do is get our bags, Sara."

"Did you bring your car?" asked Cori.

"Yes," replied Sara. "Why don't I go ahead and get a table? You won't be far behind and it will save some time in case they're crowded."

"Good idea," said Cori. "We'll see you there."

They watched Sara's back as she strode through the terminal and out the door.

"Where are the checks?" demanded Cori.

"Here, in my bag." Ellen fumbled for a moment, produced two little yellow cards and handed them to Cori, who marched off toward the baggage counter.

"Hey, wait for me," called Ellen, running a few steps to catch up.

She caught up with Cori at the counter and stood silently beside her until their baggage arrived. Cori's face was grim, jaws clamped, brow furrowed.

"What is it, Cori?" she asked, as they followed the porter with their bags.

"Wait till we get to the car," Cori snapped.

At the lot, they waited quietly until the car was brought around and the luggage stowed in the trunk. Then they got in and Cori maneuvered the car into the street.

"Now will you tell me what's wrong, other than the fact that we won't be having dinner alone?" Ellen insisted.

"I don't like the look of it. Why should Sara choose today to come shopping and why should she bother to come all the way out here to meet us just so we could all have dinner? When she comes in for shopping, she's usually back in Camsburg for dinner with Al and the kids."

"I don't see anything so grim about it, darling. What could be wrong, anyway?"

"I told you weeks ago that I had a funny feeling about Sara. She seems to be able to see through people. I wonder if she's seen through us." Cori's voice was tense, worried.

"Honey, let's not borrow trouble," soothed Ellen. "It may be nothing more than Sara's desire to have dinner in town with girl friends for a change."

"Let's hope so," said Cori, her teeth clenched.

They drove the rest of the way without speaking.

Sara had gotten a nice private booth in the back and she waved to them as they entered.

At the table, they found that she had already ordered three scotch sours.

"The Shack makes the best in town," Sara explained, "so I thought you'd approve."

The sours arrived and they all touched glasses and sipped.

"You're so right," observed Ellen. "This is delicious. Just what I needed."

"Did you get all your shopping done, Sara?" asked Cori, trying to get the conversation started. She had noticed that Sara was unnaturally quiet.

"As much as I ever do," Sara replied, smiling. "It's a job that's never finished, especially where children are concerned."

"Don't I know it!" Ellen agreed. "My boys grow so fast I can hardly keep them decently covered."

"When are they coming home?" queried Sara.

"Shortly after Labor Day and I can hardly wait. It's the longest they've ever been away from us."

"I've heard that you might send them to boarding school. Is that true?" Sara lit a cigarette and waited for Ellen's answer.

"We did consider it since they've always gone to private school, but we've decided that they're young yet to be away from home. There'll be time enough for boarding school later."

Cori thought she detected a look of relief on Sara's face as she said, "I think you're right. Our kids have always gone to public school and I dread the day when they'll have to go away to college."

The waiter came by and they ordered another round of drinks, and dinner.

When the refills came, Sara picked up her glass, eying them both intently. "I'm going to speak freely and hope that you'll take what I'm going to say in the spirit that it's meant."

"Why Sara," said Ellen, raising her eyebrows. "You sound quite serious."

Cori was quiet.

"I'm dead serious, Ellen. But before I go on, I want you both to know that I'm speaking as a friend."

"I'm sure you are, Sara. I've grown to feel close to you in the short time I've lived in Camsburg and there's no doubt about how you and Cori feel about each other. But what's this all about? Don't keep us in suspense." Seemingly unperturbed, Ellen picked up a cigarette and lit it.

Cori, unable to find any words, nodded her assent.

"Well," said Sara, with a sigh, "I'm going to be blunt and plunge right in. I'm on to your secret. I know what's going on between you."

"Sara Leggett," blurted Cori, having found her voice. "What in hell are you talking about?" She tried to sound shocked. Actually, she was stunned.

Ellen was still calm. "Cori, stop that. Sara's no fool and she's our friend. Let's hear what she has to say."

"Well," Sara began, "guess you want to know how I found out. At first I just sensed it. I might as well tell you that I'm no stranger to such things myself—that should explain my perceptiveness. But just sensing it wasn't enough. I figured I could be wrong, but then Mattie started telling me about Cameo's new schedule. You know how they talk, and I began to put two and two together. It still wasn't enough to draw a definite conclusion. The clincher was what I saw through my binoculars one day when I was practicing my little hobby of bird watching. I don't think I have to tell you what I saw."

Cori felt herself go white and knew that Sara's eyes were on her, but she couldn't bring herself to look up, nor could she look at Ellen.

"Well, Sara," Ellen finally broke the silence. "What are we supposed to say—or do, for that matter? Frankly, I don't even know how to react."

"Remember, I'm on your side. That's most important. You both know I'm no gossip and I'm not a prude either. As I said before, I've had my own experience—when I was in college—so I'm not without understanding. I just felt that you should be aware that I know because if

I could catch it, someone else might too. And another person might be quick to condemn, and also, to talk."

"Have you any suggestions as to what we should do now?" asked Ellen.

"Be careful, even more careful than you've been. I won't say cut it out. I know you can't—not now, anyway. It's good your boys are going to school in Camsburg. You won't be able to see each other quite as much and it will scotch any suspicions that may arise."

The waiter brought their dinners, but none of them seemed to notice.

Sara finished her sour, looking directly at Cori. "I do have something in particular to say to you, Cori."

Cori looked up and her eyes met Sara's. It wasn't so bad after all because she saw only kindness and sympathy.

"Yes, Sara?"

"It's about Matt. You know I'm fond of him. He's a fine man, very much in love with you, and you've no right to continue using him as a cover. He deserves better than that and you know it."

"You're right," responded Cori. "I'd planned to do something about Matt after this trip. I guess I'll just have to tell him it's all off."

Sara reached across the table and gripped Cori's arm.

"Just be sure first. Be very, very sure that you don't want what Ellen and I have. Because if you do, Matt's the man to give it to you and you may never find his equal. After all, this may be only a phase."'

"I'm afraid not, Sara," Cori was more relaxed now. "It's not the first time for me. It happened in college, too."

"Well, think it over carefully, anyway. And whatever you do, be discreet. Remember, if there's any sort of scandal, you'll get off easier than Ellen. You can always run but she has her husband and children."

For the first time, Cori turned to face Ellen, and what she saw almost dissolved her to tears, tears of relief. Ellen's eyes still shone with love and tonight, with reassurance too. Exposure hadn't destroyed their love as she had feared it might.

"Well ladies, I guess we'd better eat." Cori smiled at Sara. "I don't mind your knowing, Sara. And please don't worry. If it starts to hurt any innocent bystanders, we'll give up, won't we, Ellen?"

"Of course, Cori," Ellen answered. "You've known from the beginning that I'd never allow my family to be hurt." Looking at Sara, she added, "I'm fond of Matt, too."

They ate quietly and over coffee the conversation began again.

"I hope you two don't think I'm just an old meddler," Sara opened. "I'm concerned for you both. What you do is your own business and you can be sure I'll never mention this to anyone, not even Al."

"I'm not the least bit worried about that, Sara." Cori grinned. "You're known as a sphinx and with good reason."

Ellen's spirits were rising and she said lightly, "I hope you're the only bird watcher who's been out at the lake recently."

Sara laughed. "As far as I know, I'm the only one around Camsburg. Nevertheless, if I were you, I'd be careful in that clearing. It's not as private as you thought."

"That's for sure," quipped Cori. "Sara, it's too bad you have your car. We could all ride home together."

"I know, but I didn't dare risk it. There was an outside chance that you people might not have cared for my company after this session." Sara finished her coffee and dug into her bag. "This is on me," she added.

They tried to argue but were overruled.

"We'd better hit the road soon," Ellen said. "Walter may start to worry."

When the check was paid, they walked Sara to her car.

"Drive carefully," Cori cautioned her. "We won't be far behind you."

They waved as she pulled off, then found Cori's car and got in.

As Cori slammed the door, she emitted a long sigh.

"Whew! That was a session!"

"Yes, it certainly was," replied Ellen. "Are you terribly upset, darling?"

"Not anymore. At first I thought I'd go right through the floor but I'm all right now. She must have seen me kiss you at the lake."

"Thank heavens we didn't do anything else at the lake!" exclaimed Ellen.

"And thank heavens Sara's no ordinary bird watcher. We'd have been a real discovery." They both laughed.

The tension was broken and they had a pleasant ride home. On the straight stretches, Cori's hand sought Ellen's, and they were quiet with their memories of an almost perfect ten days that belonged solely to them forever.

The intimate story of a forbidden affair

The Whispered Sex

by Kay Martin

She had come in from the pool naked and Joyce found herself looking at the aesthetically proportioned body, then turning away, unaccountably embarrassed.

"Wait up for me tonight," Vikki had whispered—and she remembered the erratic pounding of her heart. "Take a cat nap if you get sleepy. Or read. There's a wonderful book about our kind of love..."

The Whispered Sex

It was going to be one of those oppressive mid-September days that native Angelenos explain away to visiting firemen as "unusual." It was a little past nine in the morning, but already the air lay warm and heavy. Joyce Conway crossed the Hollywood bus station, checked her suitcases, then weaved through a lethargic, travel-wrinkled crowd toward the public telephones.

Outside the booths she thumbed through a tattered Hollywood phone book. The Hub—Hubal—Hubbard. Someone back in Vale View, two hours south by Greyhound, had told her Russ was no longer touring. He had his own apartment now, his phone should be listed. But people didn't always get things straight. If Russ was staying at a hotel—!

Someone was staring at her. Joyce looked up, responding automatically to the familiar sensation. This one was short and squat, old enough to be her father, frowsy in an outdated, Palm Beach suit. He clutched a worn, simulated leather sample case and made impatient sucking noises with the cigar in his mouth.

"I'll only be a second," she mumbled.

He looked her over as though he might be taking inventory, afraid to miss any small detail. And that reaction was familiar, too. "Take your time, miss," he said. The inflections insinuated other words. It was her own fault, wearing the flesh-colored sheath that clung to her body in weather like this. Still, the man's gaping admiration was only ten percent embarrassing and ninety percent reassuring. She resumed her search.

She found his name then. Russell J. Hubbard. Repeating the phone number to herself silently, Joyce brushed past the man with the cigar and stepped into one of the cubicles, folding the door behind her. It was stifling inside the booth, but she didn't blame the lack of air for her strangled breath. She dialed, then waited, listening to the rhythmic buzz. It was a long time before the sleep-heavy voice answered.

"H'lo?"

"Is this Russ? Russ Hubbard?"

There was a pause. "I dunno. Wait'll I wake myself up and ask."

It was Russ, all right. Groggy, but unmistakably Russ. "This is Joyce Conway."

"*Who?*"

With less confidence, she explained, "Joyce Conway. From home." Silence. "Remember, you had organized your first band and you played a dance at Vale View High. You asked me out and the next Friday—"

"Oh, sure!" But his enthusiasm sounded hesitant.

"I was only a sophomore then. Little over three years ago."

"Yes, sure. I was going to call you again, but I fell into thirty bucks and headed out this way. What a gas!"

"I hear you have a small combo now. The *Vale View Reporter* had a story about you being the most promising jazz trumpet man around."

Ross's laughter came through the receiver. "Five gets you ten my mother wrote it."

She was getting nowhere, but if she could keep him talking long enough—! "Well, I believed it. You were terrific when I heard you and I can imagine how much experience you've had since."

His laughter was infectious, the way she had remembered it. "Yal. I hear ole Satchmo can't sleep nights, worrying." Then, his tone changing abruptly, "Joyce Conway. My past keeps catching up with me."

"You don't remember," she said.

"Hell, yes, I remember. Black hair down to your shoulders. You had blue eyes."

Most men would have remembered the hair and eyes second. "I still do."

He laughed again, wide awake now. "You had long black eyelashes, too. Still got those?"

"I brought all the equipment intact."

"I'll bet. Hey, what goes? You here in town to stay?"

"I'm just—looking it over." That sounded more sophisticated than telling him she had quit that crummy junior college and was hoping to find a job. Even the latter was an excuse; she had come to see Russ, tired of the prolonged daydream.

"I'd like to see you, kid. But I'm blowing up a storm at this crib in the San Fernando Valley. Vikki's."

She fought to keep disappointment out of her voice. "You don't have to brush me off politely, Russ. I only called to say hello."

"That wasn't a brush. Look, have you found a place to stay yet?"

"That's what I'll be doing today."

"I was wondering. If you aren't too pooped after that, maybe you'd like to meet me at the club around closing time. Say, quarter of two?"

"In the *morning?*"

This time, hearing his laughter, she felt she had made a genuine hayseed of herself. "I keep forgetting you're one of the day people. I guess it's a bum idea."

"Oh, no. No, I think it might be fun. Vikki's, did you say?"

"Yal, in North Hollywood. Will you be driving?"

"No."

"Oh, brother. Well, you could take a bus to the Valley and grab a hack. Just tell the cabbie Vikki's." There was another pause in which the intriguing invitation threatened to disappear in smoke. "I dunno, girl. I close at Vikki's tonight and we won't open in Long Beach until next week. After tonight I'll be free to show you around. That'll be better than—well, a kid like you shouldn't be cruising around after midnight alone."

"I'm not a child," she told him firmly. "I've been around."

And it was only after she had convinced him of that fact that Russ confirmed their date.

The tubby character with the cigar was still riffling through a phone book when she stepped out of the booth. He glanced upward and, impulsively, she smiled and winked at him. He did a fast take, but before he could speak, Joyce was clicking her way toward the checkstand. And why did I do *that*, she wondered? *But Russ had remembered and asked to see her.* The come-on gesture had been just for practice.

Vikki's club lay under a heavy blue haze of cigarette smoke. She had come too early and smoked too many cigarettes herself, adding to the dull, swimming sensation in her head. The next Manhattan, Joyce told herself, would be sipped slowly. Not gulped like the first, after which the waiter had appeared at her dark corner table like some silent genie, reappearing seconds later with the drink that sat before her now, half gone. And if she smoked less, Russ would be less apt to know she was jittery, though it helped to turn away and light up when men shuffled past her table on the way to the john. Helped to be doing something when the glassy-eyed couples appraised her on their way out of the club.

These things could be managed. The important thing was hearing Russ again, seeing him smile his recognition from the tiny wrought iron railed platform across the room. Now the spotlight caught the rust-colored crew cut and the lean, wiry frame of his body, throwing golden highlights on the horn Russ never merely played. Sang, spoke, wove poetry and sent out something of himself, but never merely played.

Shadowed behind Russ, someone caught his mood with an alto sax, twisting around his message, arguing his points in another language. Someone else made a tingling ladder of her spine with vibes. Joyce had listened to endless records, crammed books on jazz, eager, before she left home, to know something of Russ Hubbard's world. Now the technical knowledge was unimportant. You didn't have to understand his kind of music—you only had to give yourself to it. You dug it inside, the way looking at Russ made you want something wild and free that you couldn't define—something you had never experienced because none of the puerile young nowheres you had dated back home had it to give. Not that they hadn't tried. But somehow you knew they couldn't have, and so you waited, hungry, remembering one innocuous little movie date because a red-haired guy with freckles on his nose and big dreams singing in his head kissed you goodnight and let it go at that.

Now, knowing that Russ toured the country with that horn, doing all the things she pretended to know about, the second important thing was not to let him know. Starry-eyed kid getting her first glimpse of the big city. God, he'd treat her like a ten-year-old sister if he knew. Take her to another corny movie and forget she existed. Joyce drained the glass in her hand. She heard scattered applause as the music ended, and then Russ, lighting up as he walked, was making his way to her table. The skinny, sullen waiter got there first.

"Almost closing time, miss."

"She's waiting for me, Pete," Russ addressed the waiter. Then, turning that wide grin of his toward Joyce, "Hey, this was damned nice of you. And you look better than I remembered." The waiter hadn't budged and Russ spoke to him again. "Give her another of whatever she's drinking, Pete. Double scotch for me."

"Miss Prince don't go for the help drinkin'," the waiter said thinly. Joyce felt warm under the fixed gaze of little rodent eyes. "She also don't go for dames in here alone."

""Dames with *dames*, she doesn't approve of," Russ corrected him. "Look, I can't get fired because I've got one more set to play and I fold here. And, like, there'd better be a double scotch on the goddam bandstand when this break is over."

The waiter shrugged and moved away, mumbling: "Miss Prince is gonna raise hell about the dame alone."

"You know what you can do for Miss Prince," Russ said evenly.

Without turning, the sour little waiter muttered, "That'll be the day!"

Russ pulled a chair over, straddled it backwards and grinned at Joyce over its gilded back. "I can't drink with the clientele, but I'm allowed to ogle the good-looking ones. I'm trying to come up with something complimentary that won't sound like a line."

"Try a line," Joyce invited. "I'll supply any parts you forget."

"I hope Pete hasn't been giving you the needle. He's only following orders. Vikki's hypersensitive about her reputation."

"I guess I'm breaking the rules again."

"Nothingsville. You'll catch her act in a minute. The boss doesn't only make rules. She sings."

"Part of the floor show?"

"She's *it*." Russ peered over at her empty glass. "Manhattan?"

"Yes."

"That your drink?"

"When they're mixed right." Joyce leaned forward to let Russ light her cigarette. She inhaled deeply, closing her eyes in what she hoped was sophisticated boredom, giving him a moment in which to study her.

"Maybe I figured you wrong. You know what I was sorry about this morning after you called?"

"No, what?"

"Well, you got me out of the sack and my brain wasn't in gear yet. But later on I decided this idea was for the birds. Asking you to make this scene alone."

"Why did you think that?"

"I don't know. I said to myself, man, you should have waited and taken this chick to Disneyland. Bought her a hot fudge sundae, like."

Joyce laughed as though he had said something ludicrous. "Do you still think that?"

He looked at her closely. "Damned if I know."

Joyce dragged on the cigarette. "You sound like one of those cubes in the women's magazines. One of the heroes who comes home from the wars expecting the girl next door to wear pigtails. And braces on her teeth."

Russ nodded, then in a faked fervor he murmured, "You've grown up, Geraldine. You're a woman. You're—*beautiful!*"

They laughed and an overdressed bag in a nearby booth surveyed them with bleary, critical eyes.

"So Geraldine's come a long way from Vale View." Rat-eyes appeared with Joyce's drink and they were silent until he left. "'What goes on back there? Same old jazz? My folks don't write facts, only questions."

"Same old jazz," Joyce told him, pleased with the husky sound too many cigarettes had given her voice. "My dad's still setting type for the local throwaway sheet. I worked on it awhile until I got bored. I learned enough about advertising production to help me find a job. I hope."

"That's what you're planning to do in L.A.?"

"If something turns up."

"I had an idea you might be out to make Hollywood."

"Or have it make me? No, thanks."

Russ smoked thoughtfully, studying her face. "I guess you've been around enough to get wise, anyway. Though God knows around where."

"San Diego's a big town." She drank from her glass, looking directly into his eyes. Terrific the way liquor gave you courage to act the way you could only dream of acting over a sundae. "But I believe in broadening my vistas. It's sort of—a hobby."

Russ couldn't be stared down. "I collect matchbook covers m'self. But, like, this hobby of yours interests me."

"I suspected it might."

Russ shoved back out of the chair. "Later for you, honey." He stamped out his cigarette and returned to the platform.

She had done beautifully, beautifully. Russ hadn't expected her to be in the same league with girls he'd met and probably made love to, touring the country. But she had overcome that little obstacle, and there he was, with the scotch, or whatever it was he had ordered in his hand, not looking at her, but knowing she was around, Joyce told herself hopefully—really knowing she was around!

Russ exchanged the glass for his horn then, and the crew slid into a slow, heady intro—a wailing, indigo blend that did to Joyce what the third Manhattan was doing and what looking into the trumpet man's eyes had done; holding matches to the senses and making the body yearn to reach out and out—and maybe tonight for the first time, to be met halfway.

Her hand trembled as she lifted the drink to her lips. Reeling sensation, eyes following the slate-blue smoke whirling upward the length of a spotlight beam. And suddenly the minor wailing sounds, the smoke haze and the inner hunger crystallized, taking solid shape in the form of the woman on the platform—the woman Russ had called the boss—Vikki Prince.

She was tall—magnificently tall. Not with the lean, gaunt look of the model, but full-hipped and voluptuously molded. Firm, audacious breasts threatened to spill out of the silver lamé gown that plunged downward from an already abandoned décolletage, barely sheathing the nipples. There was, Joyce decided, no way in or out of that dress; it had been dropped around Vikki at birth and she had grown into it until her body strained against the shimmering metallic cloth.

And it's strange, Joyce thought, that I've noticed her body first, the way men look there and there and there before they even know I have a face. Strange because Vikki's face, almost more than her body, symbolized and carried like a standard something frankly sexual. Her eyes, accented by thick mascara, were of the distinctive yellow-green peculiar to long-haired black cats. At first you saw only the eyes and the unguarded invitation in them. Then, slowly—because you had to savor a face like Vikki's slowly—you became aware of the ripe, sensuous mouth, the strong chin, and prominent cheekbones that seemed to pull upward completing the feline effect of her eyes. Her hair was cut carelessly short but its startling color made you think of opulence, of abundance, as though it fell in cascades to her waist. For Vikki Prince's hair was silver. Not white, not platinum, not something bleached to a nondescript shade in between. It was as silver as the breath-constricting gown.

Is it because I'm woozy, Joyce wondered, or because she looks like every woman in the world sometimes wishes she could look? It made no sense to be breathing faster, staring with the same gaping fascination as the skin-headed old fool at the next table—taking in Vikki like every man in the place. She was conscious, then, of a throaty voice, low-registered and reeking of the stuff that poured from Vikki Prince's eyes. Vikki, eyelids heavy, challenging the faceless crowd, half-singing, half-murmuring:

Baby, baby, baby...let me clarify-y-y my situation!

(Mournful wail of saxophone, wild growl from the trumpet. God, what music could do to you inside!)

You were hard to come by; let me make the most of the sensation! Move slow!

(Vikki saying it now, breathless, looking out at her audience with an expression hovering between insinuation and contempt. And the sax crying its resentment.)

You hear me, baby? Move slow!

Vikki's voice and body moved languidly through two choruses of unmelodic double-entendres that passed for lyrics. Apart from an occasional lascivious snicker, the crowd gave her its rapt attention until, finally, with what Joyce had learned to recognize as a wild shake and drop-off on double G from Russ, Vikki was cut off to enthusiastic applause and wolf-whistles. She changed her pace for the encore. Something about someone never having had it so good, backed with a wild beat from the vibe man who doubled on drums. And a third selection, reverting to the heady tempo and singing voice. It was an old standard, but Vikki could have created a bedroom atmosphere singing "God Bless America."

It ended too soon. A chord from Russ and his boys signaled the finish. People strained and staggered to their feet, gradually edging out of the club. Glaring bulbs exploded into light, chairs scraped as the combo deserted the stage, hurrying out like kids on the last day of school. Pete and two other waiters piled glasses, some partially filled, onto trays, and the mood Vikki had woven was forgotten in a hurried, business-like rush to close shop. And Vikki paced the let's-get-the-hell-out-of-here activity, shouting orders, barking crisp answers to questions. Then, finally, riveting her gaze on the last, lone customer.

Joyce lighted a cigarette shakily as the sinewy figure approached her corner. "What's the matter, honey? Got no mama, no papa, no home?" The raspy, masculine voice sounded reproachful, but Vikki's smile was warm, her eyes curious.

"Am I in the way, Miss Prince? I can wait for Russ outside." Joyce got to her feet, her cigarette pack falling to the floor as her arm brushed the table. The clumsy move embarrassed her and she leaned unsteadily to pick up the white pack.

Vikki's hand stopped her, touching Joyce's arm. "Here, let me."

Vikki scooped up the cigarettes, handing them to Joyce with an amused smile. Her eyes, Joyce felt, were not smiling, but appraising. It was from nowhere to get this looped, to drop things like a stumblebum and to imagine intimacy in the smile of this silver-haired sexpot of a woman. You felt this way when Russ looked at you—felt this way with men. She thanked Vikki, a rush of warmth flooding her face.

"I hate to see Russ leave," Vikki was saying. "He blows cool horn and I shouldn't have signed him for a limited run. But I guess that's no news to you, Miss—" She hesitated significantly.

"Conway. Joyce Conway."

"I don't remember seeing you around before."

Joyce decided not to mention Vale View. "I just got in from San Diego."

Vikki continued to stare at her openly. "Tell me, do the nice girls down there sit around cribs like this alone? Waiting around for musicians who hit the bottle and haven't had a thought above the belt since they were fourteen?"

Awkwardly, Joyce explained, "I've known Russ since I was in high school. We're from the same small town."

"That's better," Vikki approved. "That sophisticated role didn't suit you at all. You're less vulnerable being yourself."

Joyce fought down her resentment. Still, there was something honest in Vikki's analysis. "If that's a warning, thanks."

"Another one. Beautiful girls come in gross lots in these parts. If you're here to beat your head against the silver screen—"

"Russ jumped to that conclusion, too. No, I'm looking for a job in advertising. Or with a newspaper."

Vikki Prince dropped her maternal concern and brightened. "I know someone who might be able to help you there."

"Oh, really?"

"Friend of mine's a fashion artist. She handles the ads for a flock of toney women's wear shops on a free-lance basis. Would that be up your alley?"

Joyce smiled. "I could make it my alley."

"Good girl. Edith's been bitching about being overworked. Maybe she could fit you in."

"Edith—?"

"Listen, don't go calling on her cold. Give me a buzz and I'll arrange a meeting. I'm in the Valley book. Vikki Prince."

Joyce was thanking her, fuzzily, for the second time when Russ joined them. He had changed to sport clothes, carrying his tux over one arm, his trumpet case in the other, "Like they say, Vikki, all good things—and all that jazz."

"Please! I can't stand these sentimental farewells." Vikki smiled. "I told Pete to put a bottle of our best scotch into your car. Check before you drive off, will you? I don't exactly trust the little weasel."

"Will do," Russ said. "And thanks."

"And come back, Russ. Have your agent call me the next time you're open. That group I've booked to replace you is from hunger." Vikki's personality flooded the club even when she wasn't performing. She's nice, Joyce thought dimly.

"Thanks again," Russ said. Then, in unexpected irritation, "Goddammit, why are you always doing things for people and making them thank you?"

Vikki turned to Joyce. "Don't they teach him manners in that little town where you grew up?"

Joyce flushed. Russ had obviously been drinking since he left her table and his rudeness made her uneasy.

"Didn't take you long to pump out her life history, did it?" Russ said, annoyed. He gestured toward the door with his head. "Let's cut out, Joyce."

They were near the door when Vikki called out, "I meant it, Russ. Come back."

"Why in hell don't you hire a girl band?" Russ said over his shoulder.

Vikki's reply was indistinct as they walked into the street, but to Joyce it sounded like, "It doesn't pay to mix business with pleasure."

She felt a vague urge to go back and apologize for Russ's surly behavior and to thank Vikki Prince again for her interest. But that would wait until she phoned her. Meanwhile, Russ was saying something about his car being parked across the street and that he hoped Pete had followed through with that scotch because, man, he had a whole week to sleep off a real tear and wasn't it like crazy that Joyce had made the scene at such an opportune moment? And saying he didn't booze it up on the job, but when a gig was over, a guy ought to let his hair down a little because, man, blowing your lungs out in these smoky dives was rough, even though it beat playing tank town one-nighters with a pop band, playing square music and ruining your eyes following the dots, and, man, Vikki might be queer, but at least she appreciated the New Sound and she had remembered him with a bottle—

Swaying against him as they crossed the deserted street, Joyce wondered why she was more conscious of the silver-haired woman she had left behind than of Russ.

"It's because I'm a little tight," she answered herself, aloud.

They reached Russ's little M.G. "Think of the time that'll save," she heard him say.

"Time?" Joyce stumbled as he helped her into the car.

"I don't imagine you teach that hobby of yours sober?"

And then she remembered that whatever Russ had in mind now had been her own idea.

Paris, the world's mistress, taught her the pangs of love

Appointment in Paris

by Fay Adams

She was very young, very American and very innocent.

Then Paris, city of light—and shadow—took her by the hand for the dangerous journey into love.

Appointment in Paris

Aunt Julia gave just a small tea for Mrs. Somerville before the latter departed. It had to be small, because Aunt Julia's doctor had forbidden excitement for his patient.

The glass doors between the two overfurnished salons were opened to make one long room, and a great sheaf of purple lilac in the front room was reflected in the large gold-framed mirror of the rear room and so did double duty and gave quite a gala effect. Aunt Julia wore her mauve georgette and the long silver Florentine earrings. She looked rested and handsome.

Aunt Julia's dowdy little English friend Miss Maple officiated very capably at the tea table. Havoc went among the guests with trays of whisky-and-soda and sherry, of *canapés* and cakes. Aunt Julia prided herself that her parties were sophisticated and gay.

The guests were mostly women of a certain age, but there was a sprinkling of men, too, elderly husbands and a few antique bachelors. There was a similarity about the women: they usually wore black and they had smart hats; and, fat or thin, they had poised but restless faces. The men often wore suits with padded shoulders and pinched-in waists; their faces, more complacent, frequently bore signs of good eating and drinking. None of these people looked quite American, but neither did they look French. They were a tribe to themselves upon this earth. The language they spoke was English with a cayenne peppering of French phrases.

Most of the curtains had been drawn so that the candles and cut-glass chandeliers might be lighted, and the two rooms were very warm. Havoc had been a model of politeness for nearly two hours and she was now numb with well-doing. It seemed as though she were confined inside a giant floating bubble, together with the hum of voices, the swim of lights, and the incense of cigarette smoke and women's perfumes; and the bubble was overdue to break. Frieda, hissing at her offstage, was a part of the bad enchantment. Frieda was handicapped by being forbidden to show herself. The drinks were out of her province, they were served from the tea table and otherwise were kept strictly under lock and key.

Havoc relapsed against the doorjamb and ate cakes from the tray she nursed. Aunt Julia, beside her, was embroidering the subject of her "little nest" on the sixth floor. "But now I am quite accustomed to looking down on the trees and having the clouds of the sky for my daily companions."

She was talking to a retired poet of private means. This gentleman—he was a bald-headed little man—moved restively.

"Havoc, fill Mr. Amory's glass, dear," inserted Aunt Julia quickly.

"Yes, Aunt Julia."

Havoc hung there in her dream. She did not know what the dream was. It had no face and no shape. Or perhaps it did. She gazed into the mirror and she did not register the lilacs or the animated room; she saw only the hypnotic smoke haze. Then she saw two bodies, wavering there, unclothed, her own and Marcelle's. Twin bodies, one flat and thin and the other fragrant and full, coming inevitably together in some curious, unknown, delicious fashion. She did not know yet, but she would soon. It was as sure as a train starting. The train could not leave its tracks; it had to go on to the end of the trip. She and Marcelle had started the voyage, they were passengers. But she had to get away from here—back to Marcelle. Dared she, now?

"Hattie, aren't you forgetting your duties? Refills, my dear!"

After more eons, only a few of the guests remained. They sat in a relaxed group and talked it over. The three Paris residents were putting on their act for the two transients—Mrs. Somerville and a Miss Pennifill from Washington, D.C., a thin, colorless creature whose only pride was her long-time marriage to the State Department.

"But do you *like* the French people?" Mrs. Somerville was probing in her downright way.

"Do we like them?" Aunt Julia mocked, looking first to Mr. Linthicum and then to Katie Richie.

Mr. Linthicum's glasses sparked out in answering humor. He was a young man with a plain, honest face that sweated a good deal. He was assistant pastor of an American church in Paris and his first name was Clarence.

Katie Ritchie giggled frankly. She was short and fat and she had the features of a nice clean little pig. She hailed from Virginia and was renowned in Paris for her mint juleps.

"Let me tell you. Several weeks ago I was lunching at Weber's—that's quite a good ordinary restaurant—with a French acquaintance," said Aunt Julia. "When she had eaten everything on her plate, she scoured the plate with a piece of bread, and ate it. Then she wiped her mouth with another piece of bread, lipstick and all, and ate that. Her hand was loaded with rings from Cartier's."

"So damn thrifty!" chuckled Katie Ritchie, pointing it.

"Yes. That's very typical. And here's another instance, though I shouldn't tell this in mixed company." Aunt Julia glinted at Mr. Linthicum. "But it is so priceless." In daily life Aunt Julia was never funny. Her long upper lip, which gave her a humorless look of great good sense, was an accurate gauge to her character. But in company she sometimes put on humor, put on daring, too, as the badge of her Parisian emancipation. "I was staying at Dinan overnight, doing the antique shops. All the hotels were full and I had to rent a room in a dreadful place near the Château. There were no usable—er—accommodations. You know, just *feet*. So I went to the public place in the center of the town. It was white-tiled and quite clean with an old harpy Frenchwoman in charge. Do you know, she counted the times the paper ripped, and when it was more than once, she shouted out, 'That will be two sous more, madame.' "

They all laughed merrily, looking at Mr. Linthicum, who laughed and blushed. Havoc, who was interested now, sat very quiet on her stool against the wall, so that she would not be sent from the room.

"But then, you do speak perfect French, Julia?" Mrs. Somerville pursued her cross-examination.

"Frankly? All right." Aunt Julia bent her head to the flame Mr. Linthicum reached out to her cigarette, and her long silver earrings swung shadows on her shoulders. "I have too much respect for any language to massacre it. And I started French too late in life to learn it properly. So, frankly, I speak French as little as possible. How is your French, Mr. Linthicum—and Katie?"

Mr. Linthicum shrugged admission of his limitations.

Katie said, "At least I'm not like Gay Smith, who doesn't really speak French, but has got so she speaks English like a person who does speak French from living here so long."

"It's such a chittering sort of language," contributed Aunt Julia.

"As I take it, then", said Mrs. Somerville, the loose-hanging water-lily bud bumping against her ear as she moved in sharp earnestness, "you do not really like the French people, any of you. You do not speak their tongue, and you do not even want to speak it. Then why do you live in France?"

The three French residents gaped at her, as a favorite child suddenly turned idiot.

"Why don't you come back to your own country—except, of course,

Mr. Linthicum, who has been assigned to this Paris post?"

"To the United States to *live?*" marveled Aunt Julia. "Never. Nothing could take me back!"

"But why?"

"You two couldn't possibly understand." The wave of Aunt Julia's cigarette in its amber holder expressed a pitying condescension for them and for all other Americans who lived in America.

"By golly," said Miss Ritchie, "I can have a maid and decent clothes in this country. What could I have in the States on my income?"

"Let us say," said Mr. Linthicum, who dealt handily in generalities, "that the charm of the life here is the constant adventure of the eternally unfamiliar."

But Mrs. Somerville had her own ministerial vein to tap. "My point is, it ought not to remain so unfamiliar. You are all outside looking in. You are outside of your own country, too—not looking in. How long have you lived in France, Julia?"

"Sixteen years."

"Well," said Mrs. Somerville flatly, "as I see it, you are all people without a country."

"We're not alone, Clara," stated Miss Horn sharply. "There are thousands of—thirty thousand, to be exact. We are the American colony in France."

"Yes, it's a sizable state of affairs. That's what makes it worth looking into. You are trying to get the best of two worlds and pay for it in neither world. You—"

"This is not a pulpit, Clara. It is Paris."

"Pass her the sherry," giggled Miss Ritchie.

"I've had three glasses already." Mrs. Somerville smirked. "Did I mention, Julia, that I'm having the time of my life in your Paris?"

Havoc passed the sherry and the sandwiches once more. Then, dismissed by her aunt, she stayed at the door separating the back rooms from the front, open a crack, waiting her chance.

Someone was coming. Havoc sped back to her room.

She was sitting before her ancient history when Aunt Julia appeared to tell her that a few of them were going out to dinner, that Frieda was saving a plate of hot soup for Hattie. Miss Horn put her hand on Havoc's shoulder. "You were very helpful, dear. Do you want a little party of your own? Want to ask some of your little school friends in for ice cream on Sunday afternoon?"

"All right, Aunt Julia," accepted Havoc indifferently.

Miss Horn stood and considered her niece with some penetration. She unscrewed an earring and massaged the ear lobe. "It's been hard on you, too," she mused. "I do try, Hattie. I...consider, I was nearly fifty, a spinster, when I suddenly found I had a child of nine," she said humorously.

Havoc moved uncomfortably in her chair.

"I wonder if I did right to bring you here. But there wasn't much money, Hattie. If anything should happen to me, you're to go back. Go to college. There's enough for that."

"Yes, Aunt Julia."

Miss Horn waited, as though expecting more of Havoc. Then she sighed. "Go have your supper, dear."

Havoc escaped like something trapped released. When finally she reached Marcelle's door, it was too late. Nobody answered her tap, not even Cushla.

It was as if a promise made to her had been withdrawn. The inexplicit dream fogged over. Havoc felt as though she had misunderstood an adult's spoken words and had imagined everything. The three days in which she could not manage even to glimpse Marcelle were forever. They were as dingy as Frieda's gas-smoked asbestos pad and as dutifully dull as Aunt Julia.

Then, on the first evening of June, Aunt Julia went out to dinner and the opera. Frieda climbed upstairs to her room with a bottle. Havoc was in the kitchen making a pickup supper, when someone ticked nails on the door.

It was Cushla. She seemed not surprised to find Havoc alone. Her round face was gripped in a misery of sternness.

"Madame Marcelle invites you to dinner. If you take my advice, you will not go."

"Oh, Cushla! When?"

"Now. She is alone. The devil is in her. A young man could not come. Also that Madame de Ste Croix. She has sent me off. But you stay away."

Already Havoc had abandoned her burned toast and cereal and was racketing down the back stairs.

"Turn off the light, Cushla, and shut the door. And don't tell Frieda."

Marcelle admitted her, in the spirit of sharing with her a gay secret. She had a glass in her hand; Havoc saw at once that she had been drinking, but not, like Frieda, too much. Her eyes were pointed with lights and hilarity shimmered on her face. Her black hair was smoothed decorously up onto her head and her delicate, luscious body might have been lacquered in the metallic gold hostess gown she wore, so tightly did it conform to her contours.

Havoc's expression was that of a little girl seeing her first Christmas tree.

"Come in, *chérie*. Are you hungry?"

"Not very."

"Me, I am a little hungry. Perhaps we should eat. Cushla has left us lobster and champagne. This man's loss, it is your gain."

The table was beautifully set and lighted with candlesticks. The lobster claws were awkward. Urged by Marcelle, Havoc tasted the champagne. She did not like it very much—it stung—but it made her feel even happier and very light. She found her laughter spangling out with Marcelle's.

They floated into Marcelle's bedroom. Marcelle leaned back on her arms on the edge of the bed and watched Havoc, all released, move around the room and touch her possessions. She had the tender, indulgent expression of a fond mother.

"That is Lanvin's new bath salts. It is suitable for a young girl. Would you like to take a bath in my tub and try it?"

"Oh, yes!"

"The good aunt is gone away for long?"

"To the opera."

"The opera?" Marcelle hooted. "Wonderful! She will not return till midnight."

Marcelle drew the bath water and doused it lavishly with the flowery bath salts. "If you are feeling modest, *chérie*—" It made Havoc laugh again, because the white nightgown Marcelle hung over a chair back was so diaphanous.

Then she was alone, lying back in the fragrant, tepid water. Then she was with Marcelle, lying back on the great bed, looking up at the gold stars in the blue ceiling. After the champagne, after the bath, she was as drowsy as a baby and ecstatically happy.

Her hand curled and uncurled against Marcelle's bare breast. Marcelle drew her closer. Marcelle's hand began that tender exploratory creeping down Havoc's spine. The shuddering began—Havoc's and this time Marcelle's, too. It was a curious sort of desperate rhythm that they played together like musicians toward some crashing finale. Havoc had no clear idea of what was happening. It was all a great rhythmic tenderness. There was no shock, no brutality. There was no part of her body that Marcelle did not explore and come to know. It was so skillful that there was no shame. Shame was a little word, it was Aunt Julia's word. This was a wonderful delight, far beyond shame.

When the rhythm crashed and ebbed, Havoc was tired. She lay against Marcelle and Marcelle richly comforted here. "*Bébé—chérie—*"

"Oh, Marcelle, I love you."

"Don't tell me *bébé*, I know. Sleep a while now."

The entire *quartier* connived in Havoc's friendship with Madame Marcelle. Two factors conspired toward this: first, a general dislike of Miss Horn; second, the Latin love of intrigue.

Julia Horn had done nothing at all to gain the esteem of her neighbors. Concierges and tradesmen called her "that Englishwoman." This was an epithet of opprobrium, for all of them knew well that she was American.

Madame Marcelle, by contrast, was the darling of the neighborhood. It was not only that she bought her way—and bought it extravagantly—so that her concierge was the envy of every other concierge on the Avenue de Versailles. Madame Marcelle was a success. She was an artiste in her field. Also, Madame Marcelle was popular in her own right. She greeted everybody gaily, and everybody greeted her. She spread a sort of bonhomie, including the poorest little delivery boy in the joy of her good fortune. The wink and the word passed that the friendship of Madame Marcelle and the little American was clandestine. The joke was on the old aunt.

No married man with a mistress could have led his double life more adroitly than did Havoc Minturn, aged fifteen. She stepped into the first-floor apartment and she was in France. She returned to the sixth-floor apartment and she was in America. She kept her two worlds separate, and she never slipped. It was "Yes, Aunt Julia" and "No, Aunt Julia," until Miss Horn gradually relaxed her surveillance over her niece and congratulated herself upon a job well done.

Havoc was inspired to this flawless performance by the first love of her life. Madame Marcelle had flooded in upon the great drought in the girl's arid existence. Havoc responded to the Frenchwoman's demonstrative affection, to the lively spirits and rich texture of this milieu with a passion that gave promise of her capacity. What she felt for her new friend was far more than a schoolgirl crush. She could not even have dreamed such delight, yet this sudden fairy tale was the truth; all else was unreal. Havoc was obsessed and jealous, and instinctively wise beyond her years in concealment of these primary feelings. She would go to any length to safeguard her meetings with Marcelle.

Cushla was the last to accept the friendship. The Irishwoman barred the door against Havoc, arms crossed, when once again Havoc knocked on the door.

"Is Madame Marcelle in?"

"No."

"Where is she?"

"How should I know?"

"Let me in, Cushla. Somebody'll come. You know I daren't be seen here."

Cushla stood solidly. "Sure, I'll tell your aunt myself, that's what I'll do!"

Havoc impatiently thrust past her. She dropped her schoolbooks on a chair. Polished surfaces gleamed from the shuttered interior, there was a smell of *eau de Javelle* and wax. Cushla had been house-cleaning. Havoc followed the sullen, plump figure to the kitchen. This was an untidy hole, littered with dirty luncheon dishes and soiled tea towels. Cushla sat again at the big kitchen range, covered with newspapers. When it was not in winter use, the stove served as a table. She had a deck of cards arranged before her, in a careful fan shape, and a cup of poisonously black tea at her elbow. Cushla's person was usually tidy in contrast to her kitchen, but today her gray hair was in shreds, her black uniform was shapeless and streaked with gluey white stains, and she smelled of sweat.

Havoc focused on the tray with two half-empty *apéritif* glasses. "Has she been gone long? Who's she with?"

Cushla slapped down the cards, muttering to herself. "Nothing but obstacles and hindrances. And love, love."

Havoc leaned out of the window, which opened upon the garden, and thought how different was the ground view here from their own sky view. She was suddenly nauseated with her hatred of a man without a face. What could Marcelle do with this man that she could not do with her, Havoc? Her sense of Marcelle's betrayal was as profound as it was wordless, because love had hit her before she had acquired even the language for it.

When she looked back at Cushla, the latter's concentration upon the cards was extreme; her round face was knotted with a look of pain.

"What's the matter, Cushla?" she asked, out of her own pain.

"I am the unhappiest woman in the world. Even the cards say so."

"Are the cards always right?"

"The cards tell true."

"Tell mine. Please—please!"

With a violent sweeping motion, Cushla scattered the cards every which way. She took a deep swig of the tea with the air of a drunkard tipping his whisky. She looked hard at Havoc with a rapt morose seer's gaze. "God loves you if He makes you ugly, mademoiselle. But He has not made you ugly. You'd better stay away from here."

Cushla shuffled the cards and invited the girl to cut. She began reluctantly to lay them down in a new circular pattern. It was not in her to deny an interest in her favorite form of soothsaying. "Hearts keep coming up. See this eight of hearts? That is the love card. Sure, you will break many hearts, mademoiselle, but one in particular. I see a great division between you and your love. I cannot tell what will come of that. I see death—death in your house. Have you made a wish?...You do not get your wish. What was it?"

"I wished Marcelle would come back soon."

"Well, she won't be back tonight, if I'm any judge. She's off with a new one that's got a *garçonnière* in the Rue de Passy."

"Is he—nice, Cushla?"

"Nice? Ho."

"What happened to Monsieur?"

"'Monsieur'?" The Irishwoman's blue eyes were almost shocked as they gazed into the girl's wide-set warm brown eyes beneath the charmingly crooked eyebrows. Havoc leaned upon the stove, teetering on her arms, her dark red hair swinging over her shoulders.

"If she's *Madame* Marcelle—"

"She has never married. The title is by courtesy." Suddenly Cushla struck the stove. "But don't you be thinking I wasn't married! I know what they say about me. I married Pierre Jardine and I married him in the church. It could have been different, because I came here green as the shamrock from near Killarney, aged sixteen. But the sisters took care of that. They'd sent me into service with a noble lady—she was the Comtesse de Reynaud—and she saw he didn't get me for less than marriage. But, faith, don't ever marry a Frenchman, mademoiselle. Marry your own kind or none. I was the unhappiest woman in the world." (Havoc was recognizing this as Cushla's stock plaint.) "It was not that he got a drop in now and then. The saints know I was used to that in Ireland. But he mauled me and he abused me. See that scar on my nose? The carving knife. He laid it open."

Havoc was speechless with fascination.

"We divorced," sighed Cushla, "and me a good Catholic."

"Did you like living in Ireland? What was it like?"

"We lived in a small little house in the country. The animals lived with us. We ate potatoes and we burned peat, and my poor mother, her life was work and children and work. The cards were always black. The winter before I left, the nine of spades and the jack of spades kept turning tip. That's sure death. That was the winter my mother died."

"My mother died, too, when I was only five. How old were you, Cushla?"

"Did she, now? And you've been with your aunt ever since?" Cushla probed.

"I lived with Grandmother Horn in Wellfleet until she died, too. That was six years ago."

"And your father, where would he be keepin' himself?"

"He died when my mother did, in a train wreck, on the way to Kansas City, where they were playing their act. My father was a magician and my mother was the girl he sawed in two. He hypnotized my mother, too—and chickens and rabbits. He did my mother a great wrong."

"Lord love me," gasped Cushla. "Weren't they married then?"

"Who—Mamma and Papa? Oh, yes."

"Then what's so wrong about that?"

"He wasn't my mother's *class*," declared Havoc flatly.

"And who would you be speakin' for now? Your old-maid aunt?"

"My grandmother said so, too. The Horns are a very old New England family. Once they had their own fleet of ships and sailed the seven seas," the girl boasted. "My mother was a college graduate, and whatever came over her to run away with a small-time vaudeville actor—of course, he was very handsome, with red hair and all that magnetic power. I take after him," she concluded simply.

"Whisht. Stop talkin' like somebody else and be yourself. And believe me, missy, worse wrongs can happen to you than ever happened to your mother if they already haven't. These Frenchmen have got different ideas about women. No girl is too young. If she's born a woman, she's man's natural prey. When God gave her her sex, He gave her the instinct to look out for herself. Then let her use it! That's the way they see it. They'll give you a lot of love fast, but very little chivalry except kissin' of your hand. Believe me," said Cushla grimly, "I know."

After this, Havoc and Cushla were unacknowledged friends. The Irishwoman continued to disapprove of and warn and berate the American girl, but her enmity lost its conviction. In Marcelle's absence, Havoc put in a lot of time in her kitchen watching Cushla at her everlasting turning of the cards.

Cushla was a comfort to her in all the black times when Marcelle rejected her. Havoc's relations with Marcelle were always off-the-earth bliss or deepest despair. She was unhappy more than she was happy. While there were no seasons in Havoc's love of her idol, she had to learn the seasons of Marcelle's desire. The girl was just the overflow of the woman's crowded life. Marcelle would hold her and love her when a date went bad, when she was disgusted with men, when she had a free evening that coincided with Havoc's ability to escape from the upstairs flat. Occasionally Marcelle was overwhelmingly kind to her, just for kindness' sake. Often she flared at Havoc, was tigerishly angry with her, cruel in her words. But Marcelle was never physically brutal with the girl. Her caresses were a great gentleness, an almost maternal tenderness.

For Havoc there was never anything like that spring and summer in Paris when she first knew Marcelle. The old city seemed just her age. There was young laughter everywhere, in the shimmer of the ethereal pale sunshine, in the very glistening showers that made upside-down silk umbrella poppies of all absurd colors bloom along the boulevards. The gushing fountains laughed musically and the slow river chuckled along its way. In street cafés the sound of glassware was a constant tittering, and the laughter was in the throats of people, too.

Though she was learning strange ways rapidly, there was a marvelous innocence to her happiness these days: The city became a wondrous sight with the flying golden horses of the Pont-Alexandre and the sugar-white domes of the Sacré-Coeur emerging from the milk-and-honey morning mists. The spill of mauve wisteria over old gray walls was a breathless thing. It seemed to Havoc that the air was softer and lighter, the flowers were gayer, and the people were more animated this spring than ever before.

When Marcelle did play with Havoc, she was the perfect comrade. They took little excursions together. They sat under a tree in the Bois, with low-hanging branches to make a little green private room, and they ate sweet buns worried by the wasps. They went farther afield by car and had tea and jam at an inn called the Coq Hardi at Bougival in a garden that had old Roman ruins overlaid by flowers.

Like every other American in Paris, Miss Horn collected addresses. These were the names and abodes of little *couturiers, modistes, coiffeurs,* shoemakers, button makers, shops where you could buy American corn on the cob or American muffin tins. She pursued these elusive addresses through cobbled courts and down dead-end alleys and up countless flights of stairs in all the odd corners of Paris.

To one of these addresses Miss Horn had been faithful for a decade. On the Rue du Bac was a little *couturier* with his little wife who made all Miss Horn's outer garments. They clothed Havoc, too, and once or twice a year the girl had to submit herself to the long bleak hours of fittings in the dark lair where the Souffrons carried on their trade.

Both Madame and Monsieur invariably greeted Miss Horn with great deference. Madame was a doll-like woman with curiously slanting Oriental eyes, and Monsieur was a beautifully tailored and mustached dummy figure. Miss Horn considered them "discreet" and "correct," qualities which, together with their command of English, she valued greatly. To give them their due, they did very well by their difficult American client. Madame Souffron hung the gaunt frame in gracious frocks that were miracles of subtle cutting. Monsieur turned her out in well-tailored suits, though you had to watch him for a tendency to fit too near to the skin.

Havoc trailed her aunt into the gloomy, gaslighted reception room and sat through the interminable commiserations on that lady's poor health. "So now my doctor has put me on digitalis," Aunt Julia concluded.

"Digitalis!" exclaimed Madame Souffron. "That is a poison which is cumulative, Mees Horn. You must measure the drops exactly or—"

"Marie!" Monsieur Souffron's sharpness was like the sudden crack of a whip. "Madame follows a doctor's prescription."

Madame Souffon cringed, then covered: "Of course, my cousin who died from taking too much digitalis may not have followed precisely her doctor's orders. She—"

Why, he's not mild at all, and she's afraid of him, Havoc discovered, thinking of Cushla's warning against French husbands.

The Souffrons, as usual, gave their first and best attention to Aunt Julia. Havoc sat by while they pored through fashion books and leafed through sample books and then courteously haggled over prices. Aunt Julia was a hard bargainer. At this point Havoc always realized again that her aunt was quite poor, and she was always ashamed before the shrewd French appraisal of them.

"You don't think the figures of that print are too large?" Aunt Julia frowned.

"But no, Mees Horn. It is extremely dignified. *Regardez*." Madame unfurled a length of the material from the bolt, threw it over Aunt Julia's shoulder, draped it and shaped it with caressing skill to the long, flat figure. "Mees Horn maligns herself if she does not know that with her height and her distinction she could carry a design much more daring."

Havoc saw the enigmatic expression in Madame's slant eyes and in the eyes of Monsieur, too, hovering in the background. For the first time, she recognized that this flattery was an act.

When finally it was her turn, the girl realized that their outward deference to Miss Horn's desires was false, too; really the Souffrons were sympathetic toward Havoc. "We must keep her *jeune fille*," Aunt Julia insisted. So they all chose for her—Havoc had nothing to do with it—a navy-blue suit with a kilted skirt, which might have been another school uniform, and another of those babyish white party frocks.

Madame Souffron suggested rather pityingly a little Scotch plaid taffeta blouse for the suit, but Aunt Julia, gazing almost in pain at Havoc's startling looks, which had flowered so extravagantly in these past weeks, said, "No, white. Let's keep it plain."

Madame Souffron was studying Havoc's young body with almost closed eyes. Monsieur Souffron, too. He brought out his tape measure.

"You have her measurements," Aunt Julia objected.

"They change," said Monsieur, passing the tape about her hips, her breasts. Though he was outwardly most impersonal in his manner, Havoc was uncomfortably conscious of his hands upon her.

Madame pressed into Miss Horn's hand the card of a friend who had opened a hat shop nearby. When they emerged, blinded, into the daylight of the Rue du Bac, Aunt Julia decided to look at these hats.

Her choice of a terrible round Milan sailor for Havoc, ready made, was literally the last straw.

Aunt Julia insisted she wear the hat. Havoc, well aware that all she lacked was a tin cup to look like an organ grinder's monkey, held on to her bursting resentment until they were home. Then she broke away from Aunt Julia and crashed into Marcelle's apartment.

Marcelle was sitting in her bedroom in a new ivory lace negligee, eating chocolates and yawning.

"My God!" She stared. "Where did you get it?"

"My aunt. She does it on purpose. She wants to disfigure me."

Havoc snatched off the sailor and flung it violently to the floor.

Marcelle sat considering her a moment. "Go on, *bébé*, be yourself. It becomes you. Hand me that Suzie hatbox from the wardrobe," she said thoughtfully. "There is a new pastel blue beret in it. There—try that on.... Hm. Sit down." Standing over her, Marcelle began to manipulate the beret, to dent it here and pinch it in there. She used pins and then she got out her sewing box and did swift, skillful things to the hat. Havoc watched her entranced; she had never before seen Marcelle in the role of active creator of styles.

She smoothed the hat down upon Havoc's head, tilting it over the left eye, and said "*Voilà*."

This was the moment when Havoc knew that she was beautiful. The soft felt hat, which was the blue of an April sky, brought out all the deep rich red of her hair, the dark warmth of her eyes, the pure clarity of her skin. The triangle of her face seemed right for her. The irregularities of eyebrows and nose were charming. The delicately flaring nostrils and parted lips spoke of eagerness and delight.

"If you were a little older," exclaimed Marcelle, "I'd be jealous of you! I would not want to compete with you. And your figure, too. Not yet, but soon. Those are the legs of a dancer—or maybe," she chuckled, "they are just the legs of an American."

Havoc stood looking at Marcelle, with a pleading intensity. "Oh, Marcelle," she breathed, "I love you. Don't—not love me back."

Marcelle pulled her down to the bed. Havoc swept off the blue hat. Still laughing at her, Marcelle probed for her mouth with a new urgency. Havoc felt she could never get near enough to Marcelle. But she tried.

Time passed over them in great waves, like a sea aroused. It had never been like this before. Marcelle had so many curious new ways of loving. But Havoc, though she lacked skill, had the bursting emotion of pure love. She knew she pleased Marcelle. She felt successful. Now striving together, they had reached that bright land where the sunshine was a white fire and the flowers were neon-colored, blinding.

The surf receded. They lay there, gasping together, the child's pale long body and the woman's rosy rounded body side by side, utterly relaxed.

"Ah," sighed Marcelle richly, "my little green fruit, you are delicious."

"Am I?" shyly.

"You are a passionate child. You will be a passionate woman. A great lover. Some man, he will have everything."

"No. *Men!*"

"What is that you say?" Marcelle's movement, turning to stare at Havoc, was brusque. "Little fool! Of course you will have men. You are a Lesbian no more than I am."

"What is that?"

"A woman who loves other women. There are those who want only each other—they are the true Lesbians. There are the others, half and half, who enjoy men quite as much as women. I am not even one of those. With me it is just a diversion, the variety that love must have. I love men, *chérie*. I must have men."

"Oh, don't!"

"Not jealous?" incredulously. "Why, *bébé, chérie!*"

Marcelle cradled her with her arms and all of her body. This was the tenderness that was always there, even in fuller moments, and was for Havoc the best of all, the lost and forever missed. Her warmth toward Marcelle swelled in her little breasts, in her throat.

"This is all for you now, *chérie*. It is enough, but not too much. You must wait. You trust Marcelle, don't you?"

"Oh, yes!"

"You will not miss the real love. Would you like to stay all night with me? Just to rest, to sleep."

"But—I can't."

"Perhaps not tonight. But what about that balcony around your apartment? Does it not go from your room to the kitchen, and could you not leave the kitchen window open? The old aunt would leave you in bed and find you in bed."

"Oh, Marcelle, could I?"

"I don't know why not. Just sometimes. Not often. You have to learn, baby, that love is not all the time. It comes, but it goes, too."

Havoc listened as to words of great wisdom, which she would never find in books, and which she must remember.

"Tell me, my own little girl that I have not yet had, you have been starved for love all your life, is it not so? Has nobody ever loved you at all?"

"My grandmother," admitted Havoc, snuggling to Marcelle.

Marcelle's laugh was a hoot. Her arms had never been so tender, so soft, so cherishing and kind.

The beautiful girl with the aura of past and future romance

The King of a Rainy Country

by Brigid Brophy

In a London bookseller's shop, Susan and her friend Neale discover a nude photograph of Cynthia, a former friend of Susan's, and together they set out to find the beautiful girl with the aura of past and future romance. Their quest takes them to out-of-the-way corners of Bohemian London, through Paris, Nice, into Italy with a busload of hilariously unquiet Americans, and finally to Venice, where they glimpse their vision, lose it, and find another. The story is a lively comedy of romantic temperament, with touches of farce, a distinctly individual tale of independent people seeking off the beaten path for the perennial romance of youth.

The King of a Rainy Country

Four lunch hours running I took the bus to Oxford Circus and inquired at the Great Portland Street post office. The fifth time I went it was my twentieth birthday. The morning grayness was trembling, about to break apart into an afternoon that would certainly be spring, or even summer. The moment's walk from the bus stop made me hot. I inquired again, and was given a letter. I could tell nothing from the handwriting; and the postmark was Bangor. I crossed to the other side of the post office, took a telegram form out of the box, and pretended to compose something. Then I opened the letter and saw it was from Annette.

> *It was nice to get your letter and hear how you are getting on. Your job sounds most interesting, and just the sort of thing that would suit you. You must tell me more about it. I am living up here in the wilds of Wales, working as a nursery teacher, believe it or not. I quite enjoy the work, but the little dears do get a bit wearing at times! I visit London in the holidays, and it would be nice to see you if you were ever free.*
>
> *I have hardly seen anyone from "the good old days" and don't expect I have any news you won't know already. Gill won a scholarship to Oxford, you know—she always was "brainy"—unlike me! I have not heard from Cynthia since we left, and I don't know what she is doing, but someone told me she was making some extra money by posing at an art school for the evening classes. I think they said it was the South-East London school.*

I went into one of the phone booths and put through a call to Neale. He took some time to answer; I reread Annette's second paragraph while I waited. When he came through, I told him about it.

"Right. We'll go there tonight. I'll give you supper out, for your birthday. I must go now. I was in bed."

All afternoon, as I sat in Finkelheim's—Neale did not come over—I was consciously but not voluntarily reconstructing life at school. Cross-fertilized by Annette's letter, my memory was stronger. Names

I had never hoped to recover came floating up like fragments of shattered tooth appearing in the gum socket. As I recalled the tenor of that life, I was amused by its incongruities: in all the relationships between the four of us, we had always seen one another unmade-up; we had never offered one another a drink or a cigarette; and every school morning except in summer I had performed what was to my present mind the masculine action of putting on my tie in front of the mirror. These, however, were only the quirks of school life. The essence was its restriction. Even imagination was restricted, by ignorance. What went on behind the closed door of Cynthia's form-room was mysterious to me. We moved in our fixed time-tables like separate planets.

At first I accepted that Cynthia was loosed on me at given times of day for short intervals. At the beginning of the autumn term I claimed her promise of walking with me, and discovered Annette was coming too. It did not occur to me that I could prevent it. But Cynthia, higher up the spiral, was more free. She contrived, the first time, to walk next to me. The second time, Annette did not appear at all. I was dazzled by Cynthia's contrivance, but also afraid; and I did not ask how she had excluded Annette.

Cynthia showed me ways of swerving out of my course into hers. I took up art: and this meant that in free lessons Cynthia and I would draw from the life—from a girl in a gym tunic posed on a desk—while Annette worked at fancy lettering in another part of the studio. I discovered for myself that if I slipped into the wrong queue at dinner time I could sit next to Cynthia. I would watch her profile; I felt unable to eat. Presently this became her feeling too. We would each crumble a slice of bread, each worked on by asceticism.

On Fridays Cynthia forwent her privilege of taking an early train and went to the after-school meeting of the French club. Annette did not belong to it. I joined it. We had a book of stories in French about various parts of the world. At the end there were questions which we dealt with verbally. The question came to me: "*Qu'est-ce que c'est qu'un bonze?*" I had no idea; the question went on to Cynthia, who answered as the book had taught: "*Un bonze est un prêtre japonais.*" In the margin of my book I drew eleven rough figures, their hands clasped inside their kimono sleeves, and gave it the caption "*Onze bonzes.*" I passed the book to Cynthia. She laughed, and then began to laugh loudly. She had to turn up the lid of her desk; and to keep the pretence going she took out a notebook and began writing in it. A minute later, however, the notebook was passed to me. Cynthia had written: "A code message. - ---- ---."

I stared down at it, knowing what I wanted it to mean.

Cynthia whispered: "Can you work it out?"

I whispered back, not daring to look: "I don't know. I'm not quite sure."

That night I walked with her to catch her late train. It was a glowing evening and already almost dark. We walked slowly, looking down at the pavements. I kicked through a drift of leaves that had blown up against a wooden fence, and turned over a horse chestnut. I picked it up and gave it to Cynthia, who put it away in her satchel. "Haven't you any gloves?" she said. "Aren't your hands cold?"

"Not very."

"Put your right hand in my pocket."

I did and for a moment walked along awkwardly.

"Do you mind if my hand comes in, too?" Cynthia said.

It lay inert in her pocket alongside my hand, each separately clenched; and then, as we went round a corner, both hands opened with the same convulsion and pressed each other palm to palm.

The next day I ran upstairs to Cynthia's classroom between lessons, stood in front of her desk, and threw down a piece of paper. I had written: "A code message in French. -- -'----." Cynthia opened the paper and read it, and then looked up at me direct for a moment. She folded the paper away carefully, and the smile she gave me seemed to be similarly folded away, carefully, into herself.

While I was shut off from Cynthia, I used Gill for amusement. In dull lessons in our own form-room I would repeat to her jokes that had made Cynthia laugh. Because repeated, they did not detonate; yet I did not care if I won no success with Gill. All was dross that was not Cynthia, and Gill especially, because she was the most familiar to me of my own familiar form. In spite of this, Gill had changed, but not enough to win my interest: she was like a thoroughly known tree which in the spring showed a number of new whippy shoots. She had suddenly grown tall; she was leggy. Her face had settled into a shape, the curly gold and pink prettiness of a painted wooden statue of an angel.

What had been Gill's childish truculence had changed into power to lash. In my own sphere I was no longer secure. I escaped from it to Cynthia, and forgot to be afraid of Gill; Cynthia became arbitress of my safety. We marched round the big field, happy when the weather was bitter because we should be completely alone. Long delayed, but always some time before the bell rang that summoned us inside, Cynthia's hand would take mine. When it rained, we were confined to the main hall. I would run for a place under the windows, up against the radiator; and there as we stood side by side, Cynthia's hand would move towards mine over the radiator's undulations and we would gaze out at the rain drenching the tennis courts and running in streams down the grass bank. Sometimes in the dinner hour I went to the chapel with Cynthia, for a meeting of the Young Christians. Sharing a song-sheet, we would stand with our hands touching while I kept silence for shame and Cynthia sang:

No need to cry, no need to whine.
Jesus is a friend of mine.
No need to wonder who I am.
He's the shepherd, I the lamb.

Kneeling in silent prayer, we held hands beneath the pew. Sitting, we gazed at one another while everyone else was embarrassed to look anywhere, as one or other of the girls made a public confession, usually of thought-crimes against the staff. Cynthia and I never confessed to anything. Once Gill came to a meeting. I saw her edge in at the back of the chapel, and was afraid for what she might do when she heard the hymn. However, she made no demonstration until confession time, when she was the first to speak. "I wish to confess to the meeting that I smoke marijuana." The gesture was not successful because I was the only person there who knew what marijuana was, and I was not prepared to help her make her effect.

Towards the end of the autumn term the rigidity of our courses began to disintegrate under an impetus that came from outside, not from Cynthia and me. The classes became less formal; girls would be sent for and taken out of lessons, unsettling those who were left; for some lessons lasses were amalgamated, for some they were dismissed unexpectedly; there was a sound of hammering in the main hall. At each tremor the first thought of Cynthia and myself was for each other. If my lesson was declared closed I would leap out through the confusion and upstairs to see if Cynthia was free too. The whole structure of school life trembled under small shock after small shock, like a stage set about to be struck. In fact, however, a stage set was going up. The platform in the main hall was under requisition; and there the headmistress conducted morning prayers beneath a cardboard arch, a bowery ornament of the forest of Arden. I wrote a play of my own, a farce set in the small French village of Mise-en-Seine, which I showed to the English mistress; she gave it me back, saying it had amused her; I was at the depth of my mind disappointed, having had some fantasy that she would drop the play of her choice and put mine into rehearsal instead.

Neither Cynthia nor I was cast. We enrolled ourselves in the studio to paint scenery and sew silk roses, and then enrolled ourselves with Miss Falconbridge as scene-shifters in the main hall. Night after night Cynthia caught the later train. We would stand at the foot of the stage, hands clasped behind a painted bush, threatened with dismissal if we so much as whispered.

"Why, cousin! Why, Rosalind! Cupid have mercy! not a word?"

"Not one to throw at a dog."

Elegant, gap-toothed, and flexed like a greyhound, Miss Falconbridge stood at the back of the hall, her arms crossed, one hand holding her paper-bound copy of the play, calling on her players to speak up.

The Celia asked: "But is all this for your father?"

"No, some of it for my child's father. O, how full of briers is this working-day world!"

The Celia was a pretty, dark-haired girl, the Rosalind a pretty, red-haired girl, both of whom I disliked. Yet even they were touched by the color of the lines they spoke. Cynthia and I moved closer to one another as we crouched behind the bush, getting a grip on it and preparing to rush it into place for the second act. But Miss Falconbridge loped to the other side of the hall and called for the first act again. The players scrambled on to the stage again, amongst them Gill, in a gym tunic now too short for her, the length of her legs conspicuous since she was standing above our level of vision. It was prefigured for her that her fair skin should be browned with grease-paint, that she should wear a pointed brown beard and a single gold earring and her long legs should be covered by a wrestler's black tights. For the moment she was in ordinary clothes: but her eyes gleamed already, as if out of the depths of grease-paint; her bare legs straddled the stage; and she roared magnificently:

"Come, where is this young gallant that is so desirous to lie with his mother earth?"

The Orlando complained to Miss Falconbridge that although Gill was technically the loser of the bout she never let herself be thrown without first twisting Orlando's arm or squeezing her ribs in realistic contention.

Neale gave me a birthday supper of fried eggs in an aquamarine snack-bar in the Waterloo Road. Afterwards we set out into south London. We sat in the lighted trolleybus; lurching and humming, it carried us through neighborhoods which lacked the characteristics of London and yet obviously, to anyone suddenly set down there, were London, if only because they could be nowhere else. Through the windows we could make out wide streets and pavements; the tall buildings were granite-grey. We got out where the conductor told us to, and found we were at an enormous road junction, at the center of which someone was changing the points on the tram lines, and someone else, just visible in the weak lamplight, was manipulating a pole to lift the arm of a trolleybus on to a new wire. Apart from an occasional clashing noise, and the whirr as an electric motor started, the place was almost silent. Very few people were on the pavements, and those there were dwarfed and formally dressed; they had an old-fashioned respectability, like figures from a pre-1914 film. We asked one of them the way, but he didn't know. We wandered round, trying to remember the directions the bus conductor had given us, and presently we found the art school. It had a dark-green notice-board outside, which we read with difficulty. We went through a wooden door and crossed what seemed to be an asphalt playground towards another door above which there was a dim light. Just before we reached it, I started: there was a fruit tree, quite tall, in full blossom, standing near the building, cemented into the asphalt; the light lay on its white upper branches gently, like light on a girl's head. We rang the doorbell; no one came. The door was unlocked. We went in, to a vestibule whose walls were painted olive-green below, yellow above, with a band of chocolate between. Neale stamped to and fro to attract attention, but no one responded. We walked along the corridor, found a door marked OFFICE, went in, and explained ourselves to the girl inside.

"I don't know, really," she said. "You'd better go up to the life class and ask Mr. Bingley."

We followed her directions: up concrete steps with an iron handrail, along unpolished wooden corridors; the building seemed to embody those institutions we had imagined in our quest by telephone. We passed doors labelled after technical processes of printing or dyeing, from behind which came a hum either of study or of light machinery; at last we reached a door marked LIFE ROOM.

We opened it, went in, and found we were staring at a blank black screen.

Gently, Neale moved one side of the screen and we stepped round it.

A woman's voice said: "I can feel that draught from the door again."

Neale moved the screen back behind us. I looked quickly at the model; but she was middle-aged and plump. She was standing with both arms raised like an Andromeda, and as she spoke she was at pains to show that she was not moving from her pose.

No one took any notice of Neale and me.

Above the dais in the center hung a big, black-enamelled light, shaped like a darning-mushroom. It threw a magic circle of brightness, round whose edges sat the students. We were beyond its pale; so were the screen in front of the door, the screens in front of each window, and the little cubicle of screens at the far end of the room. On the dais next to the model an oil-stove was burning and her left flank had become pink and spotted.

Moving round the outside of the circle, in the shadows, and coming forward behind each student to look over his head at the drawing-board he held, was a man in a tweed suit, with a peppery beard, whom we took to be Mr. Bingley. He came closer to us; I heard him say to a girl he was leaning over: "Your buttocks are wrong." He bent forward farther still and made a mark with his pencil on her drawing. He passed us. Neale signalled to me. But I said nothing.

When he had completed the circle, Bingley ordered a rest. Someone drew chalk marks round the model's feet; then she clambered off the dais, emphasizing her stiffness, and went into the cubicle of screens. Bingley lit a pipe and sat down next to one of the students. The model came out of the cubicle, wearing a tarnished kimono, and sat down on the other side of the circle. She lit a cigarette and her kimono lapsed open over her body.

We picked our way awkwardly round the outside, introduced ourselves to Bingley, and told him what we wanted.

"The name is familiar," he said. "She's not here now. But I think she was here."

"When?"

"Last year?" he wondered.

We would not let him off; we stared at him. Gesturing for help, he called: "Tom!"

A pale-faced young man came up.

"Tom, do you remember Cynthia Bewly?"

"She used to be one of the models, didn't she?"

"Yes, but when?"

"Last year," Tom said.

"'These people are trying to trace her." Bingley waved us into Tom's care. Tom asked:

"Would you recognize her?"

"Yes."

"I've got my portfolio from last year." He brought it and untied it. We began to look through a stack of prissy, academic drawings.

"You mightn't be able to tell from these," Tom said. "They're figure studies, really. Mostly five-minute sketches. I didn't do the faces in much detail—they're rather abstract in a way."

"I think we'd recognize her without the face," Neale said. He looked sideways at Tom, but Tom showed no impression.

We picked on one; the face was detailed enough to make us sure. We took the drawing out, and held it up. Bingley came and stood behind us. "Got what you wanted?"

"I remember now," Tom said. "She was a good model. There are more of her farther on." He took out the other sketches to show us. One of them was dated.

"So she was here last year," Neale said. "Is that all you can tell us? Don't you know where she went?"

Tom shook his head.

Bingley said loudly, to the whole room: "Does anyone know what became of Cynthia Bewly?"

No one answered; no one moved; no one interrupted the background noise of conversation. The question, and Cynthia's name spoken so publicly, merely rose above the room, and hung on the air like the cloud of smoke which had collected beneath the mushroom light.

I said to Tom: "What was she like? What sort of person was she?"

He held his drawing out at arm's length and concentrated on it. "It's curious. I can't remember. I can't get any clear idea of her at all." He slotted the drawing back into his portfolio.

As we went home, Neale said: "It'll be fun to see Cynthia dressed, one day." He came with me only as far as Leicester Square, where we parted, and he went off to work; but as I turned towards the Northern

Line he came running back. "I forgot to tell you. I made you a cake for your birthday. It's on top of the kitchen cupboard."

I thanked him.

"It's the first time I've ever made a cake." He grinned at me. "Any man can give a girl his virginity, but one's first cake..."

It turned out to be a sponge, lightly iced, with a few slivers of angelica on the top. It was a little doughy but not unpleasant. I lay in bed propped on my elbow and ate half of it.

The next day Finkelheim went out soon after luncheon and told me he would not be back. I sat listening for Neale. I had one or two false alarms and ran out on to the landing, but he was not there. His usual time passed. I sat on until it was within half an hour of my time to go home and I knew he would not bother to come now.

I could feel rather than see that the afternoon outside was early summer. Passages of sunshine fled past the dormer window; the sky was blue, tossed by streaks of white cloud and pools of grey. I felt sure the day would have exhausted its effort by the time I was free to go.

I surveyed our quest and decided it had got us either nowhere or into trouble. I revolted from what I now considered bungling; the real method, it seemed to me, would have been to go back to school, find Miss Falconbridge, who, I knew, organized an old-girls' society and tried to keep track of past pupils, and ask her where Cynthia was. At first I saw this as something I might have done; then, inspired by the gusty beginnings of summer, I saw I still could do it. I found myself possessed of enough moral energy, and of the stamina to endure seeing the place again. However, the plan was crippled: I should have to go on a weekday and within school hours, and I could think of no truthful way of making Finkelheim give me a day off. I felt impatient that Neale was not there to prompt me.

I stood in the middle of the office, too full of energy, annoyed by the prospect of the day's falling off without being enjoyed, and suspecting that Neale was keeping away to compensate for any advance he felt himself to have made in baking me a cake. I picked up the receiver and began to dial our number. Someone knocked at the office door.

I called: "Come in"; the door opened; I put down the receiver.

There were two men, amusingly alike. Each was about thirty-five, tall, broad, dressed in a putty-colored trench coat over a dark suit. The lapels were open, showing a blue soft collar of thick cotton and a tie striped in dull reds, golds, and gunmetal: the work of some inexpensive but safe, even dingy, outfitter. Both men had unusually large faces, rather flat, with big features; health saved them from being ugly. The one who spoke—slightly the broader, older, and healthier—had a deep voice and an accent not quite educated. He opened the door again behind him and swung it so that he could read the lettering on the outside, and then, closing it again, asked me:

"This is Finkelheim's? A bookseller's?"

"Yes."

"You were making a phone call?"

"Yes."

"Go ahead."

"No, it's quite all right. I'll wait."

We all three stared for a moment at the telephone.

"Mr. Finkelheim not here?"

"No."

"When do you expect him back?"

"Tomorrow."

"Morning?"

"Yes."

"You work for him?"

"Yes."

"Just the two of you work here?"

"Yes."

"You're his secretary?"

"More or less." I could not quite bring myself to ask who they were.

"Letters, do you do? Keep the books?" He added: "Or do you mostly work by phone?"

I said nothing.

"We'll come back tomorrow."

As they were at the door, I asked: "Who shall I say called?"

"We're police officers."

I listened to the stairs creaking as they descended; once I was sure they were out of the building I began for a second time, and much more urgently, to ring Neale. As I dialed the last number, it occurred to me not to trust the phone. I rang off, gathered my handbag and, careless of the ten minutes I still owed to Finkelheim, ran downstairs and across the road. As I opened the front door I shouted: "Neale! That woman did get the police!" Neale was out. I found a note from him on the kitchen table:

"What a pig you were with the cake. I've gone out for the evening. See you tomorrow."

We had made the telephone call to the wrong Cynthia Bewly from Finkelheim's. Now it struck me that if the police officers had watched the outside of the building after leaving it they would have learnt my home address from my flight across the road. I began to listen for them, expecting them to knock at each flat unhurriedly until they discovered me. I began to tidy the kitchen.

When they did not come, I decided to eat; but we had hardly anything in. I was afraid that the men were still in the road. I dared not go out. I poured myself a plate of corn flakes, and then found I did not want it.

I could think of no way to get in touch with Neale. His absence made me furious.

I found I could not read. At about half past nine I went to bed.

I could not prevent my mind turning at an unnatural rate, and unproductively, without gripping, like a bicycle wheel spun in the air, as I considered the alternatives of explaining or not explaining to the police. What confused me most, and threw me into tumult and hysteria, was my innocence. Of all the perversions in the world, the compulsion to make obscene telephone calls was the one I least shared.

I felt myself dropping asleep; unhealthily, since I knew I was sleeping. Suddenly I jerked awake. The image left in my mind was that I had stopped, saving myself just in time, with one foot over a steep, slippery bank.

I dozed again, and woke again, gripped by the thought that our telephone directory was evidence against us if anyone should find it with the fifteen Bewlys crossed out. I was terrified that I should have forgotten the point by morning. I forced myself to get out of bed, and wrote on a scrap of paper: "N.B. Destroy phone book."

When I fell really asleep I dreamed I was giving birth to a child—or I was the child; and the process of birth seemed be a nightmarish sliding down something in the dark.

When Neale came in next morning, I was still in bed. He stood over me. "You'll be late."

I shouted, falsetto with hysteria: "Get out!"

Presently I dragged myself up, put on my dressing-gown, and went into the kitchen. Neale was eating corn flakes. He asked: "You feeling bloody?" I told him what had happened the day before.

"It seems quite simple," Neale said. "If the police are going there this morning, you won't."

"What about Finkelheim?"

"He can cope. I'll ring him up and say you're ill."

"It's almost true."

"I'll say I'm your uncle. I doubt if that is."

I sat down and had some breakfast.

"Feeling better?"

"Yes. But rather heinous."

"Make the most of it. Enjoy it."

I left him alone to ring Finkelheim. "Look, Neale, could you tell him that if two men call he's not to worry—I'll deal with it?"

He came through into the bedroom, and I asked: "Was it all right?"

"Perfectly. He says he hopes you get better soon because he's got a lot of work."

While I dressed, Neale undressed. "Now you've got your free day, why don't you go to your school?"

"How can I? If I go out, if the police didn't see me Finkelheim might?"

Neale got into bed. "Ring for a taxi," he suggested. I hesitated.

"Go on. It's a lovely day. And I want to get some sleep."

I darted from our porch into the taxi, and as soon as I was inside I bent forward, as if to adjust my shoe, and kept my head low until we were round the corner.

I got out at Baker Street; if I had had the money I would have taken the cab all the way for the pure panache of arriving in it at school. Outside the station there were barrows of tulips, lilac, and roses. I wondered for a moment whether I would not simply go and sit in Regent's Park. However, leaving sunlight outside, I went down into the station. At once I was bewildered. I could not quite remember which of the illuminated indicator boards to consult, or what the distinction was between the Watford and the Aylesbury lines; I was certain only that there was a great distinction which I had once known so well that I scorned other people's ignorance. I felt as if I were being taken through a piece I was meant to have learnt by heart; I could not anticipate the next line, but when it was put to me I recognized it. So strong was my feeling that I ought to know, that I was ashamed to ask. I marched about the empty foyer, walking quickly to give the impression I was not lost. I moved from level to level, surprisedly coming on steps going down and steps going up to the street, with alleys of sunlight pouring down them. I moved like a person feeling his way in the dark around a room in which he knew the place of every object but where he was, temporarily, disorientated. After perhaps ten minutes I discovered the right platform.

The chestnut trees in the front garden were in flower, both the grey-white one and the deep pink which I had used to hate because it seemed to me the color of an artificial substance, perhaps marzipan. The drive had been altered in some way I could not make precise. The building did not, as I had expected it to, look smaller than I had remembered—if anything, larger. I had never really looked up at it before. What my memory had supplied as its gothicness turned out to be more debased than that: a matter of Dutch gabling, of too much red roof, like a felt hat pulled too far on, of cream pebble-dash and dark-green window frames. It was like part of an ideal farm; it was a suburban villa, or a suburban doll's-house, built on a big scale; it suggested health as it might be depicted in an advertisement, on a red-cheeked yokel.

I walked up and hesitated. I did not know which way to go in. I felt it impossible to use the girls' entrance, which led to the locker rooms; but I had never in my life gone in by the main door, and had no idea what lay immediately inside it.

At last I went up the steps. The main door was open. Inside I found a small waiting-room, and an office, neither of which I had seen before. No one was in them. I went through. I was in the main hall.

So many details I had remembered; more I had forgotten: the exact yellow of the parquet; the shape of the headmistress's chair on the platform.

I realized this must be lesson time. There was no noise, except for a voice occasionally raised in the distance.

Then footsteps approached. Although I had wanted someone to come, I walked over to the windows and stood looking out, my hand resting on the cold radiator, pretending I was waiting by appointment. The footsteps passed through the hall, and I did not see whose they were. Presently a bell rang. There was no immediate stir. At last a girl came into the hall, and I stopped her and asked if she would find Miss Falconbridge for me.

"Wouldn't you like to wait in the waiting-room? There are chairs there."

"No, I'd rather stay here, if you don't mind." I apologized: "I'm an old girl." I gave my name.

While I waited, I walked to the window again and looked out again at the tennis courts.

I recognized Miss Falconbridge's step. She came towards me across the hall, holding out her hand, smiling.

"What a lovely surprise!"

I had forgotten how much I liked her.

She seemed now, as she had seemed when I was at school, a woman of perhaps forty. Beneath the plain cardigan, despite the plain chignon, she was elegant; her lean, yellowish face would have been beautiful were it not for her teeth and would, even so, have been attractive if she had believed it.

She asked me at once if I would stay and lunch with the staff; but I said I had to go.

"Then we must make the most of these few minutes."

"Am I keeping you?"

"Yes, of course. But what does it matter?"

She led me into a corner by the far side of the platform where we were out of the way. The platform reached to shoulder height. She put her books up on it.

"Now tell me how you've been getting on."

I wondered if I should tell her about Neale, even about the police. The irony was clear in my mind of my coming back to my old school on the day when I was threatened with a criminal charge. I told her I was working for a bookseller.

"Yes, that would be the right line of country for you."

While she asked me about myself, I probed, without asking, at her. I remembered so well the tone of her voice, rather high, sounding many of the syllables clear and musical on the soft palate. Beneath her warmth of friendship, there was her old shyness, which forced her into giving this impression of enthusiasm straining on an unbreakable leash. While I turned my back on the side of the platform and leaned, she faced it, her wrists resting high on it; she looked down; she slipped her foot in and out of her black court shoe, turned it over sideways, swung it a little.

If I had told her about my life, she would never have gone beyond a conventional answer; she would never have said anything extraordinary that might have helped me. Yet in the ordinariness of all her conversation there was not bluntness but gentleness. I had always respected what seemed to me her unhappy control. My apprehension of her as a person who had given up took in the certainty that she had had something, I was never to guess what, which had been potential.

"My dear," she said at last, "I have a lesson to give."

"I've kept you far too long."

"I wish you'd stay to lunch."

"I wish I could. There's one thing. I wanted to ask you—do you know where Cynthia Bewly is now?"

"Cynthia Bewly. Yes, I know. Wait a moment and I'll get it straight."

"It's wonderful how you remember any of us."

"You're not so unmemorable. Cynthia is at the South-Eastern school of art."

"Yes," I said. "She was."

"Has she given it up?"

"Yes."

"I'm sorry, that was the last I heard."

I walked with her down the hall—she refused to let me carry her books—until she told me to come no farther. She asked me to visit the school again and stay longer—at any rate to keep in touch. As she went, she said:

"I'm sorry to hear Cynthia's given up art. She had quite a talent for drawing."

I walked back to the corner at the side of the stage. I stooped down. There was the small, square door which led under the stage. It was locked.

In this corner Cynthia and I had stood in darkness on the last night of our autumn term. A black curtain cut us off from the audience in front. At our side another black curtain, forming the wings, divided us from the stage above us; sometimes the curtain moved; once the shape of an elbow was thrust through towards us; once or twice the hem of the curtain, just on our eye level, was caught up and we saw a frill of light. Occasionally a character made her exit on our side. There would be a rent of light, rapidly healed; we would realize someone was standing on the edge of the platform—we would see the gleam of a face sweating behind its grease-paint; the figure would leap off, into us, and scuttle away; but if she had landed too heavily we would hear Miss Falconbridge—from the other side, from our side, from somewhere in the wings, actually on the stage but behind the curtain—whisper "Shhh."

During the fourth act, Miss Falconbridge was next to us, listening; she hurried away; she came back urgent. "I want two volunteers. Is there anyone here? I can't see who you are."

We whispered our names.

"Hymen's lost her crown. She needs it for the next act."

"I don't know where—"

"It must have got in with the old props." Miss Falconbridge stooped, and unlocked the door.

"I never knew there was a door there," I said. "I never knew you could get under the stage."

"You weren't meant to know."

We hunched ourselves to enter; there seemed to be steps down.

"Here, take my torch."

There was a sort of half-ladder inside: four dusty, bare wooden steps. We began to peer our way down them. Miss Falconbridge pushed the door to behind us.

Outside sounds became muffled. We were enclosed.

I led, with the torch's beam. We advanced into an enchanted hush, as if snow had begun to fall; and in the torchlight we saw fractions of dust, and sometimes a sharp but weightless splinter, continually descending as the characters above us moved about on the stage. At first we stooped; but the floor of the stage was well clear of our heads. The footfalls came to us like heavy but far-distant bumpings, and the voices, pursuing lines so familiar, seemed to reach us a moment late, distinct but laden with reverberance.

The immense stone floor had been swept, long before, with a wide broom which had left orderly furrows of brownish fluff. There was no cluttering of the space, only a few separate piles of wreckage. A painted screen lay on its side, one of its panels pierced by a gilt stick that must have been a chair leg. Elsewhere there was a bundle of masks, all tied together; and tied to them was a balloon that had withered on its string. Another heap consisted of Spanish shawls. At the far end was an artificially rustic structure, stuck over with silk roses.

"To think we had to make so many new ones, when those are here."

"Those are faded," Cynthia whispered.

Hymen's crown lay tumbled alone in a clearing. I picked it up and slipped it, like a vast bracelet, over my wrist.

Overhead, the Rosalind chided her Orlando. "I will be more jealous of thee than a Barbary cock-pigeon over his hen, more clamorous than a parrot against rain, more newfangled than an ape, more giddy in my desires than a monkey: I will weep for nothing, like Diana in the fountain...."

Cynthia tugged one of the roses out of its frame. The green ribbon which bound its stem had turned an acid yellow. She began to unpick it, exposing the wire.

I cast the torchlight round, on the dust.

Cynthia came up to me, faced me, and pushed the wire stem through the flannel of my lapel, drawing it down on the other side so that I was wearing the flower.

I slipped the gilt cardboard crown off my wrist and held it above Cynthia's head. Gently I brought it down.

She brushed it off. "Don't be absurd." Suddenly we kissed each other.

"Oh coz, coz, coz, my pretty little coz, that thou didst know how many fathom deep I am in love!"

I stood in Cynthia's arms, with my arms round her, trying to see her face. The torch in my hand shed its light casually behind her back. I had known that people kissed, but I had never involved the fact with myself. I found I had no idea how I had come into Cynthia's arms, how that space had been leapt which had always seemed sacrosanct. I had been not only without anticipation but without desire; and now all the desire I had in the world had been fulfilled beyond its own horizons.

I found that the desire had formed to kiss again. I cast my mind back to find out how it had been done, and copy it; but I could not discover any means behind the act. As my memory played on the immediately past moment, it became irrevocable.

I was left with a new moment, and with desire. Plotting clumsily, I bent my head towards Cynthia, my lips bitterly closed together.

We heard the door open and Miss Falconbridge say: "Haven't you found it yet?"

As we convulsed apart I felt a kind of guilt I had never experienced before. We filed out, handing up the torch and the crown, and I was dissimulating in an entirely new way.

As I emerged, the Rosalind spoke her departing line. "I cannot be out of the sight of Orlando; I'll go find a shadow and sigh till he come."

She stepped into the wings above me.

The Celia finished: "And I'll sleep."

The curtain at the front of the stage was rushed rattling across by the girls whose duty it was.

The morning after my day off I crossed the road to Finkelheim's in possession of my courage again, determined to treat the whole thing as casually as Neale would have done, and to explain it to the police as the absurd accident it was.

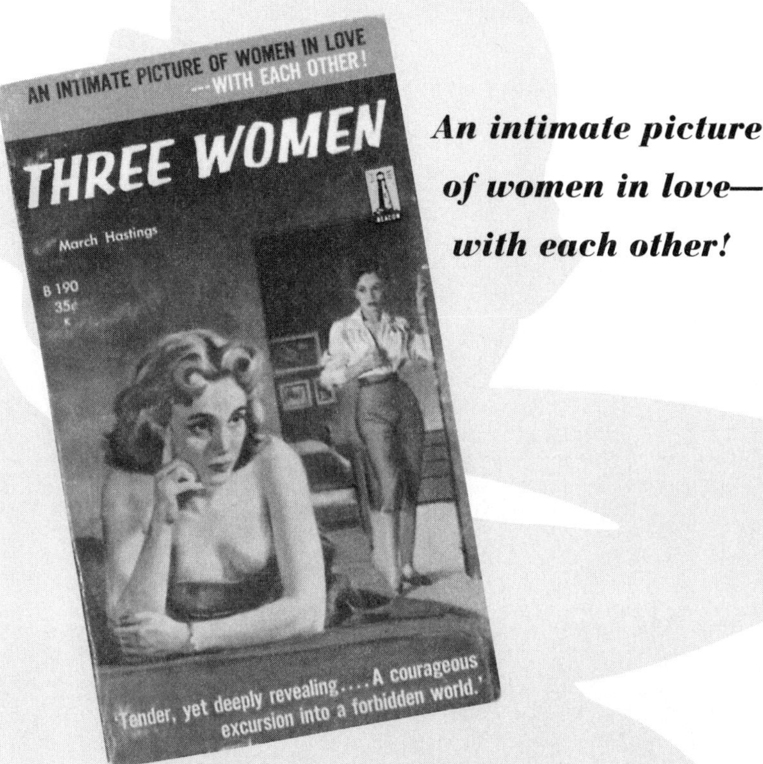

An intimate picture of women in love— with each other!

Three Women

by March Hastings

Unconventional, even unmoral, behavior certainly is not rare in Manhattan art circles. But what was going on in the menage of the Byrne woman raised the eyebrows even of the most broadminded. For she was supposed to be loving and cherishing another artist, Greta. Yet she welcomed the advances of bewitching young Paula Temple.

Of course, love between women may be considered a matter of illness, of an unfortunate warping of the personality, rather than of morality. In Paula's case, however, the guilt was there. For Paula had not only a woman to love, but also a man…

Three Women

As the first spray of dawn warmed the sky, Byrne knew that she must face Greta. How could she tell her? What could she impress upon a mind that had withdrawn so far from the ordeal of living? And yet, in all fairness to both of the women she loved, she had to do something once and for all that was decisive.

Byrne went to the bathroom and scrubbed her face as if to wash away the last fifteen years of semi-living. Had it really been that long? Had the precious time slipped by her this quickly? But there had not been until now a Paula to make time so important.

In a clean pair of slacks and a camel's hair coat, Byrne slipped out of the house. The sudden desire to be free of Greta urged her to action. Small nudges of guilt turned inside in their familiar attempt to imprison her but she thrust them aside. For Paula's sake and for her own, she had to try, now, to be a whole person.

The cab took her swiftly uptown in the emptiness of early morning streets. Memories of Greta thrust themselves into her consciousness.

How wonderful it had all been at the beginning. That delightful innocence of first passion. Yet it had been more than passion. It had been a whole entanglement of families that flung Greta and herself together.

As the cab whined along the street, Byrne could almost hear her mother saying: "Greta is coming to help you with your arithmetic."

Greta helped Byrne with homework or stayed with her when Mother went visiting at night or took her to the beach or helped her select a new pair of shoes because Mother never had the time to do any of these things. What good fortune—thought both families—their girls got along so nicely and didn't bother with boys.

They had indeed made a private island of their friendship into which no one could intrude. And little by little, Byrne found excuses to sleep downstairs or Greta found reasons to stay with Byrne all night. They would lie together under the covers and tell each other stories, aware only of the joy each found in the other's company. And then another awareness intruded.

So simply and without question Greta had leaned over one rainy night and taken Byrne's hand to quiet her fright at the jagged flashes and vibrating thunder. The storm and that hand tore open their need, spilling each into the arms of the other.

Neither one had said, "I love you."

Why did they need words or promises when there could be nothing to threaten them? The fulfillment of their bodies seemed only one more act among the thousands of acts that united them. When Byrne kissed Greta's hair, it was no different from a peck on the cheek that she might have given her at midday.

If Greta had known others thought this wrong, she had never mentioned it. No words of caution did she give Byrne. Perhaps she had not wanted to foul their beautiful dream by admitting a world that would condemn and separate. Or perhaps Greta herself did not fully realize the meaning of their closeness.

And Greta could do no wrong.

The goddess who painted like an angel and who knew all the answers to Byrne's young questions of life could only be worshipped. The heaven of their bodies' union seemed only one more proof that she was truly a goddess.

Byrne could not contain her feelings and had tried to convey to her mother the beauty of Greta's kiss.

And, to Byrne's surprise, her mother had whirled, cheeks crimson with outrage, and grasped Byrne firmly by the shoulders.

"What are you saying?"

Byrne thought her mother had misunderstood. With youthful desire to share her joy, she explained in lingering detail what happened those nights when she slept with Greta.

"Disgusting animal!" The old-fashioned collar quivered at her mother's throat.

Too late Byrne realized that she must have said some thing wrong. But what? The sneer and revulsion in her mother's eyes made Byrne leap blindly to Greta's defense. Whatever must be bad, she had to protect Greta from it.

"But you don't understand," Byrne stammered, not understanding herself what it could be that made her mother dig fingers into her shoulder as if to tear the skin off her skeleton.

With each phrase that she stammered, Byrne felt herself and Greta sinking deeper into unfamiliar quicksand.

For three days she was locked in the house.

Now her mother took her to school and brought her home and made her take a bath twice a day. She had never before received such attention, yet nothing her mother did could take Byrne's mind off Greta. She would lie awake at night, her arms around the pillow, begging Greta to forgive her.

Worst of all was the thought that she had betrayed Greta. She had to see her. She had to explain. What if she thought she had purposely betrayed her?

But there was no way to get out of the locked house.

As the days went by, Byrne's guilt grew beyond control. No matter what the price, she must see Greta just once to explain what had happened, to throw herself at Greta's feet and beg forgiveness. Her tortured mind could form no plan. She could think of only one way to get to see Greta.

And so the next day Byrne did not meet her mother after school. Instead she ran two blocks to a candy store and phoned Greta's home, praying that Greta herself would answer. Breathlessly she waited for the receiver to be lifted. And when the deep voice of Greta's brother said hello, Byrne still did not give up hope.

"Please, Jack, let me speak to Greta."

But Jack, though he wanted to, could not help her. Greta had been shipped to their aunt's house in the country.

Byrne's world collapsed. Greta had been taken out of school because of her. She was due to graduate with honors, she had a scholarship to an art school. And Byrne had destroyed it all.

She picked up her schoolbooks and trudged home, not caring if her mother whipped the flesh off her bones or threw her into a dungeon for life. Without Greta there was nothing to live for. And now that she had ruined Greta too, life became a horrible thing she could not face.

When she reached home, her mother said nothing. She merely smiled at Byrne with the superior knowledge of what Byrne had just learned.

Byrne could not eat the meal placed before her. She could only stare at the plate and think of Greta cooped up so far away from all her dreams and ambitions. How could she leave Greta alone and a prisoner?

As the days passed Byrne suffocated in self-accusation. Each time she walked out free on the streets, she thought of Greta alone. Each night she went to bed, she recalled Greta's sweet lips and thought of them wasting away unloved. When her mother took her to the movies, it was Greta's face she saw on the screen, her blue eyes gazing sadly down at Byrne.

The nightmare of trying to sleep robbed her nerves of all strength. She could not simply sit and do nothing. She must free Greta and make the world know that the fault was all her own and not that of her innocent beloved.

Homework went undone and in class her own thoughts obliterated the teacher's voice. She barely passed the mid-term examinations. Greta, only Greta lived vividly for her. She lost weight and had to move the buttons on her skirts. Nervous energy alone drove her and her mind focused on one tiny burning point—free Greta.

Until finally Byrne could no longer live with her thoughts.

In the middle of the night, she took from the savings bowl money equivalent to the allowance that had been denied her the past two months. She knew that the authorities would question a fifteen-year-old girl trying to buy a train ticket at one in the morning. She would have to wait until daylight. Carefully she unlatched the door and slipped into the hallway. For the rest of the night she could hide in the basement. Then, when daylight broke, she could go to the train station before her mother discovered that she was missing.

To see Greta again! To look at the slender fingertips that seemed to caress without touching. To hear the light footstep and the singing voice again. Just one more minute with Greta and she would be content to die.

And a minute would be all they would have. For Byrne knew that her mother would know where she had gone.

At the train station she discovered that she had just enough money for a one-way ticket. Tall men pushing carts of luggage smiled at her and an elderly gentleman helped her up the steps into the train. She found a seat near the window and prayed that the train would start before her mother could get to the station and come on board to look for her.

The trip was only an hour long and Byrne knew the route almost by heart. For she had often gone there with Greta during Christmas and summer vacations.

Listening to the clicking of the wheels, Byrne tried to relax. She watched the leafless trees whip by and tried not to think how Greta might receive her.

Maybe Greta wouldn't want to see her at all. She couldn't blame her if she didn't. But Greta had to understand. She couldn't go on for the rest of her life thinking that Byrne had said ugly things about their love.

After an eternity of waiting, the train slowed down and stopped at her station. She listened to the conductor call the name out like a great judge pronouncing her doom.

In the station house she tried to warm herself at a pot-bellied stove while she waited for the bus that went to the house. The stench of old cigars reminded her of Greta's uncle. He would look down from his great height over the cigar that stuck straight out from between his lips. But he would understand and help her.

The old bus rattled to a halt beside the station house and Byrne ran to board it, knowing that she would still have to wait ten minutes before the driver started on the return trip.

Bouncing along the dirt road she looked out at the brown stubble that grew along the hillside. For miles above her the gray sky drearily stretched. The desolate hills had long since dropped their blooms and even the occasional rabbits that hopped quickly off the road seemed lonely and desolate.

When the driver came to her stop, Byrne held her breath. Her legs were unsteady things that balanced her body with effort. But she went bravely down the gravel path toward the wooden house.

Maybe Greta would be around in the back sorting apples. Byrne passed along the side of the house and peered down between the slanted door that opened into the basement. No light was there.

"Greta?" she said softly. And silence answered her.

She went down the steps and looked around, hoping that perhaps Greta had not heard her.

Only coils of garden hose and bulging sacks of potatoes met her sight.

Greta must be upstairs. Maybe she was in her little room on the top floor that looked outward toward the hills and toward the city.

Unhappily Byrne retraced her steps and walked with uncertain determination back to the front door.

She climbed the crooked steps and listened to them squeak beneath her feet. Then she rapped on the screen door and waited. Her breath caught in her throat and her heart knocked wildly in her chest. If only she had wings to sweep Greta up and fly away from here before the adults could swarm down on them. But she still did not understand why all these terrible things had happened as a result of all the loveliness she and Greta had shared. How could it be sinful to be so content?

Byrne heard the heavy bootsteps of Greta's uncle and crossed her fingers fervently.

"Hello, little girl," he said in the slow voice that could hide surprise. He always called her "little girl" and Byrne felt encouraged.

"May I come in?" she said in a thin voice that trembled from her breathlessness.

He opened the door and tapped a long cigar ash on the ground. "Of course you can come in."

Byrne wondered why he didn't ask what she was doing here or where her mother was or anything. But she came into the inside porch where the old wicker chairs seemed to beckon her with their hominess.

"Had a good trip?" He made easy conversation while she took off her coat. "This time of year makes mighty bitter traveling." He smiled amiably and the red veins on his cheeks crinkled.

Byrne let him take her east and then followed him into the spacious kitchen.

"Nobody's home but me," he chatted. "But I can make as good a cup of coffee as anyone."

The question that leaped to Byrne's frantic mind remained unspoken. She had to conduct herself like a lady. So far, Uncle John was on her side. At least he wasn't calling her all kinds of names and acting like she was a poisonous witch.

After he placed two heavy mugs on the table, Byrne asked, "Isn't Greta here?"

"Oh, she's staying here, all right," he said gently. "But she's not here this morning. Her Aunt Nell took her over to visit with the Regans. Everybody seems to think it's about time Greta got herself a husband, you know." He stirred sugar into his coffee as if the words he'd just said were ordinary words and not the most horrible things that Byrne could hear.

Byrne knew the Regan boys. One was fat and the other one fatter. But they were wealthy and would inherit a lot of money someday. It didn't make any difference to the family which one Greta married, so long as she married one of them. The vision of Greta, who could not stand the two boys, being forced to marry one of them horrified Byrne.

"Oh, Uncle John," she blurted. "You've got to help her!"

He searched her face with the dark and kind blue eyes. He seemed to find and understand the earnestness in Byrne that had prompted her outburst.

"Everybody's got their minds made up," he said, striking a large match and moving its flame to the cigar.

"But Greta doesn't want to marry either of the Regan boys." Even if Greta didn't love Byrne, she wouldn't want one of those two.

"You don't think so?" he asked. "Well, it was her own idea that her Aunt Nell take her over this morning."

Byrne's mind went blank. Why would Greta want to do a thing like that? What must she be suffering? What horrible tortures could push her into that kind of decision?

"Greta's almost eighteen," Uncle John continued. "And I suspect she knows how to make up her own mind."

Maybe Uncle John didn't know what the trouble was. Maybe no one had told him what had happened between her and Greta. But if he did know, would he understand why Greta would want to drive herself into such a corner? If she told him, would he help? If she told him, he might just throw her out. But if she didn't tell him, he could never help Greta.

Byrne had to take the chance. For Greta's sake.

She took a long drink of coffee and then explained to him as simply as she could everything that had happened.

He listened to her story without interruption. And Byrne didn't spare herself. She repeated what her mother had said and how she had been treated as a result. She emphasized that none of this had been Greta's fault. That the blame must be hers alone.

When she had finished her story, Uncle John put down his cigar and folded the stained fingers around the strap of his overalls.

"You know," he said, "when you spend your life tending animals, you get to respect nature."

She looked at him with question, moving her palm nervously along the knicked table top.

"And the first law of nature," he said, "is that animals and men and all living things should reproduce their own. I guess that's all I can see wrong with what you're telling me. It doesn't lead anywhere except into a blind alley, seems to me. Pretty girls, strong girls like you and Greta should have homes and raise families someday."

Byrne started to protest. She had always expected to have a family. That was something simply taken for granted, even if not particularly wanted. It seemed like something you just did; everybody had a family. But why couldn't she love Greta and have a family too? Why should one get in the way of the other?

Yet Uncle John said that it would. And she trusted him enough to believe in his judgment.

"Then if Greta has to get married," Byrne persisted, "that means that I have to get married too?"

"Right," he nodded.

"So she'll get married to one of the Regan boys and I'll marry the other one." A triumphant feeling floated through her. This way, Greta wouldn't have to suffer alone. If they could both be married and have houses across the street from each other or maybe apartments in the same building, she could still see her every day and things would be all right.

Uncle John said, "Well, maybe in a few years. You're still kind of young for marrying, you know."

A few years? Separated from Greta all that time! In school she had learned that there were certain states in the union where you could get married at fourteen, and she was a year older than that. She told Uncle John.

"Just the same, I think you're safer waitin' a few years," he smiled gently.

But a plan was already beginning to form in Byrne's mind. If Greta wanted to marry one of the Regans, then she certainly wanted to marry the other. The happy prospect of being near Greta again relieved some of her tension and she finished the remains of her coffee, enjoying the warmth of it in her stomach.

She sat back against the high wooden chair and inhaled the warm odor of preserves cooking on the stove. Greta would be back soon and she could tell her all about how wonderful things would be for them again. Uncle John didn't press her into further conversation. He too sat back, contemplating things from behind the whorls of smoke that rose lazily from his cigar.

At last they both heard the crunch of footsteps coming up toward the house. Once again Byrne's nerves jumped. But the anticipation of seeing Greta again held her frozen to the chair. She clutched the edge of the table top and turned her face toward the doorway.

Aunt Nell came in first, her small mouth tied in a tiny knot of satisfaction. Behind her, Greta ambled slowly as though drawn along by an invisible rein. Her gaze was fastened on the tips of her shoes. Byrne waited excitedly for her to look up.

"What's she doing here?" Aunt Nell snorted.

The tone made Greta look up.

Byrne, grinning happily with the joy of the new plan just formed, burst her beaming gladness upon Greta. She wanted to run to her, hug her, and assure her that everything was going to be all right.

And Byrne saw in Greta's eyes a strange thing that she had never seen before. They didn't shine, those eyes. A dulling film seemed to have dropped like a curtain before them. She hardly seemed to know Byrne. It took some moments before she said hello.

Uncle John said some combination of magic words that calmed his wife's annoyance, but Byrne did not hear him speak. She could concentrate only on Greta. With a sudden burst of enthusiasm, she rushed out of the chair and over to her darling, wanting to fight her way past that unfamiliar curtain and back into the loveliness and warmth that had always been her Greta.

But Greta smiled stiffly, as though she were meeting Byrne for the first time.

"I'm getting married," she said in a voice that seemed to float over Byrne's head.

"Yes, I know," Byrne tried to be enthusiastic. "That's wonderful. And I'm going to get married too." She smiled encouragingly, hoping that Greta would change back into her old self, that she would reach out with the familiar tenderness and laugh softly with her.

Aunt Nell started to say something calculated to bite at Byrne, but her husband managed to lead her away into the parlor. Byrne was alone with Greta at last.

The two girls looked at each other wordlessly, though Byrne felt that she had a million things to say all at once.

"Greta, darling, it was all my fault," she whispered. "I didn't mean to do you any harm."

"Your fault?" Greta repeated. "I'm older than you are. You didn't know what you were doing, but I did." She couldn't seem to look at Byrne directly. Her gaze sought fugitive places up on the ceiling or over at the sink.

"But what did we do, Greta, that was so terrible?" Byrne insisted, aching to reach out and have Greta take her hand.

But Greta clasped her hands tightly together. "We sinned," she murmured without strength. "I wanted to protect you and I led you into the path of damnation instead."

"What are you talking about?" Byrne said. She recognized Greta's words as only an echo of her Aunt Nell. How could Greta believe that anything as wonderful as what they had done would be sin?

But Greta's mind roamed far away from any argument Byrne might have to offer. She seemed to have opened the door and stepped into an unreachable place where Byrne could not follow. Byrne felt an inkling of fear, for the first time. Not for herself and not because of the thing that was supposed to be sin. Yet that fear crawled along under the surface of her skin and made her cold. This Greta was not the Greta she had known two months before. Byrne didn't know what the difference was; all she could see and understand was that something horrible closed Greta away from her.

And Byrne knew it was all her own fault.

The marriage took place quickly. Everybody seemed anxious to have it occur as quickly as possible.

When the wedding ring was securely on Greta's finger, all the restrictions that had prevented Byrne from seeing her beloved were relaxed.

Of course she was living in the country now and Byrne could get away to see her only on weekends. But now, it was merely a question of patience. She went out with the other Regan boy, the thinner one. She dressed nicely and did everything to please him, hoping that he would ask her to marry him.

And she watched Greta to see what it was like to be a good housewife. Greta seemed to take on the chore without difficulty. She cleaned her new house and baked cakes and seemed to float around as if nothing touched her. Byrne prayed for that far away feeling to disappear, but instead it seemed to be getting worse. Greta hardly laughed anymore. When something pleased her, an odd smile would flit across her lips, and that was all. And one day Byrne realized that the unfamiliar odor surrounding Greta was the smell of whiskey.

They never talked about the same things anymore either. Uneasily, Byrne began to think that maybe Greta hated her.

One Saturday, when Greta's husband had gone to town for the week's shopping, Byrne confronted her.

"I've got to know the truth," she pleaded. She had taken Greta into the living room and forced her to sit down on the couch and give complete attention.

"I've got to know," Byrne choked, "how you feel about me."

She waited for the dread words to fall on her ears.

Greta said, "I'm very thirsty, dear. Can't I have a drink first?"

Impatiently Byrne got out the bottle and filled two glasses. She watched with unhappiness as Greta emptied hers and refilled it two more times.

"Don't you want to tell me?" Byrne said. "Anything would be better than this not knowing. Do you hate me for what I've done? Do you?"

Greta put down her glass. She seemed to be mustering all the forces that had scattered inside her.

"I love you, darling," she whispered. "There is nothing in this world that means anything to me except you." Thankfully Byrne relaxed against the over-stuffed sofa. "And I adore you. Worship you."

Before either of them knew what had happened, they were in each other's embrace, kissing away the tortured months that had kept them apart.

It did not seem strange to Byrne that they made love in hurried intervals. She was grateful for Greta's kisses whenever she could get them. By now the textbooks in the library had revealed to her the meaning of their feelings, and she realized too that Greta had gotten married as a protection against the evil name that went with their kind of loving.

Still Byrne knew that she had committed irreparable damage. Though Greta responded and showed her the ecstasy that Byrne had come to expect, she did not show any exuberance or even the suggestion of happiness at other times. Only when they were in each other's arms did she seem to come alive.

Greta began to bulge out of her clothes, not seeming to care about her appearance anymore. The silken mane hung in tangled masses around the housedress that gaped open at the tight buttons. The grace and the beauty that had been Greta decayed. Her carelessness began to spread through the house, too. Empty whiskey bottles rolled beneath the furniture. Byrne began to sense in herself an outrageous feeling of shame that she struggled vainly to subdue. And to hear Isaac Regan grumble about his wife's sloppiness hurt Byrne.

She tried to tell herself that Greta was bored with living so far away in the country. So Byrne brought her drawing equipment in the hope of reviving the dull spirits.

And Greta did begin to draw. She filled pages and pages with strange heads as though she were trying to loosen from within herself an anguish that could find no words. As the months drew into a year, Greta stopped doing anything else except painting and the drinking. She carried a full glass of whiskey with her almost constantly and sometimes Byrne argued with her about it, only to hear Greta laugh a strange laugh that made no sense.

The biggest shock of all came when Byrne entered the house one day to discover Greta in the process of cutting off all her hair.

She sat, not before a mirror, but in the kitchen, snipping of the back of her head and making jagged scars in the beautiful thick blonde hair.

Horrified, Byrne snatched the scissors away from her. But it was too late. As Greta looked up at her in mute helplessness, Byrne realized for the first time how much damage Greta had actually done to herself. Not just the hair. The smooth complexion had lost all its old rosiness, and the fine line of jaw had begun to sag into a slovenly mass of flesh. Byrne felt sick. She put the scissors back into the drawer and tried to ward off the depression that pressed into her mind.

She loved Greta. She would always love Greta. A fierce loyalty bound her to this poor woman whom she had so innocently betrayed. If it weren't for her own stupidity, Greta would not be suffering so. If Byrne had not interfered, Greta would be in New York, making a name for herself in the world of art, living a rich existence, full of the happiness of accomplishment. Byrne alone was responsible for the destruction of this once wonderful being, and she must stay with her. At the least, she could help fend off people's inevitable accusing looks and degrading words—cutting, painful words that even Isaac never ceased to say.

By the time Byrne graduated from high school, Isaac had started divorce proceedings.

Byrne shared the shame, and it seared through her pride. But at the same time, she was glad. Isaac was willing to give Greta a great deal of money if she would not fight the separation, and she could go to New York. Byrne would live with her there. She was eighteen now, and at last no one in the world could stop her from doing what she wanted. And maybe, if they lived together, away from reminders of blame and guilt, Greta would regain her health.

What encouraged Byrne most of all was Greta's desire to live with her. In the midst of her detachment and withdrawn isolation, this one last remnant of enthusiasm still appeared.

And so Byrne had an apartment all ready by the time Greta's divorce came through.

Since there was no problem of money, Byrne had all the time in the world to lavish on her beloved.

After breakfast, she would say, "Let's take a ride up to Bear Mountain."

But Greta would sit in the armchair and hug her knees up to her chest. She stared out the window at nothing in particular, just far away.

"Well, how about the zoo?"

Whatever Byrne suggested met with no response. With a sigh, Byrne would pick up a book and try to get interested.

Only at night did Greta seem to come alive. When they had climbed into bed, she would fling herself on Byrne and passionately dig her teeth into the soft flesh of her girl's belly. And Byrne, mistaking this for ecstasy, thrilled to the pain at first. Yet she could not bring herself to treat Greta with anything except gentleness.

They would spend almost all of the night in lovemaking. Nothing seemed to satisfy Greta. Content to sleep during the day, her energies focused in wild excitement when she held Byrne within naked reach. And Byrne accepted this kind of lovemaking, not daring to admit even to herself that it did not satisfy her, that it left her feeling base and without gladness.

But she could recognize that lolling around the house all day drained her energies into a pool of boredom. She needed to do other things besides sketch. The world sat outside on her doorstep, waiting to be explored. She ached to experience it. Nothing she could say or do excited Greta into wanting to share this with her.

After a while Byrne took to going to the movies by herself. If it were a comedy she would sit in the darkness laughing to herself, terribly aware of having no one to share the fun.

One evening Byrne came home to find Greta huddled in a corner, staring up at her like an angry animal.

"But you said I could go," Byrne protested.

Without a word Greta leaped at her. She pounced upon Byrne with surprising agility for a woman of her weight. Byrne could not protect herself without hurting Greta. She crossed her forearms in front of her face and let Greta's fists pound and the nails claw until the woman was out of breath.

"You don't love me," Greta panted in a furious whisper.

"Of course I do," she lowered her arms and sought Greta's eyes. They looked beyond Byrne and seemed to be speaking to someone far away. Tears rose and welled over on Byrne's cheeks. She could no longer deny to herself that Greta's mind was unbalanced.

But Greta did not become increasingly worse. True, she began to insist that she felt stupid in a dress, yet she would occasionally go out for a walk with Byrne or listen to the radio. She made just enough conversation to permit Byrne to believe that she didn't need to be hospitalized.

And, of course, there were her magnificent paintings. She would sometimes look at Byrne's work and, with rapid short sentences, would show her exactly what was wrong. Then and only then would Byrne feel a glimmer of the once sharp intelligence.

So Byrne continued to live this weird existence of alternating hope and loneliness. She didn't question that there could be such a thing as real companionship for her. But Greta was her first responsibility, especially now that a psychiatrist had diagnosed her case as incurable.

Their apartment became for Byrne a chamber of horrors. Two Chinese lamps that she had bought were long since smashed in one of Greta's fits. Deep holes in the plaster reminded her of the violence always lying dormant, even when the two of them were sitting quietly watching television.

It never occurred to Byrne that she should have a separate apartment where she could be alone occasionally and pull her battered spirits together. The idea came very innocently one day when a young girl in the supermarket started to talk to her.

They were both pushing carts along the frozen foods counter when the girl picked up a package of deviled crabs and said to Byrne, "Gee, I wonder if this brand is any good. Have you ever used it?"

Byrne looked at the dark curling hair and the bright vivacious eyes and felt an almost overwhelming desire just to make ordinary conversation with an ordinary person.

"I've used them many times," Byrne said eagerly. "The trick is to get them good and brown." She wished she could invite her over and show her how to prepare them.

The girl thanked her and strolled on, leaving Byrne to realize more strongly than ever how impossible it would be to make friends with anybody because of Greta's condition.

She began to look in the "apartments for rent" column, hardly realizing her own motives.

Greta had taken to sleeping more than ever. Whole days slipped by, lost to her. Soon Byrne rented a place on Eleventh Street, knowing that if she did not get away, her own sanity might be threatened too.

From this it was only a small step to having visitors. Casual friends at first, who chatted about current events. Then gradually, a woman whom Byrne would take into her arms, forgetting her past for a moment, ignoring the anchor that dragged at her heart.

How many women passed in and out of her life like this? Byrne always managed to let them know she could give nothing permanent. Susan...Phyllis...Rachel... They all came and went like sea shells rolling up on a beach and then sliding back into the ocean again...

Byrne had not expected ever to meet anyone like Paula. But when she did, her safely sealed heart knocked against the doors of its prison, demanding to be freed.

No one had insisted the way Paula insisted on the right to her loving. And Byrne, for all her responsibilities and loyalties to Greta, had succumbed.

There was nothing left but to face the idea of putting Greta into the hands of someone who could really take care of her properly. A nurse of some sort would stay with Greta during the time when Byrne must be with Paula.

For two weeks Byrne interviewed women until she found the right person to take care of Greta. But Greta was not so detached from life she did not know what was happening.

She looked at Byrne with wide eyes that could not comprehend and said, "Why don't you want to live with me anymore?" Her voice fluttered around Byrne with helplessness.

"I'll see you very often," Byrne replied and struggled to keep a bright expression on her lips.

"Where will you be living?" Greta folded her hands childlike on her lap. All the years of sitting had made a caricature of her body. The warm woman's curves lay hidden beneath pads of fat and flab now.

"Not too far." Byrne tried to reassure her, even knowing it was hopeless.

"Will you show me where?" She tilted her head up with pleading. The gesture reminded Byrne of a dog tied outside the store and waiting for its master.

"Of course."

"Take me now?" she begged eagerly.

And Byrne had not the strength to deny her request. She got a taxi and brought Greta down to her apartment and watched her wander about from room to room, looking as if she were searching for a corner in which to curl up and hide herself.

Byrne took her by the hand and led her back into the living room.

"See?" she said, pointing to Greta's painting above the bookshelf. "I've got you with me all the time."

Byrne searched in vain for some response of pleasure but Greta's eyes remained as ever dull.

"Can I come to visit you sometimes?" A tremor as of tears shook in her voice.

Instinctively Byrne pulled Greta into her arms. "Of course you can," she whispered, struggling to sound cheerful. "You can come here any time you want."

For the first time, now, Greta smiled.

"I'll wait for you," Greta said. "I always want to wait for you."

Byrne brought her back to her own apartment and then left hurriedly. She went to a small dark bar and drank to quiet some of the tearing thoughts and heavy guilt that pulled at her with such pain.

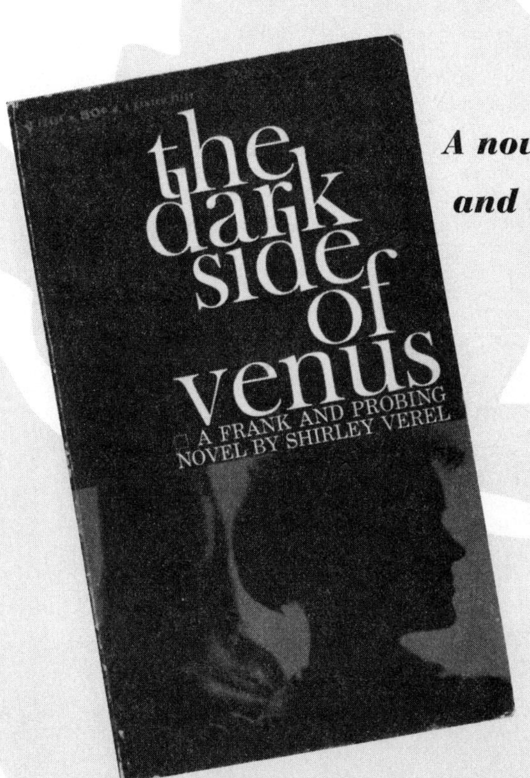

A novel of strange lusts and inbred passion

The Dark Side of Venus

by Shirley Verel

"It's too much to ask, you can't expect me to give up love, to live without it." Judith knew that Julian couldn't understand why she wouldn't marry him. She had to make it clear to him, explain to him that she was already in love—desperately and passionately—with another woman.

The Dark Side of Venus

We had driven back to Paris against the beginning of a pale gray rain barrier. The car was at a garage. Our only purpose now had become to talk.

There is a blankness about hotel bed rooms, the blankness of rooms that don't belong to anyone. She sat on the other side of the room in a small cushioned bedroom chair.

She said, "Had you stopped loving each other; you and Terry?"

"It wasn't that. It was"—I paused, for putting into words just what it had been—"that everything about her except her senses believed women need men. Whether or not they want them or can have them."

"For prestige? To be propped up socially?"

"That's less trivial than you make it sound. Though what she was really afraid of was where going on with it would lead in a relationship like ours: two unprotected old maids. Unprotected and unproductive."

She frowned.

Held together, Terry had said, by the things that do hold people together: responsibility, loyalty, perhaps love—yet hating each other at heart for their final situation. Saying it, finding I had to say it despite the part of me in open revolt against further reservation, objection, scruple, now what had happened had happened—had to say it because the life Diana would live continued inescapably and *really* to matter, if anything mattered, if human beings mattered—I had a sudden consciousness of brutality. "Women don't stop being women because they love women."

"And if it couldn't have been different? The babies—and everything. If it couldn't have been different?"

"Doesn't one always think it could have been different?"

A Velocette darted noisily by outside in the rain.

"Judith—was Terry why you married Martin?"

"I married him after her."

"I could never talk much to you about Martin. It wasn't what you said, but you looked as if you minded. Marrying Martin didn't work for you; did it?" There was a pause. Then, "Was she like me?" she asked.

"No. Not really like you."

"Often people go on falling in love with the same type, I think. In the way they keep writing the same book. Not that it was why I asked.

Did you love her more than me?"

"No. I loved her."

"Italians are passionate. What was she like?"

"Does it matter? Do you really want to know? She came from Naples. She was very—*un*tragic. And she was sure that in the end we should be tragic. That was really her whole point: that you mustn't go on long enough for that. I saw the point; but I am better at falling in love than out of it."

"People can always be miserable in the end. Gerry's mother and father are. And that Belgian woman in the train," she added suddenly; "you remember. She was as miserable as anyone I've seen, and she had a rich and doting husband—once."

"She had a reasonable chance. She didn't start off against the tide. It's a very strong tide. Leaving aside any question of babies, of things like that; of still being a woman. As a homosexual man I could have been in prison. As a woman I would automatically be thought depraved. And unsavory." For the first time she glanced away. The inward compulsion, not choice, certainly not choice, made me go on, "It's what most people feel. What they feel is terrifying. And it isn't even only that. It's—oh, all the books you ever read being wrong, all the plays you see, the talk you listen to. The whole of life the wrong way round."

She didn't look at me. Dark ends of hair curved in against her neck. I noticed the faint lines of vein running, bruise-like, upwards from her wrist.

"Diana, listen. I have nothing to lose; but if you have the least chance of doing without me, or someone like me, of arranging your life differently, take it. Don't start with me unless you must. Don't believe we shall live happily ever after."

"I don't want an affair with you," she said. She was facing me again. "Being just something that happened once. I couldn't, now. I don't want kissing you in cars and saying good-bye."

"That would be easier."

"People don't love because it's easier; or because they think they'll be happy, even. It isn't like that."

"What is it like?" I heard my tone become gentler.

"What was it like, for me?" She picked up a new packet of cigarettes, slit the cellophane; thinking. "Shall I try to tell you? It's hard, but I'll try and tell you. At first, you see, I was just interested, terribly interested—in everything to do with you. You had a kind of glamour.

Then I started getting emotional about you. I didn't know why, but it was the first time, and I didn't much care. It was the first time." She gave a brief, barely voiced laugh. "And it was something so terribly important to life. I hadn't believed it would happen to me, not like this, but it had. Everything in my life began being related to you. And everything about you mattered. What you said, whether you were happier sometimes than others; what you felt about me." She paused. "I didn't know really what you felt about me."

I was silent.

"I knew I had to see you, be with you. I began to know I needed you. As well as everything else, the kind of stillness and certainty in you."

"*Certainty?* Oh, darling."

"And I'd felt at first," she went on, "there was something about you I almost had to stand up to; overcome. Something, oh, I can't exactly explain, the way you didn't behave intimately with people, a sort of coolness in the way you behaved. Then, when there wasn't that, when you didn't do it with me, it was—oh, well." The last words she had spoken softly. "I loved being near you. I loved touching you, and if you touched me. I didn't think of any more than that. I didn't think of loving you, of making love. Not until that evening at your flat when you kissed my hair. Then I wanted us to be in love, terribly."

I was looking at her.

"I knew what it meant. Of course. That it wasn't normal. Perhaps I didn't know quite all of what it meant. Or quite think of it then as being for always. But I didn't care what it was. I was just terribly happy that you loved me." She stopped. "Only afterwards," she said, "I was sure you'd thought better of it, whatever you felt. Because you weren't the type. I thought it was why we never talked about it. Behaved as though nothing had happened."

"The type?"

"You see, I thought you'd decided not to involve yourself. That for you it was too beyond the pale. Which was why you'd lit the blue touchpaper and retired immediately."

I said at last, "So would you have just, well—let it go?"

With a sudden sharp movement she stripped the cellophane from the cigarettes. "I was afraid if I tried to do what you didn't want I might lose you. Altogether. I'd have accepted anything rather than that. I'd have accepted just what you decided we were to have. No love-making, then no love-making. Nothing had ever happened, anyway, to make me think sex was everything. Happiness for me with you wasn't going through all the motions. Then." She crumpled up the paper in her hand. "Besides, I didn't want to be a nuisance to you anymore."

"Could it really have been like that?" I stood gazing at her. Finally I added, "But it was *only* that?"

"Though it was hard all the same to think of us as anything so classified as homosexuals." She had just hesitated before the term.

"It doesn't come easily."

"Even this morning."

"I didn't mean this morning to happen."

"It was that none of it seemed to have anything to do with you; nothing that I knew, or had imagined. I'd heard it talked about; and had people pointed out to me once or twice. I remember Vic did. Funny: we could have what men like that'll ruin their lives for, and they could have either of us with shoes and rice. I'd read things in books, of course, something in a French girl's novel once about some horrible club where a lot of women in leather jerkins danced with a lot of other women and everyone was more or less drunk on gin. There was something in a war book I read, too, about sinister sisterhoods, and obscenity. And I know prostitutes are often Lesbians. And everyone's heard of touting at tubes. But none of it had anything to do with us; with you."

"I couldn't tell you anything about the clubs if you wanted me to. I suppose they exist. I haven't got a leather jerkin. And when I go into a tube it's to get somewhere; because it's less trouble than the car. There are other things I can't help having to do with. The things Terry believed women must have."

"What would I have without you?"

"Everything?—in the end?"

Her look now didn't move from my face. "I love you. You haven't only given me being loved, you've given me loving."

There was a silence which felt very long. She didn't break it, but came slowly over to where I stood. She was frowning slightly. Without coquetry she kissed my mouth.

Doesn't it seem to be rather generally believed that women in their sexual relations want to be dominated? At any rate it is a convention of thought. I didn't want to be dominated, nor did I want to dominate. There was no suggestion when we made love of the pretended masculine partner, the woman one imagines lean and mannish; we gave and we took, both of us, equally.

I hadn't known how it would be for her. There was Gerry, after all—it was with him she perhaps could have begun a taste of the senses, whether or not she was aware of it. At first I wanted above all to be emotionally sensitive to her; and adroit.

Then this became the concern with oneself of ordinary passion: melting into pleasure and the tenderness which comes from pleasure, and into gratitude.

In a successful novel about love, written with the specialist's air of knowledge, I had read once that even the most sensible of women are subconsciously rather afraid to be despised after they have let themselves be made love to. What is claimed for the subconscious is hard to deny. But if, in reverse, it is possible to feel contempt for such a reason, I am astonished.

We had gone to the impersonal bed, with its coolness and blankness. I could feel her still trembling. Her slip was white, with lace where it contained her breasts. The lace and the nylon were very white; with an odd digression of the mind at a time when one hardly thinks I remembered something she had said, amused, about being told at school that what one wore under one's dress was of greater importance than the dress.

She said, " 'At last, at last, or some such rot.' " The words broke in the middle, as if she had swallowed because her mouth was dry.

I knew I had read the words somewhere or heard them, perhaps in a film, but I didn't know where, or try to place them.

"Judith."

"Oh, darling."

I think her passion surprised me; it had in it a quality of *gladness*, I think it was, that a little surprised me.

The afternoon darkened, and the rain with it.

She almost slept.

It was her idea that we should go back to Mirrepont.

"On the spur of the moment and leaving everything behind?"

She remembered, and half smiled. "Only this time," she said, "it will be what it was supposed to be."

We went back to make love in the sun.

Everything hinged on the man who stood in the road as we approached him from Uzerche going towards Mirrepont and waved at us to stop. I probably wouldn't have stopped if I had thought about it; the road was lonely. But I braked automatically when I saw him.

He was standing by a motor-bike which had a box with tools in it instead of a side-car. That we were foreigners rather took him aback, and he explained through the window of the car with an uneasy mixture of brusqueness and embarrassment that what he wanted was petrol—just enough to get him to a garage.

I told him I hadn't any. Except in the tank.

He then explained that he had a tube he could use to get petrol from our tank to his.

When I had backed the car so that it was alongside his bike, Diana got out to watch. I heard her talking to him as he searched for his piece of tube. To begin with he merely answered her; but gradually his politeness became less gruff. He asked her where we were going, and said something or other about his sister. Most of it, however, I could barely hear and didn't follow. I knew he said his sister was a widow. "*Veuve*."

Afterwards he offered me two hundred francs.

When I refused it, he thanked me with a small movement which could almost have been a bow, and went back to his bike. He stood waving to us as we drove off.

Diana said, "His sister has a little hotel on the road to Souillac; after you get to Mirrepont. He comes from Souillac. He was quite poetic about it. I suppose he was trying to do some business for her…"

The small sunny garden, she assured me when we arrived there, the steps in rock leading up from the road to the restaurant, were just as he had said.

The restaurant was small; it had checkered tablecloths and frilly, frivolous curtains, and was full of flowers. There was a smell of hot butter and garlic. Brass and bottles were doubled in dark wood which had been polished everywhere until it had a sultry glow.

When we first arrived, new there, with nothing to explain, two women were in the garden. They were both immensely fat. One was in black, a very old lady sitting on a box in the shade, her back against a water-butt. She was trying to read a newspaper. The other, who was younger, the sister we had heard about, was doing some washing as she talked. She seemed to have a natural talkativeness.

Seeing the car, she came towards us and greeted us with phrases and gestures that amounted to elegance. Her feet bulged out of a pair of plimsolls, and the apron tied round her waist appeared to have been threaded through her.

She chatted all the time as she showed us our room.

Afterwards she made us sit in the garden, and going down into her stone cellar returned with a bottle of Monbazillac and two bottles of mineral water. She wrote the number of our room on the Monbazillac.

"*Voilà, Mesdames!*" she said.

A little later she was back with two or three postcards of the hotel, which she handed to us, smiling.

Something of the place's extraordinary charm had been caught on the postcards. I sent one of them to Helen, explaining that I should be in France longer than I had planned. Later I learnt that she kept it, and used it for making conversation. To Julian, at any rate.

Our first days with Madame Chabal were enchanted; charged with a central bliss that lit all the warm pleasures we had returned to. That I cannot convey with words my happiness at that time seems not to be important. The experience is too common to need clarifying with words. Our love in essence was like million upon million of love affairs. It was made up of such things as finding her sleepily beside me in the morning, of waking in the night to find she was awake, too; her extravagant endearments when she wasn't serious, her speaking of my name when she was. It had the hot sun and the French countryside as a part of it. And the river, now.

Afternoon after afternoon we spent in the riverside hut Madame Chabal had let to us. Her husband had used it for fishing.

We talked there; swam, and got dry again in the sun; made love; played records on a gramophone belonging to her son.

The son was in Japan, and had a collection of records, some Bach among them, and a lot of Rachmaninoff—Diana loved the Rachmaninoff, and played the Third Piano Concerto until I almost grew tired of it—his mother doubted if he would return to play again.

I read a good deal.

Our new relationship, for me, had much in it of an emancipation. I could at times now effortlessly go my own way, and read, or just lie looking at the green river verge and the smooth, clear surface of the water, thinking of anything, of things quite remote from her. I no longer had any feelings about couples in dark doorways. With so much else she had given me a balance, a new freedom. A new tranquillity.

I began even not to ask myself if the relationship between us rested on, was the result of, no more than just an accident: or whether somehow, in some fashion, the kiss would have been chosen, would have happened, anyway. It was past. It was theoretic.

And she seemed so happy.

She wrote a poem. She said it was for the first time. She didn't keep it, and she wouldn't give it to me. She just said that it wasn't very good; and that "lake" was poetic licence, "river" wouldn't have fitted—but that she had wanted to write a poem. However, I almost remember it still. I remember it began:

Out of creation for the heart's song,
For the mindless moment of delight:
A lake's blue silence,
And the wakeful night
Lain in the burnished bowl of the land.

A brush of high trees in the sun, climbing; petals, golden wings, on a hot hill; slanted summer rain, singing. I think those were the other things she chose.

It ended:

But of all things, still,
Most destined to this joy
None
More than the flesh of my love
In her summertime,
The warm flesh, and the blood's call.

The poem meant something fundamental to me.

But she laughed at herself as a poet. "If I'm going to be anything," she said, "it'll have to be a novelist. It was just that I never believed it could be like this; that's all."

Soon afterwards she took to getting up early, and writing at the window of our bedroom—slacked and sweatered, her feet on the ledge, reminding me in those moments of a model in some teen-agers' magazine.

The first time it happened I woke up, vaguely aware of being looked at. "The reason," she said, "you take up too much of the bed, I have just discovered, is that you sleep with your head on the edge of it, lulled by a misplaced sense of virtue, while the rest of you sort of arcs itself out."

"What are you doing?"

"It's all right. I am. I really am. I'm doing some work." She paused. "You know, I've never thought much of writing as a sublimation; it seems a bit irrelevant. But making yourself work and letting yourself love: that's the perfect arrangement."

Her eyes looked quite tired from writing.

It was a moment when I loved her very much.

Then for some days we couldn't make love.

"U.S.," she said.

"What is 'U.S.'?"

"It's Air Force. Or it was. My father said it. It means unserviceable."

"Oh, darling. Well, don't you say it."

"From tomorrow I will cease to have been born vulgar." Suddenly she laughed. "You're a romantic, of course."

"Do you think so?"

About a week after this we went to the hut for an entire day. We told Madame Chabal in the morning, and she packed us a picnic lunch, saying she would expect us back to dinner—as early or as late as we liked. She told us mind the sun.

By afternoon the heat had a quality of clinging velvet gold, and I lay in the doorway of the hut, half mesmerized, transfixed by a sensuous laziness; unwilling even to swim. Diana was still in the water.

There were two or three other people bathing, and she had been chatting with a thickly-built, brown Frenchman who sat on the bank most of the time, his back glistening, only his feet in the water, watching her.

When she was ready to come out, he bent down and, taking her under the arms, lifted her onto the grass. He released her at once. She smiled at him—then ran towards the hut.

It wasn't doubt that I felt, or jealousy; just the tremor of a desire to be reassured.

"I m going to get dressed now. Darling, mind your legs."

She pushed the door to.

"Diana."

She was kneeling on the sun-warm boards, drying herself.

"Come here."

She looked up, and came to me.

I pulled her down by my side, and kissed her hair, and throat, and mouth. "It's what I wanted to do that Sunday."

"You should have done."

"Do you think you will always say that?"

"Yes," she said, very softly, her body against mine.

I don't know why, when I am a woman, a woman's body should hold such magic for me. Hers was smooth, and so soft one could be cradled in it, lost; yet it was beautifully contained within its own design.

We began to caress each other.

If it sounds indecent, if it is offensive, it didn't seem these things; it seemed natural. That, I think, is the basic stumbling block: seeing as evil what one feels to be natural. I know it's been said that there's a kick to be had from feeling perverted. If it's so it's something I know nothing of. Never could passion have felt more innocent than it felt to me with her. It felt innocent and luminous from loving each other.

A small cylinder of sunlight came through the doors.

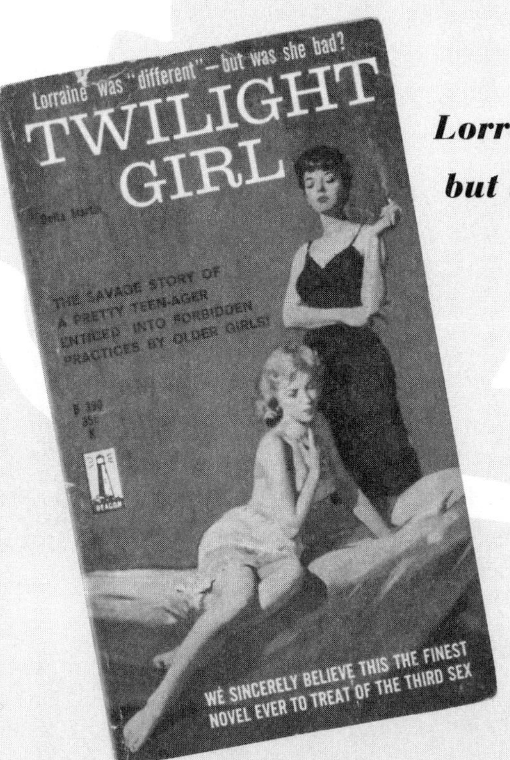

Lorraine was "different"— but was she bad?

Twilight Girl

by Della Martin

Yes, there are such girls…it's no secret. The subject is no longer taboo. Lesbianism today is discussed freely not only by physicians, social workers and teachers, but by all responsible people shocked by its rapid spread. For unless the blight is understood, it cannot be curbed. With unprecedented frankness, this sensitive novels seeks the requisite insights…

Are Lorraine and her friends just bad girls—or are they emotionally disturbed girls? For new answers and brilliant delineation of the origins of aberration, this book should be read by everyone bent on combating the lesbian contagion.

Twilight Girl

It was Rags who peered cautiously into the night, opening the drab green door of the lonely cement-block building at the end of the dark, undeveloped street. Lon knew Rags by the sharp black tux, the cerise bow-tie beneath a pallid, acne-scarred face. Rags stood sullen in the doorway, behind her an amateurishly lettered notice: THE 28%—*MEMBERS ONLY.*

"What the hell's with the pounding?" Rags was no bigger than Violet, but the tough bass sound was enormous.

"Sweetie, meet this real good friend a mine. Lon Harris."

Unsmiling, Rags nodded. "Hiya, Lon."

Lon responded, "Hi!" And apparently being Violet's "good friend" meant open sesame. Friend and proprietress led Lon into the smoke-blue dimness. Lon blinked at the strangeness of the scene.

Rags hurried ahead, circling behind the long, home-built bar. She had been interrupted apparently, by Violet's hammering. But now she backed the girl Lon judged to be a barmaid-partner against a chipped and dented bottle cooler. Grimly, she clasped the taller girl in her arms. Kissed her as though it were a life-death matter. Lon watched, something forbidden stirring inside her. "Our kind of kids," Violet had said. *"Our kind of kids!"*

Violet led Lon to the far end of the bar. She pounded amiably on the linoleum top. "Hey, quit makin' out. How's about some service?"

The girl in Rags's stranglehold laughed and pushed herself free. "That's what I'm getting! Break it up, honey. Vi wants a drink."

She came to their end of the bar, and Lon was introduced to "a real swell kid—Betty." Betty from out of a black-and-white movie; colorless, pale, like shoots that spring up from under sidewalks.

"We need a couple beers," Violet told her. "How 'bout that, Lon?"

"Right," Lon said. Using a ruggedly deep voice that came instinctively because she knew it would sound right. Betty took two brown bottles from the cooler, popped them open with a church key and set them on the bar.

"Most of the kids are in the other room," Violet said, swigging. "I'll go see if I c'n find us a table."

She wriggled her way toward the opening in the divided wall, stopping to scream, *"Hi,* doll!" to a girl in fly-front slacks and white T-shirt,

Lon's size. And Violet hugged another girl, a pug-faced peroxide blonde. Violet shrieked, "Swee-tie-eee!" at another group and made her sensuous way to the rope curtains that divided the barroom from the room in which the shadow-forms of kids danced to a recording of "Lonely Street." The kids, the kids...Violet glanced over her shoulder once to wink at Lon, to let her know, it seemed, that she knew the kids and the kids knew her and weren't they all having the craziest time? *Like Eddie,* thought Lon. *Eddie going to Disneyland with the family after having gone before with the Cubs—anxious to point out the sights and let everyone know in a loud voice that he had been there before.* Like a queer lavender Elsa Maxwell, Violet greeted the loved and the unloved, the staked and the cruising, disappearing finally into the packed room where the shadow-shapes clung to each other. Now she was singing in unison with the record: *"Perhaps upon that Lonely Street, there's someone such as I..."*

Lon sipped beer. Sipped the new bitter taste and marveled at the way dry palm fronds and a raffia backing on the bar had given an exotic air to a cement-block garage. Someone had painted a Hawaiian hula scene on the wall above the bar. Someone had sketched a likeness of Rags on the opposite wall, and had framed it with bamboo. *This is the way the clubhouse will look. This is the way we'll fix up the recreation hall on the Island!* She swigged from the bottle again, mellowing with the sense of a long-gone traveler at last arrived home. For the threesome at the other end of the bar were not unlike the traveler she had seen in mirrors, her own self.

They wore tan peggers, nonchalantly unpressed. Two in plaid flannel shirts, one sharper in an open-throated white job with a turquoise sweater vest. Lon envied them the clipped haircuts, the strong scrubbed faces. And ignored the lazy eyes and droop-cornered mouths.

"I still claim you owe me two-bits," one argued.

"The hell you say."

"You remember that girl, right here at this bar?"

"Oh, Jesus, yes."

"You bet me a quarter I couldn't make her."

"You didn't."

"Oh, didn't I?"

"I'll be damned."

"I've got a witness." The first of them turned to the silent one. "Did I make her, Chuck?"

"If you don't know, I'm not gonna tell you."

They roared at this and then the loser paid her bill. "Here's your goddam quarter. Just tell me one thing. Was she butch or fem? Christ, I couldn't tell!"

"Smorgasbord. By the time she went home I wasn't sure which I was!" Eyebrows wriggled up and down, implying secrets that could not be unveiled. Regular guys, remembering a girl and laughing it up. Regular guys, flicking kitchen matches with their thumbnails for a light, burrowing hands in the front-zipped pants for a crushed cigarette pack and belting each other in the back to punctuate a belly laugh. Regular guys, and less than twenty years before, unknowing nurses had checked the wrong box on the hospital form that offered only *Male* and *Female*. For perhaps the choice was incomplete.

Halfway thorough the brown bottle, Violet came back. "I got a place at their table. This girl, kid—Jeez, she's society an' everything. Boy, would I like to get next to her. She's here with some crazy dark one. I hate t' say this, but this girl, wow, is she sharp." Violet spilled the words breathlessly. "I got a spot at their table. Pray for me, kid." Leading Lon from the bar toward the curtained room, frenzied with her dim hope of a conquest that escaped Lon. "Make out like I'm your girl. Act real nuts about me."

They wove their way through the dancers. Pretty girls and crones at sixteen, old hands and neophytes, insatiable and satiated; Lon saw them in the darkened room where dreams were woven, seeing through the untutored, all-sensing eyes of the young, the clip-haired butches who looked as she herself must look, yet knowing the purpose of their maleness, shuffling to the agonized cry—"*Where's this place called Lonely Street?*" Big, brawl-sized butches and tiny Napoleons, out to prove to the world: *we are not small; we matter, we count!* Hands clutching their partners as though someone might doubt their talents to possess, hip grinding hip.

And Lon heard, through the unplugged ears of the young, their spicy, pungent talk, as she tacked her way through the crowd:

"...took ourselves out on the lawn and I mean, almost froze..."

"...told that witch, in the future you keep your hands off my girl. Fun is fun and I'm no prude, but I've got my standards, honey..."

"...OK, OK, we'll go home. I said we'll go home. OK, so you can't stand to see me have a little fun..."

And the shriek with its aftermath of hilarious commotion; somebody gagging somebody, everyone game for one more laugh.

Lon saw and heard with the inner awareness that transcends callow ignorance, linking phrase and gesture. So that she knew why they danced with such gay desperation, why they gathered here where a green door barred the inquisitors of that other world with a sign that warned and pleaded: MEMBERS ONLY. And Lon sympathized with the unclassified kids who needed a place "to dance." For she was of them, so must be with them and for them. Of them, and belonging to their secret.

Four perspiring bottles graced the redwood picnic table provided by the limited budget of The 28%. Side by side on one of the benches, Lon and Violet faced a twosome conspicuous not only by their post-nineteen maturity but by the vivid contrast of their coloring. Violet had introduced them as Sassy Gregg and Mavis.

The Amazon's pale-yellow hair fell in short careless waves over the wide brow of a face once deeply tanned, now faded. It was a face with the unravaged ruggedness of one who has enjoyed the outdoors in solid comfort: playing dedicated tennis, perhaps, or swimming lengths of a country club pool. Her features were carefully spaced, her gray-blue eyes unflinchingly direct. And the simplicity of her tailored shirt and slacks spoke quietly of elegance. Any doubt of her affluence was erased by the wide bracelet clamping the cuff of her long-sleeved shirt and the matching side belt-buckle of hand-wrought silver and Mexican lava. Her nickname, Lon suspected, was backwash from early childhood; Sassy looked and behaved like anything but her name. A few of her yawns were deliberate; the rest seemed genuine enough.

Violet was tying herself into tortured knots in a pathetic attempt to impress the girl. "Honest to God, I think it's terrif' about you went ta collidge. Even if you on'y specialized in gym. Ain't that what you mean by P.E.?"

Sassy's gray eyes reflected more boredom than amusement. "Yes. I majored in physical education."

"Yeah, but along with that you had ta read up on other subjecks. I'm that same way. Books! Jeez, I read 'em by the carload. Anything that has t' do with education, or if it's artistical, it makes me flip." She reached over to squeeze Lon's hand in a show of familiarity and Lon flinched.

Sassy Gregg broke her cool reserve to wink subtly and knowingly at Lon. Who smiled a vague response to the compliment, grateful that Sassy was not seeing them as a pair.

Violet chattered on, parading her concept of intellectuality, and the analytical eyes of the older girl veiled with a patronizing contempt. Lon turned her attention to Sassy's friend. "Did you go to U.C.L.A. with Sassy?"

The colored girl spoke with a joyless calm. "No, we met this place I work. Used to come round, hear me play jazz piano. Come with 'er fiancé."

Lon had missed the sparkle on Sassy's powerful hand. "Oh, sure. She's engaged."

Mavis smirked. "Reason why escape me jus' now."

Lon stared at the girl, silent while Betty brought fresh beers all around and Sassy wrangled with Violet over the two-dollar honors. Lon had never exchanged words with a Negro before—nor gazed at enigma that surpassed mere physical beauty. Mavis was slight, loose-limbed, the *café-au-lait* flesh pulled tightly over bone structure well defined. Yet it was not the effortless grace with which she moved the languid wrists, floated the slender fingers when she talked. And not the uninterrupted sweep of features, from broad, intelligent forehead past high-rising cheekbones, downward below the cherry-tinted mouth to the defiant little chin. It was in the line of blue-black hair drawn rigid to the coiled bun from which black wisps played with the back of her neck. And in the fierce pride of distended nostrils, the negroid nose. There, and in the regal tilt of her head, the impassable curtain of velvet black eyes. Eyes almond-shaped and weary from too much seen. If she rose, Lon knew, she would walk with a haughty bearing; Lon knew this with an unassailable certainty. *Born to be a Second High Priestess, born to murmur the rhythmic incantations, weave the lithe body on nights when the sky is moonless and the sea beats the time for our chant.* Lon dropped her eyes unconsciously to the heavy, snobbish breasts.

"You takin' style notes? You analyzin' my dress?"

Embarrassed, Lon shook her head. "No—I'm sorry. I didn't mean..."

What could be seen of Mavis's dress was dull black and shapeless. Lon lifted the second bottle, drinking back the chagrin.

"This dress what you call a *saque*," Mavis said tonelessly. "Been with me a long time. Man, couple years back the *modistes* caught up with me. But I pass 'em up again. Now nobody in style but me!" Flashing a snowflake grin, the whiteness melting into brown repose. "Sassy say I look beat. Them beat cats jus' catchin' up with me, too. I beat befo' they latch on Zen. Long befo' they pick up on Gide. Baby, I beat from awa-a-y back. An' don't need to make some *café expresso* scene provin' it."

Now Lon faced the new bewilderment. Mavis fluctuated between a cultured enunciation and what seemed to be deliberate parody of minstrel show dialect. Finding courage in swallows of the tart beer, she said, "You sound like you know a lot. But you don't talk like—" And stammering in the self-induced confusion, "You perplex me!"

Mavis lifted a cigarette from Sassy's case, lying on the table between them. "Trouble is, you tryin' put me in some peg-hole. Baby, go 'head an' crucify me. Go 'head an' vilify me. But don't go messin' 'round tryin' to classify me! I one thing now. Tomorrow I gonna be something else."

"Don't you want anyone to know how sharp you are?"

Sucking in the blue smoke, Mavis said, "That way I get me invited into white-color brain circles. Them folks can go home, tell they neighbors they had tea with a colored gal could quote Spinoza. Big deal! Man, I take a good ole-fashioned down-South nigger-hater over them kind." Then, staring into the dim haze, "I talk my way. I read about some decadent French cats, that Proust talk. Read about some festerin', slime-ooze creeps down South, that Faulkner talk. Ain't for me." And in a sudden spurt of animation, the heat of white-hot, white-directed resentment burned like the tip of her cigarette. "Mavis talk. That all you ever gonna get from me!"

The juke broke out with "Poison Ivy." And Sassy, obviously bored with the pressure of being impressed, lifted her brows at the Violet kid. "Dance?"

"Crazy!" Violet wrinkled the little round nose, laughed her delight.

Sassy was even taller than Lon had suspected. The statuesque and the stubby left the table to jiggle their way into the moving crowd.

An alien excitement fell over Lon. Alone with brown Mavis and too tense to express what had lain dormant in her, Lon tried to force herself. Now, now, when at long last the closed doors had strangely opened to her. Feebly offering, "I've never known anyone named Mavis. Mavis what?"

"Jus' Mavis."

"Everybody has a last name."

"Some born without 'em. Some lose the right to use 'em."

Lon sensed that she had treaded on shaky ground. And began again. "You said you play the piano."

"Yea-ah, Sassy got this Knabe grand. Used to be jus' furniture in that fancy pad where she live. That big ole piano cryin' its gut out f'lonesome till I come by."

"I thought you said she used to go somewhere to hear you play."

"Ruggio's. Baby, I play in more pi-ano bars 'n' you got years. That the last place I play before I git unemployed. Ruggio, he tie the can to me."

"Why?" Asking it indignantly, marking the faceless Ruggio a sworn enemy.

"Oh, couple gay gals start hangin' 'round. Ruggio don't want that. I tip these gals, but that don't stop 'em comin' on, comin' on, requestin' I play this numbah 'n' that numbah. Till one night he blow his stack. I gotta git!

"But it wasn't your fault, was it? Just because he didn't like..." Lon swallowed the hard core taking form in her throat. "Were they girls like these?" Gesturing to indicate the dancers.

"Man, they don't come no gayer. These gals, they both on the make. They wear a big neon sign keep flashin' what they is. Same as these cats you seein' now." Mavis dragged deeply, exhaled, cooled the smoke with draughts from the brown bottle. "I say one thing 'bout you. You look the same. But you diff'runt. You don't wait till Sass leave the table, 'nen make a pass. Too young? Too chicken?" She laughed shortly. "I perplex you? Well, you perplex me!"

The dark eyes mocked, then softened as Lon looked to the beer-wet redwood. Lon lifted her face at last to drink, thirsty swallows, drowning her lack of understanding. And still knowing. Knowing that you can belong and not belong, knowing how much and how little she knew. Until Mavis, wearying, it seemed, of the jazz-man, end-man jargon, dropped her cigarette to the concrete floor, bent to grind it under her heel and spoke with the precise diction of a speech-department pedant. "Sassy happened to be at Ruggio's the night he fired me. Strangely enough, she had come alone that night for the first time. And I could have called the agent who booked me. Complained to the union. But I was beat. You know? Sassy's folks were in Hawaii. Like when people find themselves in Pittsburgh—it's raining—it's a drag, so they get married. Later they ask themselves why." She laughed again, the quick-dying jab of laughter. Amused by her story? More likely getting a laugh from Lon's stunned reaction to the abrupt change in delivery. "Sassy's got no imagination. You see, I have this dark skin. Types me with people like her folks. So we meet this housekeeper at the door. Sassy's got one idea. I'm the new maid. Trite, but that does it! I'm still living there, making with the dustpans. Fractures me, watching Sassy cover up for the way I do a bed. It's a funny hype."

"But you can work in some other night club. Why do yon want to—to lower yourself that way?"

Almond eyes explored the table with a soft melancholy. And Mavis echoed again her cotton-patch talk. "Sass an' me, sometimes we dig each othah. Got a fine piano there. Got books. Don' know, baby. That butch needs me bad. Jus' don' know."

"You mean you're going to stay there?"

"Toss-up. Do I leave Sassy, or do she tell me leave? Don't look now like Sassy's evah goin' let up, but hard tellin'." Mavis shrugged an indifferent shoulder. "Don' nuthin' last."

"I've thought about that a lot," Lon said. The cold beer warming her inside, the words coming easily now. "I've thought about a place where people weren't always—spoiling things for each other."

"Keep tellin', baby."

"A place where—people leave you alone. I mean, where they aren't always stopping you from doing what you want to do."

"Fine place," Mavis encouraged. Picking up her rhythm from the juke.

"I decided it would have to be—well, an island."

"Now yo' makin' sense!"

"Somewhere in the Pacific." And bursting like a bag of popcorn at the dusky girl's approval, "I've never told anyone, but I have it all planned."

"Swingin'!"

"Everybody could do whatever they enjoy doing."

"Take me at once to yo' leadah!"

"I'd...temporarily, at least, I'd be in charge. Because I know all the plans. I'm doing all the preliminary work."

"It figures, baby."

Then, with the beer and the beat drowning out, hammering down the earlier timidity, "Mavis, how would you like to be the Second High Priestess? If this thing really goes through, there has to be somebody... I mean, I have all these chants written down. Really weird and...exotic. Do you think you'd...?"

"Secon' high priestess. Hot damn!"

A chill suspicion trickled down the length of Lon's spine. Was Mavis making fun of her? Fighting boredom, the way Sassy was killing time on the dance floor with Violet? They had danced by a moment before and the tall blonde had been yawning. With dampened enthusiasm, Lon said, "I still have a lot of details to work out. Transportation's my main problem. I have to figure out how to get a boat and where to find somebody that'll know how to sail it."

"Man, you talk to Sass. Her daddy, he got him a yatch. She know mo' 'bout yatches anybody you evah meet!"

And spurred again, Lon said, "Really? Does she really?"

"That cat's made the Catalina scene all by her lonesome." Mavis dropping her pose once more, like a seagull letting go of a fish. Then adding significantly, "Don't count on her, though, baby. The way Sassy's goin', don't anybody count on her for Thing One."

Lon would have asked for an explanation. But the girls returned to their table. Violet ecstatic, Sassy apparently disgusted. "God, what an obvious crowd of neurotics!"

"They neurotic," Mavis agreed.

"That's one a the kinds a persons I can't stand," Violet echoed.

And Sassy winked at Mavis, snickering behind her beer.

"They psychotic," Mavis added. "Pore chillun!"

Then Sassy, in sudden irritation, "God, will you cut that plantation bit? Talk about sounding neurotic! Where's your goddamn pride?"

Mavis sighed, shrugging once more. "Can't be queer, effen you ain't neurotic."

Lon watched Sassy's anger flare. "I detest that word, Mavis. Literally detest that word."

"'OK, baby. Yo' bi-sexual. Ain't queer nohow. Yo' bi-sexual."

Sassy leaped up from the bench, seething. "You make me so damned—" Her sudden motion upset a tray with which Betty was trying to wriggle through the narrow aisle between tables. A beer bottle toppled, rolled down Sassy's back, crashing to the concrete floor in a burst of glass and foam.

"You clumsy bitch!" Sassy whirled on the waitress in a scarlet-faced rage. "Goddamn clumsy—you did that on purpose!"

"Got her monkey wet," Mavis murmured senselessly. "That monkey gonna ketch pneumonia."

Sassy caught the muttered phrases. They meant something to her, Lon decided, for the fury turned on Mavis now. "Keep your nasty little mouth shut!"

Betty stared open-mouthed, shocked by the force of Sassy's outburst. A small, curious group gathered around the table, watching with detached interest.

And Sassy reached back to assess the damage, shrieking, "My back is soaked. Literally soaked, you goddam, stupid..."

"One more word, debutante, and you'll go home in a basket." The grim figure in the black tuxedo had materialized from nowhere. Rags, with menace written all over that pale, pitted face. Sassy towered over her. Like a eucalyptus tree in a poppy field, Lon thought. But evidently Sassy caught the threat in that throaty masculine voice. She stopped in the middle of her sentence, violence suspended in mid-air. And then Lon saw why Goliath curdled in the face of this tiny David. The something that Rags turned slowly in her hand was a breadknife. And Sassy stood still, pulsating with the hateful silence, eyes helplessly drawn to the saw-toothed blade.

No one moved. They stood around, sat around, immobile in a tableau of motionless waiting, breath suspended. And Lon caught up in a tremulous excitement of heroic battle, siding with the underdog in a T.V. writer's struggle for truth, honor and justice. *Still, it was Sassy who owned a boat—Sassy who knew how to sail. And Sassy who would bring Mavis if Mavis was to come again.* Apart from the other spectators, Lon waited for the next move.

"I suppose one should expect this sort of thing in a place like this," Sassy said, breaking the impasse with lame defiance.

One of the observers hooted, "Hey, Rags—whyn't you pick on somebody your size?" Jeering laughter routed what was left of the drama. Slowly, Rags lowered the breadknife. But her eyes had preserved the glint of its blade. "Beat it, debutante. Go do your slumming somewhere else!"

Sassy threw back her head in a gesture of contempt. "Scum. Literal, uncouth, uncivilized, neurotic scum." She edged her way past the onlookers, pushing disdainfully against the rigid wall of unfriendly shoulders. Lon sensed the blood churning invisibly inside, the gray-blue eyes deliberately unseeing, as though by her unawareness Sassy had dismissed them all. "If I thought it was worth the bother, I'd have my dad pull the right strings."

"Before you start shutting us up," Rags said, her voice deadly level, "figure out a good excuse for your daddy-O."

And picking up the cue, another voice cried, "Yeah, tell him what you were doing here, rich-bitch!"

"Are you coming, Mave?" Sassy, halfway across the dance floor. Not bothering to turn her head.

Mavis sighed. "Don' make no never-minds to me, baby."

Rags wedged herself between Mavis and the narrow aisle. "We don't hold anything against you. We don't want you to think we aren't—well, democratic." Still wearing the unsmiling mask: "Don't think you aren't welcome here because you're colored."

Lon nodded approval. The T.V. drama was going according to all the principles. Truth, honor and justice. These were great kids. Really great kids, and Violet had not been wrong. Lon found time to drain the second bottle.

"Hot damn, you sho 'nuff democratic! You so democratic man, I overwhelmed!" Mavis having herself a ball. "Heah I thought you Republican."

"If you haven't got a way home, I'll drive you myself," the poker-faced owner promised, the dusky sarcasm escaping her.

And timidly, Betty piped, "Don't mix in between them, Rags. If you were that other girl, I'd stick by you. Even you were wrong, I'd walk out of here with you."

Rags considered the protocol of loyalty and stepped aside. "I just wanted her to know how I feel."

Lon missed the next few bits of by-play. Violet clutching her arm and whispering desperately, "Jesus, kid, what'll I do? If I go out now, Rags won't ever leave me in again. But I gotta see that Sassy again. Kid, I jest went ape over her!" The lavender-blue eyes following Sassy Gregg out of the room, miserable. "If you was me, would you make up some excuse that she fergot somethin' an' follow her to the parking lot? Or what, kid?"

Mavis solved the problem before she left. "You gals give us a buzz now, heah? You call Sass an' me an' we have us a real swingin' time." Then with head held loftily, as befitted the Second High Priestess of Name-to-be-Selected-When-We-Get-There, she swept across the floor. Moving easy, as if, perhaps, at the far end of this chandeliered ballroom her ladies-in-waiting curtseyed in greeting to the Queen. Weary black sack dress drooping from the proud breasts—nobody in style but Mavis. And fat warm tears out of nowhere blinding Lon's view of her departure.

"I want to see her again," Lon said quietly. "I don't care about the other one. I want to see Mavis again.

Violet matter-of-fact. "I know how it is, sweetie. You're like me, real emotional." Then, noticing her beer was gone, watching Betty blot up the puddle on the floor, Violet added, "'Course, I should be jealous, you feelin' that way about somebody when you're out with me."

"Oh, I like you, too, Violet."

"It's OK, kid. I know how it is. Holy Jeez, wouldn't I love it if you got that chocolate girl away from Sassy? I could really go to town, hey?"

She drummed the redwood table with bird-long lavender fingernails, the idea playing around the corners of her little *O* mouth. "Trouble is, hon, you got a lot t' learn."

Still, having a lot to learn is not an insurmountable problem when the student thirsts for knowledge and the teacher is dedicated.

They stumbled into the airless living room and Violet switched on a lamp. Through the ruffled, velvet-ribboned red shade, a hideous light poured into the Polivka parlor, crammed to bursting with the monstrous mohair sofa, chair and ottoman; royal blue, the legs like a mastodon's—carved from imitation mahogany. Crocheted antimacassars protected the arms from elbows or elbows from the harsh scrub-brush fabric. A maroon carpet swirled with bilious tan feathers, a knee-high nude in simulated jade held an ashtray hopefully over her head, competing with the toilet-shaped tray on a blue-mirrored coffee table, its glazed surface inviting, "Put your ash here." An artificial fireplace held an artificial log. Across the mantel, sentimental hands had arranged cardboard-framed wedding pictures: artificial white faces over rented tuxedos and stiff taffeta gowns. Violet was represented, too; her plump little-girl figure ludicrously old in a white confirmation dress, the hair still naturally dark under the skimpy veil.

And crowning the mass of carnival bulldogs with sparkling eyes, the dime-store ceramics piled with dime-store roses, the lustrous glaze of panthers, the dancers, rosebud planters, kittens and gazelles, ersatz Hummels, genuine Tokyo parasols and *bona fide* blue-green abalone shells—crowning all these, a poignant Jesus looked out upon the grandeur from a mat of silver foil leaves and garishly dyed pressed flowers. The sacred heart was bleeding realistically red, the thorns were accusingly sharp.

Violet paused, proudly allowing the impression to register. Belittling the effect of splendor, as if modesty were called for in the face of so much opulence. "You wouldn't guess from the outside how it looks in here, would you kid?"

Lon shook her head dully. And found herself sinking into the overstuffed blue showpiece of the room. Her head felt hollow from the unaccustomed beer, yet every nerve had escaped the deadening effect and transferred to the flesh a suspenseful awareness, an acute knowledge of being alive and of wanting to be more so. She felt her breath accelerating as Violet's purple-tipped fingers rested on her jean-covered thigh, and waited through vaguely heard small talk until her hostess, softly lovely in the red-tinted light, reached at last the point where learning began.

"It's kinda mixed-up at first, but you get the hang of it. Like there's girls that're butch. I mean, they wish they could be a guy and they treat you same as they were a guy, on'y better. And there's fems, like me. See, like one is the guy and one is the girl—" And Violet laughed her beered-up starlet laugh. "So you don't have to stick to no damn rules. Like for instance. No lie, sometimes in bed I'm way ahead of those butch types." And she laughed once more at the private memories.

"Oh, Christopher, I wish I knew. Sometimes I just wish I knew," Lon said without knowing the meaning of her words.

"You're butch, Lon. You mean you didn' know it?"

"I never even heard the word before." *Yet, how the softly rounded forms had gyrated on the shore of the Island...How, always, the dancers had been girl-lovely, and to be loved!*

"Well, you're butch awright. I c'n tell a girl that's straight a mile away. What I wanna know is didn' you ever have a case on some other girl?"

"Sort of. Only it wasn't a girl, exactly."

"What the hell y'mean, not a girl *exac'ly!*"

"I mean, she was a teacher. Not what you'd call a girl anymore." Lon spoke as if the remembrance had been buried in time. But now it prodded itself into life: *This morning I was in love with Miss Chamberlin. Up until this afternoon I loved her, loved her!*

"Was she gay?"

"You mean did she..."

"Did she go fer girls?"

"I guess not."

"Get anywheres with her?"

"No." Then, shoving the ache into the dim corridors of the past, "No, and I hope I never see her again."

Violet moved closer, her fingers tracing an indolent pattern across the faded blue jeans. "Did you ever kiss a girl, hon?"

"I used to think about kissing—this teacher. I couldn't help it."

Violet shook her colorful head incredulously. And broke the quiet enchanted spell. "Jeez, it's so funny to be aroun' a sharp-lookin' butch that don't know sugar from Shinola!" Then, as though she regretted having laughed: "Boy, I'd like t' get next t' you about five years from now. Wowie!"

"I was hoping," Lon said earnestly, "that we could get to be friends right away, Violet." Sassy Gregg would have said it in a more commanding voice, she reflected. And envied the other girl's height, though she, Lon, sat inches taller than Violet. *And would stand inches taller than Mavis, too.* "Why would you want to wait five years?"

Violet's eyes narrowed. "Hey, are you snowin' me? Is this some kinda line or somethin'? Not that I give a crap, kid. If you got it in your head t' make me, you don't ketch me fightin' you off. What I wanna know is, are you as dumb as you act?"

If she denied it, the lesson might end. Sheepishly, Lon said, "Nobody knows everything about everything."

"Well, one thing you oughta know about gay kids. Some practic'lly get married. Even, they give a ring. But mostly the kids I know, 'specially the butches, they get fed up with one girl. Know what I mean? They keep cruisin', lookin' fer kicks."

"Mavis told me something like that. She said she'd get tired of Sassy or Sassy would get tired of her."

"Don't I know it, kid! See, even if you wear rings, who you kiddin'? The straight married people, they got kids or they're payin' on a house an' a car. They're stuck. But if you're gay an' you get fed up...pow! You take off. You don' have t' cruise long an' somebody else shows up."

Thinking—and it seemed strange to be thinking of Mavis—Lon said, "But if you really love somebody, you wouldn't want to break up."

There was a momentary sadness, it seemed to Lon, in Violet's shrug. "Who wants t' be stuck? That's how you know, honey. I bet you never got it from a guy, even."

Got it. The words dredged up another fevered recollection; the thick brown medical book buried under nightgowns and girdles in her mother's dresser drawer. Lon remembered reading furtively and with a fascinated horror, wondering why anyone would want to perform the intimate and humiliating rites at which the secret pages hinted. And knew in this moment the flushed exhilaration that had drawn her back to the book time and again when the house had been empty, feeling the tensed band around her chest that had constricted her breath in those forbidden hours. Yet free of the mystifying crudeness of the male body, here where the excitement concerned itself only with the graceful and familiar, Lon did not fear.

"You heard me. I bet you never got it from a guy."

"No," she told Violet. "One kissed me, though."

"Is that all?"

"And started—you know—petting. That was all."

"Did you get a charge?"

"It scared me. It made me sick."

"If it was a girl, you wouldn' of got sick, sweetie," Violet said wisely.

"I don't know. I get this lonesome feeling sometimes. In a way, I'd sooner be friends with a girl, but in another way—well, I can talk to boys. That part's all right. We can discuss cars or sports, almost anything, and I feel sure of myself. But the other part of it, with boys—I don't know, it gets me disgusted just to think about it. Trouble at school was, most of the other girls acted like I was some kind of—" Lon swallowed the bitter taste. "Some kind of freak. Tonight was the first time I was around girls and didn't feel that way."

"Gay girls. Sure."

"And I kept having a peculiar feeling that somewhere, with somebody, I would fit in. I still don't know all I want to know, but at least, with you, I can talk about it. I never could talk about—about things like this—with anybody. I still feel mixed up, but whatever I've been looking for...Gosh, I won't say I've found it. But I think I'm going to." Lon made the sound of laughter. "Christopher, doesn't that sound whacky?"

"Don't be ashamed a havin' real deep feelings," Violet said somberly. "I don't look the serious type, but I take a lotta things serious like that."

Encouraged, Lon said, "Sometimes I think I'm going to bust up inside. I get these wild urges to..." And dropping her voice to a grim whisper, "I get to thinking about somebody and I love them so much, I want to—grab them and smash them. Oh, nuts, that's stupid! I don't even know what I mean. It's just that I have to love somebody, no matter how they feel about me." Lon spoke slowly then, with paced deliberation. "Before this teacher I told you about, there was a girl in my gym class. We weren't in the same squad, so there wasn't any reason for me to talk to her. I never got up enough nerve to say anything to her, just kept watching and finding out all I could about her from other kids. I guess it got to her that I was asking questions and she told another girl—and that girl told me that I was a creep and should mind my own business."

"Jeez! I know how you musta felt."

"It hurt a lot, but I didn't stop thinking about that first girl. I have a diary at home. I write everything down in a code that I made up, so my mother won't be able to read it."

"Whatta ya mean, a code?"

"Oh, you exchange letters. I use *H* for *K* and *K* for *G*. I'll explain it to you some time. Anyway, last year that diary was full of nothing but Joan, Joan, Joan. I never once talked to her. After vacation, last year, I didn't see her around and somebody said she'd moved back East."

Violet looked genuinely touched. "Jeez!" Then, curiously, "Didn' ya ever think about her that way, Lon?"

"What way?"

"Do I have to name it?"

"She was another girl, and I didn't know—" Lon wrestled with the new confusion. "All I remember is, she was a tiny thing and I always felt...Oh, this is crazy! I had a feeling I should take care of her. I'd think about some other girl saying mean things to Joanie—or sometimes it would be a boy. Joanie would be crying and I'd come along and belt the other person in the mouth. I thought about that a lot, but nothing ever happened. I just thought about it a lot."

"Yeah. I usta think about I was a big movie star. I know whatcha mean."

"I almost—feel that way now."

"About me?" Violet asked, coy. Her hand moved, rested where no hand had rested before, and still the coarseness of thick denim between them. Lon shuddered.

"Maybe you'd rather be with Sassy—"

Violet shrugged once more. "Oh, I dunno. You're jest as good-lookin'. She got a better car, prob'ly, but you're jest as good-lookin'. The way you act so hard to get, you get me all steamed up, honey."

"I'm not playing games, Violet. I'd like to be a friend of yours." *But I'm haunted by a proud tan face,* Lon thought, *by almond-shaped eyes staring indifferently.*

"There's a lot more to it than jest that, hon." Violet's arms lifted to encircle Lon's neck. "Want I should do *everything?*"

And it was like poetry, suddenly, with Violet's coarseness melted away in the brush of the pink velvet cheek against Lon's face and the deep forest sweetness of violet cologne. Suddenly like poetry and music, this softly surprising glow of intimacy, with a wave of attraction beyond Lon's understanding undulating between them, rushing toward some destination fearfully, sacredly, irresistibly unknown. And she wondered in that hesitant moment, *what would Sassy Gregg do? If Mavis should lift the cherry lips, what would Sassy do?* And Lon trembled with not knowing.

"Jeez, honey, loosen up. I ain't poison."

"Oh, God, Violet—I don't know..."

"Go ahead an' kiss me, Lon. You wanna."

"I don't know...!"

"Holy cow, quit shakin'. Lookit how easy!"

The little mouth that was so like an *O* mashed against Lon's lips. Too late for a sudden intake of needed air. Violet's face fused with her own and the world around them floated in a nest of lavender spun-glass. It was like holding a delicate Christmas angel in your arms; pastel-tinted and yielding, when always before, when she had reached out to touch, her hands had met the unrelenting coldness of steel and the heart had returned, bruised and uncomprehending, to its hiding place. There to wait for this moment in time.

Twined and thrown off balance in the exquisite suffocation of their embrace, Lon emerged with a sobbing cry. Yet Violet's excitement appeared to be well-disciplined. Practically, she said, "This damn sweater's so hot. Lemme get it off, hon."

"Sure," Lon said, breath coming hard.

"How 'bout you kid? Jeez, it's roastin' in here." Violet's words muffled in the bulky white wool as she pulled the sweater carefully over her vegetable-colored claim to glamour.

"It's warm, all right." Lon hesitated.

"It'll be OK, jest with me." And sliding with an economy of motion out of the purple toreador pants, taking with them all that separated her from Lon's eyes.

Lon was aware of the beer-daze, yet submitted to it in mechanical, zombie movement. Until, naked and fearful in her muddled anxiety, she stood opposite the Easter-egg roundness, the pink and white and lavender prettiness that flooded her eyes.

They faced each other for what may have been an eon or perhaps only a grace note in time. And then the coil-spring that had lain wound and waited freed itself inside Lon. With a cry that culminated all the cries suppressed within her, that echoed the muffled sobs of lonely nights when the softness was only a pillow, she grasped at the proffered body. Her sudden movement threw them to the couch, Violet squealing her delight. And Lon's kisses were the repeated, thirsty gulps of a body parched, a spirit long dehydrated. Kisses prodded into frenzied repetition by the tinny, ecstatic sound that reached her ears: "Oh, Jeez, Lon! Oh, Christ, you're ketchin' on—" Violet voicing her approval, the beer-numbness shutting out Lon's fear of venturing to where Violet's approval became an inarticulate sound, like the moaning of wind.

Long afterward, like a dreamer shaken from sleep, she heard Violet speak again, this time with an awed reverence. "Holy Mother, you're the livin' end!"

And with a calm that had not fallen upon her in all the years she could remember, Lon observed that the bleeding heart on the wall had been treated with luminous paint. If the lamp light had been turned off, she thought, it would have glowed in the dark.

Women who dare to live in that outcast world of "twilight" love

Edge of Twilight

by Paula Christian

Sophisticated, witty, attractive Val MacGregor was one of Inter-American's most popular stewardesses…

Then one day lovely, dark-eyed Toni was assigned to be her co-stewardess. From their first moment of meeting Val sensed something oddly disturbing about the girl. Not until later did she realize what it was—and then it was much too late!

Edge of Twilight offers a refreshingly realistic treatment of women who are "different." Without the usual tragic and doomed atmosphere, Paula Christian has created a memorable and moving story about a difficult and much abused subject.

Edge of Twilight

In her room, Val quickly changed and applied fresh makeup for dinner. She was glad to see Don, very glad. But she felt stifled.

I'm being silly, she decided. Best thing that could happen to me would be a quiet marriage to Don. I've given in to my caprices long enough. Time I settled down and lived a normal and average life. I won't be young forever.

It will be so dull, though. I'll either evaporate or I'll unintentionally crucify him. Oh well, still lots of time to decide.

She rejoined him in the bar and explained to him her plans for returning to New York—carefully omitting why.

"Is there any good place to eat around here?" Don asked.

"Frankly, I wouldn't know," Val said. "When I buy my own dinner I go to the little diner down the street or the motel coffee shop." She laughed and added, "When the boys are buying, I'm too tipsy to notice where I am by the time I get to the place."

It was the sort of humor she knew didn't appeal to Don, but he tried not to show it now.

They hailed a cab and climbed in. "Know of any quaint little restaurants not too far from here?" Don asked the driver, a husky young woman with a deep voice.

"Depends on what you want, mister."

"Something with unusual atmosphere," Val suggested.

"Lots of them places." The driver hesitated, looked at Val, then added tentatively, "Want something really different? But I mean really?"

Don looked at Val inquiringly. She gave a what-can-we-lose shrug. "OK, driver. Let's go."

From the outside the place looked like a neighborhood bar and grill. An enormous white notice was on the entrance wall: NO ONE UNDER TWENTY-ONE ADMITTED. Don opened the door and they were met with a blast of romantic juke box music, conversation and laughter.

The room was large, but so dimly lighted and smoke-filled they were at first unable to find a table. Don spotted a clearing and led Val to it.

A tall attractive girl in slacks was wiping up an empty table. Val and Don sat down while she stood waiting for them.

"What'll it be?"

"Do you have a menu?" Don asked.

"This is a bar. Sandwiches only."

Don looked helplessly at Val.

She shrugged and suggested, "Let's have a drink and then we can leave. We're already sitting down." She looked up at the waitress and smiled. "Two scotch on the rocks."

"Right." The girl sauntered away.

"Bet she's wondering how we ever found our way here." Val laughed. But she felt a certain excitement about the place, an aliveness.

"I don't like this place, hon," Don insisted. "Let's leave."

"Why?"

"Because I don't think it's the sort of place I should bring my future wife. What if someone came in here whom I knew, whom we knew?"

"Oh, Don! Have you no sense of adventure? In the first place, who's going to know you in here, and in the second place, even if someone should it would be to everyone's mutual advantage to keep quiet. What's wrong with it?"

"There's something funny about the people here."

"Of course. That's what the cabby said. Remember? Really different." Val looked around the room, her eyes adjusting to the dim light. "Probably an artists' banquet."

A young man minced by their table and tripping slightly, bumped into Don. "Oh, excuse me, dear. I'm so sorry," he lisped, then walked away.

"Val! This is a homosexual hangout. That boy was a queer if I ever saw one!"

"Will you relax?" Val said sharply, but the idea appealed to her. Their drinks were served and the waitress said, "That will be two bucks. You pay when served here."

Val turned and began studying the people in the room. What had appeared before to be normal couples sitting at the tables, now turned out to be girls, one of whom was dressed as a boy. The young men at the bar were actually robust girls completely manly in their posture and actions.

So these are the "butches" Toni was telling me about, Val thought silently.

Two boys, their arms entwined around each other, were dancing to the music in a dark corner of the room. Little by little, Val watched first a boy-girl ask a girl-girl for a dance and then ease off into the back room; then other "couples" rose. Biologically, there appeared to be by far more girls than boys.

Don remained sullen and silent. He had hardly touched his drink and kept his eyes on the table top. In a way, she could understand his embarrassment, but then, too, she wanted to stay and see what went on in a "queer bar."

"Shall we leave now?" he said.

"No, Don. I want another drink." She knew she was being stubborn and taking unfair advantage of his good nature. But she had always gone where he wanted, whether it amused her or not. Now it was her turn. If I go to Toni, she thought, this may very well be how I'll end up. I may as well know what I'm letting myself in for. Maybe this place will cure me once and for all. She found it disgusting and fascinating at the same time.

Don called the waitress over and brusquely ordered one drink for Val. The waitress smiled for the first time and glanced at Val appraisingly.

"We got a real nice place about a mile from here. High-class customers—money crowd." She winked at Val as though sharing a greater knowledge, then seemingly offered for Don's behalf, "They get dinners over there."

Don coldly said, "Thanks."

The girl saluted lazily and walked away.

It made Val feel uncomfortable and daring at the same time.

"Why do you want to stay here?" Don demanded. "I don't see any point to it."

"Why do you enjoy watching the monkeys in the zoo?"

"Because they're funny. But these freaks aren't very funny."

"Not because they're funny, Don, but because it's fascinating to see something you can recognize in yourself and yet feel superior to."

"You mean you feel a kinship to these, these..."

"In a way."

"But how in earth can you..."

"Oh, Don! Stop being so stuffy! We're not the only people in the world, you know. You act as if the sun shines only in your direction. How about letting me have a good time once in a while."

"This is a good time to you? Since when? And besides, I always ask you what you want to do."

"Oh, sure. Thanks."

"What's that mean?"

"It means that I'm tired of Loew's main features, and nice rides from Manhattan to Brooklyn, and solid respectable night clubs where I may indulge in not more than three drinks and only a very discreet waltz for convention's sake!" She was surprised at the words that came out of her mouth. Am I really saying all this, she wondered.

But she couldn't seem to stop now that she'd started even though she knew he wasn't at fault. "And that goes for your mealy-mouthed friends who'd have me living in a stove, too!"

Don stared at her in complete bewilderment. "I don't understand what's gotten into you. Who wants you to...to live in a stove? What are you talking about? And you know I can't waltz."

"See? That's what I mean! You can't even waltz!"

"You're drunk, Val. And I'm going to get you out of here. Come on, I knew I shouldn't have let you have that third drink."

Val stared at him for a moment, then remembering all she had had to drink in the past few weeks, burst out into almost uncontrollable laughter. She was tempted to say that he was lucky it wasn't her third bottle.

"You're hysterical, hon. Please. Please let me take you home. It's this place that has upset you." He put his hand gently on her arm.

She pulled her arm away roughly and for an instant hated him. "Who are you pulling?" she asked furiously.

"Whom."

"Who-whom. Just *whom* the hell do you think you're pulling?"

"Val," Don said quietly, "we're in a public place."

Her tension found release in inflicting pain on Don. "Poo poo. So self-righteous, aren't we."

He looked at her pleadingly. "Please lower your voice."

"Scared to let loose and be human, aren't you? Scared to get mad and tell me off. Scared to death you'll feel something stronger than hunger and thirst. Go ahead, Don," Val goaded, "get mad. It's fun. Look at me. I'm having a ball!"

"Val," he said sternly, "listen to me. I'm leaving and I expect you to come with me. I'll give you sixty seconds to make up your mind. Otherwise, I'll leave alone."

She followed his movements as he took out his watch and stared at it. Why am I doing this, she asked herself, not really caring. I know I'm not drunk, not really. She couldn't help humming cheerfully along with the music in sadistic delight over his obvious discomfort.

He looked at her impatiently. "Are you ready to go now?"

"Did you say something?" she asked with complete indifference. Don pulled out his wallet and threw a ten-dollar bill on the table. Without saying a word, he got up and left her.

She made no effort to stop him.

The waitress came back and grinned. "Will your friend be back?

"I hope not," Val said before she realized it. She was surprised to discover that she meant it. It had been a good fight and she had won—although she was a little uncertain on what score—and she felt purged, even a little giddy with this strange new freedom. The nagging old feeling of always having to act under obligation was gone.

Val looked up at the girl still standing by her table, and repeated, "I certainly hope not." She smiled a little smugly.

The waitress smiled back. "Can the house buy you a drink? That was some fight you two had."

"Thanks. I could use one. I hope we didn't disturb anyone." Val suddenly realized that she had been talking louder than necessary.

"Not at all. We're used to arguments here, only not usually between a boy and a girl." She laughed casually and walked away.

Val sat quietly watching the couples on the dance floor. Why is it that all of a sudden I run into this type of thing? Where was I before? Is it that I've only now become aware of it? Maybe I've been in a hundred places like this and never knew it.

Val felt someone looking at her, and for a moment had the sensation that she should get out. But it was too late, the woman was already walking over to her table.

She was very handsome, dressed in a man-tailored suit which fit her beautifully. "Maxie tells me you've just had a fight with your boyfriend. Asked me to bring you your drink." She placed it on the table. "May I join you?" Her voice was well modulated and soft.

Val looked at her swiftly. Her face was a little too long, but it was interesting. Especially her dark gray eyes which held just a trace of a twinkle.... Or were they blue?

"Certainly," Val answered, feeling suddenly alone. Then asked, "Who's Maxie?"

"The waitress." She sat down gracefully.

"Oh."

They were silent a moment, and Maxie brought a drink for Val's guest and a plastic bowl crammed with pretzels.

"Been in Miami long?" she asked. "By the way, my name is Clare."

"Mine's Val. About two weeks."

"Know what kind of a bar you're in?" she asked gently.

"Yes."

"And you brought your boyfriend here?"

"We didn't know when we first came in." Val felt very stupid and awkward.

"Well, baby, if you don't feel like talking would you like to dance?"

She was tempted to say no at first, then feeling a little reckless said, "Well, I guess it can't make me pregnant."

"No, baby. You won't get pregnant." Clare stood up and led Val to the floor.

She was just Val's height, and held her loosely, leaving Val to decide how close she wanted to be. May as well have the whole works, Val decided silently. She closed the space between them and rested her cheek against Clare's. It felt strange that there was no beard. Strange and nice.

She could feel Clare's body mold to her own and realized that Clare was breathing very fast. It was exhilarating to feel that she could excite another woman.

This was different from Toni.

And a lot different from Mrs. Summers.

Val closed her eves and let Clare's body lead her to the music. Lead and lead and lead…

Nothing was said. It was unnecessary.

Val opened her eyes slowly and tried to focus them as Clare led her into a fast turn.

Suddenly, there was a tall shadow just inside the entrance. Val stopped, pulled away from Clare, and stared.

His name came to her lips, but she couldn't quite say it.

Don just stood there, his face white with anger and shock, looking at her as Val watched helplessly from the dance floor. Finally, the word came out, "Don…"

But it was too late.

He turned and went out the door without glancing back.

Val felt a sudden twinge of regret. That was the finale. Don would never be back.

"What's the matter, baby?" Clare asked.

"What?" Val muttered. "Oh, nothing," she said flatly. "Just a shadow… from the past."

She excused herself and called a cab. The place made her sick now and she wanted to leave.

Where can I go?

To the motel.

And then?

The week that followed dragged slowly. Girls were interviewed to replace Val, and it would look as though they were really going to hire one. Then, for one reason or another Al Newman or Summers would decide against her.

Val's nerves were ragged with the suspense.

Toni phoned her every night. Drunk, or crying, or simply pleading for her to return to New York. Her letters were the same: morbid, frantic, and filled with pleas for love.

For Val the nights were long and tormented. Sleepless, unable to think, she spent bitter hours castigating herself for lack of character, for not being able to decide what to do.

She tried to forget herself with the crew. She drank every chance she had, and indiscriminately made love. Coldly, impersonally. Seeking physical contact only as a means of forgetting and escape.

She couldn't even remember with whom she had slept from one night to the next.

Each morning, she grew accustomed to having a jigger of scotch with her cigarette before she was able to get up. The shadows under her eyes deepened and the corners of her mouth were tense with nervous fatigue.

The crews noticed the change but discreetly said nothing, worried lest they lose their relationship with her. Some attributed her behavior to their individual manliness, their overpowering effect upon her.

Yet her only drive was to keep busy, to so exhaust herself that she could sleep. But it never seemed to help. Toni was always on her mind.

Val laughed too hard, talked too much, and made love too violently. It was as though she were trying to convince herself of her own existence. To Janice's and Ralph's questions she flatly replied that it was because she couldn't be with her lover in New York.

She was moody, tired on the flights, and then given to sudden hectic gaiety.

Stewart naturally assumed it was due to his failure and tactfully kept out of her way as much as possible.

At last, a girl was hired to replace her and Val's last trip to Panama was over—forty-eight hours short of the two-week period she had promised Toni on that first phone call. It seemed so very long ago.

She returned to the motel room to pack. She would get the first plane out of Miami. She had to settle her life once and for all and she knew that it could be done only in New York—face to face with Toni.

Tired and weary, unable to carry herself erect, Val finished packing and tried to make reservations on the first plane available.

By luck she managed to obtain a canceled space on a 4:15 flight that afternoon.

Good thing I've already said good-bye to the crew. No time now. "Out of here, at last," she told herself aloud.

She forced herself to look in the mirror, staring at the hollow face that peered back at her, asking herself, "Can this be me? Once you thought you were smart, didn't you? Thought nothing would ever touch you, make you suffer. Look at yourself now. Take a good look. Decide something soon or you won't have enough mind left to make a decision."

She took out the bottle of scotch, then replaced it in the drawer. The time for drinking was past. It wouldn't help anymore. She had to help herself. No matter what I am, she thought, I'm not a lush and don't intend to become one.

Turning away from the mirror and the tempting bottle of scotch, she decided to lie down for a few minutes of rest.

The room was very still; only the dull hum of the air conditioner sounded over her breathing. She closed her eyes, and for some reason her mind went back to an experience she had not thought about for a long time.

It had been strange and eerie.

She and the boys had to ferry an empty plane out of Fargo, North Dakota, one icy winter night. They had taken a load of G.I.'s there and were to pick up another group in Spokane. Once aloft, Val had turned off the cabin lights and sat alone in the center of the plane, smoking a cigarette before trying to get some sleep. The entire crew was up front in the cockpit.

She was all alone.

Completely alone.

The plane suddenly became a huge flying tomb taking her on and on. Forever.

They would never land, she was certain, never see earth or people again.

Looking out into the night, she glimpsed the reflection of the cold clear moon on the wings. Everything was so brilliant; the cotton clouds looming in the distance were unreal against the inky sky; stars seemed very close, so much closer than the earth so far below, not visible from their altitude because of the gray-blue blanket of soft downlike clouds beneath them.

It didn't seem to matter that she was neither dead nor alive. It didn't seem to matter that this, after all, was all that there was to eternity.

Shadows danced and darted within the cabin, making the seats seem grotesque in their yawning emptiness. The engines would drone on forever, the ghosts in the cockpit could not affect her for they were not of the same world, and the sun would never shine again for she was going away; on and on and on, into darkness.

Cool, peaceful, quiet darkness.

The Stewardess Crew Call buzzer from the boys had startled her back to reality that night and she had shuddered, pushing off the cold shadows of the moon that had held her captive.

What would startle her back to reality now? This was not fantasy. And what would now help her to push off her fears and uncertainties?

Val opened her eyes and sighed heavily.

It was a room in a motel. It was Miami.

And she was going some place in particular. New York.

She would land, and she would see people. Toni.

And she would have to make a decision.

She got up and called for the bellhop and had him take her luggage to the lobby.

She smiled half-heartedly at the desk clerk, mumbling thanks for his service. A cab was waiting with her luggage.

Her plane would leave in half an hour.

Val sat in the plane pensively, trying now to understand what had happened since she had first met Toni that rainy night several weeks ago. It had seemed like many other nights, nothing really unusual about it. What happened? What made it different? What had happened to her? She tried to reconstruct the past few weeks in an effort to find herself.

There had been no warning—or had there been one?

Of course there had been signs, but she had not known then how to recognize them, nor their full significance.

Here I am, she thought, on my way to New York to face something that I know nothing about. Am I in love with Toni?

As she silently said the words, she felt her body respond. The tenderness and urgency, the need and freedom, the desire and peace, all seemed so new and so contradictory. But wonderful.

She tried to understand herself and what it was she was so avidly seeking from life, struggling, fighting, and never comprehending her own motives, but still searching.

She wondered what she would gain and what she would lose by a conversion to a way of life which was socially outcast.

She would have to be careful of all her social relations, find new friends, discover herself in a strange and different atmosphere.

Her relations with the crews would be a problem in itself.

She would have to learn to accept disdain and jibes, and injustices because of the few homosexuals who had to advertise themselves so grotesquely, rubbing society's nose into a puddle they would otherwise step right over. She tried to estimate if these sacrifices were worth the tender and consuming love to be achieved only between women.

As they circled the field to come in at La Guardia, Val wondered what she would say if Toni were there. She had sent Toni a wire from the airport advising her of arrival time and flight number.

It was drizzling when they landed, and Val could hardly believe that she was home at last; she felt alive and invigorated.

Walking into the terminal, she saw Toni scanning the crowd eagerly. Then she saw Val and ran toward her, stopping in front of her abruptly. She was still a moment.

"Hello, darling," she whispered, kissing her on the cheek.

Her perfume penetrated Val's nostrils, and awareness crept through her as though the scent were a blood transfusion. They stood helplessly in the throng, just looking at one another, unable to speak or show in any way that they were more than good friends to one another.

Val collected her wits at last and led Toni to the baggage counter, making trivial conversation about her trip and the Miami flights, asking questions about the European flights she had missed. She felt as though she were standing outside of herself watching her own actions with amazement.

"You mean you still want to go to Europe?" Toni asked despondently.

Val picked out her luggage for the attendant. "Nothing could make me change my mind about going to Europe."

Tears filled Toni's eyes. She squeezed Val's arm tightly. "Don't mind me. I'm just so happy to see you. And I was so sure that when you came back it would be just to be with me. Sorry."

"I came back because I was going insane running away from you. Come on, let's go pick up my little Ford. Then I'll drive you home and we'll talk." Val smiled. Now she felt controlled again, self-confident, and honest with herself and with Toni. Things would soon be settled.

They took a cab to the Idlewild parking lot where Val had left her car. The ride was short. Toni sat very close to her, snuggling her hand into Val's, seeking some gesture of reassurance.

Val asked the cabby to wait while she tried to start her car. To her amazement, she had no difficulty. She waved the taxi away, leaving them alone in awkward silence.

Val started a light conversation, reminding Toni of how much this ride seemed like their first, as though she had never been away. They were parked near Toni's apartment before they realized it.

"Is your friend still staying with you?" Val asked quietly.

"Florence has gone away for the weekend," Toni told her.

They ran through the rain to the door and then up the stairs. They were both breathless when they entered the apartment. Toni turned on the phonograph, playing soft mood music and left Val in the semidarkened room while she made a pot of fresh coffee in the cramped kitchen.

Val found that she was smiling to herself, asking herself questions and answering them.

Do you know what you are doing? Do you really know? I know, she told herself, and I don't care. It's a question of existing miserably for a society that really doesn't give a damn as long as I don't flaunt it, or grasping a chance for happiness. There's no murder involved. No rape, no perjury. Just love. What I do in bed should be private and only between the one I love and me.

Children? Security? There's no guarantee that I would ever have these things: If not satisfied your years cheerfully refunded. And as for scandal, would it be any worse than my current past?

"What are you thinking about, Val?" Toni asked quietly, returning from the kitchen.

"About whether you make good coffee or not." Val laughed lightly.

"Please, Val. I'm miserable. Tell me."

"All right. Come here." She pulled Toni down on the couch next to her, inhaling her warmth, and unbuttoned her dress.

"Val!" Toni demanded tremulously. "What are you doing?"

"You're going to make love to me."

As Toni undressed, Val studied her body in the dim light, savoring it, noticing the full curves and the soft firm flesh. Her young breasts, her abdomen, even the shape of her bones, excited Val.

Val pushed herself against Toni's body, running her hand over the smooth flesh, letting Toni's closeness thrill her, fill her with a passion she had never known before.

Toni pushed her away. "You, too," she begged.

"Me too, what?"

"Get undressed."

"Must I?"

"Yes."

Val smiled. She pulled her clothes off quickly, her body throbbing with desire.

Lying close to Toni, she allowed herself to become lost in the soft soothing warmth of their merging bodies.

"Kiss me!" Val commanded.

Toni suddenly became coy. "Say it first."

"Kiss me! Kiss me, I said." Her lips twitched slightly, her mouth hungered.

"Say it!" Toni's eyes were half closed, with a look of infinite wisdom on her face. "Tell me first why I should..."

Val brought her mouth to a fraction of an inch from Toni's, letting the closeness torture her, completely smother her.

She whispered, "Because I love you...I adore you... Oh, God, I want you so much."

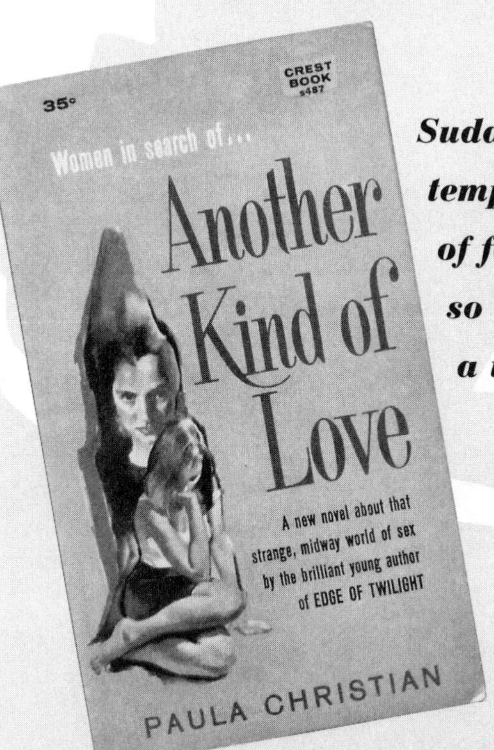

Suddenly that shadowy, tempting dream-world of forbidden desires—so long denied—became a terrifying reality

Another Kind of Love

by Paula Christian

Laura was young, lovely, intelligent. A successful Hollywood writer, she had everything a man could want in a woman. Except the most important thing—the capacity to love a man.

Laura was no innocent. She had had affairs with men. There were even moments when she convinced herself she was truly in love.

But always something had been missing. Until she met Ginny.

Never would she forget the wild shock of pleasure at the look of naked yearning in Ginny's smoldering green eyes.

Another Kind of Love

At six P.M. exactly, Laura signaled a passing cab in front of the office. She couldn't bear the bus today—it was too nice a day. As she rode down Fifth Avenue, Laura sat pensively reviewing these past weeks and how much of a routine it had become for her to frequent the Village "rounds" almost nightly. The bartenders now knew her along with the other steady customers.

At the office she worked herself mercilessly each day, as her department took shape and more responsibility came. Then she ate a hurried dinner and lost herself in her new world.

It hadn't helped her to forget Ginny—she could never do that and accepted it now. But it did help her to find a place for herself in the world—a place that was both a sanctuary and a strange source of rebellion.

She knew that Madeline did not approve of what she was doing, and of the hours she kept. But Madeline had made it quite plain that she understood what was happening to Laura, that it was a phase of "coming out" and that it would pass. It annoyed Laura occasionally that Madeline seemed to take such a superior attitude, particularly when Madeline would make some comment about Laura going out "to punish yourself."

But it was also quite clear to Laura that she needed Madeline, needed a friend....

She paid the driver and looked around the now familiar street before walking into the apartment building. It seems as if I've lived here all my life. Palm trees and freeways are a long way off.... It all happened to someone else—not me, she thought.

She looked up at the trees and saw the branches in their need to bud and grow. There was no doubt about it: spring had finally arrived in New York.

Sighing, she wondered if Ginny realized that spring had come. Or if Ginny knew she was thinking of her. She wondered how Ginny was doing and if she needed anything—or if she had found someone new.

It's strange, she thought, how you can numb your feelings about people yet can never really rid yourself of them. Some silly little incident or random association and...wham!... They were back, raw as ever.

Instant amnesia—and anesthesia—for painful memories. That's what the world needed. Only it should be permanent as well. Liquor didn't really do the job. Not really.

"Just in time for soup," Madeline yelled as Laura let herself into the apartment.

Reliable, sweet Madeline, Laura thought with a comfortable sigh. "I'm going with you tonight," Madeline announced. With a mischievous smile, she asked, "How do you like my drag outfit?"

Laura had to laugh. Madeline couldn't have looked masculine no matter what she did, and the jersey blouse with matching slacks she had on did very little to make her manly.

"You'll be the butch of the ball," Laura said.

"My. Aren't we learning the trade jargon!" Madeline laughed. They sat down to a hurried dinner, and Laura speculated about what was making Madeline so chipper this evening. Not just weather.

"Have you seen Edie lately?" Madeline asked.

"No," Laura answered. "Why?"

"She's doing a bit in some awful thing at Actor's Playhouse. Thought you might like to catch part of the rehearsal tonight."

"Why?" Laura asked cautiously.

"Friend of mine is in the show, too—kind of a friend, that is. Anyway, it won't kill you, and Edie does have quite a thing for you."

"Sure," Laura laughed. "She's loved me for twenty-five minutes. That's a five-minute edge over her old girlfriends." She stood and walked into the kitchen, balancing her dishes. "All right. I'll be a sport. Do I have time to clean up?"

"Yes. But make it fast." Madeline began to wash the dishes, whistling merrily.

"Why don't you get a maid?" Laura called from the bedroom.

"How would I advertise? Gay and personable?"

Laura shrugged her shoulders in mock helplessness and took a shower, briefly enjoying the sheer luxury of the spray of water.

Drying herself, she looked at her reflection in the mirror impersonally and realized for the first time how tired she looked, and how much thinner.

"The wages of sin," she murmured to herself, and turned her back to the mirror. She dressed quickly and applied her makeup with hasty efficiency.

"You about ready, Laura?" Madeline called.

Laura went into the living room smiling. "In the flesh. What's your hurry?"

"You'll see."

They left the apartment just after dark and walked briskly to the small playhouse on Seventh Avenue.

A lanky youth with tight-fitting chino pants sat at a small table as they entered. He had the glazed look of the devout failure. Madeline smiled at him benignly.

"Max said it was all right for us to watch the rehearsal," she told him.

He looked at them both momentarily. "The producer?"

"Of course."

"Go on in," he said, as if he had a beer with old Maxie every evening. "You've missed about fifteen minutes of the first act."

Madeline walked down the narrow stairway and into the darkened theater. She paused by the refreshment stand inside the theater long enough for Laura to get accustomed to the dark, then led Laura to a seat in the last row.

Laura leaned over and whispered, "This better be good."

"You may never know how true that is," Madeline answered.

In the dim light from the stage, Laura could make out Madeline's expression. Gone was the mischievous look and the bright little smile. In their place were concern and speculation. Laura wondered if Madeline had sunk money into this show, but decided against it—Madeline knew better.

Laura settled back in the uncomfortable seat and wished she had a drink. Glancing around the room, she saw a cluster of people sitting off to the right and several leaning forward in the first row center.

"How does the audience see anything when there's no dais?" she heckled softly.

"Shh," Madeline ordered.

Laura shrugged and tried to listen to the gaunt young man on stage who was talking to a blue spotlight behind a blue sheer backdrop with modernistic foliage sewn on it.

She sat back and sniffed happily. Yes. It was there. That special, intoxicating smell of the theater—that kind of velvety, faintly perfumed, warm-dust aroma.

There was something curiously soothing about it all. Gradually Laura began to succumb to the wonderful mood a darkened theater always aroused in her. It struck her then that this was the first time she had ever really been in an honest-to-God New York theater, even though it was off-Broadway. She must come more often—she'd almost forgotten what a delicious experience it was.

Absently she watched the blue light dim and move to the edge of the stage. Somewhere music came through in a rhythmic, fragmented drumbeat. The figure of a woman began to emerge slowly from the offstage shadows. Laura found herself straining to see. She was barely conscious of Madeline, who had turned to watch her.

All Laura's attention was focused on that shadow figure that was now undulating to the center of the stage. There was something about it that sent a strange, warning thrill through her. She could not have said what it was exactly.

She wished they'd turn the damned spot up so she could see.

When it did happen, it was so swift Laura was unprepared.

"Ginny!" It was a full moment before Laura realized that the stifled gasp was her own. She stared in frozen realization at the crown of soft red hair that shimmered in the soft, ghostly light—at the pale, anxious face, the small, supple body that not even the ill-fitting costume could obliterate. So familiar, yet so unreal.

"Steady, old girl," whispered Madeline, closing her fingers around Laura's arm so tightly it was almost painful.

By this time Laura was almost standing up.

A thousand impressions and arguments flew through her mind, and the scene became a blur to her except for Ginny's small figure making stage gestures, walking upstage and, for some reason, into a man's arms.

The sight of her there was all too odd, too unexpected.

Laura picked up her purse mechanically and without a backward look left the theater. She was halfway out the street exit when she heard Madeline's voice calling her.

She turned on her heel and stopped. "That was a pretty cute trick," she said tightly.

"It wasn't meant as a cute trick," Madeline replied softly.

"What did you mean by it?"

"I...I just wanted you to know she was in town, and I thought this way you could see her without being discovered."

"You're lying." Laura said flatly.

Madeline took Laura by the shoulder gently. "You're not angry with me, are you?" She sighed. "I guess it was the actress in me—the dramatic approach. I'm genuinely sorry."

Laura felt the tears creeping into her eyes, and the back of her throat was aching. She fought them back and gained control of herself.

"No," she said finally. "I'm not really angry. It was just such a shock..."

They walked in silence past Sheridan Square. Laura wanted to get drunk, to just lose herself inside a bottle of scotch until she drowned.

She paid no attention to Madeline. She tried to place the event in its proper perspective, tried to see the situation objectively. So what if Ginny was in town... Maybe she didn't know that Laura was here, too, or maybe she hated Laura after finding that she had run out.... Maybe many things.

But what reason did Laura have for staying away from Ginny? Laura led the way up the steps to the bar and, without even saying hello to Georgie, marched into the back and sat down. She half saw that Madeline paused to talk to Georgie, a terse conversation punctuated with stern expressions and lifted eyebrows. Then Madeline was walking toward her and sitting down at the table with Laura.

"How did you know who she was?" Laura asked.

Madeline smiled as if to admit that "she" could only be one person. "From your description, and knowing her name. When Max told me that she had been Saundra Simon's protégé, there could be no doubt." She sat silently a moment. "I talked with her yesterday."

Laura looked up at Madeline quickly.

"I was having lunch with Max." Madeline paused while Georgie set their drinks in front of them and walked silently away. "He was telling me about this girl in the show, and he said she was going to join us a little later. Seems he's taken a fancy to her and thought that with my new pull at *Fanfare* I might get a good plug in for both the show and her."

Laura nodded and, with a slightly shaking hand, took a deep swallow of her drink.

"The long arm of coincidence," she mumbled, savoring the harsh taste of the whisky.

"I didn't put two and two together until after she arrived and Max made some comment about Saundra and Ginny." Madeline laughed mirthlessly. "After that, my brain was going like a rampant IBM tabulator."

"And you concocted this little plot?"

"I'm afraid so. I thought the shock would stir you out of this waste of time in bars...and here we are."

Laura sat back and said nothing. She looked about the room at the few faceless girls coming in or already seated. Someone fed the juke box, which glittered hungrily in its corner; an old Frank Sinatra ballad began. Too early for the rock 'n' roll crowd, Laura thought.

"What are you going to do?" Madeline asked quietly,

"Probably nothing," Laura answered with a wry smile. "Did you tell her I was in town?"

"I didn't have to. She already knew."

"How do you know?"

"She asked if I knew you." Madeline stared at the lamp on the table, then reached out to straighten the shade.

"Stop playing with that thing, damn it," Laura commanded tersely. "What did you tell her?" She was sorry immediately; she hadn't meant to sound so harsh.

But Madeline accepted Laura's manner with calm understanding. "Only that I had met you," she said gravely. "And that was all. I changed the subject. There was no point in lying about it, was there?"

"No. I suppose not." Laura relaxed again.

"Why don't you call her? I'm sick of looking at you moping around."

"Would it do any good?" Laura signaled to Georgie for another round. "She probably hates me."

"You'll never find out at the rate you're going. If you do still love her, do something about it! Why are you building up such a 'thing' about it?"

"Shut up!" Laura demanded. She desperately wanted to call Ginny, and Madeline's urging didn't help. But Laura was afraid to—afraid of this emotion that Ginny aroused in her. She feared that if she called Ginny, somehow, in some mysterious way, she'd be "hooked" again and this time not able to break away. Laura felt trapped by her own desires—desires she didn't understand much less control.

Later, Laura looked up and suddenly realized that the bar was full of people. There were several wet ring spots on the table, and Laura realized that she must have been drinking steadily, without thinking or keeping track of the drinks or the time.

Madeline was standing at the bar, talking to a very attractive blonde but keeping her eyes on Laura.

Laura looked at the clock over in the far corner of the bar. It was a quarter of eleven. She felt as if she had been unconscious and was awakening in some alien, bawdy place. But there was Madeline to remind her she was not alone, that she had a friend, someone who cared what happened to her and what went on inside her.

Madeline smiled at the blonde, touched her arm, and, circling the dancing couples, walked back toward Laura.

"How do you feel?" she asked, sitting down carefully.

"All right." Laura tried to clear her head as waves of fuzziness came at her. "Thank you, Madeline. Have I thanked you yet for being so wonderful? Have I?"

"Do you want me to take you home?"

"Be it ever so humble...but ours isn't. How come the words and the truth don't agree, Madeline?" She gripped the edge of the table with all her strength. "Yes...I want to go home...I may as well..."

Laura's voice broke off as she looked over Madeline's shoulder. "Oh, no!" Laura whispered. She shook her head violently and looked again.

"What is it?" Madeline asked with real concern.

"Look..."

Madeline turned and sat motionless for a moment. "What's she doing here?"

She glanced at Laura sympathetically, then stood up effortlessly and walked away.

Madeline nodded as she passed Ginny.

⁂

Ginny stood very still and stared at Laura with no visible expression on her face. Then, slowly, she walked to her.

In spite of herself Laura began to shake. She felt as if someone had hooked up her stomach to a vibrator. Her arms and legs were weak. She couldn't take her eyes away from Ginny's, yet she was unable to really look at her.

"May I sit down?" Ginny asked in a low, soft voice.

Laura said nothing, afraid that she would both cry and laugh if she tried to talk. She wished she had not drunk so much.

"I saw you leave the Playhouse," Ginny said. "One of the girls in the show knows you...Edie. She said you come here regularly." Ginny sat down. It seemed to Laura that she had changed in some unfathomable way.

"I just wanted to say hello." Ginny smiled and carefully pushed her hair from her face. "It never occurred to me that you might be in a place like this." She seemed amused.

Laura still said nothing. A confusion of emotion swept over her, paralyzing all response. She had a maddening urge to throw her arms around Ginny, feel her warm, young body, hear Ginny tell her that they would never be apart again.... But the amusement in Ginny's voice chilled her, held her in check.

"How are you?" Laura managed to ask finally.

"Fine," Ginny said. "Shouldn't I be?"

Her coolness jolted Laura. The times when Laura had imagined their reunion, she had prepared herself for hurt accusations from Ginny, for tight-lipped fury, for scalding rejection—anything but this blankness, this indifference.

Laura leaned forward, her voice harsh with tension. "Are we going to make conversation like strangers on a train?"

"Are we anything else, really?" Ginny asked.

"We were plenty else!" Laura snapped, the drinks loosening her usual reserve. "Do you know what I've been through staying away from you?"

"Who asked you to?"

"My blind instinct for self-preservation," Laura muttered. "And my fears, my appalling ignorance."

"Perhaps it's just as well," Ginny replied levelly. "This would have been much more difficult if you had really fallen in love with me."

Laura's face seemed to freeze. "Really fallen in love? What in God's name did you think it was I felt for you?"

For an instant, Ginny's face softened. There was a flicker of compassion in her eyes as she raised them and looked directly at Laura.

"Not love, Laura. Not really."

Laura couldn't answer. She had known for some time that this was true. She was not sure just how she felt about Ginny.... There was a wild kind of craving to hold her, to breathe her in. Ginny made her feel so goddamn physical.

She must have loved Ginny in a rather special sort of way—certainly not everlasting, but intensely. Even now, with Ginny sitting so near to her, the old feelings...

"Besides," Ginny continued, "we got what we wanted from each other."

Laura wanted to ask Ginny what she meant by that, but just then Georgie walked up to the table and picked up the empty glass in front of Laura, depositing a fresh one. She wiped the top of the table with exceptional care, then, without looking at either of them, asked, "You Virginia Adams?"

"Yes."

Georgie gestured toward the bar. "Some dame on the phone for you. Says she's Saundra Simons," Georgie laughed. "I should've told her I was Rudolph Valentino."

Georgie walked away still chuckling, stopping to tell another couple the joke.

Saundra...Saundra... The name kept repeating in Laura's mind over and over. She could feel rage, hurt, resentment pyramiding inside her.

Ginny stood up slowly, wordlessly, and went to the phone near the bar.

Laura tried desperately to keep calm.

A moment later, Ginny came back and sat down on the edge of the chair. "I have to leave."

"Saundra?" Laura's voice was knife-edged.

Ginny nodded. "It's funny," she said with a slight curl on her lips, "but of all the times Saundra could have made a scene or been jealous of me, the only time she ever really gave any possessive signs was with you in the picture. She was jealous for the first time—of you."

"I'm laughing," Laura commented tightly. She could feel the heat rising inside her, strained to hold back the anger choking in her throat. "Why did you go back, Ginny? Why?"

"Why not?" Ginny answered resignedly. "Sure, I was attracted to you—no point in denying that. As a matter of fact, I felt a lot more for you than I ever did for Saundra. So when you left I was pretty hurt and pretty disappointed. But it was too damned frustrating lugging a torch around—getting circles under my eyes. After all, if I lose my looks, not only would Saundra not want me, but neither would any producer. It sure as hell wasn't any reason to ruin my career, was it? For what? No, Saundra, no career and no you. I just didn't see any point to it."

"So you went crawling back to Saundra? Only Saundra didn't know you'd ever been away; is that it?"

"More or less," Ginny answered. "Does it matter?"

"No. I guess it doesn't." Laura stared at her glass and lapsed into silence.

Ginny gave an irritated cluck. "Well? What would you have thought if I'd done it to you? Run away, I mean."

Laura just shook her head and shrugged.

"Actually," Ginny went on, "I didn't go back to Saundra—that way—for quite a while. It didn't seem to matter much to her at the time. She was on a kick of her own. That's the way it's been with her, anyway—

she doesn't care what I do...as long as I'm there when she wants me. So I started dating an agent, remembering what you had said about making it on my own."

Numbly, Laura raised the fresh drink to her lips, unable to look at Ginny but listening to her with a kind of morbid fascination.

"The gang used to say he was a great lover and a big promoter. What did I have to lose? He took me to some parties and I got sick of him. Besides, he never did anything for me at all—not even one crummy bit part."

"Sorry I didn't bring my violin," Laura remarked bitterly.

Suddenly, with detached insight, she realized that Ginny was acting.

Watching her now, she wondered if Ginny was capable of just a plain unvarnished emotion—no spotlights, no Academy Awards. She didn't doubt that Ginny had been unhappy in her way, upset even, but she obviously was now milking this scene for all it was worth. She was giving Laura the four-star pitch. Laura's feelings toward Ginny at this point were a mixture of indifference and amused disbelief. She felt like asking, "So what else is new?" but didn't.

"Are you interested, or am I boring you?" Ginny asked sarcastically.

Laura smiled carefully. "Go right ahead," she answered. "This may save me a lot of research when I have to do a write-up on you someday."

"Oh, Laura, don't be this way. Try to see my side just for once. You didn't leave me much choice, you know."

"Go on, I said I'm listening," Laura replied, trying to sound sincere.

"Then I ran into Saundra one day, at one of those crazy parties up on Beechwood Drive. She was apologetic, understanding, charming—you know how she can be."

Laura nodded but found her attention wandering. She kept thinking what a fool she had been to let this girl take such a hold of her life and turn it upside down.

Suddenly she looked up to see that Ginny was watching her with tear-filled eyes. "Laura...could we...I mean, maybe we could still make it together. I've never forgotten you."

Laura was too startled to answer. Besides, she felt cold inside now, and tired.

"I was so glad," Ginny went on when Laura made no reply, "when Saundra got this chance to do a tour using New York as her base. And then when she got me this part on off-Broadway, I kind of figured I'd run into you again...somehow."

Still Laura said nothing. Even Ginny sat quietly now, and the silence between them grew visibly strained. It was amazing how very little they had to say to each other. It must be me, Laura thought, not just her. I'm the one who's changed, hardened. Good! She praised herself, maybe I'll know better next time. Next time what? Next time I fall in love...

She looked around the room and wondered how many of the people there were saying the same kind of desperate, hungry lies to cover an unbearable emptiness. She saw Ginny out of the corner of her eye and contemplated what they had been to each other, wondering what they had wanted from each other so urgently.

But it was too much to understand right now, and she searched for Madeline, hoping to draw reassurance from her, some measure of reality. That was it, Laura thought, this scene has no reality—it's just like a book or a movie. It's almost rehearsed.

Just as phony as what she had had with Ginny. It couldn't have been love—it had been too consuming, too sick, for love. It had been a compulsion, a springing loose of long-hidden fears and yearnings twisted and forged together into a mad kind of fascination...physical infatuation.

Ginny had been the one to touch the spring, and that was all. As if out from nowhere Madeline appeared and stood behind Ginny's chair. "Am I intruding?" she asked hesitantly.

Madeline! Laura thought with relief. My better half... Then she immediately felt embarrassed, as if she had no right to such a thought. My best friend, she corrected herself.

Ginny twisted in her chair and looked, coldly at first, at Madeline; then her eyes brightened and she smiled. "Oh, hello again, Mrs. Van Norden."

She turned to Laura. "We met yesterday at lunch with Max Geisler. You know, the producer."

Laura cringed inwardly. That familiar, fawning tone of voice, she thought—the hopeful starlet.

Madeline sat down next to Laura. "Why don't you call me Madeline," she suggested.

Laura had a bristling response to Madeline's words. It was so out of keeping with her honest personality. It had that Hollywood quality of "Stick with me, baby, and we'll go places."

Ginny responded energetically to Madeline's presence. She sat forward and leaned on the table with calculated ease and began a conversation about the show she was appearing in, how Max had great deal of confidence in her and, with lowered eyes, how she hoped she would fulfill his expectations.

Madeline came to her rescue gallantly with reassurances and told her that although she had not seen much of her rehearsal tonight, she thought Ginny showed real talent.

"Of course, I know I still have a lot to learn," Ginny commented with ritual modesty.

"Nothing that some real experience, and a little help, wouldn't take care of," Madeline replied sweetly.

Christ! Laura cursed silently, this isn't an interview! Madeline doesn't have the least intention of giving Ginny any help. Or does she? Suddenly Laura turned and scrutinized Madeline, searching for signs of sincere interest in Ginny's career. She was annoyed and confused by Madeline's behavior. It wasn't like the Madeline she knew, who was considerate, loyal, the Madeline who had kissed her that night long ago to show...to show what? This attitude toward Ginny didn't become her at all—it was beneath her! There was an excuse for Ginny. After all, she was looking to get ahead and she didn't care how—her behavior befitted her character.

But there sat Madeline, drinking it all up, playing straight man to Ginny's dialogue. Don't tell me she's falling for Ginny's line!

All at once, Saundra loomed over them, cloaked in vengeful wrath. Laura almost laughed, she looked so grotesquely menacing. Like the villain in a comic opera.

Saundra snapped, "Next time you intend to go slumming, Ginny, you might tell me. I don't enjoy having to smoke you out this way!" Saundra's voice was exquisitely acid.

With someone else the situation might have been honestly tragic, but Laura had the distinct impression that Saundra was enjoying herself—that she had summoned to this new role of the injured lover all the counterfeit passion of a summer stock celebrity playing to a packed house of adoring fans. Laura tried to feel resentment at the way Saundra spoke to Ginny, tried to feel protective, but couldn't—not even for old times' sake.

She looked at Madeline instinctively to share this amusing moment. Madeline had settled back in her seat and folded her hands neatly on top of the table. She looked up into Laura's eyes, and very swiftly an expression crossed her face that made it quite clear to Laura: Madeline had expected this meeting, had expected Ginny to show herself for what she was beyond any possible doubt. An impish curl came to Madeline's lips, and Laura was torn between wanting to burst out laughing and punching Madeline in the nose.

Ginny had simply shrugged her shoulders at Saundra's opening sentence. An empty look filled her large eyes, and Laura was appalled as she looked at her.

This is Ginny, she told herself; this is the girl you once loved...the girl for whom you've been drowning your sorrows, the girl that made your flesh tingle whenever you thought of her....

Saundra glanced down at Laura icily. "I thought I'd find you here," she sneered. Her catlike stare had not failed to encompass Madeline. For a moment she seemed puzzled, faintly contemptuous.

Laura momentarily suspected that Saundra and Madeline might know each other, perhaps had met through Max, especially since Saundra's face held a rigid expression of not deigning to acknowledge Madeline. The woman's arrogance was infuriating.

Anger and liquor had robbed Laura of all caution. "What do you want, Saundra?" she heard herself ask. She wasn't quite sure why she bothered, unless it was just because of Saundra's nuisance value, or her own curiosity as to the outcome of this situation.

Saundra threw back her head and laughed coldly. "I think you know the answer to that. Let's not play games."

"Why not? Afraid you won't win this time?" Laura's quiet sarcasm shook Saundra's form-fitting composure ever so slightly.

"You are a miserable young snot, aren't you," she rasped.

"You're not so bad yourself," Laura parried.

Saundra stared at her with unblinking eyes.

For a moment Laura had the impression that she was a large, jeweled snake.

"I advise you to stay in your own backyard," the snake hissed softly. "With playmates more suited to your level." Her glance flicked over to Madeline, and the insult was unmistakable.

No one moved.

Saundra laughed maliciously and placed her hand on Ginny's shoulder possessively.

"Mrs. Van Norden is rather well known for her charity among lonely young women," Saundra baited venomously.

"You bitch!" Laura half rose from her chair. She found herself almost hypnotized by Saundra's dazzling viciousness—she could almost see the mechanism of that calculating brain making something sordid out of her relationship with Madeline.

"What would you know about charity, Saundra—or love, either, for that matter?"

"How clever you are." Saundra's reply was like the lash of a whip.

Laura ignored it. "What I might have felt for Ginny has nothing to do with my moving in with Madeline," Laura whispered hoarsely. "What happened between Ginny and me..." and suddenly Laura couldn't say anything more.

She could hear Saundra laughing, but she seemed miles away. It seemed to Laura that her brain had been turned inside out. She felt herself sit down, and she looked at Ginny, stared at her, tried to see through her.

But Ginny simply sat there and looked back at her. "You've been living with her ever since you arrived here?" Her tone was edged with reproof.

"There has been nothing between us," Laura said wearily, and felt as if she were lying. "Anyway, it's none of your business."

All at once Laura was struck by the peculiar paradox of her situation. In a way, there had been a great deal between her and Madeline. But nothing physical. It was only that she had needed Madeline, had needed her friendship, her understanding. Nothing more. What more could there have been? Nothing! Goddamn it, nothing!

Ginny stood up slowly. Laura watched her, unmoved. She was so filled with her own emotions that nothing else seemed to matter—she simply had to straighten herself out, had to put things back into some kind of order, some semblance of reality.

Reality. Madeline would give her that; she always had. Madeline could keep her in this world without making it impossible to endure...

"And to think that I chased you the way I did," Ginny pouted the way she would over a faulty purchase. "That I offered myself to you again because I thought you would be different, would have learned about yourself—I even kidded myself into thinking you would be everything I'd ever want or need." Tears welled up in her eyes. "You even sat there and let me...let me suggest we try again."

"That'll be enough, Ginny!" Laura snapped angrily. She wished to hell that Ginny would shut up and stop making an ass of herself. But that wasn't it, either. It was more that she herself felt like an even bigger ass for once having loved this shell of a human being. She wanted to get away from the sight of Ginny...and Saundra. Away from the sickness of it all.

It didn't seem to matter to Ginny that Saundra was there and heard all she said. Ginny sobbed, "All right, then. You keep your affair! I'll keep mine and we'll be square. But can't we see each other once in a while? Can't..."

"Oh, Christ!" Laura cursed aloud. "All of a sudden I'm the most wonderful thing that ever happened to you. How come? We'll double-date, Ginny. All right? On all the legal holidays—just the four of us."

"But, Laura..."

"But what?" Laura asked without expecting an answer. She stood up and hastily put on her coat, motioning to Madeline to do the same. It didn't occur to her to inquire if Madeline wanted to leave or not—she was leaving and that automatically meant that Madeline would leave, too.

She roughly pushed Madeline in front of her, and they exited, leaving Saundra and Ginny to complete their little drama alone.

Laura experienced an inexplicable sense of relief, as if a great, pressing weight had somehow been lifted from her. She no longer had to feel guilty for having run away, or think that she'd genuinely hurt Ginny. And she was no longer burdened with her love for Ginny.

There was a kind of justice in what had transpired. Laura had the fatalistic sensation that life had evened itself out. She was certain now that Saundra and Ginny deserved each other in some neurotic way. Saundra talked of love as if it were chattel to be bargained for—bought and sold and bought again. And Ginny made it sound like a necessary evil—a sexual and economic convenience that would last until the next conquest, a new sponsor for her aspirations and random passions.

She glanced over at Madeline, walking beside her. The look of concern and unhappiness on her face surprised Laura. It's been a rough night for her too, she thought, suddenly stricken with the cruelty of her own self-absorption. But she found Madeline's pained look oddly pleasing.

Let her suffer a little, Laura thought with a trace of sadism.

She wasn't sure why she wanted Madeline to suffer at all, unless it was because Laura believed that she had known all along that Laura's "torch" had been in vain, that what Laura had been going through was not really the agonies of denied love.

They walked silently and slowly. It was almost as if they would lose something if they walked too quickly or arrived too soon at the apartment. Something that was hanging, waiting to be said or understood... Something Laura was convinced she knew but couldn't think clearly enough to force into the open.

Arriving at the apartment, they entered wordlessly.

At last, Madeline broke the long silence.

"I'm sorry, Laura. Really sorry." Her voice was low and tender.

"Why?" Laura asked abruptly.

"If...if Ginny hadn't thought that there had been something between us, you might have...won her." Madeline said it as if there were no other way to describe Ginny.

Laura shook her head. "You might still," Madeline continued to soothe. "You could call her later, after...things cool off a little...."

"But I don't want to," Laura interrupted vehemently. "Not now, not later...not ever!"

Madeline sat down and stared at Laura. "What do you mean? After all these weeks of...of denying yourself your big chance at happiness, and you don't want it any more?"

Laura turned and looked at Madeline, appraised her as if really seeing her for the first time.

"That's right."

"But..." Madeline protested.

Laura grinned. "All I want to know is how long you've known."

"Known? "Known what?"

Laura didn't answer at once—she was glimpsing now what it was she had felt on the way home and had been unable to mask. "How long have you known that my torch had gone out?"

"Oh...that!" Madeline said. It seemed to Laura that she sounded both disappointed and relieved. "Does it matter, Laura?"

"Not really," Laura answered honestly. "Did you arrange for us all to meet tonight?"

"Of course not," Madeline replied indignantly. Then she laughed. "But the idea did occur to me."

Laura walked over to where Madeline sat, and perched on the arm of her chair. She could feel Madeline tense up. But she offered no comfort; she was enjoying her moment of revenge, of having Madeline in the position that Laura herself had occupied so many times herself.

"There is something else I'd like to know," she said with a half-amused tone, despite the fact that she was actually very serious and felt strangely elated.

Madeline didn't move, didn't even raise her head to look at Laura. "What's that?" she asked in a whisper.

"How long you've known that I would fall in love with you."

Laura's voice was low, and she could feel her temples throbbing. She leaned close toward Madeline, feeling her warmth and drawing a secure kind of comfort from it—a feeling of complete naturalness.

Calm, poised Madeline looked up with moist eyes. "I didn't know..." she said tightly. "I only hoped. Oh, God! How I hoped."

"And now—what happens now?"

"What do you want to happen now, Laura?"

She looked hard into Madeline's dark, questioning eyes. The love she saw there was so undemanding, so real and simple, that Laura felt herself filled, tranquilized with trust and security.

She took Madeline's face into her hands and kissed her forehead gently, then her eyes and the tip of her nose. "I'm going to let myself go and love you—and never lose you."

Laura touched her cheek to Madeline's, then reached for the slim, vibrant body. She could feel their bodies merge, their hearts pounding against each other. Their flesh leaped with the excitement that charged through them, intermingling.

Laura clung to her—motionless, savoring the painful sweetness. "Are you going to kiss me, or are you going to torture me to death?" Madeline asked huskily.

"Both," whispered Laura.

She pulled Madeline's warm searching mouth to hers. The shock of pleasure was almost unbearable. All consciousness was blotted out in that first drowning moment.

The last thing Laura remembered before she went under was thinking how wonderful it was not to feel guilty anymore—or unwanted...or strange.

She was where she wanted to be at last.

She was home.

She came to Greenwich Village and found the love that smolders in the shadows of the twilight world

Beebo Brinker

by Ann Bannon

She landed in New York, fresh off the farm, the hayseed still showing—along with the bewilderment and desperation of a girl whose only certainty was that she was "different" from other girls with their…healthy flirtations with normal young men.

That was the Beebo Brinker who slowly, searchingly came to know what she was and finally discovered the kind of love she needed—in a whirlwind affair with a famous Hollywood beauty, an affair that was as dangerous as it was glamorous. But Beebo was young and innocent. She knew only that she was in heaven—and never once considered that it might turn into a fool's paradise.

Beebo Brinker

The bartender brought her another drink while she searched for the last cigarette in her pack. It was empty. The girl sitting next to her immediately offered her one, but Beebo declined. It was partly her shyness, partly the knowledge that it was better to be hard-to-get in the Colophon.

"Do you have cigarettes?" she asked the bartender.

"Machine by the wall," he said.

She got up and sauntered over, ignoring the outrage on the face of the girl at the bar. The machine swallowed her coins and spit out a pack of filter-tips. Beebo noticed the juke box, looked at her change, and fed it a quarter, good for three dances. She liked to watch the girls move around the floor together, now that the initial revolt had worn off.

But when she regained her seat, she found most of the patrons paying attention to her, not the tunes. She looked back at them, surprised and wary. The cigarettes in her hand were an excuse to look away for a minute and she did, lighting one while the general conversation died away like a weak breeze. She lowered her match slowly and glanced up again, her skin prickling. What in hell were they trying to do? Scare her out? Show her they didn't like her? Had she been too aloof with them, too remote and hard to know?

She had started the music, and it was an invitation to dance. They were waiting for her to show them. It wasn't hostility she saw on their faces so much as, "Show us, if you're so damn big and smart. We've been waiting for a chance to trap you. This is it."

She had to do something to humanize herself. There was an air of self-confidence and sensual promise about Beebo that she couldn't help. And when she felt neither confident nor sensual, she looked all the more as if she did: tall and strong and coolly sure of herself. She had turned the drawback of being young and ignorant into a deliberate defense.

It didn't matter to the sophisticated girls judging her now that she was a country girl fresh from the hayfields of Wisconsin, or that she had never made love to a woman before in her life. They didn't know that and wouldn't have believed it anyway.

Beebo recognized quickly that she had to start acting the way she looked. She had established a mood of expectation about herself, and now it was time to come across. The music played on. It was Beebo's turn.

The match she held was burning near her finger, and because she had to do something about *it* and all the eyes on her, she turned to the girl beside her and held out the match.

"Blow," she said simply, and the girl, with a smile, blew.

Beebo returned the smile. "Well," she said in her low voice, which somehow carried even into the back room and the dance floor, "I'm damned if I'm going to waste a good quarter." She got up and walked across the room toward the prettiest girl she could see, sitting at a table with her lover and two other couples. It was exactly the way she would have reacted to student-baiting at Juniper Hill High. The worse it got, the taller she walked. Her heart was beating so hard she wanted to squeeze it still. But she knew no one could hear it through her chest.

She stopped in front of the pretty girl and looked at her for a second in incredulous silence. Then she said quietly, "Will you dance with me, Mona?"

Mona Petry smiled at her. Nobody else in Greenwich Village would have flouted the social code that way: walked between two lovers and taken one away for a dance. Mona took a leisurely drag on her cigarette, letting her pleasure show in a faint smile. Then she stood up and said, "Yes. I will, Beebo." Her lover threw Beebo a keen, hard look and then relapsed into a sullen stare.

Beebo and Mona walked to the floor single file, and Mona turned when she got clear of the tables, lifting her arms to be held. The movement was so easy and natural that it excited Beebo and made her bold—she who knew nothing about dancing. But she was not lacking in grace or rhythm. She took Mona in a rather prim embrace at first, and began to move her over the floor as the music directed.

Mona disturbed her by putting her head back and smiling up at her. At last she said, "How did you know my name?"

"Pete Pasquini told me," Beebo said. "How did you know mine?"

"Same answer," Mona laughed. "He gets around, doesn't he?"

"So they say," Beebo said.

"You mean you don't know from personal experience?"

"Me?" Beebo stared at her. "Should I?"

Mona chuckled. "No, you shouldn't," she said.

"Did I—take you away from something over there?" Beebo said.

"From some*body*," Mona corrected her. "But it's all right. She's deadly dull. I've been waiting for you to come over."

Beebo felt her face get warm. "I didn't even see you until I stood up," she said.

"I saw you," Mona murmured. They danced a moment more, and Beebo pulled her closer, wondering if Mona could feel her heart, now bongoing under her ribs, or guess at the racing triumph in her veins.

"Did you ask Pete about me?" Mona prodded.

"A little," Beebo admitted. And was surprised to find that the admission felt good. "Yes," she whispered.

"What did he say?"

"He said you were a wonderful girl."

"Did you believe him?"

Beebo hesitated and finally said, huskily, "Yes."

"You're a good dancer, Beebo," Mona said, knowing, like an expert, just how far to go before she switched gears.

"I dance like a donkey," Beebo grinned, strong enough in her victory to laugh at herself.

"No, you're a natural," Mona insisted. "A natural dancer, I mean."

"I don't care what you mean, just keep dancing," Beebo said.

Mona put her head down against Beebo's shoulder and laughed, and Beebo felt the same elation as a man when he has impressed a desirable girl and she lets him know it with her flattery. Mona—so elusive, so pretty, so dominant in Beebo's dreams lately. Beebo was holding her tighter than she meant to, but when she tried to loosen her embrace, Mona put both arms about her neck and pulled her back again.

For the first time, Beebo had the nerve to look straight at her. It was a long hungry look that took in everything: the long dark square-cut hair and bangs; the big hazel eyes; the fine figure, slim and exaggeratedly tall in high heels. But it was still necessary for her to look up at Beebo.

"It's nice you're so tall," Mona told her.

"Who's the girl you're with?" Beebo said. "I think she wants to drown me."

"No doubt. Her name's Todd."

"Is she a friend?"

"She was, till you asked for this dance," Mona smiled.

Beebo didn't want to make trouble. "I'm sorry," she said.

"Are you?" Mona was forward as only a world-weary girl with nothing to learn—or lose—could be. And yet she seemed too young for such ennui—still in her twenties. "Are you sorry about Todd?" she pressed Beebo.

"I'm not sorry I'm dancing with you, if that's what you mean," Beebo said.

"That's what I mean," Mona smiled. "Would you like to dance without an audience, Beebo?"

Beebo frowned at her. "You mean ditch your friends?"

Mona could see that Beebo was offended by such a suggestion of two-timing; and Mona was interested enough in this big, beautiful, strange girl not to want her offended. "They aren't true friends," Mona said plaintively, "that you can count on, anyway. It's all over between Todd and me, too. We just came here to bury the corpse tonight. This is where we met five months ago."

"Five months? That's not very long to be in love with somebody," Beebo said.

"I wasn't," Mona said.

"Was she?" It seemed indescribably sad to Beebo that one partner be in love and the other feel nothing. She wanted everyone to be happy on this night full of sequin-lights and clouds of music: even Todd.

"I never meant much to Todd," Mona said. "Talk about ditching, Beebo. I'm the one who's getting ditched."

"You?" Beebo held her tightly, glad for the excuse. "How could anyone ever do that to you?"

Mona swayed against her, smiling with her eyes shut, and Beebo was too immersed in her to notice the look on Todd's face.

"She likes to torment her lovers," Mona whispered. "She uses them, as if they were things. When she gets tired of them, she puts them in a drawer and pulls them out to show off, like trophies. That's all she does—collect broken hearts."

"She sounds like a female dog," Beebo commented. And yet the little speech recalled disturbingly some of Jack's remarks about Mona; as if Mona were amusing herself by describing her own faults to Beebo and pretending they were Todd's.

The music ended and they stood on the floor a moment, arms still clasped about each other. "Wait at the bar," Mona whispered into Beebo's ear. "I'll get my coat." Beebo glanced doubtfully at the table, but Mona said, "It'll be better if I tell her alone. Go on."

Beebo released her reluctantly, went to her seat, and sipped at her drink till Mona came up. She let Mona lead the way, feeling a sudden wild exhilaration as she followed, lighting a cigarette, holding the door for Mona, taking the street side when they reached the sidewalk.

"Was Todd angry?" she asked.

"No one wants to look the fool," Mona said lightly, with a smile.

"I'm sorry. I wouldn't like to get you up the creek, Mona," Beebo said. "I didn't want trouble."

"I make my own trouble, Beebo. I thrive on it. The way I see it—" she paused to give Beebo her arm, and Beebo took it smoothly, with a sense of power and burgeoning desire, "—life is flat and dreary without trouble." Mona dodged a puddle, then continued. "Good trouble. Exciting trouble. You can't just walk across the Flats forever, doing what's expected of you. Excitement. That's everything to me." Mona stopped in her tracks to look at Beebo with bright sly eyes. "Being good isn't exciting. Right?"

"I'm no philosopher," Beebo said.

"I'll prove it to you. You're a good person, aren't you? You felt bad about Todd. You've been good all your life. But are you happy?"

"I am right now. Are you telling me to be bad?" Beebo said, laughing.

"Would making love to me be bad?" Mona asked her, so directly that Beebo wondered if she were being made fun of. There was no respect in Mona for the innate privacy and mystery of every human soul. She saw them all as part of the Flats—unless they could make beautiful trouble with her. Then, she was interested. Then, she saw an individual.

"Making love to you," Beebo said slowly, "would have to be good."

"I'll make it better than good." Mona reached up for Beebo's shoulders, pulling her back into the dusk of a doorway. They stood there a moment, Beebo in a fever of need and fear, till Mona's hand slid up behind her head, cupped it downward, and brought their lips together.

Beebo came to life with a swift jerking movement. Mona's kiss had been light and brief, until Beebo caught her again in a violent embrace and imprisoned her mouth. She forgot everything for a few minutes, holding Mona there in her arms and kissing her lips, pressing her back against the doorway and feeling the whole length of her body against Beebo's own.

It wasn't till she became aware that Mona was protesting that she let her go. She stood in front of Mona, still trembling and weak-kneed, her breath coming fast and her head spinning, and she felt oddly apologetic. Mona had started it, but Beebo had carried it too far. "I'm sorry," she panted.

"Stop saying you're sorry all the time," Mona told her in a sulky voice. And, with a briskness that all but shattered the mood, she turned and started walking off, her heels snapping against the asphalt. Beebo stared after her, shocked. Was this the end of it?

But Mona turned back after a quarter of a block and called her. "You aren't going to spend the night there, are you?" she said crisply.

Beebo hurried after her, and they walked for two more blocks without exchanging a word. Beebo could only suppose she had done something wrong. Yet she didn't know what, or how to make amends.

Mona stopped at a brownstone house with six front steps. "I live here," she said.

Beebo glanced up at it. "Shall I leave?" she said.

"Do you want to?"

"Don't answer my questions with more questions!" Beebo said, a tide of anger releasing her tongue. "Damn it, Mona, I don't like evasions."

"All right. Don't go," Mona said, and smiled at the outburst. She went up the steps with Beebo coming uneasily behind her, opened the door, and went to the first-floor apartment in the back. At her door she pulled out her key and waited. Beebo was looking around at the hall, old and modest, but cleanly kept. The apartments in a place like this could be astonishingly chic. She had seen some belonging to Jack's friends.

Mona let her take it in till Beebo became aware of the silence and turned to her quizzically.

"Approve?" Mona said.

Beebo nodded, and Mona, as if that were the signal, turned the key in the lock. She walked over the threshold, switched on a light, and abruptly backed out again, preventing Beebo from entering.

"What's wrong?" Beebo said, surprised.

"There's someone in there," Mona said.

Without thinking, Beebo made a lunge for the door. She had thrown prowlers out of her father's house before. A situation like this scared her far less than being in that room alone with Mona—much as she wanted it.

But Mona caught her arm. "It's a friend of mine!" she hissed. "Beebo, please!" Beebo stopped, irritated, waiting for an explanation. "It's a girl. I told her Todd and I were breaking up," Mona shrugged. "I guess she came over to cheer me up. We've been friends a long time. Oh, it's nothing romantic, Beebo."

"Well, send her home," Beebo said. It was one thing to be afraid of Mona, but another entirely to forfeit the whole night in honor of a hen party.

"I can't." Mona looked up at her in pretty distress. "She's my one real friend and I owe her a lot. She's had some bad times in her own life lately. Beebo, look—here's my phone number. Call me in an hour.

Maybe we can still make it." She took a scratch pad from her purse and scribbled on it.

Beebo took it, feeling rebuffed and insulted. But Mona stood on tiptoes and kissed her lips again. And when Beebo refused to embrace her, Mona took her wrists and pulled them around her and gave Beebo a luxurious kiss. "Forgive me," she said. "It would be tough if she knew I'd brought someone home—it really would." She slipped out of Beebo's arms and put a hand on the doorknob. "Be sure to call me," she said. And then she disappeared inside her apartment.

Beebo stood in the hall a while, leaning on the dingy plaster and trying to make sense out of Mona. There was no sound from the apartment. Perhaps Mona and the girl had gone into a bedroom to talk. The idea made Beebo angry and jealous. She went slowly down the front hall. There was a pay phone by the entrance. Beebo went outside and sat on the front stoop for about forty-five minutes, and then went in to call.

She had lifted the telephone receiver and was about to drop in a dime, when she heard a bang from the end of the hall, as if someone had dropped something heavy. It seemed to come from Mona's door, and Beebo rushed toward it. But at the threshold, she froze.

Mona's voice, muffled as if through the walls of several rooms, but discernible, penetrated the wood. "And you! You sneak in here like a rat with the plague! God damn, how many times do I have to say it? *Call* first. Are you deaf or just stupid?"

Beebo's mouth opened as she strained to hear the answer. It came after a slight pause: "Rats don't scare you, doll. You already got the plague."

Beebo whirled away from the door as if she had been burned, and stood with her knuckles pressed angrily against her temples.

The voice belonged to a man.

It was several days before anything happened. Beebo went back to work as usual. There were no calls, no notes, no effort on Mona's part to get in touch with her and explain. Or apologize.

Beebo worked dully, but gratefully. Keeping busy was a balm to her nerves. She took pleasure in driving, taking corners faster and making deliveries in better time as she learned the routes. During the morning she took out groceries. In the afternoon, it was fresh-cooked, hot Italian food in insulated cartons.

Mona and her male visitor were on Beebo's mind so constantly that she didn't even take time to worry about Jack, or the possibility that he might fall in love with Pat. She saw them every evening, but said little and saw less.

She was full of a boiling bad temper: half-persuaded to go out on the town with as many girls as she could find, sure that Mona would hear about it; and half-toying with the idea of dating a man out of sheer spite. It would be nice irony—almost worth the embarrassment and social discomfort.

She was mad enough at Mona, in fact, to be nice to Pete. After all, Mona had stood him up too, long ago. He was still under her feet, and although he had never made any indecent proposals, he managed to always look as if he were just about to. Beebo was comforted to see that he gave the same look, and likely the same impression, to every woman in range of his sight, except his wife.

One day at noon, she went deliberately to the table in the kitchen where he was eating and pulled up a chair, while Marie served them. Pete looked at her with his somber eyes and stopped munching for a minute. She ordinarily managed her schedule so she could eat before or after he did. Marie noticed the change, as she noticed everything, but whatever she thought, she kept her own counsel.

"How is it with Jack and Pat?" Marie said conversationally.

Beebo straightened around. "How did you know about that?" she said, surprised.

"They was in earlier. Pat says he knows about bugs. Maybe he can stomp out my roaches.... He is a nice boy? I never did trust blonds."

Beebo felt threatened, as if Marie had just announced the end of Beebo's life with Jack. "Sure. Very nice," she said, and swallowed her stew. She was conscious of Pete's piercing gaze on her face.

"So?" Marie said, nodding. "He got a friendly style."

Beebo recounted mentally her evenings in the past week. Since Jack and Pat had met they had been together every night. Pat was in the apartment all day—no matter what hour Beebo dropped in during her deliveries. What about his job? And Jack? Jack Mann was a charming and persuasive man, and the fact that his face was plain did not alter the fact that his strong body was clean and pleasing, nor that his wits were quick and could make you learn and laugh.

"What's the matter, Beebo? You don't like rabbit?"

She started at Pete's voice and pulled away. His face was too close. But she was glad for the diversion. He aimed a big spoon at her stew. "Maybe you like a cheese sandwich?"

"No, this is fine," she said, forcing a social smile...and then wishing it were possible to retract it. Pete was examining her curiously.

She ate with concentration for several moments, still seeing Pat and Jack in her mind's eye. Pat liked Jack already. He was afraid of the city, and he abominated his job. If he didn't get back to it fast, he wouldn't have it anymore, and she knew he didn't give a damn—as long as somebody fed and loved him. He was like a pet: a big lovable goddamn poodle. She knew his liking for Jack would grow to fondness, if not love. She could see it coming, especially at night when Jack let him talk his heart out. Nobody listened or comforted more intelligently than Jack.

And when they fall in love—then where do I go? Shack up with Mona and her stable of strange men? she wondered. Jack's remarks about Mona's past were haunting her days and ruining her nights.

"Beebo," said a quiet male voice into her ear. "You want the afternoon off?"

It was an indecent proposal, all right. His voice made it one.

"No thanks," she said frostily.

"You look bad."

"I'm all right," she snapped.

"You could've fooled me," he said. And when she didn't answer, he went on, unwilling to let the conversation die, "The way you was acting, I thought you was sick."

"Maybe I am," she said sardonically. "I've got the plague."

"The plague?" He stopped eating, his teeth poised around a bite, and grinned. "Plague, like the rats bring?"

"Yeah." Beebo frowned at him.

"I got a friend with an obsession about rats," he said. "You seen her in here once or twice. Mona. You know?" Beebo nodded, her eyes fixed on him. It was the longest she had looked at him squarely. "She tells every man she knows—and that's plenty—he's a rat. I asked her why once. Want to know what she said?" He paused, building suspense, while Beebo held her breath. "She says they're all hairy...filthy...and stupid. And they'll sleep with anything ain't already dead. You agree?" He grinned at her.

Beebo turned away. "I don't know any *men*," she said pointedly.

Pete threw his hands out. "Is that nice to say?" he demanded. "Jack, I can understand. All he got of man is his name. Your father, who knows? Another fag." Beebo got halfway out of her seat, but he protested elaborately at once. When she simmered down, he added confidentially, "But *me*...even Marie will admit that much, when she's feeling honest."

"Marie's in a position to have an opinion," Beebo said acidly. "But I don't think that's *it*."

Pete folded his arms on the table and leaned on them, unoffended. "You want to be in that position too, Beebo?"

"Not for a million bucks," she said, and drank down her milk in a gesture of scorn.

"I know a lot of good positions," he said cozily, laughing at her.

Beebo had enough sense not to get visibly angry; not to make a scene. It wasn't worth it and it would only tickle Pete. If it did no more than embarrass the two women, he would be satisfied.

She put her glass down. "What do you do with all your women, Pete?" she asked him, making no effort to keep her voice from Marie. "Line them up in half-hour shifts? It beats me how one mighty male can keep so many women happy."

She picked up her plate and took it to the sink.

Marie tossed her a grin. "You tell him, Beebo," she said. "To hear him talk, he's sold out till next March."

"I'm selling nothing, bitch," Pete told her sharply. "What I got, I give away."

"Listen to Robin Hood," Beebo cracked, and walked out of the kitchen toward the truck with a load of Marie's packaged foods. Pete followed her. Marie turned and took a step toward them, thought better of it, and returned to brood over the stove. Beebo could handle him. She didn't need any help.

In the parking area, Pete took some of the load from Beebo and helped her put it in the truck. "You think I brag a lot, Beebo?" he said.

"I think you're a creep," she said.

He waited a moment, chagrined but not about to show it. "That mean you don't like me?" he said finally.

"Let's drop it, Pete."

"You *do* like me?" he pestered her.

"What do you want, a friendship ring?" she demanded.

Pete shrugged, staring at the low clouds, taking out a toothpick to spear the food specks stuck in his white teeth. "Just an opinion," he said.

"I told you. That's Marie's department. Now, if you'll get out of my way, I have some deliveries to make."

He turned to her. "Everybody got an opinion, Beebo. You worked for me over two months now. So say it. Say the truth."

Beebo swallowed her aggravation. This was a game of wits, and the first man to blow off, lost. She put on the same casual cloak Pete was wearing. "You're my boss. You keep clear of me, I keep clear of you, and we get along."

"You make a big thing of keeping clear," he said. "I smell bad, or something?"

"I wouldn't know. I never get that close," Beebo said.

Something in his eyes made her swing up into the driver's seat with unusual speed. She started the motor, but he came around the truck and pulled her door open.

"You want to know where Mona hangs out?" he said.

Beebo set her jaw. "Not from you," she said tautly.

Pete grinned. "Why not? My information is as good as the next guy's."

It made Beebo wildly impatient. She gripped the steering wheel in hard hands. "You through now, Pete?" she said, gunning the motor.

But he stood there, angled into the truck doorway so that she couldn't move without bending some of his bones the wrong way.

"It's OK, Beebo, don't get sore," he said, and put a hand on her knee. She picked it up and dropped it like a knot of worms, and he laughed. "You know why I do that?" he asked. "'Cause you put on such a good show. It really bugs you, don't it? When I touch you."

"You get the hell out of my truck or I'll roll you flat!"

He chuckled again. "OK," he said. "I just got one piece of news for you, butch. Listen: 121 McDonald Street—Paula Ash. Tonight. For those as wants to locate Mona." He pulled away from the truck, and Beebo backed out in a rumble of dust and gravel.

It was nearly midnight before Beebo could bring herself to the McDonald Street address. She had debated it tempestuously throughout the evening, but without confiding in Jack. She could have gone to Mona's apartment instead, or called her and demanded an explanation. But something told her Pete Pasquini had an interesting motive for sending her here. She might get hurt; but she might also learn the truth, whatever that was, about Mona. So she took the chance.

She was in a don't-give-a-damn mood, expecting to find Mona with a man in the apartment, rented under an assumed name; or Mona making love to Paula Ash, whoever the hell she was; or even—best joke of all—Mona waiting for her alone, while Pete peeked through the keyhole.

She stood at 121 McDonald Street in a light drizzle, partially sheltered by an inset doorway, her hands shoved into the sleeves of her windbreaker, and tried to make up her mind to call the jest.

At last the chill drove her into the foyer to look at mailboxes. There was a Paula Ash, all right. Apartment 103. Beebo took a deep breath and pushed the buzzer.

The answer came after so long a wait that Beebo was just leaving in disgust, and had to turn back quickly to open the inner door. She had scarcely entered the hall when a door opened ahead and a girl looked out.

"Yes?" she said. She appeared very sleepy, as if she had been in bed for many hours already, even though it was not quite midnight.

"May I come in?" Beebo said. She walked down the hall looking Miss Ash over candidly. If Mona were going to stand her up, and Pete play jokes on her, the least she could do was fall into the pit with as much bravado as possible—and perhaps a pretty girl in her arms.

"I don't know," the girl said doubtfully, opening her eyes very wide as if the stretch would keep the lids up a few minutes more. "Who are you?"

"I'm Beebo." Beebo looked at her, standing about three feet away in the door, wondering if her name would register. The living room behind Paula looked inviting after the gray rain outside.

"Beebo Who?" The girl was beginning to wake up, staring at her visitor.

Beebo smiled. "Didn't Mona tell you?"

The girl gasped and rubbed her eyes open earnestly. "Mona!" she said, her voice husky. "Did Mona send you here?"

"Not exactly," Beebo said. "But I was made to think I'd find her here." The girl was so distressed that Beebo began to think Paula was the victim of whatever joke was afoot, and not herself. She was moved to apologize. "I'm sorry, Miss Ash," she said. "There must have been a mistake. I came expecting some sort of practical joke. I guess nobody let either one of us in on it."

"Will you come in, please," Paula Ash said unexpectedly. She was shy and looked at Beebo's shoulder when she spoke.

"Thank you," Beebo said, walking past her into the living room. "It's pretty cold outside." She took off her jacket and handed it to Paula, who hung it in her front closet.

"Will you have coffee?" Paula said.

"Thanks, that sounds good." Beebo watched her curiously while the girl busied herself in a small doorless kitchen. She had a delicately pretty face, different from Mona's slick good looks and more appealing to Beebo.

Paula ran an uneasy hand through her hair and bit her underlip as she stood by her stove, waiting for the water to boil. "Would you tell me," she asked timidly, "just what Mona told you?"

"I haven't seen Mona for a week," Beebo said. "A mutual acquaintance told me she'd be here tonight."

"Well, your mutual acquaintance has a queer sense of humor," Paula said. "Mona and I were never good friends. And lately we've been pretty good enemies."

"So that was it," Beebo said. "That's a hell of a note. I'm sorry, Miss Ash, I—"

"Paula, please. Oh, it wasn't your fault," Paula said. "Mona has done crazier things than meeting her new lovers in my living room. I've known her almost five years." She came back with two cups of hot coffee. She still seemed half-conscious, and when she stumbled a bit, Beebo got up and rescued the coffee.

Paula made a hissing sound of pain, pulling air between her teeth and looking at her left thumb.

"Did you scald it? Here. Under the cold water, quick." Beebo left the steaming cups on an end table and took Paula by the arm to the sink. She turned on the tap full force and held Paula's burn under the healing stream. Paula tried to pull away after a few seconds but Beebo held her securely. "Give it a good minute," she said.

And as they stood there, Beebo studied Paula at close range. She was a lovely-looking girl, even though she seemed *non compos* at the moment. "Are you sick, Paula?" Beebo asked kindly.

"No, no. Really. I'm just terribly tired. And then I took some sleeping pills. Probably too many. I haven't been sleeping well."

"If you're so tired, why do you take sleeping pills?" Beebo asked.

Paula's dainty face contracted around a private pain. "The doctor gave them to me. It's harder to sleep when you're too tired than when you're just tired." She weaved a little, and Beebo put an arm around her.

"Are you supposed to take so many they send you into a coma?"

"No. But one pill doesn't work. Three or four don't work anymore. I just keep swallowing them till I drop off."

"That's dangerous," Beebo said. "One of these days you'll drop too damn far." She turned the water off and reached for a paper towel, blotting the injured hand gently. Suddenly, to her dismay, Paula pulled her hands away and hid her face in them to cry. Beebo watched, frustrated with the wish to touch and comfort her.

Paula's sobs were short and hard, and she pulled herself together with a stout effort of will. All Beebo could see for a moment was the top of her head, covered with marvelous rich red hair. And, when she looked up, a trail of pale freckles across her cheeks and nose. Beebo handed her a tissue from her shirt pocket, and Paula blew her nose and wiped her eyes.

She was a fragile, very feminine and small girl, wearing a pair of outsized, plaid-print men's pajamas.

Beebo took a bit of sleeve between her fingers with a smile. "You always wear these?" she asked.

"Only lately. They aren't mine. A former roommate left them behind when she moved."

"Oh," Beebo said. "I didn't think they were your type."

"They're not. They're hers. And she's gone, and this is all I have left of her." Paula shook out her smoldering curls and cleared her throat. "I'm better now. Shall we have the coffee?" she said. It was obvious that she had humiliated herself with the unplanned personal admissions, and Beebo did her the courtesy of dropping the subject and joining her in the living room.

They drank the coffee in preoccupied silence a while. Beebo lighted a cigarette and offered it to Paula, who refused. Finally she said lightly, hoping to cheer Paula up, "Seems to me those pajamas are the answer to your insomnia."

"What? How?" Paula looked at her as if suddenly remembering her presence in a room where Paula had thought herself alone with a ghost.

"Switch to nighties—your own—and get some rest," Beebo said. "If I had to wear a plaid like that, I'd have nightmares all night."

Paula smiled wanly. "I know," she said. "They're silly. I just needed somebody else to say it, I guess. It's hard to break away from a person you've been close to. You hang on to the stupidest things."

"Well, her old sleep gear won't bring her any closer," Beebo said. She pulled a sleeve out full length. "Did she play basketball?" Beebo said, and they both laughed.

"She wasn't a shorty," Paula admitted. Her laughter made her wonderfully pretty. She stopped it suddenly to say, "That's the first time I've laughed in a month." She gazed at Beebo with grateful astonishment.

"Looks like I got here just in time," Beebo said, not realizing till after she spoke what a hoary come-on that was. Paula's pink blush clarified things for her.

"I suppose you want to be getting home," Paula said shyly, rising from her chair. She was struck for the first time with Beebo's size. Stretched across the sofa, with her long legs thrusting out from under the cocktail table, Beebo looked too big for a nine-by-twelve living room.

To her surprise, Beebo found she didn't want to be getting home at all; not even to run interference between Jack and Pat. And thinking of Pat brought a flash of recognition to her mind. "You remind me of a friend," she told Paula, sitting up to scrutinize her. "A boy named Pat. A lovable thing. Shy and just a little childish. In the nice way, I mean."

"I remind you of a *boy*?" Paula stared.

"More of a child than a boy."

Paula didn't know quite how to take it. "In the nice way?"

"Yes. Trusting, affectionate. Still curious about people and life. It's a very—endearing quality."

"And you think *I'm* like that?" Paula asked.

"You obviously don't," Beebo chuckled.

"I've been told I'm nasty and spoiled and selfish...childish in the bad way."

"Who told you that? Your friend with the plaid pajamas?"

"Yes."

"If you were that way with her, she must have done something to deserve it. You look like a natural-born angel to me," Beebo said, surprising them both with her frankness.

"That's a very nice thing for a stranger to say," Paula said. "Thank you."

"My pleasure," Beebo said, blanketing her sudden confusion with an offhand nod.

There was a pensive pause while Beebo tried to remember the books she had read about Lesbian love. It wasn't always a question of sweeping girls off their feet and carrying them away to bed, as Mona had made it seem at first. How did you approach a sensitive, well-bred girl like this one? Mow her down with kisses? Certainly not.

Beebo began to wonder how to make herself welcome for the night. It seemed far better than going back to Jack's and stewing again until dawn about her future. She would be leaving Jack and Pat alone together all night for the first time, and yet it seemed less painful now than it had before. It would suffice Beebo if she and Paula did nothing but sit and talk all night.

"I suppose somebody's waiting for you?" Paula said.

"Nobody."

Paula frowned at her. "Your roommate?" she asked.

"My roommate is having an affair with a man," Beebo said and shocked Paula, until Beebo smiled at her and made her think she was kidding.

"Well...Mona?" she asked.

"Mona could be on the moon for all I know. I thought I'd find her here."

"And now you're disappointed," Paula said diffidently.

"Not at all. I'm relieved."

Paula drained her coffee cup and put it down with a nervous clink. "It must be—awkward—if your roommate is really in love with somebody else," she said, in a voice so soft it was its own apology for speaking.

"It is," Beebo said. "I hate to go home. I'm too long to sleep on the damn sofa."

"I'm afraid you're too long for mine, too," Paula said. There was a pause. "But I could sleep on it and you could take my bed, if you will."

It was such a completely disarming—almost quaint—invitation that Beebo smiled at her, prickling with temptation. Paula's bashfulness was enough to make Beebo self-assured.

"At least you're not too long for the pajamas," Paula said.

"I can't put you out like that," Beebo said.

Paula was flustered. She looked at her hands. "I don't mind," she said. "It's long and I'm short. We're used to each other."

"You and the sofa?" Beebo said, and stood up. She went to the closet and found her jacket. You can't take somebody's bed away just because you told a lie about sleeping on your own sofa. She pulled the jacket on and zipped it.

"You're a sweet girl, Paula," she said, not looking at her. "Miss Plaid Pajamas must be nuts. Find somebody who deserves you, and she'll never make you sleep alone on the sofa."

She started for the door but Paula, recovering suddenly, jumped up and put a restraining hand on her arm. Beebo turned around, a shiver of sharp excitement radiating through her. She was not—she was *never*—as sure of herself as she seemed.

"Beebo," Paula said, whispering so that Beebo had to bend her head to hear her. "I'd like you to stay. Make yourself welcome. Please."

Beebo was afraid to believe her ears. It had seemed almost easy, in retrospect, to storm the Colophon. She was not unaware that Mona was something of a catch, and when she went over the events of that night, she was satisfied at the way she had acted. Nobody, not Mona herself, knew how inexperienced and uncertain Beebo was, and nothing she had done gave her away. Unless it was her exuberance when Mona kissed her.

But now it seemed incredible that this exquisite stranger should reach out for her from the middle of nowhere. "Paula," she said, "I think we're both just lonely. I think it would be best if I go. You don't want to wake up tomorrow and hate yourself." She was still hedging about the ultimate test with a girl.

"I *was* lonely. I will be again if you go."

"Maybe you'd be better off lonely than sorry."

"Beebo, do I have to beg you?" Paula pleaded, her voice coming up stronger with her emotion.

Beebo reached for her in one instinctive motion, suddenly very warm inside her jacket. "No, Paula, you don't have to beg me to do anything. Just ask me."

"I did. And you didn't want to stay."

"I didn't want to scare you. I didn't understand."

"I thought it was Mona. She can make herself so—so tempting."

"I can't even remember what she looks like."

"Aren't you in love with her?"

Beebo's hands, with a will of their own, closed around Paula's warm slim arms. "I met her last week for the first time. You can't be in love with someone you just met."

"You can't?" Paula demurred cautiously, looking down at her big pajamas.

"I never was," Beebo said, feeling sweat break out on her forehead. She pulled gently on Paula and was almost dismayed when Paula moved docilely toward her. Beebo became feverishly aware that the plaid pajamas did not conceal all of Paula Ash. The sweeping curve of her breasts held the cotton top out far enough to brush Beebo's chest with a feather touch. Beebo felt it through the layers of her clothes with a tremor so hard and real it tumbled eighteen years of daydreams out of her head.

She held Paula at arm's length a moment, looking at this lovely little redheaded princess with a mixture of misgivings and want too powerful to pretend away. Paula took her hands and held them with quivering strength, returning Beebo's gaze. Beebo saw her own doubts reflected in Paula's eyes. But she saw desire there, too; desire so big that it had to be brave: it hadn't any place to hide.

Paula kissed Beebo's hands with a quick press of her mouth that electrified Beebo. She stood there while Paula kissed them over and over again and a passionate frenzy mounted in them both. Paula's lips, at first so chaste, almost reverent, warmed against Beebo's palms...and then her kitten-tongue slipped between Beebo's fingers and over the backs of her broad hands until those hands trembled perceptibly and Paula stopped, clutching them to her face.

Beebo reclaimed them, but only to caress Paula's face, bringing it close to her and seeing it with amazement.

"I never guessed I'd feel love for the first time through my hands," she murmured. "Paula, Paula, I would have done this all wrong if you hadn't had the guts to start it for me. I would have manhandled you, I—"

Paula stilled her with a finger over Beebo's mouth. "Don't talk now," she said.

And Beebo, who had never done more than dream before, slipped her arms around Paula and pulled her tight. It was a marvel the way their bodies fitted together; the way Paula's head tipped back naturally at so beckoning an angle, and rested on Beebo's arm; the way her eyes closed and her lips parted and her hair scattered like garnet petals around her flower-face.

Beebo kissed her mouth and kissed her mouth again, holding her against the wall with the pressure of her body. Paula submitted with a sort of wistful abandonment. Everywhere Beebo touched this sweet girl, she found thrilling surprises. And Paula, coming to life beneath Beebo's searching hands, found them with her.

It was no news to Beebo that she was tall and strong and male-inclined. But her voluptuous reaction to Paula shocked her speechless. Paula began to undress her and Beebo felt herself half-fainting backwards on the sofa into a whirlpool of sensual delight. The merest touch, the merest flutter of a finger, and Beebo went under, hearing her own moans like the whistle of a distant wind. Paula had only to undo a belt buckle or pull off a shoe, and Beebo responded with a beautiful helpless fury of desire.

It was no longer a question of proceeding with caution, of "learning how." The whole night passed like an ecstatic dream, punctuated with a few dead-asleep time-outs, when they were both too exhausted to move, even to make themselves comfortable.

Beebo had only a vague idea of what she was doing, beyond the overwhelming fact that she was making ardent love to Paula. She seemed to have no mind at all, or need of one. She was aware only that Paula was beautiful, she was gay, she was warmly loving, and she was there in Beebo's arms: fragrant and soft and auburn-topped as a bouquet of tiger lilies.

Beebo couldn't let her go. And when fatigue forced her to stop she would pull Paula close and stroke her, her heavy breath stirring Paula's glowing hair, and think about all the girls she had wanted and been denied. She was making up, this night, for every last one of them.

Paula whispered, "Do you still believe you can't love someone you just met?"

"I don't know what I believe anymore."

And Paula said, "I love you, Beebo. Do you believe that?"

Beebo lifted Paula's fine face and covered it with kisses while Paula kept repeating, "I love you, I love you," until the words—the unadorned words—brought Beebo crashing to a climax, rolling over on Paula, embracing her with those long strong legs.

She felt Paula sobbing in the early dawn and raised up on an elbow to look at her. "Darling, did I hurt you?" she asked anxiously, not stopping to think that she had never called a girl "darling" before, either.

"No," Paula said. "It's just—I've been so unhappy, so confused. I thought the world had ended a month ago, and tonight it's just beginning. It's brand new. I'm so happy it scares me."

Beebo held her tenderly and brushed the tears off her cheeks. Paula put her head in the crook of Beebo's arm and gazed at her. "You must have been born making love, Beebo."

"How do you know?" Beebo had no intention of setting the record straight just then.

"I don't, really. It's just that I never reacted to anybody the way I have to you. I never did this with anybody before."

"Never made love?" Beebo said, surprised almost into laughter. *The blind leading the blind,* she thought.

"No, I've made love before," Paula said thoughtfully. "With men, too. It's just that I never.... You'll think I'm making this up, but it's the truth. I never—oh, God help me, I'm frigid. I mean, I was, till tonight."

Beebo lay there in the dark, holding her, torn between the wish to accept it and the suspicion that she was fibbing.

"You don't believe me," Paula said resignedly. "I shouldn't have told you. It's enough that it happened."

Beebo petted her, smoothing her hair and letting her hands glide over Paula's silky body. "OK, you never came before," she said. "Now I'll tell you a fish story. I never made love before."

Paula laughed good-naturedly. "All right, we're even," she said. "That's a real whopper. Mine was the truth."

Beebo laughed with her, and it didn't matter anymore whether she had been lied to or not. It was the truth in spirit, and only Paula knew if it was the truth in fact. Her attraction to Beebo was so real that it took shape in the night, surrounding her like the aura of her perfume. Beebo kissed her while she was still laughing. "You have such a mouth, Paula. Such a mouth..."

"Does it please you?"

"You please me. All of you," Beebo said, and she meant it. Paula was wholly feminine, soft and submissive. She was finely constructed, looking somehow as breakable, as valuable—and as durable—as Limoges china. Beebo wanted to protect her, accomplish things for her.

She kept touching her admiringly. "You're so tiny," she said. "I'm going to feed you lasagna and put some meat on your bones."

"Will you buy me a new wardrobe when I get too fat for my old one?"

"I'll buy you anything. Mink coats. Meals at the Ritz. New York City," Beebo said.

"All of it?"

"Just the good parts."

Paula clutched at her suddenly, first laughing, then trembling. "Beebo, don't leave me," she said. "I do love you." She seemed dumbfounded. "It frightens me, it makes me believe all over again in my childhood dreams. Did you ever feel like that?"

"Only on the bad days. My childhood wasn't that pretty," Beebo said.

"When are the bad days?"

"Never anymore. Not with Paula around."

They got up at noon the next day, and it was some time before Beebo could think rationally about her job. She should call Marie, she should call Jack and tell him where she was. But it was impossible to get out of the bed while Paula was in it. And every time Paula sat up, Beebo pulled her down.

"Let me make breakfast," Paula smiled, and after wrestling a moment, pulled free and scampered halfway across the bedroom, pulling a sheet after her. She stood with her dazzling naked back, delicately sugared with freckles, to Beebo, who admired it in infatuated silence.

Paula ruffled through her closet looking for a negligee until Beebo said, "Paula, are you in love with me or that sheet?"

"I don't want you to see me," Paula confessed. "You said I was too thin."

"I said 'tiny.' And beautiful. Honey, I felt you all over; I know you with my hands. Would it be so awful if I know you with my eyes, too?" When Paula hesitated, Beebo threw the covers off and stood by the bed.

Paula studied her in silence. "You're wonderful," she breathed at last.

"I'm homely," Beebo answered. "But I'm not ashamed of it."

"You are many things, Beebo, but homely isn't one of them," Paula declared. She faced Beebo sheet-first, like a highborn Roman girl in her wedding chiton. "How many girls have admired you like this?"

"Never a one," Beebo said. She crossed the room toward Paula and saw her flinch. "Are you afraid of me?" she said, surprised.

"A little."

"No, Paula." Beebo reached her, touching her with gentle hands. "I'd never hurt you. Don't you know that?"

"Not with your hands, maybe," Paula said, bending her graceful neck to kiss one. "But I'm so in love...it would take so little. And scores of other girls must want you, Beebo. It would hurt me awfully if you ever wanted *them*."

"What girls?" Beebo scoffed.

"Well, for a starter—Mona."

"Paula, I kissed Mona twice. She stood me up twice. That's the end of that," Beebo said flatly. Abruptly, she pulled Paula's sheet off and gazed delightedly on the fresh fair curves beneath. And before Paula had time to blush, Beebo picked her up, grateful at last for the uncomely strength in her arms, and placed her on the bed.

"Beebo," Paula whispered, her arms locked tightly around Beebo's neck. "How old are you?"

Beebo couldn't blurt idiotically, "Eighteen." Instead she asked, "How old do I look?"

"Like a college kid," Paula sighed. "Which makes me older than you. I'm twenty-five, Beebo."

"An ancient ruin." Beebo kissed her nonchalantly, but she was secretly surprised. Nonetheless it pleased her to have won an older girl.

They made love again, lazily now. There was no wild rush, no fear on Beebo's part that it would hurt and disillusion her. They rolled in caresses like millionaires in blue chips...ran their fingers over each other, and kissed and tickled and laughed and blew in each other's ears.

And all the while Paula kept repeating, with the transparent affection that is the crown of femininity, "I love you, Beebo. I love you so much."

Beebo couldn't answer. She couldn't have been happier, or hotter, or more rapturously charmed with the girl. She could hardly believe she had found one so lovely, so generous, so responsive, so single.

But there was a lot of roaming restless curiosity in Beebo, and while she was willing and eager to make love to and romanticize Paula, she was not willing to fall in love with her.

It wasn't Paula's fault, though Paula, with a woman's quick awareness of emotions, sensed the situation. It was just that Beebo wasn't ready for it. Paula had come too early in Beebo's life. And that fact alone made Paula realize how young Beebo must be.

Beebo had caught Paula in a vulnerable state, on the rebound from an unhappy love affair with the girl in the plaid pajamas. But it was the culmination of a lot of bad affairs with both sexes that had left Paula drained and skeptical; hopeless about her future and unable to cope with her present. She had nearly taken the whole bottle of sleeping pills the night before, instead of the four that knocked her out.

Beebo was too good to be true, too young to know herself, too masculine to be faithful. But how strong she was, how sensual and sure; in some ways, wise beyond her years with that hard-won maturity Jack had perceived months before.

Paula tried to tell herself, as she lay in Beebo's embrace, that she had nothing more than a hot crush that would end as suddenly as it began, and make her laugh to think she had called it love. She wanted very much to believe it, because it would have spared her the pain of losing Beebo Brinker to another girl—a pain she was in no condition to take safely then.

They ate together in Paula's kitchen, and Paula obligingly sat on Beebo's lap and let Beebo feed her. They were enchanted with each other. It was the kind of day everybody ought to have once in a while; if you knew it was coming, you could bear the boredom and solitude in the interim.

Paula told Beebo about her young years in Washington, D.C., and the shock that accompanied her suspicions that she was a Lesbian.

Because it was Paula speaking, and because Beebo had never talked heart-to-heart with another Lesbian, the story seemed remarkable. She held Paula on her knees, answering with sympathy and affection, troubled and touched by it...and stirred by the warmth of Paula's close, firm bottom.

They were startled when the phone cut in on them late in the afternoon.

Paula answered it over Beebo's protests. "Hello?" she said, and as she listened her eyes went to Beebo in surprise. Finally she held out the receiver. "It's for you," she said. "Jack Mann."

Beebo stood up, concerned. "How did he know I was here?"

"You're his roommate, he says. Roommates ought to keep track of each other," Paula said, teasing but with just a trace of chill in her voice. "Why didn't you tell me you were straight, Beebo?"

Beebo took the phone with a comical grimace. "You would have guessed, anyway," she said. "Hey—do you know Jack?"

"Everybody knows Jack," said Paula.

Into the receiver Beebo said, "Jackson?"

"I hear you've been out stupefying the female population of Greenwich Village," Jack said. "You must have something. Paula's usually a deep freeze."

"How did you know I was here?" Beebo said.

"My spies are everywhere. And a damn good thing, too. I would have given you up for dead. Listen, pal, I just got an S.O.S. from Marie. There's a very large customer on Park Avenue who wants a very large pizza right now. Marie is whipping it up and Beebo will whip it over to said customer."

"Park Avenue is Pete's territory," Beebo said. "He won't like it."

"He's out somewhere, as usual. Marie can't find him and besides, she's afraid to look."

"You want me to leave now?" Disappointment growled in her voice.

"I know Paula, honey; she's a good girl. If she likes you enough to sleep with you, she likes you enough to wait for you."

"You mean you knew this beautiful girl all along and didn't tell me about her?" Beebo said, grinning at Paula.

"Well, hell, you waited two months to tell me you *wanted* one. Come on, Marie's in a hurry. Show her what you're made of."

"I'm made of sugar and spice, like the rest of the girls," Beebo said sourly. "It doesn't mix with cheese and anchovies."

"Get your ass over there, Beebo," Jack said. "This order goes to Venus Bogardus."

The name rang in Beebo's head. "The actress?" she said, frowning. "She's not one of our customers."

"She is now."

"But Jack, my God. Venus Bogardus!"

"The original. The girl with the bosom that just won't stop. Can you take it?"

"It's worth it just for a look," Beebo grinned. "OK, call Marie and tell her I'm coming. And Jack—I know I should have called you. I'm sorry."

Beebo hung up and walked to Paula, expecting to embrace her and explain. But Paula was quite pale. "What's all this about Pete and Marie? Do you mean the Pasquinis?"

"Yes. I work for them. Marie wants me to deliver a pizza to—"

"—to Venus Bogardus. I heard. Beebo, why didn't you tell me about Pete?"

"There's nothing to tell," Beebo said, mystified. "Honey, are you mad at me? Why?"

"Pete and Mona are thick as thieves. What Mona does, Pete does; what Mona thinks, Pete thinks—unless they're quarreling. If they don't like you, they'd as soon exterminate you. They wouldn't cut you down if you were hanging."

Beebo laughed a little at this explosion. "I know you don't like Mona, honey. But Pete's just a twerp. He's the one who sent me over here last night. I'll admit it wasn't exactly ethical."

"Then Mona knows you're here. How charming," Paula said sourly.

"So what's Mona, the Wicked Witch?" Paula scowled and Beebo said, "OK, Pete's a slob; and my opinion of Mona is slipping fast. But I can't be mad at anybody who sent me to you, Paula, no matter what their motives were."

"Now they'll do everything to take you away from me," Paula said, looking fearfully at Beebo.

"There's no way they could do that, sweetheart," Beebo said, pulling Paula down beside her on the bed. "Paula, I'll be back in an hour. I won't do anything but deliver the pizza."

Paula clung to her. "Promise," she said. "And if Milady Bogardus walks into the room, you have to shut your eyes and run."

"At the same time?"

"Yes."

"You want me to break my neck?" Beebo laughed.

"Better your neck than my heart," Paula whispered.

At the door Beebo took Paula's hands and kissed them the way Paula had first kissed hers. "I never liked Venus Bogardus," she said. "I read somewhere that her curves are built into her clothes. She's about as sexy as a hat rack under the finery—and a cool forty-eight years old."

"Come back," Paula said seriously. "That's all I ask."

They parted and Beebo left the building with a soaring pride and satisfaction that seemed to lift her clear off the pavement.

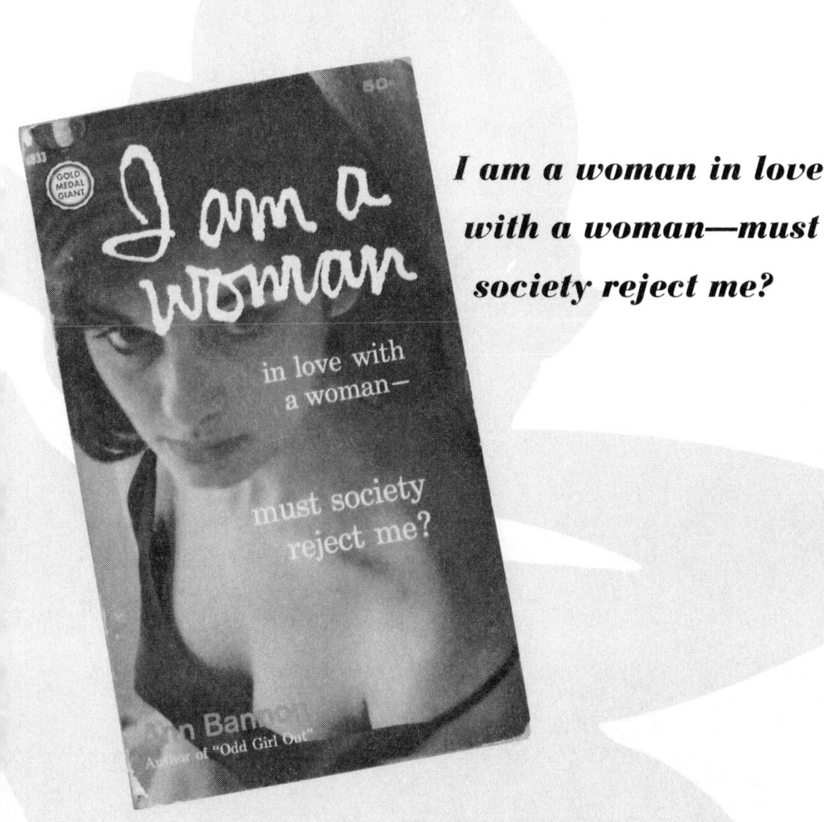

I am a woman in love with a woman—must society reject me?

I Am a Woman

by Ann Bannon

Home to Laura was not an apartment or a house with a fashionable address. Home was a dimly lit and badly ventilated bar on a back street in Greenwich Village. She understood the customs. Only forbidden desires were recognized and love rarely lasted more than a night. The tormented and lost women met there, and Laura, slim and boyish, found happiness for the first time in her life.

I Am a Woman

Laura had to look then. She turned her head slowly, reluctantly. Her face was cold and composed. Beebo chuckled at her. She was handsome, like a young boy of fourteen, with her smooth skin and deep blue eyes. She was leaning on her elbows on the bar, and she looked sly and amused. "Laura's afraid of me," she said with a quick grin.

"Laura's not afraid of you or anybody else. Laura thinks you're a bitch. That's all."

"That makes two of us."

Under her masklike face Laura found herself troubled by the smile so close to her; the snapping blue eyes.

"Where's your guardian angel tonight?" Beebo said.

"I suppose you mean Jack. I don't know where he is, he doesn't have to tell me where he goes." She turned back to the bar. "He's not my guardian angel. I don't need one. I'm a big girl now."

"Oh, excuse me. I should have noticed."

Laura's cheeks prickled with embarrassment. "You only see what you want to see," she said.

"I see what I want to see right now," Beebo said, and Laura felt her hand on the small of her back. She straightened suddenly.

"Go away," she said sharply. "Leave me alone."

"I can't."

"Then shut up."

Beebo laughed softly. "What's the matter, little girl? Hate the world tonight?" Laura wouldn't answer. "Think that's going to make it any prettier?" Beebo pushed Laura's whisky glass toward her with one finger.

"I'm having a drink for the hell of it," Laura said briefly. "If it bothers you, go away. You weren't invited, anyway."

"Don't tell me you're drinking just because you like the taste."

"I don't mind it."

"You're unlucky in love, then. Or you just found out you're gay and you can't take it. That it?"

Laura pursed her lips angrily. "I'm not in love. I never was."

"You mean love is filth and all that crap? Love is dirty?"

"I didn't say that!" Laura turned on her.

Beebo shrugged. "You're a big girl, lover. You said it yourself. Big girls know all about love. So don't lie to me."

"I didn't ask you to bother me, Beebo. I don't want to talk to you. Now scram!"

"There she stands at the bar, drinking whisky because it tastes good," Beebo drawled, gazing toward the ceiling and letting the smoke from a cigarette drift from her mouth. "Sweet sixteen and never been kissed."

"Twenty," Laura snapped.

"Excuse me, twenty. Your innocence is getting tedious, lover." She smiled.

"Beebo, I don't like you," Laura said. "I don't like the way you dress or the way you talk or the way you wear your hair. I don't like the things you say and the money you throw around. I don't want your dimes and I don't want you. I hope that's plain because I don't know how to make it any plainer." Her voice broke as she talked and toward the end she felt her own crazy tears coming up again. Beebo saw them before they spilled over and they changed her. They touched her. She ignored the hard words Laura spoke, for she knew enough to know they meant nothing.

"Tell me, baby," she said gently. "Tell me all about it. Tell me you hate me if it'll help."

For a moment Laura sat there, not trusting her, not wanting to risk a word with her, letting the stray tears roll over her cheeks without even brushing them away. Then she straightened up and swept them off her face with her long slim fingers, turning away from Beebo. "I can't tell you, or anybody."

Beebo shrugged. "All right. Have it your way." She dinched her cigarette and leaned on the bar again, her face close to Laura's. "Try, baby," she said softly. "Try to tell me."

"It's stupid, it's ridiculous. We're complete strangers."

"We aren't strangers." She put an arm around Laura and squeezed her a little. Laura was embarrassed and grateful at the same time. It felt good, so good. Beebo sighed at her silence. "I'm a bitch, you're right about that," she admitted. "But I didn't want to be. It's an attitude. You develop it after a while, like a turtle grows a shell. You need it. Pretty soon you live it, you don't know any other way."

Laura finished her drink without answering. She put it down on the bar and looked for the bartender. She wouldn't care what Beebo said, she wouldn't look at her, she wouldn't answer her. She didn't dare.

"You don't need to tell me about it," Beebo went on. "Because I already know. I've lived through it, too. You fall in love. You're young, inexperienced. What the hell, maybe you're a virgin, even. You fall, up to your ears, and there's nobody to talk to, nobody to lean on. You're all alone with that great big miserable feeling and she's driving you out of your mind. Every time you look at her, every time you're near her. Finally you give in to it—and she's straight." She said the last word with such acid sharpness that Laura jumped. "End of story," Beebo added. "End of soap opera. Beginning of soap opera. That's all the Village is, honey, just one crazy little soap opera after another, like Jack says. All tangled up with each other, one piled on top of the next, ad infinitum. Mary loves Jane loves Joan loves Jean loves Beebo loves Laura." She stopped and grinned at Laura.

"Doesn't mean a thing," she said. "It goes on forever. Where one stops another begins." She looked around The Cellar with Laura following her gaze. "I know most of the girls in here," she said. "I've probably slept with half of them. I've lived with half of the half I've slept with. I've loved half of the half I've lived with. What does it all come to?"

She turned to Laura, who was caught with her fascinated face very close to Beebo's. She started to back away but Beebo's arm around her waist tightened and kept her close. "You know something, baby? It doesn't matter. Nothing matters. You don't like me, and that doesn't matter. Someday maybe you'll love me, and that won't matter either. Because it won't last. Not down here. Not anywhere in the world, if you're gay. You'll never find peace, you'll never find Love. With a capital L."

She took a drag on her cigarette and let it flow out of her nostrils. "L for Love," she said, looking into space. "L for Laura." She turned and smiled at her, a little sadly. "L for Lust and L for the L of it. L for Lesbian. L for Let's—let's," she said, and blew smoke softly into Laura's ear. Laura was startled to feel the strength of the feeling inside her.

It's the whisky, she thought. *It's because I'm tired. It's because I want Marcie so much. No, that doesn't make sense.* She caught the bartender's eye and he fixed her another drink.

Beebo's arm pressed her again. "Let's," she said. "How about it?" She was smiling, not pushy, not demanding, just asking. As if it didn't really matter whether Laura said yes or no.

"Where did you get that ridiculous name?" Laura hedged.

"My family."

"They named you *Beebo?*"

"They named me Betty Jean," she said, smiling. "Which is even worse."

"It's a pretty name."

"It's a lousy name. Even Mother couldn't stand it. And she could stand damn near anything. But they had to call me something. So they called me Beebo."

"That's too bad."

Beebo laughed. "I get along," she said.

The bartender set Laura's glass down and she reached for her change. "What's your last name?" she said to Beebo.

"Brinker. Like the silver skates."

Laura counted her change. She had sixty-five cents. The bartender was telling a joke to some people a few seats down, resting one hand on the bar in front of Laura, waiting for his money. She was a dime short. She counted it again, her cheeks turning hot.

Beebo watched and began to laugh. "Want your dime back?" she said.

"It's your dime," Laura said haughtily.

"You must have left home in a hurry, baby. Poor Laura. Hasn't got a dime for a lousy drink."

Laura wanted to strangle her. The bartender turned back to her suddenly and she felt her face burning. Beebo leaned toward him, laughing. "I've got it, Mort," she said.

"No!" Laura said. "If you could just lend me a dime."

Beebo laughed and waved Mort away.

"I don't want to owe you a thing," Laura told her.

"Too bad, doll. You can't help yourself." She laughed again. Laura tried to give her the change she had left, but Beebo wouldn't take it. "Sure, I'll take it," she said. "And you'll be flat busted. How'll you get home?"

Laura went pale then. She couldn't go home. Even if she had a hundred dollars in her pocket. She couldn't stand to face Marcie, to explain her crazy behavior, to try to make herself sound normal and ordinary when her whole body was begging for strange passion, for forbidden release.

Beebo watched her face change and then she shook her head. "It must have been a bad fight," she said.

"You've got it all wrong, Beebo. It wasn't a fight. It was—I don't know what it was."

"She straight?"

"I don't know." Laura put her forehead down on the heel of her right hand. "Yes, she's straight," she whispered.

"Well, did you tell her? About yourself?"

"I don't know if I did or not. I didn't say it but I acted like a fool. I don't know what she thinks."

"Then things could be worse," Beebo said. "But if she's straight, they're probably hopeless."

"That's what Jack said."

"Jack's right."

"He's not in love with her!"

"Makes him even righter. He sees what you can't see. If he says she's straight, believe him. Get out while you can."

"I can't." Laura felt an awful twist of tenderness for Marcie in her throat.

"OK, baby, go home and get your heart broken. It's the only way to learn, I guess."

"I can't go home. Not tonight."

"Come home with me."

"No."

"Well..." Beebo smiled. "I know a nice bench in Washington Square. If you're lucky the bums'll leave you alone. And the cops."

"I'll—I'll go to Jack's," she said, suddenly brightening with the idea. "He won't mind."

"He might," Beebo said, and raised her glass to her lips. "Call him first."

Laura started to leave the bar and then recalled that all her change was sitting on the counter in front of Beebo. She turned back in confusion, her face flushing again. Beebo turned and looked at her. "What's the matter, baby?" And then she laughed. "Need a dime?" She handed her one.

For a moment, in the relative quiet of the phone booth, Laura leaned against a wall and wondered if she might faint. But she didn't. She deposited the dime and dialed Jack's number. The phone rang nine times before he answered, and she was on the verge of panic when she heard him lift the receiver at last and say sleepily, "Hello?"

"Hello, Jack? Jack, this is Laura." She was vastly relieved to find him at home.

"Sorry, we don't want any."

"Jack, I've got to see you."

"My husband contributes to that stuff at the office."

"Jack, please! It's terribly important."

"I love you, Mother, but you call me at the God-damnedest times."

"Can I come over?"

"Jesus, no!" he exclaimed, suddenly coming wide awake.

"Oh, Jack, what'll I do?" She sounded desperate.

"All right now, let's get straightened out here. Let's make an effort." He sounded as if he had drunk a lot and just gotten to sleep, still drunk, when Laura's call woke him up. "Now start at the beginning. And make it quick. What's the problem?"

She felt hurt, slighted. Of all people, Jack was the one she had to count on. "I—I acted like a fool with Marcie. I don't know what she thinks," she half-sobbed. "Jack, help me."

"What did you do?"

"Nothing—everything. I don't know."

"God, Mother. Why did you pick tonight? Of all nights?"

"I didn't pick it, it just happened."

"*What* happened, damn it?"

"I—I sort of embraced her."

There was a silence on the other end for a minute. Laura heard him say away from the receiver, "OK, it's OK. No, she's a friend of mine. A friend, damn it, a girl." Then his voice became clear and close again. "Mother, I don't know what to say. I'm not sure I understand what happened, and if I did I still wouldn't know what the hell to say. Where are you?"

"At The Cellar. Jack, you've just got to help me. Please."

"Are you alone?"

"Yes. No. I've been talking to Beebo, but—"

"Oh! Well, God, that's it, that's the answer. Go home with Beebo."

"No! I can't, Jack. I want to come to your place."

"Laura, honey—" He was wide awake now, sympathetic, but caught in his own domestic moils. "Laura, I'm—well, I'm entertaining." He laughed a little at his own silliness. "I'm involved. I'm fraternizing. Oh, hell, I'm making love. You can't come over here." His voice went suddenly in the other direction as he said, "No, calm down, she's not coming over."

Then he said, "Laura, I wish I could help, honest to God. I just can't, not now. You've got to believe me." He spoke softly, confidentially, as if he didn't want the other to hear what he said. "I'll tell you what I'll do, I'll call Marcie and get it straightened out. Don't worry, Marcie believes in me. She thinks I'm Jack Armstrong, the all-American boy. The four-square troubleshooter. I'll fix it up for you."

"Jack, please," she whimpered, like a plaintive child.

"I'll do everything I can. You just picked the wrong night and that's the God's truth, honey. Where's Beebo? Let me talk to Beebo."

Laura went out of the booth to get her, feeling half dazed, and found her way back to the bar. "He wants to talk to you," she said to Beebo, without looking at her.

Beebo frowned at her and then swung herself off her seat and headed for the phone. Laura sat down in her place, disturbed by the warmth Beebo left behind, twirling her glass slowly in her hand. She was crushed that Jack had turned her down.

Perhaps he had a lover, perhaps this night was so important to him that he couldn't give it up, even though she had all his sympathy. These things might be—in fact, were—true. But Laura could hardly discern them through her private pains.

Beebo came back in a minute and leaned over Laura, one hand on the bar, the other on Laura's shoulder. "He says I'm to take you home," she said, "feed you aspirins, dry your tears, and put you to bed. And no monkey business." She smiled as Laura looked slowly up into her face. It was a strong interesting face. With a little softness, a little innocence, it might have been lovely. But it was too hard and cynical, too restless and disillusioned. "Come on, sweetie pie," Beebo said. "I'm a nice kid, I won't eat you."

They walked until they came to a small dark street, and the second door up—dark green—faced right on the sidewalk. Beebo opened it and they walked down a couple of steps into a small square court surrounded by the windowed walls of apartment buildings. On the far side was another door with benches and play areas grouped in between on the court. Beebo unlocked the other door and led Laura up two flights of unlighted stairs to her apartment.

When they went inside a brown dachshund rushed to meet them and tried to climb up their legs. Beebo laughed and talked to him, reaching down to push him away.

Laura stood inside the door, her hands over her eyes, somewhat unsteady on her feet.

"Here, baby, let's get you fixed up," Beebo said. "OK, Nix, down. Down!" she said sharply to the excited little dog, and shoved him away with her foot. He slunk off to a chair where he studied her reproachfully.

Beebo led Laura through the small living room to an even smaller bedroom and sat her down on the bed. She knelt in front of her and took her shoes off. Then, gently, she leaned against her, forcing her legs slightly apart, and put her arms around Laura's waist. She rubbed her head against Laura's breasts and said, "Don't be afraid, baby." Laura tried weakly to hold her off but she said, "I won't hurt you Laura," and looked up at her. She squeezed her gently, rhythmically, her arms tightening and loosening around Laura's body. She made a little sound in her throat and, lifting her face, kissed Laura's neck. And then she stood up slowly, releasing her.

"OK," she said. "Fini. No monkey business. Make yourself comfortable, honey. There's the john—old, but serviceable. You sleep here. I'll take the couch. Here! Here, Nix!" She grabbed the little dog, which had bounded onto the bed and was trying to lick Laura's face, and picked him up in her arms like a baby. She grinned at Laura. "I'll take him to bed, he won't bother you," she said. "Call me if there's anything you need." She looked at Laura closely while Laura tried to answer her. The younger girl sat on the bed, pale with fatigue and hunger, feeling completely lost and helpless. "Thanks," she murmured.

Beebo sat down beside her. "You look beat, honey," she said.

"I am."

"Want to tell me about it now?"

Laura shook her head.

"Well..." she said. "Goodnight, Little Bo-peep. Sleep tight." And she kissed her forehead, then turned around and went out of the bedroom, turning out the light on her way.

Laura had gotten off the bed without looking at her, but feeling Beebo's eyes on her. She shut the door slowly, until she heard the catch snap. Then she turned, leaning on the door, and looked at the room. It was small and full of stuff, with yellowed walls. Everything looked clean, although the room was in a state of complete confusion, with clothes draped over chairs and drawers half shut.

All of a sudden, Laura felt stronger. She undressed quickly, taking off everything but her nylon slip, and pulled down the bedclothes. She climbed in gratefully.

She didn't even try to forget Marcie or what had happened. It would have been impossible. Mere trying would have made it worse. She relaxed on her back in the dark, her arms outflung, and waited for the awful scene to come up in her mind and torture her.

Her mind wandered. The awful embrace was awful no longer—only wrong and silly and far away. The damage was irreparable. She stared at the ceiling, invisible in the dark, and felt a soft lassitude come over her. She felt as if she were melting into the bed; as if she could not have moved if she tried.

Time flowed by and she waited for sleep. It was some time before she realized she was actually waiting for it. It didn't come. She turned on her side, and still it eluded her. Finally she snapped the light on to squint at her watch. It said five of four. She switched it off again, her eyes dazzled, and wondered what the matter was. And then she heard Beebo turn over in the next room, and she knew.

An old creeping need began to writhe in Laura, coming up suddenly out of the past and twisting itself around her innards. The pressure increased while she lay there trying to ignore it, becoming more insistent. It began to swell and fade with a rhythm of its own; a rhythm she knew too well and feared. Slowly the heat mounted to her face, the sweat came out on her body. She began to turn back and forth in bed, hating herself and trying to stop it, but helpless with it.

Laura was a sensual girl. Her whole being cried out for love and loving. It had been denied her for over a year, and the effects were a severe strain on her that often brought her nerves to the breaking point. She pretended she had learned to live with it, or rather, without it. She even pretended she could live her whole life without it. But in her secret self she knew she couldn't.

Beebo turned over again in the living room and Laura knew she was awake, too. The sudden realization made her gasp, and she could fool herself no longer. She wanted Beebo. She wanted a woman; she wanted a woman so terribly that she had to put her hand tight over her mouth to stop the groan that would have issued from it.

For a few moments more she tossed feverishly on her bed, trying to find solitary release, but it wouldn't come. The thought of Beebo tortured her now, and not the thought of Marcie. Beebo—with her lithe body, her fascinating face, her cynical shell. There was so much of Beth there. At that thought, Laura found herself swinging her legs out of bed.

Moonlight glowed in two bright squares on the living room floor. Laura could see the couch, draped in blankets. She wondered whether Beebo had heard her and waited breathlessly for some sign. Nix lifted his head but made no sound, only watching her as she advanced across the room on her tiptoes, her white slip gleaming as she passed through the light.

Laura stood and hovered over the couch, uncertain what to do, her heart pounding hugely against her ribs. Beebo was on her side, turned toward Laura, apparently asleep. Nix was snuggled into the ditch between the back of Beebo and the back of the couch.

Beebo stirred slightly, but she didn't open her eyes. "Beebo," Laura whispered, dropping to her knees and supporting herself against the couch with her hands. "Beebo?" she whispered again, a little louder. And then, sensing that Beebo had heard her she bent down and kissed her cheek, her hands reaching for her. Beebo was suddenly completely roused, coming up on her elbow and then falling back and pulling Laura with her.

"Laura?" she said huskily. "Are you all right?" And then she felt Laura's lips on her face again and a shock of passion gripped her. "Oh, God—Oh, baby," she said, and her arms went around Laura hard.

"Hold me," Laura begged, clinging to her. "Oh, Beebo, hold me."

Beebo rolled off the couch onto Laura and the abrupt weight of her body fired Laura into a frenzy. They rolled over each other on the floor, pressing each other tight, almost as if they wanted to fuse their bodies, and kissed each other wildly.

Laura felt such a wave of passion come up in her that it almost smothered her. She thought she couldn't stand it. And then she didn't think at all. She only clung to Beebo, half tearing her pajamas off her back, groaning wordlessly, almost sobbing. Her hands explored, caressed, felt Beebo all over, while her own body responded with violent spasms—joyous, crazy, deep as her soul. She could no more have prevented her response than she could the tyrannic need that drove her to find it. She felt Beebo's tongue slip into her mouth and Beebo's firm arms squeezing her and she went half out of her mind with it. Her hands were in Beebo's hair, tickling her ears, slipping down her back, over her hips and thighs. Her body heaved against Beebo's in a lovely mad duet. She felt like a column of fire, all heat and light, impossibly sensual, impossibly sexual. She was all feeling, warm and melting, strong and sweet.

It was a long time before either of them came to their senses. They had fallen half asleep when it was over, still lying on the floor, where Nix, after some trepidation, came to join them. When Laura opened her eyes the gray dawn had replaced the white moonlight. She was looking out the window at a mass of telephone and electric wires. She gazed slowly downward until she found Beebo's face. Beebo was awake, watching her—no telling for how long. She smiled slightly, frowning at the same time. But she didn't say anything and neither did Laura. They only pulled closer together, until their lips touched. Beebo began to kiss Laura over and over, little soft teasing kisses that kept out of the way of passion, out of the way of Laura's own kisses as they searched for Beebo's lips. Until it was suddenly imperative that they kiss each other right. Laura tried feebly to stop it, but she quickly surrendered. When Beebo relented a little it was Laura who pulled her back, until Beebo was suddenly crazy for her again.

"No, no, no, no," Laura murmured, but she had asked for it. A year and a half of abstinence was too much for her. At that moment she was in bondage to her body. She gave in in spite of herself, rolling over on Beebo, her fine hair falling over Beebo's breasts in a pale glimmering shower, soft and cool and bringing up the fire in Beebo again.

Once again they rested, half sleeping, turning now and then to feel each other, reassure themselves that the other was still there, still responsive. Now and then Beebo pushed Nix off Laura, or out from between them, where he was anxious to make himself a nest.

It was Saturday afternoon before they could drag themselves off the floor. It was Laura who pulled herself to her knees first by the aid of a handy chair, and squinted at the bright daylight. For a few moments she remained there, swaying slightly, trying to think straight and not succeeding. She felt Beebo's hand brush across her stomach and looked down at her. Beebo smiled a little.

An elusive feeling of shame slipped through Laura, disappeared, came back again, faded, came back. It seemed uncertain whether or not to stay. She swallowed experimentally, looking at Beebo. After a minute Beebo said, "Who's Beth?"

"Beth?" Laura was startled.

"Um-hm. She the blonde?"

"No. That's Marcie."

"Well, baby, seems to me like it's Beth you're after, not Marcie."

Laura frowned at her. "I haven't seen Beth for almost a year. She's married now. It's all over."

"For her, maybe."

"I won't discuss it," she said haughtily, getting up and walking away from her, while Beebo lay on the floor admiring her body, her head propped comfortably on her hands. "It happened long ago and I've forgotten it."

"Then how come you called me Beth all night?"

Laura gasped, turning to look at her, and then her face went pink. "I—I'm sorry, Beebo," she said. "I won't do it again."

"Don't count on it."

Laura stamped her foot. "Damn you, Beebo!" she said. "Don't talk to me as if I were an irresponsible child!"

Beebo laughed, rolling over and nearly crushing Nix, who reacted by licking her frantically and wagging his tail. Beebo squashed him in a hug, still laughing. Laura turned on her heel to leave the room, looking back quickly to grab her slip, and went into the bedroom, slamming the door. Within seconds it flew open again and Beebo leaned against the jamb, smiling at her. She sauntered into the room.

"Now, don't tell me you didn't enjoy yourself last night, Little Bo-peep," she said.

Laura ignored her, moving speedily, suddenly embarrassed to be naked. In the heat of passion it was glorious, but in the morning, in the gray light, in the chill and ache of waking up, she hated it. Her own bare flesh seemed out of place. Not so with Beebo, who sprawled on the bed on top of the underwear Laura wanted to put on.

"Did you?" said Beebo. "Enjoy yourself?"

"Get up, Beebo, I want to get dressed."

"After all, it was your idea, baby."

"Don't throw *that* in my face!" she exclaimed angrily, ashamed to remember it.

"Why not? It's true. Besides I'm not throwing it in your face, I'm just saying it."

Laura turned away from her, unbearably conscious of her own slim behind, her dimpled rump, and her long limbs. She yearned to be shrouded in burlap. "Beebo, I—I couldn't help myself last night." She worked to control her voice, to be civilized about it. "I needed—I mean—it had been so long."

"Since Beth?"

Laura fought down a sudden impulse to strangle her. "I was a fool," she said, and her voice trembled. "A fool with my roommate and now with you. It got so I couldn't stand it at home. It got intolerable."

"So you came down here. And I was a nice convenient safety valve."

"I didn't mean that!" she flared.

"Doesn't matter what you mean, baby. It's a fact. Here you were, desperate. And here was I, ready and willing. You knew I wouldn't turn you down."

Laura's face began to burn. She had a wild idea that her back was blushing with her cheeks.

"What would you have done if I *had* turned you down, Laura?" Beebo spoke softly, insinuatingly, teasing Laura, enjoying herself.

But Laura was too humiliated to tease back. "I don't know," she exclaimed miserably. "I don't know what I *could* have done." And she covered her face with her hands.

"I'll tell you, then. You'd have begged me. You'd have gotten down on your knees and begged me. Sometime you will, too. Wait and see."

Laura whirled toward her, insulted. "That's enough!" she said harshly. She pulled her underthings forcibly from under Beebo, but Beebo caught the shoulder strap of her brassiere and hung on to it with both hands, her heels braced against the floor, laughing like a beautiful savage while Laura yanked furiously at it.

"You're going to get about half," she said. "If you're lucky. I'll get the other half. Half isn't going to hold much of you up, baby."

Laura let go suddenly, and Beebo fell back on the bed, grinning at her.

"Laura hates me," she said, "Laura hates me." She said it slowly, singsong, daring Laura to answer her.

Laura glared at her, defiant and fuming. "You're an animal!" she hissed at her.

"Sure." Beebo chuckled. "Ask Jack. That's his favorite word. We're all animals."

"You're nothing but a dirty animal!"

"What were you last night, Miss Prim? You were panting at me like a sow in rutting season."

Laura's eyes went wide with fury. She grabbed the nearest thing—a hairbrush—and flung it violently at Beebo. Beebo ducked, laughing again at her young victim, and Laura turned and fled into the bathroom. She slammed the door so hard it bounced open and she had to shut it again. With frantic fingers she tried to turn the lock, but Beebo was already pushing on the other side. Laura heaved against it, but Beebo got it open and she fell back against the wall, suddenly frightened.

"Don't touch me!" she spat at her.

Beebo smiled. "Why not? You didn't mind last night. I touched you all over. Did I miss anything?"

Laura shrank from her. "Let me go, Beebo."

"Let you go? I'm not even touching you."

"I want to leave. I want to get out of here." Laura tried to push past her but Beebo caught her, her strong hands pressing painfully into Laura's shoulders, and threw her back against the wall.

"You're not going anywhere, Bo-peep," she said. And began to kiss her. Laura fought her, half sobbing, groaning, furious. Beebo's lips were all over her face, her throat, her breasts, and she took no notice of Laura's blows and her sharp nails. Laura grabbed handfuls of her hair, wanting to tear it out, but Beebo pulled her close, panting against her, her eyes hypnotically close to Laura's. And Laura felt her knees go weak.

"No," she whispered. "Oh, God no. Oh, Beebo." Her hands caressed Beebo's hair, her lips parted beneath Beebo's. All the lonely months of denial burst like firecrackers between her legs. Once it had started her whole body begged for release. It betrayed her. She clung sweating and heaving to Beebo. They were both surprised at the strength and insistence of their feelings. They had felt the attraction from the first, but they had been unprepared for the crescendo of emotion that followed.

It was a long time before either of them heard the phone ringing. Finally Beebo stood up, looking down at Laura, watching her. Laura turned her face away, pulling her knees up and feeling the tears come. Beebo knelt beside her then, the hardness gone from her face.

"Don't cry, baby," she said, and kissed her gently. "Laura, don't cry. I know you don't want to make love to me, I know you have to. Damn that phone! It's not your fault. Laura, baby, you make beautiful love. God grant me a passionate girl like you just once in a while and I'll die happy."

"Please don't touch me. Don't talk to me." She was overwhelmed with shame.

"I have to. I can't help myself any more than you can. I had no idea you'd be like this—Jesus, so hot! You look so cool, so damn far above the rest of us. But you're not, poor baby. Better than some of us, maybe, but not above us."

Laura turned her face to the wall. "Answer the phone," she said.

Beebo left her then and went into the living room. Laura could hear her voice when she answered.

"Hello?" she said. "How are you, doll? Fine. Laura's fine. No, I didn't rape her. She raped me." Laura sat straight up at this, her face flaming. Beebo was laughing. "Tell her what? It's all fixed up? You mean I can send her home to Marcie?" Her voice became heavily sarcastic. "Well, isn't that too sweet for words. OK, Jack, I'll tell her. You what?...With who?...Oh, Terry! Yeah, I've seen him. You got a live one there, boy. Hang on to him, he's a doll...OK, don't mention it. It's been a pleasure. Most of it. She's lovely...So long."

When Beebo returned to the bathroom, Laura was standing at the washbowl, rinsing her face, trying to compose herself.

"What did he say?" she asked Beebo.

"It was Jack."

"I heard."

Beebo put her arms around Laura from behind, leaning a little against her, front to back, planting kisses in her hair while she talked. "He says you're forgiven. He handed Marcie some psychological hocus pocus about a neurosis. You are neurotic, love. As of now. As far as Marcie's concerned, you have attacks. She should have a few herself."

"Don't be so sarcastic, Beebo. If you knew what I've been through—how scared I was—"

"OK, no more sarcasm. For a few minutes at least. God, you're pretty, Laura." Like Jack, like Marcie, like many others, she realized it slowly. Laura's singular face fit no pattern. It had to be discovered. Laura herself had never discovered it. She didn't believe in it. She grew up convinced she was as plain as her father seemed to think, and when she looked into the mirror she didn't see her own reflection. She saw what she thought she looked like; a mask, a cliché left over from adolescence. It embarrassed her when people told her she was pretty.

"Don't flatter me," she said sharply to Beebo. "I hate it."

Beebo shut her eyes and laughed in Laura's ear. "You're nuts," she said. "You are *nuts*, Bo-peep."

"I'm sane. And I'm plain. There's a poem for you. Now let me go."

"There's no rush, baby."

"There is. I want to get home." She twisted away from Beebo, turning around to face her.

Beebo let her hands trail up the front of Laura. "Home to Marcie?" she said, and let them drop suddenly. "OK. Go home. Go home, now that you can stand it for another couple of days. And when the pressure gets too great, come back down again. Come back to Beebo, your faithful safety valve."

"You said you wouldn't be sarcastic."

Beebo wheeled away, walking into the bedroom. "What do you want me to do, sing songs? Write poems? Dance? Shall I congratulate you? Congratulations, Laura, you've finally found a way to beat the problem.

Every time Marcie sexes you up, run down to Beebo's and let it off. Beebo'll fix you up. Lovely arrangement."

She turned to Laura, her eyes narrowed. "Laura gets loved up for free, Beebo gets a treat, and Marcie stays pure. Whatever happens, let's not dirty Marcie up. Let's not muss up that gorgeous blonde hair."

"Don't talk about her!" Laura had followed her into the bedroom.

"Oh, don't get me wrong, Bo-peep. I'm not complaining. You're too good to me, you know. You give me your throw-away kisses. I get your cast-off passion. I'm your Salvation Army, doll, I get all the leftovers. Throw me a bone." She was sitting on the edge of her rump on her dresser, legs crossed at the ankles, arms folded on her chest—a favorite stance with her.

Laura was suddenly ashamed of the way she had used Beebo. Beebo was hurt. And it was Laura's fault.

"Everything's my fault, Beebo," she said. "I'm sorry." There was silence for a minute. Laura was acutely aware that "I'm sorry" was no recompense for what she was doing to Beebo.

Beebo smiled wryly. "Thanks," she said.

"I am, Beebo. Really. I didn't come to you last night just because of Marcie." It was suffocatingly hard to talk. She spoke in fits and starts as her nerve came and left her.

"No?" Beebo remained motionless with a "tell-me-another" look on her face.

"No. I came—I came because—" She covered her face with her hands, stuck for words and ashamed.

"You came, baby. That's enough," Beebo finished for her, relenting a little. "You came and I'm not sorry. Neither are you, not really. The situation isn't perfect." She laughed. "But last night was perfect. It isn't like that very often, I can tell you."

Laura looked at her again. Then she moved toward her clothes, afraid to stay naked any longer, afraid the whole thing would start over again.

Beebo came toward her, pulling the slip from her hand and dropping it on the floor. "There's no hurry," she said.

"I'm going, Beebo. Don't try to stop me."

For a moment Beebo didn't answer. Then she scooped up some of Laura's clothes on her foot and flung them at her. "OK, baby," she said. "But next time, you don't get off so easily. Clear?"

"There won't be a next time." Laura concentrated on dressing, on getting her body covered as quickly as possible. "I'm grateful to you, but I'll never do it again. It isn't fair, not to you."

Beebo laughed disagreeably. "Don't worry about being fair to me, baby. It didn't bother you last night."

"I couldn't think last night! You know that."

"Yes. I know that. I'm glad. I hope I drive you out of your mind." Beebo's eyes bored into her and made her rush and stumble. She was afraid to confront her, and when she had her clothes on she caught her jacket up with one hand and headed for the door without looking back.

Nix pranced after her. Before she got the front door open, Beebo caught her and turned her around. "Good-bye, Beebo," she said stiffly.

Beebo smiled, upsetting Laura with her nude closeness. "You'll be back, Little Bo-peep. You know that, don't you." It was a statement, not a question.

I'll never come back, she told herself. *I'll never open this door again.*

And, confident that she meant what she said, she turned and walked away. Within minutes she was riding uptown on the subway. In less than half an hour she was climbing the flight of stairs to the penthouse, her heart pounding.

A remarkably candid treatment of a particularly controversial theme

Enough of Sorrow

by Jill Emerson

The totally absorbing and somewhat shocking story of a beautiful young woman, elevated from the depths of despair and self-destruction by the strange friendship of another female.

Seldom has any writer so dramatically ripped away the veils of mystery that obscure the emotional and physical aspects of lesbianism.

Seldom has any writer so completely reflected an understanding and appreciation of the kind of relationship that exists between women.

Seldom has so difficult and elusive a subject been handled with such startling candor…

Enough of Sorrow

Twice she had seen Rachel Cooper. Once from her window. She was sitting at the window, just sitting and thinking, and she saw the blonde girl emerge from their building and walk to the curb, the wind whipping the long coat tight against her legs, the wind tossing the golden hair. A cab pulled up and Rae opened the door and got inside, and the door closed and the cab pulled away and was gone.

Another time they passed in the building's entranceway. Neither of them spoke. Karen had felt the rush of blood to her face. Her hands trembled like leaves in a windstorm. And for a moment Rae seemed on the verge of speaking, as if groping for a phrase, for the right words. They passed in silence.

One night she heard footsteps in the corridor. The steps halted at her door, and she waited for the knock but no knock came. There was a long moment of silence, and she ached to say something, anything, and then at last the footsteps resumed and Rae walked past her closed door without knocking.

Rae could have knocked. Or she could have called out, inviting the knock. But they had both waited.

In bed, waiting for sleep to come, she decided that she was glad the blonde girl had made no move. Rae had to desire her—this was important—but still she did not want to be pushed into anything, neither pushed nor pulled. She thought of this and smiled at the darkness and slept.

There were some thoughts to think about, so many thoughts to examine, so many feelings to mull over and attune to. One had to take time, she thought, because a mistake would be a disaster and she could not afford much more in the way of disaster. Yet there was not an eternity of time. Rae would not wait forever, and she herself could not wait forever.

At times, sitting over dinner, dreaming in her room over a book, she would feel a burst of longing and sit bolt upright, trying to define and appraise it. Sometimes she identified it as loneliness. When one is always silent, when one neither speaks nor is spoken to, when one carries on wordless conversations with one's self day in and day out, loneliness becomes a living thing to be contended with. She would react to a thought or a sight or anything at all and have no one with whom to share it. She would think so many things and have no opportunity to give them voice. She had never been the type to speak with strangers, to bandy small talk with shopkeepers. The thoughts and ideas stayed locked up inside and the loneliness grew like cancer.

Or there would be the sexual longings. These always came when she was not ready for them. Often in bed, late at night or early in the morning, when she was either awaiting sleep or drugged with it, there would be a tingling itch at the tips of her breasts or a quivering warmth at her loins, and her mind would begin to swirl away into dark fantasy before she knew quite what was happening. At times her hands would go to the source of discontent, embracing her breasts or groping for her loins, less to caress than to somehow reassure, and then she would redden with solitary embarrassment and force her mind and body away from lustfulness.

The loneliness and the longings all pointed the same way, toward a girl with golden hair and knowing hands and eager lips. It was just a question of time, and she knew this and knew it well. It was just a question of time, and, one Friday evening, one sweet evening, the time had come.

A dark night, thoroughly dark, moonless and starless. She sat a long time at the window, and she was still sitting there when a taxi stopped at the curb and Rae stepped out of it. Her heart gave a sudden almost painful throb, and her loins went instantly warm, and she knew it was time. For a horrid moment she was positive that she had waited too long, that there was someone with Rae. But no, the girl was alone.

She waited. There were footsteps on the stairs, and she heard them reach her floor and pass on upward. She waited, and she lit a cigarette and put it out after a single drag, and knew that it was time. In the bathroom she scrubbed her face clean and put on rouge and lipstick and a hint of eye-shadow. She checked the result and fussed with her hair and knew that she did not look at all pretty, that she was really a frightfully plain thing.

She trembled as she climbed the stairs. She walked softly across the floor to Rae's door, and she stood there for a few eternal seconds, and then she knocked, twice.

"Yes?"

"It's Karen," she said. She did not recognize her own voice. It sounded wholly unfamiliar, foreign.

The door opened. Eyes caught her own eyes. She stepped inside and drew a breath and pushed the door shut.

"I'm afraid I'm a silly person," she managed to say. "A stupid person, actually. There are too many things I just do not know. About myself, about...everything."

She caught her breath. Her head was whirling. "I'm sorry for being such a fool," she said. The words came a little easier now. "I want to be here. Now. With you."

⁂

"Would you like to talk, Karen?"

"No."

"Can I get you anything to drink? I have a little scotch left in the bottle, not very much, but—"

"No, thank you."

Tell me, Rae's eyes were saying. *Cue me in, let me know how you want me to play it. Fast or slow, hard or soft, let me know and we'll play it your way.*

"Just love me," she heard herself say. Her words surprised her, startled her. She took an involuntary step backward, surprised by what she had said, the boldness of her words, the stark nakedness of desire that underlay them. Was she then so very much in need? Was her desire that raw?

"Oh..."

There was a moment telescoped in time, a moment of hands reaching and flesh groping. She was transfixed, a bird hypnotized by a snake, a doe caught in a car's headlights at night. Until Rae caught her and held her and kissed her and tore the image forever out of focus.

Rae's lips on her own were feathers upon silk, hummingbird wings beating against the petals of a rose. Rae's hands held her shoulders, then moved down along her arms to her elbows, then caught her waist and passed around her back to draw her close. At first Karen's eyes were open, staring blindly at the closed eyes of the girl who was kissing her. Then, easily, her eyes fluttered shut and her heart beat audibly and her throat grew dust-dry, a deep burning aridness running all the way back from her mouth. Her knees melted. She thought she might fall, and she clutched Rae as if to keep herself from losing her balance entirely.

They kissed again. Now she gave herself up wholly to the kiss, her arms tightening around Rae, her lips parting of their own accord to accept the fullness of the kiss. She felt and was enormously conscious of the pressure of their bodies together, two fine and beautiful girl bodies, thighs pressed against thighs, breasts against breasts, mouths glued wetly together.

The fear and trembling died and melted away. The awful nameless anxiety drifted off. Rae's hands released their grip, Rae's lips withdrew, and Karen stood for a moment, eyes still shut, waiting. For an instant it was like waking at dawn, waking up from a good dream and hugging the pillow, reluctant to meet the day, reluctant to give up the warmth and sweetness of the dream.

When she let go of it, when she opened her eyes, she saw Rae still standing in front of her, the ghost of a smile upon her lips.

"I'll turn out the lights."

"All right."

Rae crossed to the doorway, flicked the switch to turn off the bare lightbulb overhead. Karen did not move. Rae took her hand, and the two of them moved through the half-darkness, moved quickly and silently across the uncarpeted floor to the small bed. She sat on the bed and Rae sat beside her and they kissed. She turned in Rae's arms. Rae's tongue stroked Karen's lips, probing, seeking, searching. Yearning took wings and turned to passion. They clutched each other, moved on the bed, tumbling awkwardly until they were stretched out full-length upon the narrow cot, their arms around one another, their mouths drawing nourishment from each other.

While she lay there, while Rae made love to her, her hands so skillful and lips so knowing, she felt a sort of detachment that was almost schizoid in nature. A Karen Winslow was upon her back on a bed in a dark room while a beautiful blonde girl unfastened a button and worked a zipper and touched here and kissed there. That Karen Winslow felt it all and responded to it all, stirred by each kiss, provoked by each touch, drawn ever more deeply into the rhythm of passion.

But at the same time another Karen Winslow, ethereal, amorphous, sat or floated somewhere across the room, somewhere in space. And this alien Karen Winslow did not participate but merely observed, watching and knowing all while feeling nothing at all...

Hands touched her bare breasts, cupped them, felt their weight. Lips brushed over her lips, over her cheek, nibbled at the hollow of her throat. Moved down past her shoulder, moved down across satin skin toward the perfection of her breasts.

She had grown naked. Rae's clever hands, so quick, so gentle, had removed every stitch of Karen's clothing. The air was cool on her bare skin, cool in sharp contrast to the fire of Rae's mouth, of Rae's hands, of Rae's warm body...

Where their flesh touched, fire spread. Warm, glowing fire, hot coals in a campfire's residue. Ashes to ashes, lust to lust—the Karen Winslow who sat observing picked up this bit of doggerel and played with it like a cat with yarn. Ashes to ashes, lust to lust, belly to belly and breast to breast.

Somewhere the alien Karen, the untouched observer, the shapeless voyeuse, went forever away. Somehow passion and desire took complete control. The well of hot blood surged in her loins. Her nipples, alert with hunger, rose to Rae's lips and tingled at the touch. Her thighs trembled, sprang apart like startled fish. Her hips were caught up in a rhythm too long forgotten, a rhythm that had already been ancient when the world itself was young, rocking straining writhing rhythm of love...

Before she had wanted only to be loved. Now she yearned to love and be loved, to do and be done, to have and be had, to possess as she was in turn possessed. Her own hands sought, her own lips searched and joyfully discovered. Her hands filled themselves with Rae's breasts, twin cones of warm yielding flesh, and she thrilled alike to the feel of Rae's flesh in her hands and to the sharp intake of breath that signaled Rae's urgent excitement.

I am doing this, she thought. I am exciting this girl, this beautiful marvelous girl. I am making her happy. I am doing this, I, I...

The special feel of slippery flesh drawn across flesh. The sharp scent of sweat mingling magically with the odors of passion. The taste, the glorious taste, of Rae.

Their bodies moved on the bed. She was no more than barely conscious of this. Her hands, her lips, her whole body seemed to act with a will all its own. She did things without thinking of them or willing them, did things she had never known she knew how to do. It seemed as though she were proceeding by some deep instinct, as though the rituals of their lovemaking were somehow inborn. And their bodies melted and flowed together like twin streams of lava flowing down the sloping sides of a volcano.

She was a flower opening to a bee.

She was a bee draining nectar from a blossom.

Magic...

"I thought you would never come back, Karen."

"I couldn't stay away."

"I thought I'd scared you."

"The wine..."

"I know."

"It would have happened sooner or later. It had to. I wanted you at once, you know."

"I didn't know."

"I saw it in you when we first met. Your eyes, perhaps. I didn't trust myself. Afraid to. People see what they want to see, you know. A play I saw once—I forget the title, something in Eden—*Winter in Eden?* That sounds close enough. A musical version of Adam and Eve. In one scene Satan is temping Eve and she says he looks like a snake, and he says *Women see snakes everywhere*. Get it? The Freudian symbol. Women see snakes because that's what they look for, only for *snakes* you read *phallic symbols*. A lovely line, really, but you have to think about it before it makes sense. Which might explain the play's monumental impact upon the world of theater. The audience walked out humming the Freudian symbols. Where was I?"

"Here. With me."

"Mmmmm. Well—people see what they look for, so I suppose I thought you were gay because I wanted you to be gay. It happens constantly downtown. You think you're getting a long-drink look from the most with-it kid since Sappho and she turns out to be a devoutly heterosexual NYU coed, and the stirring stare doesn't mean she's warm for your form, just that her contact lenses are making holes in her eyes. Am I talking coherently?"

"Not especially."

"I had that feeling. Love gives me tons of things to say while it renders me utterly inarticulate. How do you feel?"

"Mmmmm."

"Happy?"

She opened her eyes, closed them again. The room was still, the night outside dark and silent. Rae was curled up on the bed, her long legs tucked under her, one knee brushing but not quite touching Karen's hip. Karen lay prone on the bed with her head on a pillow. She felt somehow strange, relaxed and enervated all at once, satisfied and wholly content and yet on edge.

"Happy," she said at length.

"You don't sound too certain."

"But I am."

"Silly question, this, but I'll ask it. Was this your first time?"

Half a smile with eyes still shut. "The first time was a few nights ago. With you."

"Ah, yes. I knew the answer, you know. That you hadn't been with another girl before me. But I had to ask the question. I'm not an enormously secure person, dear. What was the man's name? The one who made you cut yourself?"

She opened her eyes involuntarily, moved one arm and looked at her scars. "Ronnie," she said quietly. "Why?"

"I don't know why I asked. Did you...was it good with him? The bed part of it?"

"You want to know too much."

"I—"

"I'm sorry," she said quickly. She signed, sat up, yawned. "That didn't come out right, did it? I didn't mean it the way it sounded."

"I ask too damned many questions."

"It's just that I don't want to talk about it."

"I know."

"It's all...history, really. Do you have another cigarette?"

Rae handed her the pack. She took a cigarette out and Rae lit it for her. She drew on it, inhaled, blew out smoke, sat for a moment, then drew a second time on the cigarette. "Do you want to know something? I can't remember what it was like. I honestly cannot remember, can't picture it. Not the sex in particular. The whole affair. Living with him, the life we had, everything. I could tell you what I did and the people I knew and where I worked and how I spent days and nights, all of that. I don't mean I've lost any memories. But I can't feel it. Do you know what I mean? As though it happened long ago, ages ago, and I can't get the handle of it."

"As though it happened to somebody else?"

"Yes. Almost that way."

"It did, you know. You *were* someone else, Karen."

"Because it was before tonight?"

Rae shook her head. "No. Much as I'd like to take the credit for the transformation, I'm not nutty enough to believe that one little experience could work that complete a change."

"It wasn't a little experience."

"What I mean is—"

"It was a big one," she broke in.

"Clown. Braggart. No, not because of tonight. Because of the way you were shaken up, and the way you almost killed yourself, and the way you came out of it—everything, all of it. People don't live through all of that and come out the same as they were when they started. My older brother was in the Korean War. He was eighteen when he went in and twenty when he came home, and eighteen from twenty is two, and if you think he had only aged two years in Korea then you must have rocks in your head. It was more like ten years. He looked older and he talked older and he acted older. Everything. It's not how long you live that changes you. It's what you live through."

She thought of Ted. "I have a brother," she said. "He's in the service now. Somewhere down South. I don't even know where."

"Honestly?"

She nodded. "We're not very close. I don't know why not. He's all I have left, really, but we don't keep in very close touch. He's not the type to write letters. I actually don't know where he is."

"My brother and I were very close."

"What happened?"

"He died."

"Oh, I'm sorry..."

"Don't be silly. It happened ten years ago. He was in all of those battles in Korea, he was shot at day after day, he killed...oh, too many Chinese to keep track of. I mean it was just constant slaughter from what he told me. Three times he killed men with a bayonet. He was wounded twice. All of this, you know, and nothing killed him, he got through all of it."

Rae put out her cigarette. "Then he came home and in a couple of years he died of a ruptured appendix. Isn't that ridiculous? People don't die of that anymore. But his appendix ruptured without any warning and he didn't know what it was and didn't get to a hospital soon enough. They operated, and there was a post-operative infection, and they just couldn't knock it out. They always can, you know. They use antibiotics and that's the end of it. But nothing worked, and he was in that silly hospital for three weeks, and I kept telling myself that he would get better because that's what happens, people get better. Then he...well, then one morning he just died, actually. That's what happened. And it has never made the slightest bit of sense to me."

She looked at Rae and tried to think of something to say. The silence was overpowering but there were no words with which to break it. She had a lump in her throat and a dull pain at the back of her eyes as if she might begin to weep at any moment. She crushed out her cigarette and the moment for tears passed.

Rae said, "Well. I don't know why I got on that kick. The special Rachel Cooper finesse. Always get a love affair off on a firm footing by turning the conversation to the most morbid topic conveniently at hand. I wonder why I went on like that. I suppose it's like any old wound. You have to pick at the scab from time to time to see if it still bleeds. I think it still does. Karen? Could we sort of lie together now? I just want to be held."

And then they were suddenly lying on the bed. She held Rae in her arms and felt the warmth of flesh pressing flesh. She looked into the blonde girl's eyes, and their gaze locked, and suddenly Rae began to weep. Karen held her close, very close, until she was at once crying herself. Weeping uncontrollably, shedding gritty tears for a nameless loss.

It was good to hold another and comfort her while she wept. It was good to be held in turn and sob out all the hurt and fear and acid that was so bad when kept too long inside. Their nakedness was sexless. Their breasts touched, their loins were in warm proximity to one another—and yet, new as this all was to her, she was entirely unconscious of any taste of passion. Sex was simply not a part of it now. Just warmth and need and tenderness.

The tears came for a long time. And when they stopped there were no words. Just the closeness, the warmth.

The love.

This was love, she thought. This, she told herself, was what it really meant. Just this—far more than the kissing and stroking and the rest. Just this. This was love as she had never known it and had not even been capable of imagining it. Not what she had had with Ronnie—that seemed in retrospect like a nasty caricature of love at best. This was something new, something rather glorious.

I am in love with a girl, she thought. And incredibly enough I am not bothered by it. I do not think it is wrong or evil or awful or dirty. I am not afraid of it. I, square and unworldly Karen Winslow, am in love with a girl.

A lesbian.

No, that was too easy. She could not be so easily labeled like a bug impaled upon a pin and mounted on a board. She could not simply identify herself with a tag reading *Lesbian*, a handy name-tag to tell herself and the world who she was. There was more to her than that. She was not simply a lesbian. She was a girl who happened to be in love with another girl.

Her mind swam in idle circles. She was warm and comfortable and wanted to stay just as she was forever.

"I don't want to go," she murmured.

"Don't go."

"I just want to go to sleep."

"Yes."

"Like this."

"Yes."

"In your arms, like this."

"God yes."

"Rae? I love you, Rae. Isn't it fantastic? I love you, dear, darling, darling Rachel."

"I love you, too. Go to sleep, baby."

"I am in love with Rachel Cooper. Do you really hate it when I call you Rachel? I think it's a beautiful name, really. But I won't say it if you don't like it. I won't do anything you don't want me to do and I'll do absolutely anything that you do want me to do. I am so silly. I am really very silly, you know."

"Go to sleep, silly."

"Yes. Yes, I think I will go to sleep now."

There was something else she wanted to say but she couldn't figure out just what it was. She hugged Rae tight and searched her mind for the thought and swam slowly off into sleep.

Bibliography

Titles are listed by original publication only unless otherwise noted.

*Denotes original hardcover fiction.

Adams, Fay. *Appointment in Paris*. New York: Fawcett, 1952.

Bannon, Ann. *Beebo Brinker*. New York: Fawcett Gold Medal, 1962. Tallahassee, FL: Naiad Press, 1983. San Francisco: Cleis Press, 2001.

——. *I Am a Woman*. New York: Fawcett Gold Medal, 1960. Tallahassee, FL: Naiad Press, 1983. San Francisco: Cleis Press, 2002.

——. *Journey to a Woman*. New York: Fawcett Gold Medal, 1960. Tallahassee, FL: Naiad Press, 1983. San Francisco: Cleis Press, 2003.

——. *Odd Girl Out*. New York: Fawcett Gold Medal, 1957. Tallahassee, FL: Naiad Press, 1983. San Francisco: Cleis Press, 2001.

——. *Women in the Shadows*. New York: Fawcett Gold Medal, 1959. Tallahassee, FL: Naiad Press, 1983. San Francisco: Cleis Press, 2002.

Barnes, Djuna. *Nightwood*. New York: Harcourt, 1937.

*Bedford, Sybille. *A Compass Error*. New York: Alfred A. Knopf, 1968.

Britain, Sloane. *These Curious Pleasures*. New York: Midwood Tower, 1961.

*Brock, Lilyan. *Queer Patterns*. New York: Greenberg, 1935.

Brophy, Brigid. *The King of a Rainy Country*. New York: Alfred A. Knopf, 1957.

Bronski, Michael. *Pulp Friction*. New York: St. Martin's Griffin, 2003.

*Casal, Mary. *The Stone Wall*. Chicago: Eyncourt Press, 1930.

Castle, Terry. *The Literature of Lesbianism*. New York: Columbia University Press, 2003.

Christian, Paula. *Another Kind of Love*. New York: Fawcett Crest, 1961.

——. *Edge of Twilight*. New York: Fawcett Crest, 1959.

——. *This Side of Love*. New York: Avon, 1963.

Clanton, Carol. *Gay Interlude*. New York: Midwood Tower, 1961.

*Cowlin, Dorothy Whalley. *Winter Solstice*. New York: Macmillan, 1943.

*Craigin, Elisabeth. *Either is Love*. New York: Harcourt, 1937.

*Davenport, Marcia. *Of Lena Geyer*. New York: Scribner, 1937.

*De Jong, Dola. *The Tree and the Vine*. New York: Lyle Stuart, 1963.

*Donisthorpe, Sheila. *The Loveliest of Friends*. New York: Claude Kendall, 1931.

*DuMaurier, Angela. *The Little Less*. Garden City, NY: Doubleday, 1941.

Ellis, Joan. *Gay Girl*. New York: Midwood Tower, 1962.

——. *In the Shadows*. New York: Midwood Tower, 1962.

——. *The Third Street*. New York: Midwood Tower, 1964.

Emerson, Jill. *Enough of Sorrow*. New York: Midwood Tower, 1965.

——. *Warm and Willing*. New York: Midwood Tower, 1964.

Emory, Carol. *Queer Affair*. New York: Beacon, 1957.

Evans, Lesley. *Strange are the Ways of Love*. New York: Fawcett Gold Medal, 1959.

*M. J. Farrell (Molly Keane). *Devoted Ladies*. Boston: Little, Brown, 1934.

*Fisher, M.F.K. *Not Now, But Now*. New York: Viking, 1947.

Foster, Jeannette. *Sex Variant Women in Literature*. New York: Vantage Press, 1956. Baltimore: Diana Press, 1975. Tallahassee, FL: Naiad Press, 1985.

*Fredericks, Diana. *Diana*. New York: Dial, 1939.

Gardner, Miriam. *My Sister, My Love*. New York: Monarch, 1963.

——. *The Strange Women*. New York: Monarch, 1962.

Grier, Barbara. *The Lesbian in Literature*. Tallahassee, FL: Naiad Press, 1981.

*Harris, Bertha. *Catching Saradove*. New York: Harcourt, Brace & World, 1967.

Hastings, March. *Three Women*. New York: Beacon, 1958. Tallahassee, FL: Naiad Press, 1989.

Herbert, Anne. *Summer Camp*. New York: Beacon, 1963.

*Highsmith, Patricia (pseud. Claire Morgan). *The Price of Salt*. New York: Coward-McCann, 1952.

*Jackson, Shirley. *The Haunting of Hill House*. New York: Viking, 1959.

*——. *Hangsaman*. New York: Farrar, 1951.

*Kilpatrick, Sarah. *Ladies' Close*. New York: Doubleday, 1968.

Knight, Dorcas. *The Flesh Is Willing*. New York: Midwood Tower, 1962.

*Laurence, Margaret. *A Jest of God* (title later changed to *Rachel, Rachel*). New York: Alfred A. Knopf, 1966.

*Lindsay, Joan. *Picnic at Hanging Rock*. Australia: Cheshire, 1967. New York: Penguin, 1970.

*Mahyere, Evaline. *I Will Not Serve*. New York: Dutton, 1959.

Martin, Della. *Twilight Girl*. New York: Beacon, 1961.

Martin, Kay. *The Whispered Sex*. New York: Hillman, 1960.

McManus, Yvonne. *The Reunion*. New York: Award, 1965.

Morgan, Nancy. *City of Women*. New York: Fawcett Gold Medal, 1952.

*Olivia (pseud. of Dorothy Strachey Bussey). *Olivia*. New York: Sloane, 1949.

Packer, Vin. *The Evil Friendship*. New York: Fawcett Gold Medal, 1963.

——. *Spring Fire*. New York: Fawcett Gold Medal, 1952. San Francisco: Cleis Press, 2004.

*Renault, Mary. *Friendly Young Ladies*. London: Longmans, Green, 1944.

*Rendell, Ruth. *Down with Doon*. Garden City, NY: Doubleday, 1965.

*Rinser, Luise. *Rings of Glass*. Chicago: Henry Regnery, 1958.

*Rule, Jane. *Desert of the Heart*. New York: World, 1965.

——. *Lesbian Images*. Garden City, NY: Doubleday, 1975.

*Sackville-West, Vita. *Daughter of France*. Garden City, NY: Doubleday, 1959.

Salem, Randy. *Chris*. New York: Beacon, 1959. Tallahassee, FL: Naiad Press, 1989.

——. *Honeysuckle*. New York: Midwood Tower, 1963.

——. *The Sex Between*. New York: Avon, 1962.

——. *Tender Torment*. New York: Avon, 1962.

*Sandburg, Helga. *Wheel of Earth*. New York: McDowell, Oblensky, 1958.

*Sarton, May. *Mrs. Stevens Hears the Mermaids Singing*. New York: W. W. Norton, 1965.

Sellers, Connie. *Private World*. New York: Newsstand, 1959.

Server, Lee. *Encyclopedia of Pulp Fiction Writers*. New York: Checkmark Books, 2002.

Sherwood, Danni. *So Strange a Love*. New York: Midwood Tower, 1964.

Smith, Artemis. *Odd Girl*. New York: Beacon, 1959.

——. *The Third Sex*. New York: Beacon, 1959.

*Stein, Gertrude. *Things as They Are* (also known as *Q.E.D.*). Pawlet, VT: Banyan Press, 1950.

Stryker, Susan. *Queer Pulp: Perverted Passions from the Golden Age of the Paperback*. San Francisco: Chronicle Books, 2001.

Taylor, Valerie. *The Girls in 3-B*. New York: Fawcett Crest, 1959.

——. *Return to Lesbos*. New York: Midwood Tower, 1963.

——. *Stranger on Lesbos*. New York: Fawcett Crest, 1959.

*Tey, Josephine (pseud. of Elizabeth McIntosh). *Miss Pym Disposes*. New York: Macmillan, 1947.

Torres, Tereska. *Women's Barracks*. New York: Fawcett Gold Medal, 1950.

Verel, Shirley. *The Dark Side of Venus*. New York: Bantam, 1962. Reissued as *The Other Side of Venus*. Tallahassee, FL: Naiad Press, 1988.

*Wilhelm, Gale. *Torchlight to Valhalla*. New York: Random House, 1938. Tallahassee, FL: Naiad Press, 1985.

*——. *We Too are Drifting*. New York: Random House, 1935. Tallahassee, FL: Naiad Press, 1985.

Zimet, Jaye. *Strange Sisters: the Art of Lesbian Pulp Fiction*. New York: Viking Penguin, 1999.

KATHERINE V. FORREST is the author of fifteen novels, including the lesbian classic *Curious Wine*, the lesbian-feminist utopian trilogy that began with *Daughters of a Coral Dawn*, and the Kate Delafield mystery series, winner of two Lambda Literary Awards. She has edited numerous anthologies, and her stories, articles, and reviews have appeared in publications worldwide. She was senior editor at Naiad Press for ten years, and continues to edit and teach classes on the craft of fiction. She lives with her partner in San Francisco.